Praise for *New York Times* bestselling author Nalini Singh and the Guild Hunter series

'Paranormal romance at its best' — *Publisher's Weekly*

'Sc[illegible]borate [illegible]mpelling [illegible]iews

'I don't think there's a single paranormal series as well-planned, well-written, and downright fantabulous as Ms Singh's Psy-Changeling series' — *All About Romance*

'Terrifyingly, passionately awesome . . . you'll love it'
#1 *New York Times* bestselling author Patricia Briggs

'I loved every word, could picture every scene, and cannot recommend this book highly enough. It is amazing in every way!' — *New York Times* bestselling author Gena Showalter

'Ms Singh's books never fail to draw me in and keep me enthralled until the very end' — *Romance Junkies*

'It's a given that when readers open up a Singh book they will be transported to a unique world filled with genuinely unforgettable characters . . . Singh's novels never disappoint!'
Romantic Times

Also by Nalini Singh from Gollancz:

Guild Hunter Series

Angels' Blood
Archangel's Kiss
Archangel's Consort
Archangel's Blade
Archangel's Storm
Archangel's Legion
Archangel's Shadows
Archangel's Enigma
Archangel's Heart
Angels' Flight (short story collection)

Psy-Changeling Series

Slave to Sensation
Visions of Heat
Caressed by Ice
Mine to Possess
Hostage to Pleasure
Branded by Fire
Blaze of Memory
Bonds of Justice
Play of Passion
Kiss of Snow
Tangle of Need
Heart of Obsidian
Shield of Winter
Shards of Hope
Allegiance of Honour
Wild Invitation (short story collection)
Wild Embrace (novellas collection)

Psy-Changeling Trinity Series

Silver Silence
Ocean Light

OCEAN LIGHT

A PSY-CHANGELING TRINITY NOVEL

NALINI SINGH

First published in Great Britain in 2018 by Gollancz
an imprint of the Orion Publishing Group Ltd
Carmelite House, 50 Victoria Embankment
London EC4Y 0DZ

An Hachette UK Company

1 3 5 7 9 10 8 6 4 2

A CIP catalogue record for this book is available from the British Library.

ISBN (mass market paperback) 978 1 473 21763 8
ISBN (eBook) 978 1 473 21764 5

Printed and bound in Great Britain by
Clays Ltd, Elcograf S.p.A.

www.nalinisingh.com
www.gollancz.co.uk

OCEAN LIGHT

Winter

THE YEAR 2083 dawns in the icy shadow of winter's crystalline wings.

Snow is falling.

Flowers have gone dormant.

And a man sleeps in an endless winter of the mind.

Does he dream? Does he remember that humans are the bridge?

A truth brought to light by Adrian Kenner, the eighteenth-century peace negotiator who ended the territorial wars that had drenched the world in changeling blood.

The Psy were thought too condescending in their belief that their telepathy and telekinesis, psychometry and foresight, made them stronger, better.

No changeling negotiator could take on the task, for they all had their alliances and enemies. A leopard would not trust a bear, a bear would not countenance being at the same table as a wolf, a wolf refused to accept an eagle's authority . . . So many broken, splintered packs and clans, so much enmity.

Only the humans, caught in between the two violent powers and considered impartial, were trusted.

Only Adrian was trusted.

And in designing a peace accord that ended the wars, he repaid that trust a thousand times over.

But it has been more than three hundred years since that historic signing.

And people have forgotten that humans are the bridge.

Humans have forgotten.

Chapter 1

Bowen Knight: Status unknown. Location unknown. Condition as noted in final verified medical report: "Persistent comatose state. Brain functional, but no evidence or indication of increase in brain activity regardless of all measures taken."

—Human Alliance Internal Register

KAIA HATED HOSPITALS.

The sharp antiseptic scent, the quiet beeps occasionally uttered by the machinery of life, the stark lack of color on the walls, the carpetless floors, even the perfectly blameless pale blue sheets on this particular bed—it all caused her gut to churn and air to tighten in her chest until the pain was a constant.

This patient was breathing on his own, so at least she didn't have to listen to the quiet whisper of the apparatus that forced air in and out of the lungs.

Shh. Shh.

Such a soft sound. Such a terrible sound.

Fisting her hand just below her breastbone, she pushed in hard in an effort to dislodge the agonizing knot. "Breathe, Kaia," she ordered. "This isn't even a hospital."

It was only a small clinic and it had only a single patient. A single *subject*.

The reminder did nothing to calm her heart or warm her skin, her breaths still shallow inhales followed by jagged exhales. She should've told Atalina no when her cousin asked her to step in to check the subject's vitals and status. She should've pointed out that she was the *cook* for the entire station and had lunch to prepare. But then Atalina wouldn't have agreed to get off her feet and have a rest despite her advanced pregnancy.

And Kaia had once been a scientist who worked alongside her cousin. She could do this simple task that Atalina did multiple times a day. It wasn't as if Attie had asked her to titrate the subject's medications or run complicated neurological scans. Though, if she had, Kaia was trained in both.

Becoming a cook hadn't wiped out her years of study and experience.

It had just made her happy that she no longer had to pretend to be something—someone—that she wasn't. She'd leave the science to the Kahananui branch of the family, and surrender to her own artistic lineage. Because while Elenise Luna had been a doctor, Iosef Luna had made his living as a lyricist. And the smallest "Lunatic" of all, their baby daughter, Kaia, had once thrown a tantrum in a toy store because she wanted the toy oven so very much.

"Procrastinating won't get this done any faster," she muttered under her breath before closing the short distance to the end of the bed. A complex piece of machinery, that bed featured a large computronic panel at the foot. Data about Atalina's motionless subject glowed quietly on that panel.

It had been updated thirty seconds earlier, the bed set up for constant monitoring.

It was also programmed to alert Atalina if anything changed beyond acceptable parameters, but Kaia's cousin was too meticulous a physician and scientist to put all her faith in technology. She did a manual check every hour except the six hours when she slept. And then, she had the feed going to an organizer beside her bed, with multiple types and levels of alerts built in.

It was a good thing her mate loved her so much.

Kaia scanned the data, saw nothing problematic. The subject was stable, but his neurological profile remained unchanged—Attie would be disappointed. The well-built male was still in as deep a comatose state as he'd been in when they'd transferred him to this facility. Technically speaking, Kaia and the others had kidnapped him—she'd been roped into the team of felons because Atalina couldn't move that fast right now and they'd needed someone with the necessary medico-scientific expertise to safeguard the subject.

A flicker on the screen.

Frowning, she looked more closely and spotted another blip in the graph that charted the subject's neural activity. The profile was changing at last. Though from what Kaia could see, the change was minor. Nothing that would instigate an alert to Atalina. Satisfied all was as it should be, Kaia made a couple of notes on the organizer Atalina had given her, then slipped the slim computronic device into the pocket built into her ankle-length sundress and moved to stand beside the bed.

Though that bed was designed to monitor every possible function, it remained good practice to physically check the status of a subject. After releasing the transparent "shell" around the subject's chest and lower body—a shell that protected and monitored at the same time—she made sure the sheet that covered him was undisturbed, then placed her fingers carefully on the inside of his wrist and began the quiet mental count of his pulse.

He might be human, might be the enemy, but right now, he was her responsibility.

His skin was surprisingly warm and healthy, though it looked to have lost its natural depth of color. She wondered absently what shade it became under sunlight. A deep golden-brown? More bronzed? The tawny color of that flowering plant she'd seen in the hydrogardens when she ducked in to grab a handful of fresh herbs?

Whatever shade it became, it was currently interrupted by hundreds of tiny "bugs" hooked into his system. Strangely adorable, the dull silver objects worked to ensure that the subject's muscles would remain strong and flexible despite his inactive state. The bugs were currently in the beta test phase but showed every sign of having surpassed their creator's initial targets.

Should Atalina's subject wake, he'd be capable of movement within a relatively short period.

Kaia's eyes went to his face.

He was pretty, she supposed—though the thought made her want to scowl. Square jaw, high cheekbones, tumbled black hair that made her fingers itch to touch. And an unexpected softness to his lower lip, as if his smile would be playfully sensual. She snorted inwardly. This was not a playful man. His reputation made it clear he was one of the most ruthless humans on the planet.

His pulse jumped under her fingertips.

Snapping her eyes to the machines around them, she saw sudden, dangerous spikes appear in front of her eyes. *Everywhere.* "Shit."

She broke contact with his wrist and took a single step toward the data panel to make sure it had shot an alert to Attie.

That was when Bowen Knight, Human Alliance security chief, and a pitiless man with a beautiful mouth, parted his lips and spoke.

Chapter 2

Kaia, if you don't put Mr. Puggles in his travel box, he'll get hurt feelings and think you don't want him to come with us.

—Iosef Luna to his only daughter, Kaia

THE LAST THING Bo remembered was smashing through the bridge wall and into the canal, the cold Venetian water closing over his head as his heart exploded in bloody shards inside him. He'd almost been able to feel the pieces of the bullet piercing and devastating the vital organ, had known he was a dead man.

He'd said something to Lily before he died. He'd told his sister to use his brain.

Maybe he wouldn't have said that if he'd realized he'd still be conscious while his brain was being chopped up.

"I am *not* chopping up your brain."

Bo frowned . . . Could a brain frown? And why was his brain talking back to him in such a coolly affronted tone of voice? Had it gone insane while being a disembodied brain in a jar that someone was experimenting on?

"And I'm not experimenting on your brain, either!" A long pause. "Someone else, however, *is* experimenting on it. But Attie needs your entire living brain for research, so you're safe from being sliced up."

For some reason, those words—spoken in a feminine voice as lyrical as it was husky—weren't very reassuring. Also, why was his brain suddenly replying in a woman's voice? Was that a side effect of getting shot and dying and having your brain scooped out to be put in a jar?

He'd really thought he could trust Lily to make certain he was actually dead when his brain was put into a jar. He'd have to have a serious chat with his sister when she made it to the afterlife. If he ever made it to the afterlife himself—because if he was stuck as a brain in a jar—

His foot jerked up hard before slamming back down to the bed. The reverberation pulsed up his entire body, disrupting his train of thought and making his shoulders jerk. *Wait a minute.* If he had shoulders, then he couldn't be a disembodied brain in a jar.

"That's what I've been trying to tell you," said the female voice that held an undertone of ice.

His breath kicked hard in his chest . . . No, that was his heart. But his heart had been fatally damaged, he was sure of it. Or maybe . . .

Things had been chaotic after the shooting, his memories a jumble of shocking pain entwined with raw fear for Lily. Maybe he'd gotten it wrong. Maybe his heart hadn't been destroyed after all.

But he *knew*. Bo was a security specialist; he understood weapons and he had zero doubts that what had gone into his chest had been a bullet designed to fragment and cause catastrophic damage.

Hearts didn't regenerate from that brutal an assault.

He shouldn't be feeling anything inside his chest, but he was, and he was having thoughts inside his head, which meant his brain hadn't exploded, either. Was it possible the medics had him on some sort of life support?

Yet he felt too alive to be nothing but a vegetable hooked up to a machine.

He needed to open his eyes. But he couldn't.

"Hold on a minute," the frost-kissed female voice said. "You have tape over your eyes."

A sliding sound, a new and breathless woman's voice saying, "He's awake?"

"Yes, and thinks he's a brain in a jar. Can I take the tape off his eyes?"

"Do it. I need to monitor his vitals as he rises. It's possible he might not make it all the way out." More huffed breaths. "This is incredible. I never expected this response. The compound clearly works on human neural tissue far more efficiently than it does on ours."

Bo wanted to scowl. He was right here. Could they please stop talking about him as if he couldn't hear them? And if they weren't human, where was he?

"I think you're speaking Italian now," said the one with the cool but throaty voice. "I only speak Hawaiian, Samoan, English, Japanese, and a bit of very bad Cantonese and French."

Bo felt a whisper of movement against his face, caught the edge of a lush scent that made him draw in a deeper breath. Some kind of exotic flower . . . and sugar. *Cinnamon.* He liked cinnamon.

"Good to know. But don't start thinking I'm going to bake you a cinnamon cake, Security Chief. I save that for friends."

Bo tried to settle his brain. But he kept on being distracted by the waves of luscious scent rippling across the air. That scent had nothing to do with the otherwise astringent smell all around him.

Hospital.

It was a hospital smell he'd been ignoring. Every single person in the world probably knew that smell. Whatever antiseptic they used to clean hospitals, it seemed to be the same regardless of location. Maybe they got a bulk discount.

Flowers and cinnamon whispering across his perception again.

A tug on the skin of his face near his eyes.

"I'm sorry"—an unexpectedly gentle touch, her fingers stroking back his hair—"the tape isn't meant to stick so hard."

"Here," the other woman said. "Use this to warm it up first. It's probably stuck because I used a new roll. Christ, his vitals are insane."

"Good or bad insane?"

"Phenomenally good."

"Permanent?"

"Unlikely. He could come up only to dive back down."

A sensation of warmth against his skin, then the tug again. "Keep still—moving your head's just making it harder."

Bo was coming to the realization that he was alive, very alive, and the woman with the gentle hands, frost-coated voice, and luscious scent appeared to be a medical technician or a doctor. If she was, her bedside manner was terrible.

"Of course you're a critic," was the distinctly annoyed response. "And for your information, I'm a cook. An excellent one."

He had to be hallucinating. Why would a cook be taking medical tape off his eyes?

He also didn't recognize either woman's voice, and he knew every single senior medic in the Alliance, knew each and every one of the doctors to whom his grievously wounded body would've been taken. So where was he? Was it possible the Alliance had brought in others to help? They had allies now, friends.

"I'm going to prick your feet. It won't hurt." Words spoken by the woman whose voice didn't make his skin . . . itchy.

His leg jerked seconds later. It had been a test, he realized, to see if he had sensation in his feet. Breath held, he flexed both his fingers and toes.

Everyone had their nightmares and Bowen's was to be helpless. He'd been exactly that once, a long time ago. He'd never forget the agony of the telepath's psychic fingers shoving into his brain while he fought helplessly against her control.

It had all ended in blood.

Hers and his.

He'd made it clear to Lily and his parents that he'd never want to be kept alive only by machines, his body and mind beyond his control. It was the most vicious horror he could imagine. But his brain seemed to be functional, and as the last of the fog flickered away, he confirmed he had no physical blank spots, no numbness.

It was odd but he could also sense hundreds of tiny objects on his skin, and it felt as if they pulsed his muscles.

The tape disappeared. "Okay," said the cook with the smoky, bluesy voice that held an inexplicable anger, "try to open your eyes—don't force it. They may feel heavy."

Bo could be patient when he needed to be, but he found he didn't have that control today. He flicked open his lashes.

Chapter 3

KL: Mal, are you sure this is safe? I know we have to let Attie run her experiment, but Hugo's information changes things. Bowen Knight is a cold-blooded murderer and he's targeting our people.
MR: If he doesn't wake, all we've done is give Attie what she needs. If he does, then we have him under our control.

—Messages exchanged between Kaia Luna and Malachai Rhys

THE ANGRY COOK had huge brown eyes that snapped with electricity against skin of a softer brown, her long dark hair in a loose braid that had fallen over one shoulder. She'd tucked a creamy white flower behind her right ear and her features reminded him of a movie he'd once seen about a Tahitian princess. Except this woman was no princess. She was a warrior. One Bo was dead certain was fighting the compulsion to stab him.

Fingers touched his left shoulder, followed by a small press against it. "That should help clear your head."

Bo went to say his head was fine . . . only he hadn't sensed the other woman's approach. And he was a security chief with supposedly hair-trigger instincts. Which meant the fog hadn't all dissipated.

When he turned to face the medic, he saw that her white-threaded black hair was cut sharply into a bob, her body covered by a white lab coat. His mind caught on the disconnect between her hair and her face—

the white strands spoke of age, but her face was unlined, her light brown skin plump with youth.

Her eyes, however, they were familiar. They reminded him of Lily's eyes, even though the medic's were a dark shade where Lily's were gray. No one knew Lily's past before two years of age, but genetic tests done as part of a routine medical check for latent diseases had put his sister's ancestry as Eurasian. The medic also had a strangeness to her shape. As if she had a bowling ball hidden under her coat.

When the woman with the young face and odd shape held a straw to his lips, he took a draw of the cold and slightly sweet liquid within. "How long?" he asked afterward, his brain sloshing itself back together as it shook off another layer of sleep.

"You've been in a coma for the past eight weeks and four days. Ever since you were shot on the bridge in Venice."

Two months.

As he struggled to accept the lost time, Bo looked right to confirm he hadn't imagined the warrior cook with the deadly look in her eye.

There she was. Crossed arms, scowling face, and dangerous curves.

Around her was a hospital suite. Pure glowing white except for the blue sheet over his body and on the bed. All kinds of lines went from his body to various machines on either side of the bed, and the tiny things he'd sensed on his skin? That hadn't been his imagination. Small objects of a muted silver clung to his bare arms, and he could feel them on his legs, chest, everywhere.

They looked like robotic bugs.

"Muscle trainers," the brown-eyed cook said without warning. "It means you won't be confined to bed because your muscles turned to noodles while you were in a coma."

"They're on my back, too?" He could feel the lumps now.

"Smaller version. Bed's designed to exercise that part of your body and keep the blood circulating." She moved to the end of the bed, touched something on the panel there. "Attie, I've turned off the exercise cycle. It would've started again in an hour."

He became aware of a fine metallic sensation against his skull. "Am I bald?" He could swear she'd brushed back his hair, but the warmth of her fingertips on his skin could've been an illusion created by his sluggish mind.

It was the old-young doctor who answered. "No. I'm monitoring your neural activity through a network of fine wires placed directly against your scalp—there was no need to shave off your hair to get them into position."

Another burst of clarity, another part of his brain roaring to full consciousness. "I need to tell Lily I'm awake." The aftermath of the shooting would've devastated her. He'd put himself in the line of fire to protect her, would do so again in a heartbeat, but he knew Lily—she'd have been beating herself up over it.

Poor Lil. She didn't understand that his choice had been selfish; Bo had seen the red dot on her forehead and felt a rush of terror such as he'd never known. The idea of burying his little sister? No, just *no*.

Oh, fuck. "Is she alive?" He'd been in a coma for two months—while the chips in Lily's head and the heads of all his closest friends continued to degrade. "The others?"

"No one is dead," the doctor confirmed. "Ashaya and Amara Aleine were able to come up with a solution that slowed the degradation, but it's limited in scope. The person implanted after you has another two to three months."

All of them still dying, just a little slower. It had been the Aleines who'd figured out how to create a psychic shield for human minds—a shield that protected them from telepathic coercion and violation by the Psy—but Bowen didn't blame the two scientists for the countdown to death; he, Lily, and their closest friends and associates had chosen to be implanted over the Aleines' objections that the chip hadn't been fully tested.

Knowing they'd die free from psychic manipulation had been worth the risk. But their choice had a cost. It'd leave wreckage behind.

He fisted his hand. "Do my parents know what's happening to me?"

"No. This entire operation is highly confidential."

"Experimental?" Though it was the doctor who'd answered, his eyes went to the angry-eyed cook again.

She stared back at him in flinty silence.

Lab coat rustling, the doctor walked into his line of sight. She was rubbing her back with one hand. "Are you sure you want to talk about this now? Wouldn't you rather get your bearings first?"

Bo began to push himself up into a sitting position, waving off her offer of help even though his muscles began to quiver almost at once.

Rolling her eyes, the cook with the body of a centerfold—*fuck, where had that come from?*—walked over to rearrange his pillows so he could brace his back against them.

It was only when the sheet fell to his waist that he realized he was naked under the crisp blue fabric. His skin, a fusion of his Scottish and Brazilian ancestry, was at least a couple of shades paler than normal—and covered in the silvery bugs that allowed him to move even after two months of nothingness.

The cook froze for a heartbeat before finishing with the pillows and returning to stand by the panel at the end of the bed. A whisper of cinnamon and that exotic flower lingered in her wake, the scent just light enough to be frustrating.

Clenching his jaw, he kept an eye on the sheet to make sure it wouldn't crumple any further as he got himself positioned against the pillows. The wires flowing from his body were just long enough to permit the move, but he was breathing as if he'd run a marathon by the time he got himself into an upright seated position.

Obviously the bugs couldn't totally ward off the effects of two months in a coma, but they'd done enough. An intensive regime calibrated to his current state of health and he'd build himself back up quickly enough. "Who are you?" he said when he could speak. "And where am I?"

"I'm Dr. Atalina Kahananui," said the woman in the lab coat, her focus on one of the monitors beside his bed.

Bo knew he should concentrate on her, but the other woman in the room was a furious force of nature he simply could not ignore. His instincts labeled her a threat—for reasons as yet unknown, this woman saw him as the enemy. And there was something deadly about her, a subtle danger that was prickles against his skin.

Bo couldn't tell if that was because of his current state . . . or because of the visceral physical reaction he'd had, and continued to have, toward her. "Planning to be a woman of mystery?"

A long pause, her eyes unblinking, before she folded her arms again. "Kaia. Dragged into this entire insane situation because I can't say no to family."

"And because you were my assistant before you decided you preferred the kitchen to the lab," Dr. Kahananui said. "Kaia was part of the team that kidnapped you."

Bo considered that revelation, factored in that he'd likely been in a highly guarded Alliance facility, and added in that neither woman moved like a soldier. "Did Lily help you?"

Kaia shot Dr. Kahananui a speaking glance. "His brain's definitely working again."

"You're right about Lily," the doctor said. "Your sister cares only for your well-being. We could trust her to maintain our confidence and to get us the medical files we needed."

Yes, that was Lily. She was blood loyal to the Alliance, but her first and fiercest loyalty was to Bo. She was no politician, Lily, and she'd never learned to weigh up costs and benefits. But who was he to question her choice—had their positions been reversed, he'd have made any deal that promised to save her life.

"Where am I?" Neither woman struck him as Psy; there was too much of humanity in their expressions, their emotions—especially Kaia's—worn as a second skin. They hadn't recently emerged from over a century of coldly emotionless Silence.

Yet . . . they weren't human. He knew that the same way he knew the most effective move during hand-to-hand combat, or the best strategic option in a firefight. Years of experience and trust in his gut. Both of those things sensed a simmering wildness under Kaia's skin, as if her humanity were a coat she could shrug off at any instant.

Not Psy. Not human. *Changeling.*

Dr. Kahananui slipped her hands into the pockets of her lab coat. "You're on a BlackSea installation."

Chapter 4

Two more of our people have vanished.

—Message from BlackSea security chief Malachai Rhys to Bowen Knight

BOWEN KNIGHT SUCKED in a breath.

Kaia watched him with dogged focus, though she knew he'd reveal nothing he didn't want to reveal. The slightly dazed—and frighteningly adorable—man who'd emerged from the coma was gone. In his place was the hard-eyed security chief of the Human Alliance.

"In that case," he said, "I'd like to talk to Malachai Rhys."

"Cousin Mal isn't on station." Kaia knew Mal had begun to build a relationship with his counterpart in the Alliance, but her cousin could be closemouthed at times. On Bowen Knight, he'd said very little—but he'd said enough that Kaia knew he was taking Hugo's warning dead seriously. "He's on a search for one of our vanished."

Kaia's beloved clan had lost and was still losing too many of their distant and most isolated people. Some of the vanished had already been found dead, while the majority had disappeared without a trace. And the man in front of her was the master of a lethal two-faced game.

"How many after Leila Savea's return?" A razor-sharp edge in his voice.

Of course he'd mention Leila, their delicate water dancer. A human trucker had helped rescue a battered and nearly broken Leila and return her to the sea that was her home. That just meant the human in question was a man with a good heart. It said *nothing* about the security chief who'd been quietly building a paramilitary force behind the public front of creating a strong business network for humans.

"Three more of our people have been taken." Kaia barely managed to keep her response civil—because one of those three was Hugo. Her friend from before they could toddle. A man with a wicked sense of humor and an addiction to poker that he kept under shaky control. Messy and bright and foolish and handsome Hugo.

Gone without a trace.

"I need to run some tests." Atalina's voice was deliberate, the thin beam of light she shot into Bowen Knight's eyes as deliberate.

Her older cousin believed Kaia was allowing her emotions to get in the way of a groundbreaking scientific experiment. Kaia felt nothing but frustrated affection for Attie's stance—that was who Attie was; for her, science came first. She couldn't care less about Bowen Knight's political maneuvering and ruthless stratagems.

No, that wasn't fair. Attie cared about their lost clanmates just as much as Kaia. She'd cried tears of joy at hearing of Leila's return, but when it came to her work, to her science, Attie shut out the world.

Right now, that was a good thing. Without this experiment to distract her, Attie would be obsessing over her pregnancy—and the bleak possibility that she might suffer another miscarriage. BlackSea's First, their alpha, had greenlit this risky experiment *because* Attie had been putting such stress on herself with her anxiety.

Atalina couldn't worry if she was preoccupied by an experiment unlike any other.

Kaia was happy for her cousin, but she couldn't shut out reality. She couldn't look at Bowen Knight without remembering the last words Hugo had spoken to her, without imagining her friend's pain and horror. She wanted to shake the Alliance's security chief and demand he tell her

Hugo's location. Because Bowen Knight was involved in the vanishings up to his neck.

Hugo had found proof.

Now Hugo was gone.

And Kaia's body had reacted with a scalding rush of blood at the sight of Bowen Knight's bare chest.

As Attie began to test his reflexes, Kaia dug her fingers into her biceps, the pain welcome. It reminded her not to let down her guard and begin to view the man on the bed as just a man. Her physical response to him might be uncomfortable, but it was nothing more than a function of biology. The animal that lived under her human skin was a sensual creature who reveled in skin privileges.

Yet even as she thought that, she knew she was lying to herself. The reason she was standing at the foot of the bed rather than near Atalina was that her response to an awake and aware Bowen Knight had been a violent one.

He was staring at her again.

"I'm going to test your mental acuity," Attie said into the frozen silence before calling out the first of a number of equations. She progressed from there to complex logic puzzles presented on an organizer.

Bowen Knight completed each one without hesitation, his response times faster than the vast majority of the population. No wonder Hugo had been so terrified of him—the man's intelligence was more lethal a threat than any bomb or gun. "It worked," Kaia said to Attie.

"What?" The harsh demand of someone who wasn't used to being kept in the dark. "A straight answer would be nice."

Attie shoved her hands into the pockets of her lab coat. "The last words you said to your sister were for her to use your brain—she understood you meant for it to be used to help your people figure out a solution to the chip implanted into your brain."

From what Attie had told Kaia, that implant was designed to block telepaths from digging into the human mind because, unlike changelings, humans had no natural shields. The chip worked. It apparently also had a very short shelf life, and when it failed, it'd take Bowen's dangerously intelligent brain with it.

Kaia dug her fingers into her biceps again.

"You have a solution?" Bowen's words were ragged at the edges, the first hint of humanity she'd seen in him. "I was the first implanted, but I'm not the only one."

Taking a step back from the panel, Kaia told herself not to be taken in by his concern for his sister and the others who had the chip. How a man treated his own people didn't necessarily translate to how he treated outsiders.

"We're only in stage one of the experiment," Atalina responded. "In layperson terms, a big reason for your extended coma was that the shock of the shooting threw your already degrading chip into an ever steeper decline. We've managed to not only halt that decline but reverse the attendant brain swelling."

Bowen Knight was too much a strategist not to ask the next question. "Can you freeze the chip in time, so it degrades no further?"

Atalina's gaze met Kaia's.

"I think he can take it." Kaia didn't think many things scared the man in front of them.

"Take *what*?"

"Stage two of the experiment is intended to stabilize the chip, so that stage three can take place. Attie's run endless computer models stopping the experiment at stage two—they all end up with the chip failing and you brain-dead in approximately three to four weeks." That chip *always* kicked back in, carrying on in its fatal path until it exploded inside Bowen Knight's brain.

Eyes as close to black as she'd ever seen on a human caught hers, his charisma potent. "What's wrong with stage three?"

Atalina thrust her fingers through hair that had begun to show strands of white when she'd been only fifteen. Most teenagers would've been mortified. Attie had made the pragmatic decision to just accept the change and—quite accidentally—turned it into a fashion statement. "Stage three models all predict success in permanently stabilizing the chip."

"But?"

"The hundred percent chance of success is paired with a ninety-five percent likelihood of severe brain damage."

Kaia flinched inwardly. Bowen Knight was the enemy, but he was also a dynamic, intelligent creature. The idea of his eyes going dull, his mind stopping to function . . . Her gut clenched. "Not from the chip," she told him. "It's the compound Attie's using. It'll stabilize the chip, but there's only a slim margin you'll come out of it with the same brain function you go in with."

"Five percent." Bowen Knight whistled quietly. "Christ." Those midnight eyes locked with Kaia's again. "Lily told you the boundaries?"

Kaia nodded. "No machines if you're brain-dead." She should've left it at that, but he had to know the truth—if she kept it from him, she was no better than the security chief who had helped steal her people. "The models don't show you suffering brain death. Only severe brain *damage*."

"Your autonomic nervous system would still function," Atalina explained quietly. "You'd be able to breathe on your own, be able to swallow. There would be no need for machines."

Kaia's gaze was still locked with Bowen's, so she saw the slow creep of horror within the living obsidian. And she suddenly understood Bowen Knight's deepest nightmare: to be helpless against the world, his sense of self erased to leave only a hollow shell.

Chapter 5

My mind is who I am. Do not prolong my life by artificial methods should my brain suffer an insult that leaves me a flesh and blood ghost of myself.

—Living will written and signed by Bowen Knight. Witnesses: Lily Knight and Cassius Drake

HORROR CLAWED AT Bowen.

He'd christened himself in blood to protect his mind against a savage telepathic violation, had spent his adult life attempting to find a way for humanity to do the same. He'd fought so no human would ever again be turned into a mindless doll . . . but he'd forgotten that the Psy weren't the only threat to that integral component of his self.

"I can stop the experiment right now." Dr. Kahananui's voice, softer and less bluntly scientific than it had been to this point.

Bo wrenched his gaze from Kaia's, her inky pupils having flared against the brown of her irises—as if she'd seen his nightmare and understood it. "What would that mean?"

"All I have are the computer models—and I'll be able to refine them with more data now that you've woken," the doctor answered, "but to summarize, you'd have approximately a month to six weeks at full function before your chip goes into catastrophic failure."

She checked something on a monitor. "According to models the

Aleines have run during your coma, you'll know when it begins—the migraines will be excruciating. Then will come the nosebleeds and the ocular degeneration. At which point, you can shut yourself up to die in peace, no chance of anyone disobeying your clearly stated decision to not be put on life support should you suffer brain impairment."

Four to six weeks of life versus an entire lifetime.

But that wasn't the real choice and never had been. "If I don't accept the risk"—if he didn't put his mind on the line for a meager five percent chance of success—"someone else will end up here, end up deciding to continue to stage three." Lily or Cassius or Heenali or Ajax, maybe even scared-of-his-own-shadow-but-brave-despite-it Zeb.

When Dr. Kahananui hesitated, he looked to Kaia. He already knew she'd give him the unvarnished truth. Unraveling her folded arms, she gripped the edge of the panel at the end of his bed. "Yes. The compound is unlike anything we've ever seen. Models can only tell Attie so much. She needs data from a living subject."

"Did you manufacture this compound? How much can you access?"

Dr. Atalina was the one who answered. "It's natural, created by a deep-sea creature as part of its life cycle. We have approximately a hundred grams—"

"No, Attie." Kaia put a hand on the doctor's arm. "What he wants to know is how many people it could save if it works."

"Oh." Dr. Kahananui glanced down at the organizer she'd picked up, but he had the feeling it was more a reflex action than anything—she had the information in her head. "If it works, we have enough to stabilize every individual who already has an implant."

Bowen's heart shuddered. Lily, Cassius, Heenali, Zeb, Domenica, Ajax, the others, they'd all be safe. "Will you be able to get more?" The world had so many vulnerable human minds.

"No, to harvest it again anytime within the next century would be to harm the being who created it. But," the doctor continued, "with the data from a successful experiment, I can take the first step toward attempting to replicate and manufacture the compound—it's so complex and rare that the task is apt to take decades, maybe my entire lifetime."

She could give him no quick answer for humanity's desperate need, but she could save the lives of people he loved. All he had to do was risk everything that made him Bowen Knight. "Five percent is better than no chance," he said, his voice like gravel. "Right now, we're all on the fast highway to death."

"What will you do if it fails?" A soft question from Kaia.

"I won't be able to do anything," he said flatly. "I'll be too brain damaged."

Her fingers clenched even tighter on the edge of the panel. Because while Dr. Kahananui might take his words at face value, Kaia was a darker creature. She understood that he'd make his choices, put contingencies in place. Cassius and he, they were bound by blood and horror. His best friend wouldn't struggle with fulfilling Bo's choice, wouldn't hesitate to run a blade across his throat.

That was when Dr. Kahananui spoke. "Even if it fails," she said, "you'll have the compound in your brain. I'll be able to study its interaction with your neural tissue over the years and gain critical data that could one day lead to a long-term solution."

Bowen stared at her. She was trying to comfort him, but she'd just slammed the prison door on his personal hell, then locked it and thrown away the key. He couldn't ask his best friend to put him out of his misery, not without stealing the chance of psychic safety from future generations.

His sister and friends would all be dead. But countless humans would still be walking around in a world where human minds were considered easy prey. And a slim chance was better than no chance.

Fuck, fuck, *fuck*.

"Do it," he said. "All three stages." For some reason, he'd looked at Kaia as he spoke . . . and he caught her slight flinch. For him? Because of him? Not that it mattered. In making this choice, he'd put himself in a purgatory where his life couldn't go forward or backward for—"How long will it take to get to stage three?"

"Not counting today, exactly two weeks," Dr. Kahananui answered.

His heart thudded at the ruthlessly short time frame. A man could do many things in two weeks, but he couldn't live an entire lifetime. He couldn't make promises, couldn't dance with a woman under a moonlit sky and know that tomorrow and every tomorrow to come for decades, he'd wake up by her side.

And the security chief of the Human Alliance couldn't set up a framework that would protect his people for untold years to come. But he could damn well try. His brain was working right now, and his heart was strong—

Wait.

Raising his hand, Bo spread his fingers over his chest, felt the powerful beat of that heart, sensed the life-giving rush of blood pumping through his arteries. "My heart was punctured by shrapnel. I didn't imagine that."

"No, you didn't," Dr. Kahananui said. "You went into total heart failure soon after the shooting."

"There was nothing left," Kaia added. "No way for the surgeons to patch you back together."

Dr. Kahananui gasped at that instant, gripping at her belly. Bo jerked instinctively toward her, but his body wasn't ready yet; it reacted sluggishly. Kaia, however, had her arm around the other woman. "You in labor?" It was a sharp question.

"No." The doctor came fully upright again. "Just a muscle spasm." She patted Kaia's cheek when the cook with a scientist's background made a distinctively suspicious face. "I have plans to take this baby to full term and to birth in the ocean and not even the resurrection of Bowen Knight will stop me."

Bo looked at the heavily pregnant woman. "In the ocean? Won't the baby drown? I know changelings don't shift until about a year of age." It had taken time and an excruciating amount of patience to learn that fact—changelings were remarkably insular for a people who had a reputation for being wildly affectionate.

"Maybe not all changelings are the same," was the enigmatic response from Kaia.

Dr. Kahananui, meanwhile, was back beside him, running a scanner over his chest. "As for your heart, it's functioning at perfect efficiency.

Your primary physicians attempted to clone one, but for whatever reason, the cloning process failed multiple times."

Bo had to concentrate to keep his attention from drifting to Kaia—it was as if he were connected to her by an invisible cord. She moved and his gaze wanted to follow. "Then what is it I have inside my chest?"

"A mechanical heart. A cutting-edge piece of tech."

Bowen spread his fingers over his chest again . . . and realized this heart would keep on beating if the experiment failed. It'd keep his mindless body moving, keep him from dying. "I haven't heard of this technique before," he said in an effort to exist in the here and now rather than the unknown future.

"It's a rare procedure because of the complexity of creating hearts and because only a single biomech company has done it successfully." Dr. Kahananui continued to take readings as she spoke. "You're the first living recipient of this latest and most stable version. It's a prototype not intended for transplantation into a living subject for another two years at least, but Silver Mercant was able to cut through the red tape for you."

Across the room, Kaia's gaze held only ice, only distance. "You have powerful friends, Bowen Knight."

"No," he said after thinking through the unexpected piece of information, "it's Lily who knows Silver." She worked most often with the telepath in charge of EmNet—the worldwide Emergency Response Network. "This tech is Psy?"

Kaia raised an eyebrow. "Is that a problem?"

"Just a fucking irony." After all that the Psy had done to humans, *stolen* from humans, after all that Bo had done to make sure a telepath could never again get into his head, he now had a piece of expensive Psy technology inside his chest. "The experiment with the compound"—he touched the side of his head—"did the Psy have a hand in suggesting that?"

Before the shooting, he'd had a meeting with Kaleb Krychek, in which the staggeringly powerful telekinetic had told Bo that the PsyNet—the psychic network the Psy needed to live—was on the verge of collapse. In another magnificent irony, it was the sustained lack of human energy in the network that had led the psychic race to the brink of disaster.

The Psy desperately needed humans. *Cooperative* humans.

Coercion wouldn't work.

Mind control wouldn't work.

Krychek needed Bo to tell humanity to trust the Psy.

Bo wasn't heartless, but the Psy had caused too much horror for him to let his heart overrule his head. He'd asked Krychek for a specific gesture of good faith, an act done with no assumption of a return—but simply because it was the right thing to do.

"Put humans and Psy on equal footing when it comes to psychic privacy," he'd said. "Then, maybe, we can talk."

This might be Krychek's response.

But Dr. Kahananui shook her head. "No, this is a purely BlackSea operation."

Which meant the Psy might still be working on their attempt at a solution. But, even if they were, it was impossible that they'd magically come up with an answer in two short weeks. This was the throw he had to play. "Did you tell my sister about stage three?"

Again, he looked to Kaia for the answer. She understood him, would know exactly what he was asking beneath the straightforward question.

"No," she answered. "There was no point if stage one didn't bring you to consciousness. If it did, the choice had to be yours."

"Don't tell her," Bo said, the words an order. "Lily, my parents, Cassius, *none* of my people can know. But especially not Lily. And if the experiment fails, you tell them I died and that you had me cremated because the compound made my body toxic. *Never* let them see what I become."

Chapter 6

Lil, I got you the special holographic concert tickets you wanted. After *four hours* lining up in the rain. This better be the concert of the century.

—Message from Bowen Knight (17) to Lily Knight (13)

KAIA HEARD FAR too much love in Bowen Knight's harsh demand. It wasn't pride that made him ask to be hidden away. It was a fierce love that sought to protect his sister from the consequences of the choice she'd made to enroll Bowen in this experiment. Lily Knight might mourn her brother, but she'd die without guilt, without horror.

And Bowen's parents would pass on never knowing their son was trapped in a living hell.

Kaia took another physical step backward.

No one had warned her that the cold and merciless security chief of the Alliance was also a protective brother and stalwart friend. No one had told her that the man building a deadly army would also be willing to walk into his darkest nightmare for a minuscule chance at giving his people an answer.

Shoulders stiff, she clenched her stomach.

Remember Hugo.

It was a brutal reminder that this same loyal and loving man had had a hand in the abduction and probable torture of her childhood friend.

Remember.

This time the reminder was older and steeped in a child's anguish, for humans had been responsible for all the terrible losses of Kaia's life. Bowen Knight's people liked to think of themselves as the underdogs, but Kaia knew too well that humans could be cruel and self-serving and murderous.

"We'll meet again for a further assessment after I've had time to review all current data," Attie said to Bowen after agreeing to his stipulations about what to do should the experiment fail. "In the meantime, I assume you'd like to get out of bed?"

A curt nod. "I want to have a shower."

"I'll have an orderly come and assist you."

"I'm sure I can do it myself once you unhook all these wires and tubes."

No, Bowen Knight was not a man who'd ever be anything other than in control. Even fresh out of a coma, there was an authority to him that had Attie hesitating. Kaia stepped into the breach—her cousin was brilliant but didn't do well with confrontation of any kind. "If you fall on your face and drown in two inches of water, it makes the entire experiment moot."

His eyes flashed dark fire at her. "A compromise, then. I'll get myself to the shower, but the doctor can position an orderly outside the room."

Attie frowned. "I'll increase the pulse on the muscle trainers." After doing that, she took him through the mobility tests a second time around. "Hmm, you should be able to move well enough to take a short shower." She glanced over. "Kaia, can you grab the alarm?"

Knowing exactly what her cousin wanted, Kaia stepped out of the room and made her way to the medical supplies closet inside the lab farther along the corridor. As she walked, she breathed deep. In and out. And she made herself remember.

The hazy summer nights on the beach when her papa had rocked her to sleep while her mama read her a story.

The laughter as her mama dived with her into the deep, Kaia swimming in the slipstream created by her larger body.

The delight when her papa let her fingerpaint on his big white canvas. The stomach-aching fun at Hugo's poker parties where they bet using toothpicks and unshelled peanuts.

All three were gone now and there was only one common denominator: *humans.*

Kaia wrenched open the closet to retrieve the alarm.

Attie had removed most of the wires and tubes connected to Bowen Knight's body by the time she returned. The only ones remaining were on his arms—and Attie was currently decommissioning those one by one.

Kaia accidentally met his gaze when she entered. He broke the contact almost at once, a dark reddish flush on his cheekbones.

She nearly stumbled.

Gaze going to the connections Attie had thrown into a biohazard container, she realized this dangerous and intelligent man was embarrassed. So much so that he was still avoiding her gaze even though he'd never once looked away previously.

Kaia busied herself going over to the far wall, keeping her back to him while Attie finished. "If you decide you want a view," she said, "put your hand on this hidden panel." She lifted up the square cover cunningly camouflaged into the wall. Beneath was the black matrix of the panel.

"But," she warned, "you'll probably have an audience, so make sure you want to be seen when you open the window." It was hard to keep a secret on Ryūjin. Everyone knew Atalina's subject was the security chief of the Human Alliance. Some—the ones Hugo had trusted with what he'd found—were angry.

Others were as curious as a nosy pod of dolphins.

There were apt to be a few "casually" waiting around nearby right now—people would've noticed Attie's rush to Bowen's room and how long she'd been in here.

"There." The sound of the biohazard container being shut. "You're no longer tethered. I've also removed the two muscle trainers you had on your face, as your facial muscles are reading as fully mobile."

Turning, Kaia went to hand Attie the alarm, but her cousin had picked up the biohazard container and said, "I'll dispose of this and organize an orderly. Make sure you explain how the alarm works, Kaia."

Kaia wasn't prepared for the suddenness with which she found herself alone with a half-naked Bowen Knight who still had a hint of red on his cheekbones. Her fingertips tingled. She wanted to brush them across the red, soothe his discomfort.

Squelching the impulse, she held her breath and slipped the strap attached to the small personal alarm over his head. Her thumbs brushed accidentally through his hair, the soft strands sliding across her skin like a caress. And his eyes, they watched her with a focus that wasn't as ruthless as it should've been.

She withdrew her hands as the flat disk of the alarm settled against his chest. "Squeeze it if you need assistance," she told him, "and the orderly will respond. It's waterproof so you can take it into the shower."

He set his jaw, nodded.

And Kaia knew that despite his intelligence, he had a pride as idiotic as all six of her male cousins. "Wait—I'll be back in three minutes."

She was breathless by the time she returned . . . and he'd managed to swing his legs over the side of the bed in the interim, the hair-rough skin of his lower legs and thighs capturing her gaze. The edge of the blue sheet hovered far too high up those thighs, his hand fisted in it to keep it across his hips.

Skin threatening to burn, Kaia snapped her focus to his face.

He was breathing hard, his other hand braced on the bed and his head slightly lowered. She dared look down, saw that he was flexing his feet back and forth. Already checking his strength, already figuring out his capabilities, already becoming a risk to the station and all the people within it.

Her blood chilled.

"Here." She thrust the cane toward him. "Use it. Even if you only lightly hit your head in a fall, it could ruin the experiment."

Bowen Knight closed the fingers of his free hand over the smooth head of the cane. “What would I do without your tender care?” he said with the faint hint of a smile on his lips.

Narrowing her eyes, Kaia stepped back. He hadn’t spoken to her in a biting or harsh or even sarcastic tone. It had been . . . She didn’t know what it had been, and—she told herself—she didn’t care. “Shower cubicle is there.” She pointed out the doorway about ten feet from the bed and to the left. “Any questions?”

The ebony of his hair caught the light as he shook his head, the waves of it far too soft for this hard man.

Fingers curling into her palms, Kaia spun on her heel and headed to the door. She was about to step out when he said, “Kaia?”

She halted but didn’t look up, not trusting her body and its stunningly traitorous response when it came to the security chief of the Human Alliance.

“Thank you for the window.”

Chapter 7

SR: Did you hear Atalina's brain is awake?

JG: Atalina's brain is always awake, genius.

SR: Ha ha. No, doofus, the human brain she's being all mad scientist on.

JG: Whoa! Seriously?

SR: Yeah. Wanna go look in his window?

—Messages exchanged between Scott Reineke and Jayson Greer on Ryūjin Station

THE WOMAN WITH the angry eyes and the gentle touch who, instead of reveling in his embarrassment, had turned away and given him a distraction just pulled the door shut behind herself.

Her scent, however, lingered in the room, cinnamon and a lush tropical bloom. His chest expanded on the inhale, eased on his reluctant exhale. For a heartbeat there when she'd put the alarm strap over his head, he'd caught the scent directly from her skin—it had been richer, deeper, more innately sensual.

"Focus, Bo. And not on the warrior princess who wants to fillet you."

Leaning heavily on the cane with one hand, his other on the bed, he levered himself down to the ground. Just as well that he'd braced himself because his knees nearly crumpled. Breath harsh, he stood there for long minutes until his muscles stopped spasming. Then he stretched out his legs one at a time—and very carefully.

The muscles felt like jelly, but they held.

Regardless, it took him five long minutes to navigate his way to the shower. The air was cool against his skin—likely because he was covered in a layer of fine perspiration. As if he'd pounded the pavement for miles when he hadn't even made it a few short feet. Bo wasn't complaining; that he could walk at all right after coming out of a coma was a miracle.

His fingers were bone white on the head of the cane by the time he stepped inside the doorway, and his breathing had gone from uneven to flat-out ragged. Bracing his free hand against the wall, he took in the spacious area with towel railings and a narrow but tall shelf filled with amenities to his left. To the right was a short passageway that held a washbasin attached to the wall and ended in a smoked glass door.

That had to lead to the john.

As for the shower, it was straight ahead. No separate door because the floor had been designed to ensure that water would flow away from this entrance area. Shoulders in knots, fingers stiff, and his teeth tightly clenched, he walked in another step. It gave him just enough maneuvering room to shut the main door behind himself.

Once inside the shower space, he didn't even pretend not to need the seat fitted within. Collapsing down onto it, he reached forward and managed to hook the cane to an empty towel rail, then sat back and tried to catch his breath. At this rate, the orderly would be checking on him before he'd even turned on the shower.

Bo frowned, realized it might be a good idea to wait.

Staying in place, he gently exercised his muscles group by group; the bugs seemed to work with him, as if programmed to follow a patient's lead after that patient became active. By the time the orderly knocked on the door, he had his breath back. "I haven't even got the water going yet, man. Give me twenty more minutes."

"You sure you don't need help?" The other man's voice had a grittiness to it that hovered on the right side of too much. "Name's KJ and I swear

I've seen it all before. You can't compete against a colossal squid clanmate who refused to shift into human form for treatment. Tentacle hooks and meter-long arms everywhere."

Bo stared at the closed door even as his brain helpfully presented him with an image of an uncooperative giant cephalopod clinging to the towel rail. "I just came out of a coma, KJ. Stop trying to mess with my head."

"I wish I were joking," was the world-weary statement. "Asshole wrapped one of his tentacles around a bolted-in piece of furniture and used his free tentacle to push me away. I tell you, I've never before wanted to eat calamari, but that day, I was ready to become a goddamn calamari chef. *Especially* after the fucker started squirting ink at me—those assholes swim so deep their ink isn't black. I ended up glow-in-the-fucking-dark."

Laughter built inside Bowen's chest, a slow-rolling wave. "You have to finish the story now. Was he high?"

"Nah, just scared of needles."

And the laugh burst from him in a throb of aching muscles. "I don't have tentacles," he said after it passed, "but I'm pretty sure I can handle turning on the shower while seated." The controls had been deliberately placed for such access. "Kaia will also brain me if I slip and knock my head, so trust me, I'll be careful."

KJ's chuckle was as gritty as his voice. "All right. Just press the alarm if you need an assist back to the bed—I've got the receiver tucked into my ear."

Bo heard the sound of the door to the room shutting seconds later.

Confident now that KJ wouldn't burst in on him without warning, he took a few minutes to examine the metal bugs attached to his body—each about a quarter inch wide and twice as long, they were literally hooked into his skin. He was guessing they'd shot in fine tendrils that reached all the way down into his muscles.

Curious, he touched one of the bugs, pressed a little.

Nothing. No pain. No change in the pulse.

As for the sensor wires laid directly against his skull, Dr. Kahananui had left them in place but they were so fine he could only feel them if he rubbed his fingers directly against his scalp. The doctor had also confirmed they were waterproof, built to be put on a subject and left in place for the long term.

Satisfied he knew about all the tech currently on—and inside—his body, he activated the large square touchpad placed on the right wall. The system came online, asking him for his water temperature preference and suggesting a "comfortable" range.

Bo slid it up to this side of boiling, then pushed Go.

Blissful hot liquid poured over him, the thin needles stabbing deliciously into his scalp and skin. The last time he'd consciously felt the touch of water had been in that Venetian canal, cool dark closing over his head. He couldn't actually remember hitting the water, but he remembered Lily's frantic eyes and searching hands, remembered the starburst in his chest, remembered the water sliding into his mouth and into his lungs.

Not about to be held hostage to an act of violence, he raised his face deliberately to the droplets raining from the showerhead. As they sluiced away the past, running over his face and down his shoulders to his chest, his mind flashed to that semisecond when Kaia had been within touching distance, the curves of her a siren song.

His body stirred.

Shoving his hands through his hair, he shook his head to dislodge the sensory impact of her. But no matter what he did, her scent continued to haunt him. Even after he used the shampoo and soap from the dispensers on the wall, a hint of cinnamon and the luscious bite of a tropical flower lingered on his tongue.

As did the black wave of her fiercely contained rage.

Bo shut off the water with a frown. He let himself drip dry for several minutes before he leaned forward and dragged a towel from the rail. Rubbing his hair with the towel, he considered everything Kaia had said and done. She was angry with him, *incredibly* angry, yet she'd helped Dr. Kahananui secure Bo for the experiment.

". . . I can't say no to family."

That explained her cooperation, but not her fury.

His instincts stretched awake. Bo had spent his adult life unearthing secrets and unraveling enigmas. It seemed fitting that he spend what might be his final two weeks as Bowen Knight attempting to solve the mystery that was Kaia.

His gut twisted.

And he made a decision—he wouldn't waste the time he had and he wouldn't focus on the ninety-five percent chance of failure. He'd live. Protect his people. Laugh with his sister and his friends. Cross swords with a cook with long dark hair and a scent that frustrated and haunted.

If Bowen Adrian Knight was to cease to exist, he'd go out on his own terms.

Chapter 8

Baby girl, while it's just us two, let me tell you a secret. One day, you'll start to like boys, or maybe other girls, as more than friends. When that happens, watch out for the crazy in your bloodline.

—Elenise Luna (29) to her newborn daughter, Kaia

KAIA, HER SKIN cold from the inside out, arrived back at Bowen Knight's room to find KJ just coming out of it. "Any problems?"

The short and compact male who looked deceptively normal in terms of strength, shook his head, the reddish blond strands of his hair glinting brightly under the simulated sunlight. "In bed and out for the count."

She quietly released a breath she hadn't realized she'd been holding. "I'll take over from here." Attie needed a couple of specific scans that could be done with a handheld, but her back was killing her today.

Ordering her cousin to rest, Kaia had volunteered to return to the human who threatened to make her a traitor to herself. "I saved you a piece of pie."

KJ pumped a fist into the air. "You're the best!" After smacking a kiss on her cheek, the scent of the peppermint gum to which he was addicted a cool wash, he all but ran off down the corridor.

Kaia's responsive smile faded nearly as quickly as it had appeared. Even though she knew Bowen was asleep, those penetrating eyes no danger to her, she had to take a second before she could step inside his room. The first thing she noticed was the scent of soap, the second that her cousin's experimental subject was once again half-naked.

He'd obviously found the duffel bag she'd asked KJ to drop inside while Bowen was showering. It was Lily Knight—petite and with skin and eyes that made it clear she wasn't Bowen's sister by blood—who'd thrust that bag into the arms of one of the kidnapping team. "Clothes for Bo," she'd said, her cheeks hollow and the shadows beneath her eyes bruised purple. "So he'll have his favorite things when he wakes."

Kaia hadn't had the heart to let Malachai tell her they'd planned to bring Bowen and only Bowen back with them. She'd put the duffel on the stretcher and silently dared Mal to take it off. He'd just shaken his head very slightly and mouthed *marshmallow heart* at her while Lily was distracted saying good-bye to her brother.

Kaia would've decked the big smugface if she could. She *did not* have a marshmallow heart. It was pure cast iron with only tiny apertures for those who were her own. She didn't care about humans or what happened to them. But Lily . . . she'd been so sad. And Kaia had stood in the other woman's shoes once, helplessly watching two people she desperately loved slip away from her.

It had just been a momentary burst of sympathy, that's all. "Nothing whatsoever to do with marshmallows." Pushing the open duffel safely to the side against the wall, she made herself look at the human who'd caused her to burn a pie, she'd been so preoccupied.

He'd fallen asleep on his front, with a pair of dark gray sweatpants hanging off his hips and his black hair not so much damp as still wet. He'd also fallen asleep *on* instead of under the blanket she'd given KJ at the same time as the duffel. In order to get it out and make him more comfortable, she'd have to interrupt KJ's pie eating. It might even take two orderlies to move Atalina's subject.

Bowen Knight was a big man.

Strange, how he'd gained size after waking. As if the vital energy that burned in his blood had affected her perception. Then there were the tattoos that covered his back, the biggest a dragon in flight, one wing stretched out over his right shoulder, the other dipping lower on the left side of his back, while the creature's sinuous tail spiraled down the right side of his back.

Kaia could *feel* the movement, sense the dragon's powerful turn.

Color drenched every inch of the design, the mythical being flawlessly rendered in shades of orange, rust, and a deep bronze. It was a piece of living art and it was another thing that didn't fit: what kind of pitiless security chief thought about fantastical creatures like dragons? It was strange, too, how well his tattoo fit on Ryūjin.

The station logo was a woodblock print of a dragon rearing to strike.

Kaia knew she shouldn't, but she gave in to the compulsion to press up against the side of the bed and examine the lines of the tattoo more closely—only to keep becoming distracted by the silken brown of his skin. Even the muscle trainers hooked all over his back didn't detract from the look of him.

Curls of sensation deep inside her, the creature that was her other half rubbing against her skin as it swam in inner waters.

Bowen Knight shifted.

Jumping back, Kaia stared at him. But he didn't wake, didn't catch her betraying Hugo and all the others. She pressed the heels of her palms to her heated cheeks in a futile effort to erase the burn before she went to the data panel and checked his stats.

He was in a deep natural sleep.

Deciding to forget about the blanket, she increased the room temperature instead. Then—teeth gritted against her disturbing response to him—she went and found a fresh towel, since the one he'd used was crumpled near where he'd abandoned his bag.

"It's like a disease that crosses racial boundaries and is confined to the male sex—use towel, drop it," she muttered to Hex as she began to dry the hair of the enemy.

Her pet white mouse popped his head out from the specially sewn top pocket of her apron, his tiny paws on the edge and his nose twitching with interest. When he clambered out of the pocket and down her arm to sit on Bowen's lower back, she scowled at him. "You know you're not supposed to do that." For some reason, big, strong men were often scared of Hex.

What did they think he'd do? Nibble them to death?

Unrepentant, Hex curled up against Bowen's lower spine and closed his eyes.

Ignoring her troublemaking pet for now, Kaia continued to dry the human security chief's hair with gentle motions. She knew it was soft, with a wave in it when dry. Wet, it licked the bottom of his neck, the strands appearing longer than they did when dry. The softness of that hair was a lie, of course.

Even in sleep, Bowen Knight had a tension to his face.

"Stratagems and double crosses," Kaia said softly, her eyes falling on the beaded wooden bracelet around her wrist that had been a gift from Hugo. "That's what he's dreaming about."

She went and hung up the towel in the bathroom a short while later, then picked up the dirty one and placed it in the small laundry basket tucked at the bottom of the shelving unit that held extra towels, razors, toothbrushes, and the like.

Walking over to Atalina's dangerous living experiment afterward, she scooped Hex's relaxed form into her palm . . . and the back of her hand brushed the molten heat of Bowen's back. She nearly dropped Hex. No wonder her pet liked snuggling up against the security chief's back.

The man was burning hot.

She quickly put Hex in the pocket where he liked to spend his time when he wasn't making her clanmates shriek by appearing on their bookshelf or in their shoe without warning, then checked the data panel.

Bowen's temperature read as within a normal range for humans.

Yet the back of her hand continued to sizzle from the contact.

"*Damn it*, Kaia." Her particular direct family line had always been known for bad choices when it came to lovers. Look at her highly intelligent mother. Before mating with a brilliant musician with a sly sense of humor, she'd dated two bad-boy convicts who'd ended up back in the slammer, an unemployed drifter who'd drifted away with most of her ready cash, an older man who'd had fluid feelings about fidelity, and a professor who'd cheated on her with a graduate student.

All before Elenise had turned twenty-three.

The only reason Kaia knew about the bad boys was that she'd pretended to be asleep in back of the family caravan while her parents shared a bottle of wine and rehashed their dating histories, both of them giggling tipsily. She hadn't understood most of it at the time, had just liked listening to their happy voices while she lay tucked snugly into her bunk, but as an adult, she understood very well that she had a line of crazy in her bloodstream when it came to men.

"No." She rubbed the back of her hand against her dress with harsh movements as the memory faded into pain as it always did. Because her mother had never had a chance to teach her about boys or about watching out for the crazy. She'd been dead and buried in the deep long before Kaia had come of age.

Her murderers had all been human.

As human as the sleeping male who caused a tug deep inside Kaia that she refused to acknowledge. She knew *exactly* who Bowen Knight was to her and it had nothing to do with that disturbing sense of intimacy. It had to do with war.

A war in which Bowen Knight was the brutal enemy general.

Chapter 9

"Sweetheart, why did you decide to climb down into such a big hole in the first place?"
"I wanted to see what was down there."

—Leah Knight (38) and her filthy, muddy son, Bowen (7)

THE NEXT TIME Bowen woke, it was to an insistent gnawing in his stomach accompanied by a sense of heaviness in his muscles that told him he'd slept long and hard. When he stretched out his arms on a yawn, those arms didn't quiver. Though he didn't feel anywhere as strong as he was used to feeling, he'd improved from the last waking.

Rubbing at his face, he sat up in bed.

The machines hummed, the air was warm, and he was alone.

He took a quick but comprehensive scan around the room out of habit. He had no weapons and his physical status made him easy prey—yeah, that was a hard pill to swallow—but he couldn't simply turn off that part of his nature. It was as much a reflex as breathing.

Having confirmed that the room was free of threats, he swung his legs over the side of the bed, then—abdomen tensed and hands braced on the bed—got out onto his feet. His legs held. Not as well as he would've liked, but well enough to keep him upright and mobile for a short period.

He'd use the cane; pride was useless if it kept him confined to this room in an unknown location. A "BlackSea installation" could mean anything, but as he hadn't felt even a slight sense of movement under him, he didn't think he was on one of their floating cities. Which meant he must still be on land—and unquestionably near water.

Ocean or lake, he'd have to see.

His gaze went to the opposite wall, but—Kaia's warning about curious clanmates in mind—he decided against sliding open the window panel. Not only did he need to get out of this room, he wasn't keen to feel like a sideshow attraction at a carnival.

Having stretched out by then, he reached for the cane. He'd forgotten to look at the time on the data panel before he crashed, so he had no idea how long he'd been out—but his hair was dry and he felt a deep sense of refreshment, so it must've been two, three hours at least.

Making his way to the bathroom, he did what needed to be done. Hands washed and dried, he was about to turn away from the washbasin when his eyes caught on the image in the mirror. The midbrown of his skin was paler than usual, the color having faded without sunlight, lines creased the left side of his face from his heavy, unmoving sleep, his jaw was stubbled, and he was thinner through the face and in the body.

But there was no sign of the ticking time bomb in his head.

Holding to his decision to focus on the chance of success—the chance of *life*—he didn't linger on that thought. Instead, he made his way out and spent a few minutes getting properly dressed.

He'd already put on his jeans and was pulling out a short-sleeved navy shirt with stud detailing from the duffel when he realized his back left jeans pocket felt slightly stiffer than the right. Shrugging on the shirt but leaving it unbuttoned, he reached into the pocket. At first, he felt nothing . . . and then his fingers caught on the edge of a seam that shouldn't be there.

His lips curved.

Going into the bathroom just in case he was interrupted, he removed the jeans and tore open the top of that false pocket to retrieve a paper-thin phone with very few metal components. "Thank you, Cassius," he muttered, dead certain it was his best friend who'd made sure he had a way to contact the outside world.

Malachai's people must've checked the bag before bringing it onto their installation, so either their scans hadn't picked up the minor metal components, or they'd left it inside in an act of good faith. On the flip side, the phone could've been hacked so BlackSea could track all data sent and received, but Bo knew this model and how to check for signs of tampering.

After pulling the jeans back on and buttoning up his shirt, he examined the phone with a critical eye. It bore zero signs of tampering—and the plas was designed to be easy to mark for exactly that reason. Satisfied the physical phone itself hadn't been touched, he turned it on to check that it hadn't been remotely hacked.

A security icon glowed on the screen. He touched it and it asked for a retinal scan. Then it asked him Cassius's middle name.

Cassius didn't *have* a middle name, but Bowen had often said his best friend should add the word "cynical" to his name. He input that answer . . . and got asked the name of Lily's doll that he'd accidentally decapitated with a hedge trimmer one long-ago summer. After that came a question asking for the date a woman on a balcony had accidentally nailed him with a ripe tomato while attempting to hit the man in front of him—a date Cassius knew because he'd also been hit by an awry missile.

Neither one of them could ever get the date wrong, not when it had happened the night of Cassius's twenty-first birthday: February 14, 2072.

Bowen's shoulders shook.

His sister and best friend had made it impossible for anyone but Bowen to get through the encryption. Regardless, he went deep into the phone's programming to search for any indications of trouble. It appeared pristine and the battery was fully charged. The phone also proved to have satellite access—though it had taken an unusually long time for it to forge a successful uplink and that link was weak.

He must be in an isolated region. A remote island?

He'd find out soon enough.

Inputting a familiar call code after stepping out of the privacy of the bathroom, he lifted the phone to his ear as he walked slowly around the room with the aid of the cane to further stretch his muscles. The room was antiseptically clean, could've been a clinic room anywhere in the world except for the high-spec data panel. His most recent readings sat glowing on the screen—as did the period of time he'd been asleep: *3 hours and 47 minutes.*

The phone was picked up on the other end.

"Who is this?" A sharp question.

"Your favorite bionic zombie."

Lily's gasp trembled. *"Bo?"*

Switching on the image feed, Bo turned the phone so it became a miniature comm. The link was bad, the image pixelated, but he could tell Lily was Lily, which hopefully meant she could see his face well enough to know beyond a doubt that he'd woken. "Hello, Lilybit."

The image blinked to black, then cleared for a single second.

It was long enough for Bo's mind to take a snapshot of the lines of grief and pain that scored her creamy skin. He wanted to reach through the wavering connection and crush her against his chest, tell her it would be okay, that he'd fix it. From the moment his parents had walked into their house with the silent, gray-eyed little girl they'd adopted from an orphanage in Guiyang, China, Bo had looked after her.

"Bo," Lily repeated in a teary whisper, touching her fingertips to the screen on her end. "You're really awake."

"I'm not all that steady on my feet yet, but I'm walking, too." Leaning against the bed, he lifted up the cane to show her. "My new style accessory."

She wiped away her tears, grinned. "Distinguished." The slick black of her hair was longer than he remembered, her fine facial bones more obvious, but her smile the same quietly joyous gift.

"How are Mom and Dad, Lil?"

"Not good." Her smile faded. "They're furious because Cassius and I helped disappear you and won't tell them where."

When Bo raised an eyebrow, she shrugged. "Malachai Rhys came directly to me with the proposition. He said one of their scientists might have a partial solution to our problem—and no, I have no idea how he figured out the problem in the first place."

Bowen did. The security chief of BlackSea was fully capable of inserting moles into the Alliance. Bo would've done the same with BlackSea except that by the time of the shooting, he hadn't found a water changeling who might be open to negotiation. "Spying's expected among new political friends," he said. "You can't expect two security chiefs to take each other at face value."

Lily pursed her lips together and tried on a scowl, but her happiness kept peeking through. "I only told Cassius what was happening." Pointed chin set firmly, she said, "You were *dying* and no one else was offering any solutions. So Cassius disabled the security systems and I put the guards on your door to sleep by giving them doctored coffee."

"I keep telling people not to trust a pretty face, but do they listen?"

"Ha!" Lily's smile peeked out again. "Can you *please* get better so I can stop having to fight everyone? Right now, every single knight but Cassius is mad at me."

"Bowen's Knights"—that's what his nine closest friends and compatriots in the Alliance had named themselves. He'd thought they'd been messing around, but the nine—Lily included—had been dead serious. And they'd stuck by his side right into hell and back. "I'm working on it," he said to his sister, his hand clenching hard on the head of the cane. "The shooter?"

"No longer a threat," Lily said. "I'm going to send you a report that breaks it all down." After giving him a summary of events, she swallowed audibly. "I made Dr. Kahananui promise that if the experiment failed, she was to bring me in and we'd shut off the machines together."

Bo's heart might've been mechanical, but it ached at that instant. "You've done everything I asked, Lil. I'll take it from here."

Chapter 10

Reception is notoriously unreliable at this location for reasons of geography even the most sophisticated modern technology can't fully ameliorate. I appreciate your patience and apologize in advance for any delays in getting back to you.

—Dr. Atalina Kahananui in a confidential message to M-Psy Ashaya Aleine, regarding the status of their mutual subject Bowen Knight

ENDING THE CALL with Lily, Bo slid his phone into a pocket, then dug in the duffel to pull out a pair of socks and the scuffed brown boots he wore as often as not. It didn't take him long to pull them on.

His stomach grumbled, the sound insistent.

It was time to track Kaia to her lair and see if he could talk her into feeding him.

Pulse quickening, he put his hand on the scanpad beside the door, and the door slid smoothly back to reveal a wall approximately five feet away. Painted a smooth off-white, it revealed absolutely nothing of his wider surroundings. Bo listened hard before he took a step outside. One glance and it was obvious he was alone in an internal corridor.

His room was located at the very end, nothing to his left but another wall.

He headed right, leaning on the cane as necessary but doing everything he could to support his own weight. The quicker his muscles fully rehabilitated, the better. Challenging a certain angry changeling would go much better for him if he could duck any projectiles she decided to throw at his head.

Bowen's lips tugged up; truth was, he'd prefer such volcanic anger to cold distance—instinct whispered that Kaia wasn't a cold or unfeeling creature. Because someone had turned up the temperature in his room, and only two people were authorized to access the data panel that controlled everything in the suite: Dr. Atalina Kahananui and Kaia Luna.

Bo had noted the names when he glanced at the panel. It made sense to him that a panel made for medical use would have that information out in the open—it functioned the same way as a hospital chart, albeit with more data. Which was also why he'd been able to see that the last access had been a few minutes after he'd fallen asleep—by Kaia.

The woman who treated him as the enemy had also kept him warm while he slept.

Fascinated though he was by the mystery of her, Bo never lost awareness of his surroundings. If this was a clinic, it was an atypical one. First of all, it was silent, with no calls over the public comm, no nurses rushing by, no beeps from other rooms. He could actually only see one other door that might lead to a room and it was situated halfway down the corridor.

As for the left wall, the majority of it was covered in a vivid mural of water shot with light, in the background of which swam a dark shadow—he could swear the creature was a sinuous water dragon. Intricately painted, the brushstrokes smooth, the mural wouldn't have looked out of place in an art gallery or a museum . . . but there was a youth to it, too. A sense of unfettered life. So maybe not anywhere as formal as a gallery or museum.

Sounds finally slivered into the quiet after he passed the other door, were at first echoes he felt rather than heard. A few more steps and he could nearly make out distinct words. Multiple people talking—not a crowd, but more than two. However, he'd still not heard a single announcement over the comm system.

It solidified his growing belief that this installation was a private clinic. Probably the only patients were experi—

"Jesus." Bowen froze.

The corridor had poured him out into a thickly carpeted atrium set up as a lounge area, complete with small tables and comfortable-appearing chairs and sofas—some with backs, others without. Beyond the generous open-plan space was a curving wall of what looked like glass.

And what lay on the other side of that glasslike material was water. Deep blue-green water lit by lights that must have been attached to the building in which he stood. "Venice," Bo whispered to himself, his skin settling back into place. He had to be in Venice. The lower level of Alliance HQ also boasted transparent walls that looked out into the water.

He didn't know how BlackSea had managed to build an installation this big right under Bowen's nose, but what mattered at this instant was that he was close to home.

Walking through the currently sparsely populated atrium, he ignored the eyes aimed his way as he went to stand directly in front of the transparent wall. Murmurs sounded from behind him, but no one approached. Not even the hard-jawed man with dark blond hair whose expression had gone cold and flat when Bo appeared out of the corridor.

Tall and wide, the other man probably thought he could take Bo, but he moved with a heaviness that said graceful movement wasn't his default. Neither was it Bo's at present, but he'd already calculated how he could use the cane and a table or a nearby chair to incapacitate the male. The strongest man in the room didn't always win the fight.

Not if the other party used his brains.

Bo made sure to keep the possible threat in his peripheral vision as he drank in the sight of the waters of home. Except . . . He frowned. Nothing looked as it did from the Alliance building. There was no sign of the piles that anchored Venice, or the remnants of buildings that had sunk prior to the building of the network of below-the-waterline biospheres that kept Venice a thriving city even as the waters rose. And, beyond the diffuse glow of the lights, the water appeared deeper and infinitely darker than in the Venetian lagoon.

Could it be an illusion caused by the way this structure had been constructed? Or a shield of some kind?

Bo had barely begun to consider that idea when a battle-scarred humpback whale swam by on the other side of the transparent wall, one huge eye looking balefully at Bo before the mammoth being disappeared into the endless darkness.

"Not Venice." It came out more as air than sound.

Chapter 11

The deep is eternity.

—Iosef Luna

KAIA HAD RECEIVED a notification the instant Bowen Knight opened his door. With Atalina currently asleep on strict orders from Ryūjin's resident healer, Kaia was on watch for experiments who got up and began walking around. Attie did have an assistant, but George preferred the clean edges of data and had gone a "bilious green" when Attie suggested he might want to interact with their subject.

Entering the communal living area of the atrium, she found the disturbingly attractive security chief of the Human Alliance in front of the seaward wall, his eyes trained on the deep. She understood his fascination—every single room in the habitat except for those in the central core had access to a seaward view. The latter were for non-BlackSea contractors uncomfortable with being reminded they stood countless fathoms deep.

Kaia empathized with their fear as most of her clan couldn't. Terror and hunger entwined in her heart each time she looked out at the deep. She craved the cold slide of it as much as she feared the dangers of leaving safe waters. Monsters existed beyond BlackSea's guarded territorial borders, and the worst of it was that they didn't look like monsters at all.

Her pulse thudded, her breath threatening to turn shallow.

Bowen Knight's face held not even a whisper of the fear that had dug its roots into Kaia's soul, only a shocked wonder that made him appear suddenly young. The way his overlong hair fell across his forehead and kissed the top of his collar just added to that impression.

As she watched, Filipe did another sweep only inches from the edge of the habitat before swimming away and probably up to get air into his lungs. Ryūjin Station's semi-retired handyman found it boundlessly funny to startle unsuspecting clanmates by appearing outside the seaward wall when they were just going about their business—or taking a sip of a well-deserved coffee.

You'd think a whale his age would be more mature, but no.

Hex poked his head out of her pocket at the same instant that Alden caught her eye. His jaw worked as he nudged it toward Bowen's form. Frowning, Kaia shook her head before she began to cross the distance to him.

A close friend of Hugo's, Alden knew the same horrific details as Kaia did. The difference was that Alden was six feet five inches tall and two hundred seventy pounds. If he decided to get violent, Bowen was in no condition to take him on. Unfortunately, Alden was a walrus with a serious problem controlling his temper.

So Kaia played dirty. "Do you want Atalina to go into premature labor?" she hissed at him when their paths crossed.

The big man's shoulders hunched forward in the same curve as his thick handlebar mustache. "He hurt Hugo."

Patting Alden's shoulder, Kaia whispered, "We'll find Hugo." It was a wish as much as a promise. "But you can't harm Bowen Knight—Attie's entire experiment would fail and you know how she is." Kaia's cousin put her soul into her work, would be heartbroken at the loss. "We have to be careful with her feelings—especially now. Go on."

Alden shot Bowen Knight another dark glance before accepting her instruction to leave. Kaia made a mental note to have a quiet word with his supervisor—a good friend of hers—suggesting that Alden should be kept busy for the foreseeable future; as an engineer, he was a godsend and, when in a good mood, a total teddy bear.

It just so happened that he'd been in a bad mood for the past six months. *Walruses.* It was like they turned thirty and lost their minds if they hadn't yet found a mate. After that, it was sulking, temper, and general snarkiness. Hugo's disappearance had just exacerbated Alden's already black temperament.

He could kill Bowen with a single unthinking blow.

Skin suddenly chilled, Kaia took the final steps to Bowen's side. The scanner was already in her hand. That hand happened to be covered in flour—she'd been mixing dough when this dangerous man had decided to mess with her schedule.

"What are you doing out of bed?" She synced the scanner with the fine "smart-mesh" that lay against his scalp, hidden by the soft ebony waves of his hair.

His readings were exceptionally good for a man who'd suffered such a grievous insult to his body. According to Attie, it helped that he'd been in prime physical condition prior to taking a bullet to save his sister's life.

"I think I'm hallucinating," he said, his eyes trained on the water. "I could swear that whale was laughing as he swam by."

"Filipe has a strange sense of humor."

Bowen Knight angled his head to search her face, as if he wasn't sure if she was serious or not. But when he spoke, it was about another thing entirely. "I could've taken the big guy with the mustache."

The hairs rose on the back of Kaia's neck; she'd been sure he was utterly absorbed in the deep while she chewed out Alden. Hugo had been right to warn his friends to not let down their guard around Bowen Knight should they ever end up in his presence. "Fine. I'll let Alden pound you into paste next time," she said, forcing an ice into her voice that didn't come naturally. "Try to do it away from here. Blood is hell to clean out of carpet."

Bowen smiled. It lit up his whole face, the dark, *dark* eyes suddenly warm and the creases in his cheeks devastatingly attractive. "Thank you, Kaia Luna," he said in a solemn tone. "I appreciate being protected."

The other part of her poked up its head at the possibility of a playmate. Kaia sternly told it to stay underwater. According to Hugo, Bowen Knight was the kind of playmate who'd leave them both broken. "Are you hungry?" she asked curtly. "Attie won't thank me if you faint because you're starving."

"I've never fainted in my life." The affront in his expression reminded her so strongly of her male cousins that Kaia's defenses nearly cracked.

Careful, Kaia. He's a master at manipulation.

He was also putting out "bad boy" pheromones that spoke to her crazy—and to the wild, playful, and curious core of her nature. But Kaia had seen the photograph Hugo had found, and no charm onslaught was going to make her forget the carnage.

"You'd better come into my kitchen so I can get on with work while babysitting you." She put away the scanner, then turned and walked toward the back end of the atrium without waiting for his response. The kitchen area was located behind a partial wall that protected it from the atrium foot traffic but left it accessible to the clan.

Once in her domain, she moved past the large table on which her kitchen hands regularly put out fruit, cookies, sandwiches, and other "in-between" snacks. In a station this big, someone was always hungry.

She ruffled the messy golden brown curls of a ten-year-old trying to sneak a cookie out of the jar and put an apple in his hand instead. "You've already had three."

Bodie gave her a long-suffering look out of big hazel eyes. "You got the cookie jar under surveillance, right?"

"I'll never tell."

Sighing, the ten-year-old trudged off . . . but she heard him bite into the apple before he disappeared from view, her hearing plenty sharp enough to catch the sound even in the midst of the other noises in the air. Of Bowen Knight, there was no sign.

Kaia frowned, nearly took a step back out before shaking her head and striding onward to the currently empty working heart of the kitchen. As she'd reminded herself only minutes earlier, the security chief of the Human Alliance was far from helpless. He might even be the deadliest person on Ryūjin.

Washing, then drying her hands, she returned to the counter where she'd been working on the dough. And ignored the jerk in her pulse when he finally came into view. His progress was slow but he didn't appear to be leaning on the cane. And when he pulled himself up onto a stool on the other side of her work counter, she noticed that while his skin was flushed, he wasn't sweating.

Rather than tired, he looked vividly, potently alive.

"So," he said, his gaze watchful in a way that wasn't a threat but that made her skin prickle and his voice full of complex layers that sank deep into her with unsettling ease, "do I have to worry about poison?"

Kaia would *never* use food to hurt anyone—for her, food was warmth, was how she showed her love even when the scars inside her stole her voice. "I wouldn't ruin Atalina's experiment." Firmly ignoring the electric sensations crackling across her skin, she dished him up a plate, then poured him a glass of water. "Eat slowly unless you trust me to save you if you choke."

He forked up a bite, his eyes closing as he savored the taste.

And Kaia's toes curled into the rug she kept below her workbench. Wearing shoes had never come easy to her, and she still tended to kick them off as soon as she could.

Exhaling gustily, Bowen lifted his lashes. "Damn, you could bring me to my knees with food alone."

Heat bloomed in her core, her gaze locked to his. She had to fight to shape a response that didn't betray her visceral and unwanted reaction to his presence, his voice, *him*. "Charm and flattery don't work on me," she said in her most cutting tone. "Eat, then leave so I can work in peace."

Kaia had scared off more than one would-be suitor with that tone, but Bowen Knight didn't even blink. "Any particular reason why you think I'm the spawn of Satan?"

The blunt question hit her hard in the center—and she responded without thought, her heart thundering and her cheeks hot. "You're the security chief of the Human Alliance, and humans are heartless, cruel creatures who love pretending to be the underdog. Like a wolf putting on a sheep's fleece."

Silence hung in the air, a sword about to fall.

Not about to back down from the ugly truth, Kaia sealed and set aside this lot of dough to rest, and opened up a batch that was ready to use. She got busy rolling out the circles for the dumplings she intended to make as part of dinner. Her kitchen hands would be arriving in thirty minutes and she'd put them to work prepping other items, but these dumplings needed a more expert touch.

She tore off small hunks of dough, rolled them into patties, then picked up the rolling pin and got to work. Circle after perfect circle, her body moving automatically even as a storm churned inside her, the being who swam under her skin as agitated as the human heart of her.

"What did humans do to you?" Bowen Knight's voice continued to please her ear on the innermost level, the deep tones of it flawlessly balanced.

Angrily rolling out another circle, she said, "Do you know that before water changelings banded together to become BlackSea, become strong, humans caught and *ate* us?" No one ever talked about that particular piece of gruesome history, but that didn't erase it.

"Changelings can shift very quickly." A steady voice, unflinching attention.

Kaia slammed the rolling pin down on the counter. "I don't have to lie when the truth is so awful."

Wrenching off another ball of dough, she began to shape it into a patty. "A harpoon through the heart does a fantastic job of ending any chance of a shift." Kaia had seen the pictures, read the heartrending memorials. "A water changeling killed in its animal form will remain in that form."

Putting down his fork, Bowen stared at her. "Tell me it doesn't happen anymore." The words came out harsh, raw.

"Only because BlackSea controls its borders with deadly force—and even then, humans creep at the edges with their illegal nets and rusting ships." Kaia's skin crawled with the remembered terror of the child she'd once been. How the hard plas fibers of the net had cut into her delicate skin, how her cries had been unheard . . . and how she'd nearly drowned after panicking and shifting back into the form of a human child.

Bowen's eyes didn't leave her face, and she knew he saw too much, this man who was far too intelligent to trust. "I'm sorry for the crimes of other humans. There is no excuse for what was done to your people—but I swear to you, I've never knowingly taken part in any such evil."

It was a pretty thing to say, but Kaia had seen Hugo's proof, knew that at least two of their vanished would never again be coming home. The tears she'd shed that night had scraped her down to the bone. Even now, each time she closed her eyes, she saw their bruised and mutilated bodies, and she heard Hugo's voice telling her how the Alliance was playing a horrific game with BlackSea's most vulnerable as chess pieces.

Chapter 12

Kaia, I think humans might be the enemy masquerading as our friends. I have proof that Bowen Knight and the Alliance are deeply involved in the vanishings.

—Hugo Sorensen in a message to Kaia Luna

"HOW MANY PEOPLE in this habitat?" Bowen asked when she said nothing in response to his attempt to separate yesterday from today.

"A hundred right now, but this kitchen services all five residential habitats on Ryūjin, so that's approximately four to six hundred people, depending on who's in and who's out." Kaia had no reason to hide the facts from him—as Mal had pointed out, once on Ryūjin, Bowen had no way to escape.

If he *did* somehow manage to summon help, there were hundreds of heavily armed people on the floating city above who'd shoot down anything before it ever reached the deep. And, after a ruthless campaign run on multiple fronts, BlackSea had cornered the market on submersible vehicles. Others might build them, but they'd never match the deadly grace of the ones on patrol in BlackSea territory.

It was only once her people ventured beyond their territorial borders that they became prey—and BlackSea was made up of countless creatures who ranged across the world's oceans. They *couldn't* always be safe . . . but Kaia still didn't understand why Hugo had broken the border when he knew human ships were prowling.

Why had he put himself at risk?

"Four to six hundred people." Bowen Knight's voice was deeper and rougher than her friend's smooth tenor, and right now it rubbed over her skin like sandpaper. "Lot of people for you to feed."

"I try not to fade away from overwork." Having prepared the filling earlier, she dropped a spoonful on each rolled-out skin before accordioning them into dumplings.

"I hate to point this out, but you seem to have a mouse problem."

Kaia glanced down to see that Hex was poking his nose out of her pocket, his paws on the edge. He knew better than to jump out in the kitchen, but he clearly wanted freedom. "His name is Hex, and he's healthier and cleaner than anyone else on this station." She put him on the counter beside Bowen, then washed her hands again and got back to work.

In front of her, Bowen and Hex seemed to be taking each other's measure.

Catching a halting movement out of the corner of her eye, she picked up a plate she'd kept on the counter, took off the thermal cover, and walked over to thrust it into a skinny teenager's hand. "I better see a squeaky clean plate when you're done."

Scott's grin cracked his face, the starburst birthmark on the top of his left cheekbone crinkling with the movement. "You made my favorite." After pressing an enthusiastic kiss to her cheek, the boy who'd recently had a run-in with a wild inhabitant of the sea—and come out worse off—grabbed a fork and began to stuff his face. His eyes, however, were on Bowen Knight.

Kaia put her hands on his bony shoulders and physically turned him around. "Go sit in the atrium." He was sure to find a friend out there; a thirty-strong group of children lived in the habitats because their parents worked on Ryūjin. The kids could've stayed in the city on the surface, but they chose to live and play in the deep—because family was life, was heart.

Kaia's own heart pulsed with decades-old pain as she returned to her counter. Sometimes she forgot her grief for long periods, but it was always there. And this hurt was one she wanted to feel, because when she did, she also remembered the love that had enclosed her, the warm arms and soft kisses, and a bearish laugh far too loud for a BlackSea changeling.

She was conscious of Bowen Knight watching her with security chief concentration, but though the tiny hairs on her body rose in warning, she ignored him to finish this set of dumplings.

The other dough had rested enough by now that she could prep the second set. Her kitchen helpers could be trusted with the cooking part of the process, with her supervising.

While they did that, she'd get to work on a batch of cookies. Her last lot had been hoovered up so fast she was half-convinced certain cookie fiends were hoarding them in their rooms. Might be time to send Hex on a spy mission.

"Kid was limping."

"Scott's a teenager who can swim in the black." Kaia rolled out another circle. "More sensible than most, but his brain's still developing its danger sense."

"What did he do? Try to wrestle a shark?"

She flicked Bowen a glance—and felt a nearly physical shock of sensation when their gazes collided. "I'm fairly certain he wasn't looking for trouble." Her heart thudded. "But neither did he get out of the way fast enough."

Eyes of such a deep brown they appeared black in this light continued to hold her own, the currents arcing between them white fire she could almost see.

"Kaia."

A shiver rippled over her skin.

Forcibly breaking the eye contact, she dived back into work. But her mind was racing, spinning. Why was her body reacting to him? Why was *she* reacting to him? It wasn't as if she was starved of choice should she want skin privileges. Ryūjin's population aside, the station had visitors from the city on a regular basis. Kaia, too, could swim up whenever she pleased.

More than one clanmate had made her an invitation. And yet . . .

"Shit." Metal hitting china, Bowen's fork clattering onto his plate. "Muscles are spasming." Rising from the stool with a wince, he began to stretch with slow, intense attention to detail.

Kaia wondered if he ever did anything any other way as she kept an eye on him. Should he begin to topple over, she'd summon one of the group of clanmates who'd come in to grab coffee a couple of minutes earlier and were now lingering nonchalantly in the external part of the kitchen.

The five women were too scared of Kaia's wrath to invade her domain, but that didn't stop them from staring in Bowen Knight's direction with unabashed interest. BlackSea might've managed to convince the rest of the world that they were mysterious and aloof loners, but everyone seemed to forget that a great number of water creatures preferred to hang about in large groups.

Forget mysterious, the oceanic flow of gossip was second only to the massive currents that formed the North Atlantic Gyre.

Her eyes narrowed as she noticed the precarious way Bowen's jeans were hanging off his hips.

"Does your mouse eat human food?" he asked after shaking out his body like a large dog settling its skin.

The curious cats—all of whom were single females—made eyes at each other.

"Give him a hunk of that yellow cheese on your plate," Kaia said absently as she finished accordioning the last dumpling. "I'll be back in a moment." She headed to the knot of watchers. "Drooling over a man just out of a coma?" She glared at them. "Shoo."

"But Kaia," one whispered, "he's so . . . rough looking. That stubble, the tumbled hair."

"Yeah. Like Malachai. He can dive with me anytime."

Kaia shook off a shudder at the image—Mal was like her brother; she did not want to visualize his love life. "Fine. Keep drooling, but do *not* go near him." The instruction had nothing to do with her painfully uncomfortable response to him; Bowen needed to eat, not fend off amorous offers. "And *especially* no offering him tentacle skin privileges." She pinned the most likely offender with her gaze.

Oleanna giggled as she stole a flower from a friend's braid to tuck behind her right ear. "Not my fault so many humans have a fetish."

Throwing up her hands, Kaia took the risk of leaving Bowen alone with the horde while she went to her quarters. It didn't take her long to find the belt Edison had forgotten the last time he'd visited. The oldest of Atalina's five younger brothers—and the cousin to whom Kaia was closest—had crashed in her room on a mattress on the floor.

He'd kept her awake half the night with hysterical stories from the city, his sense of humor so dry most people saw him as stoic and quiet. But that quiet existed, too; Edison had a deep well of silence within, an unshakable inner peace. As a heartbroken little girl, it was fifteen-year-old Edison whom Kaia had allowed to hold her, Edison whose hand she'd clutched when the clan consigned her parents' bodies to the deep with a song of mourning that pierced her childish heart.

Returning with the belt to find Bowen unmolested but all the watchers giggling and blushing, she thrust the battered black leather at him over the counter. "Put this on before you give your fan club a strip show." He'd obviously lost weight during the coma and his jeans were barely hanging on to his hips.

A slow smile that reached the darkness of his eyes and made her stomach clutch . . . and had certain people fanning themselves. Lifting her rolling pin, Kaia tapped it against her other palm. The fan club continued to watch, unrepentant and gleeful.

"Thanks." He got off the stool and, lifting up his shirt, began to slip the belt through the loops on his jeans. The action revealed the still-hard plane of his belly, though it was more concave now than she guessed was normal for him. A dark line of hair arrowed down and into his jeans. It was a view available only to Kaia . . . who didn't look away.

"Done."

Dumplings all prepped for cooking, Kaia made a production out of checking her recipe organizer. "Shortbread," she said aloud.

"Oatmeal raisin, too!" cried she-of-the-tentacles. *"Please."*

"If you scat right now."

A pause, but Bowen's admirers finally decided they really wanted the cookies. "Bye, Bo." The women waggled their fingers in his direction.

"Ladies." Waiting until they were alone once more, he sat back down on his stool.

Hex chose that moment to scramble down the counter and to the floor. "You want me to grab him before he makes a grand escape?"

"No. Hex knows the way home." Her pet moved quickly out of the kitchen. She knew he'd find his way to the seaward wall and sit there watching the deep in rapturous quiet.

"Odd pet for a cook."

Kaia could see no risk in sharing this truth with him. "My boy cousins put a mouse in my bed when I was twelve." None of the six had played a single trick on her while she was in the black hole of grief, instead surrounding her in warmth and affection and more compassion than most people would believe possible from a bunch of rowdy boys.

"They thought I'd scream. I didn't." The miscreants had been trying ever more devious tricks since then—every so often, the younger four could still talk Edison and Mal into joining in.

"Hex doesn't look a day over one or two."

"His full name is Hex Luna the seventh. The mouse life span is sadly short." Flippant words, but Kaia had mourned the death of each Hex. She would've never adopted Hex II if Edison hadn't turned up with the mouse six months after the first Hex's death.

"Love him, Kaia. He needs it."

Her big, tough cousins kept doing that, and she kept not being able to give the new Hex back. Each one had their own personality, their own way of being. This Hex was mischievous and loved to explore where Hex VI had been a homebody who mostly enjoyed sleeping—with *very* rare excursions to run on his wheel.

And though Kaia *hated* death, she'd come to terms with it with the Hexes—because when they died, it was after their natural life span. And in that life span, they were pampered and protected and loved.

It was the unexpected or unnatural losses that destroyed her.

Her eyes landed on Bowen and she thought of the ticking time bomb in his head . . . and of the untested compound in his brain. If the chip imploded or the compound failed, there'd be nothing natural about it.

It would destroy Bowen Knight right in the prime of life.

Chapter 13

"We can bandage up his physical wounds, but it's the damage done to his heart and his mind that'll scar him."
"My gentle, sweet boy. What will this do to you? Who will this make you?"

—Jerard and Leah Knight on their son, Bowen (13)

BO THOUGHT OF the plate of Scott's favorite food, of the cane thrust under his hand, of a room made warm so he could sleep comfortably and wondered how Kaia expected him to believe she just shrugged off the deaths of her pets.

"I was thirteen when my pet hamster died," he found himself telling her. "I cried for a week at night, when no one else could see me." It had happened four days after he killed in desperate defense of himself and his best friend, four days after his mind was violated so badly that he'd still been suffering ice-pick migraines, blood vessels bursting in his eyes from the pressure.

Kaia's expression stilled. "That's not a very macho admission."

"You've seen me flat on my back in bed, a million wires coming out of my body," Bowen said with a shrug, though he could feel a dark flush creeping onto his cheekbones. "I figure that ship has already sailed far, far away." Unfortunately.

"What was your hamster's name?"

"Toric the Destroyer."

A twitch of Kaia's lips. "Did you ever get another hamster?"

Bo deliberately forked up a bite of food, took his time chewing then swallowing. "No. Guess I grew out of it." He'd buried Toric in his parents' back garden and planted a tree over his small body.

That tree now provided a home for birds, and shade on a sunny day. And it reminded Bo of the boy he'd once been, a boy who'd held long conversations with his pet about the best way to lay siege to the ogre's castle in his favorite game. That boy seemed a mirage of the past now. A ghost who had never really existed.

"No, you didn't." Kaia looked at him with a disturbing intensity. "You were too sad to get another pet."

How could he explain to her without tearing open scars he'd spent a lifetime ignoring? "Some things were for the boy I was," he said at last. "The man has other priorities."

A sudden blink . . . and a stiffening of her features. "Why are you pursuing a friendship between humans and water changelings? It's not like we often cross paths."

"Water changelings do live on land," Bo pointed out. "Generally near lakes and rivers and the ocean, but they have definite land-based residences. Including many in my home base of Venice."

"You know what I mean."

"Yes, our paths *don't* often intersect," he admitted. "Water changelings tend to stick pretty close to their own." It was rare for them to even make contact with other changeling groups, far less humans. "How's the alliance with the leopards and wolves working out?"

"The wolves upgraded all the lighting in the station." Kaia pointed up. "We didn't have the simulated sunlight and moonlight till then." She closed her eyes, took a deep breath, and released it with pleasure. "That's the one thing I used to miss about the surface—the light."

Bo had gone motionless the instant she raised her face, the softness of her catching him in its steely grasp. So much pleasure in such a simple act, her entire body worshipping the glow of sunlight. "What did you think of them?" he asked when she returned to her recipe.

"Engineers are engineers everywhere, but I've never seen such powerful dominants go so green." Laughter in the backs of her eyes. "Station commander says they set a speed record with the installation, they were so antsy to leave."

"Yeah." Bo found wonder in being down in the deep, and he had no claustrophobic tendencies—but he was also very conscious that it'd be nearly impossible for him to leave without BlackSea cooperation.

He had only a single ace to play: Kaleb Krychek.

Of course, calling the cardinal telekinetic for an assist would put the Alliance in debt to the Ruling Coalition of the Psy—which made his ace useless. "Humans and water changelings have a lot in common."

Kaia's scowl was a storm cloud. "Oh?" She put a jar of walnuts on the counter.

"What are those for?"

"Walnut coconut snowballs. The orcas like them and they haven't broken anything this week."

Orcas, sharks, women with tentacles who purred suggestive promises at him across the room, it all sounded like a drug-fueled dream. "They the bull-in-a-china-shop of the sea?"

"Walruses hold that title. Mostly because they're too bad-tempered to watch where they're going."

Bowen couldn't help but think of the mustachioed male who'd seemed ready to pound him into paste in the atrium. If anyone should be a walrus, it was him—especially with that mustache. "Do you want me to chop up the walnuts for you?"

Kaia passed him the jar along with a knife and a wooden cutting board—and when their fingers brushed, she drew back with jagged speed. "Unless you can swim underwater for hours, I doubt we have anything in common."

Heart thundering, Bo began to twist open the jar. "We're spread out across the world." It was hard to focus when his fingers burned with an echo of sensation, but he had to make her listen; only then might he get an answer on the cause of her anger and that of the man in the atrium. "It makes us less able to defend ourselves."

Jar open, he picked out a nut and crunched it between his teeth. "The DarkRiver leopards, for example, have well-defined and comparatively compact territorial borders they defend with blood and fury. Same with the StoneWater bears—huge territory but defined down to the wire. Cross their boundaries at your own risk."

Kaia crouched down to look for something in a lower cupboard. "What do you know about the bears?"

"One of my cousins just mated into StoneWater."

Kaia popped up from her crouch so fast she almost hit her head on the edge of the counter. "You're making that up."

Bo didn't take her disbelief personally. "I nearly fell down when Phoenix told me. He's so shy he couldn't even approach a gazelle changeling."

"A shy human with a *StoneWater* bear." Kaia sounded like she was being strangled. "Is he still alive?"

"Not only alive but deliriously happy." In love in a puppyish way Bo simply couldn't imagine. To trust that deeply, so without fences or walls, to let yourself fall . . . he wasn't capable of it.

He'd seen masks on too many faces, had learned too well never to trust based on instinct alone. It had begun at thirteen, in an act of boyish trust that had almost cost his best friend his life and turned Bo into a killer.

Chapter 14

If a bear or a wolf tries to feed you, you wild women know to be on your guard. If an eagle suddenly turns up spic-and-span and wearing a pretty suit, you know to lift an eyebrow. But humans . . . humans don't follow any kind of a pattern that we've been able to work out despite *extensive* investigation on your behalf, so you'll have to be on your guard. Or you might end up in your sneaky human's bed before you know it.

—From the December 2081 issue of *Wild Woman* magazine: "Skin Privileges, Style & Primal Sophistication"

BOWEN KNIGHT WAS very good at hiding his thoughts and emotions, but nothing could erase the black cloud hanging over his head. Yet they'd been talking about a happy subject, about love, about a bear mating a—*Oh*.

Kaia swallowed hard as she grabbed the oatmeal she needed for the oatmeal raisin cookies, her skin suddenly frigid. Because it struck her that Bowen was probably caught in the vicious reality of his own existence, where he had only a five percent probability of surviving beyond two weeks with his mind intact. His chances of falling in love, mating—

"Does BlackSea have a relationship with the Moscow bears?"

Flinching inwardly at the sound of his voice, she stood to find he'd banished the blackness and was focused on chopping up the walnuts. His hair fell across his forehead, and the lines on that forehead were of concentration. She wanted to shake her own head—he even chopped walnuts with a dangerously intent absorption.

She curled her fingers into her palm when they threatened to reach out and push back that lock of hair. "You'll have to ask Mal or Miane about the politics, but I've never met a bear." Apparently the bears had been acting secretive for a while.

Malachai had mentioned it to her once, while muttering about how bears drove people crazy and those crazy people liked it. It had been on the heels of three of their young going missing—only to turn up gigglingly drunk in the Caspian Sea, on a boat with a bunch of bears.

That had been before the vanishings, before they'd lost their innocence.

"Here's what I do know," she said, fighting the sadness threatening to crush her; her kitchen hands would be here soon and they were only youths, deserved better than to exist in a clan mired in constant mourning. "Last week the bears threw a party so raucous it covered half of Moscow." She found the vanilla pods and set them out; she liked having all her ingredients at hand before she began to bake. "It was in the latest In the Know column of *Wild Woman* magazine."

Bowen looked up. "What magazine?"

She waved away the question to tell him something far more interesting. "Kaleb Krychek attended and the column had a photo of him dancing with his mate." The Psy couple had been surrounded by large bears in bear form wearing party hats.

"Any reason for the party?"

"Mating celebration for their alpha." She realized something. "You probably don't know, do you? Valentin Nikolaev mated Silver Mercant."

The knife thunked to motionlessness on the cutting board. "Seriously, Kaia," Bowen said with a pained look, "you all *have* to stop messing with me. My coma-brain is going to explode. The last person Silver Mercant would ever mate with is a *bear*."

A laugh bubbled up inside her at his expression. "Here." Picking up the organizer she generally used to make recipe notes, she brought up the most recent edition of *Wild Woman* and flicked to the article about the mating. "They even managed to get a short Q&A with Silver for their story."

Kaia had a feeling the powerful woman had agreed in order to humanize herself, breaking down barriers that might stand in EmNet's way. She had to admire the telepath for that—because Silver Mercant had a sense of containment about her that said she valued her privacy. Yet she'd given that up for the good of people across the globe who might one day need assistance from the Emergency Response Network supported by all three races.

Bowen took the organizer, spent the next five minutes reading the article. "One measly coma and the world turns upside down. Silver Mercant with a bear. What the hell am I going to find out next? That Psy Councilor Nikita Duncan has fallen madly in love and eloped?" Shaking his head as he muttered that ridiculous scenario, he turned a few pages, then seemed to get engrossed in another article.

Kaia wondered what he was reading; *Wild Woman* was aimed at changeling women for the most part, though she knew her cousin Armand had a subscription. Ask him around other men and he'd smirk and say it was for "research on women," but Kaia knew full well he loved the fashion and beauty editorials. He'd even asked her to help him make the natural skin-softening cream described in one issue.

"I have the worst stubble rash," he'd said, scratching at his jaw with black-painted fingernails.

Amused at Bowen's fascinated concentration and speculating whether he'd found a beauty tip of his own, she bent down to grab the jar of raisins she had to hide behind pungent spices so people wouldn't steal them. No, not the kids. Grown adults who should know better, but who kept purloining her cooking supplies—as if there weren't perfectly fine packets of snackable raisins in the huge "goody" jar she had out front.

Apparently, her cooking raisins were "juicier."

Bowen had put down the organizer by the time she rose back up to her feet. As she watched, he threw a walnut into his mouth.

"How about eating more actual food rather than my walnuts?" She looked pointedly at his half-full plate.

"I'm taking a break." He continued to chop the walnuts.

As Kaia began to measure out the ingredients for the first set of cookies, he said, "You lost someone, didn't you? In the vanishings?"

Kaia's spine went ramrod straight at the quiet question. God, the man was *dangerous*—he might have just come out of a coma, but the security chief part of his brain was fully functional. And she'd let down her guard in the silliness of a conversation about bears and walnuts.

Chapter 15

The Consortium wants Trinity to fail. Peace and cooperation between humans, Psy, and changelings hurts their bottom line and their posited ambition of being shadow powers who treat us all as their puppets. As we come from all three races, so do the members of the Consortium. None of us can wash our hands of this scourge. They are the enemy of peace, of unity, of Trinity.

—Message sent to all signatories to the Trinity Accord

"MY BEST FRIEND, Hugo." Kaia measured out the sugar with jerky hands. "He went out for a long-range swim and never came back."

"Consortium." White lines around Bowen's mouth, his jaw hard. "Those bastards want to use water changelings to get into places they can't."

Kaia had heard all the theories. It didn't matter that she wasn't in security. Three of Atalina's brothers were—and then there was Mal, Miane's right hand and one of the deadliest men in the clan. But when the cousins all gathered together, Mal and the others spoke openly on many things. They knew nothing they said would ever leave the room.

And it wasn't as if Mal was going behind Miane's back in sharing the information; she was often right there with them.

In the beginning, it had been strange to have her in the group—

Miane was their First, their alpha, the most powerful person in BlackSea and capable of bloody retribution against those who harmed her own. The distance, however, hadn't lasted long under the force of Miane's charisma and incredible warmth.

Kaia now knew that Miane had a weakness for salted caramel bites, basil-infused pasta, and strong Turkish coffee. During those dinners full of conversation and laughter, she became just another clanmate, albeit one who hummed with so much power that Malachai alone could handle the full force of it.

So Kaia knew full well that everyone was blaming the Consortium for the vanishings—but they weren't the only nasties in the water. "Or maybe," she said, too angry to watch her words, "illegal human fishers are murdering our people and blaming the bogeyman of the Consortium." What she didn't say was that those fishermen also gave Bowen Knight and his people plausible deniability.

Bowen's hand tightened on the wooden hilt of the knife she'd given him. "No." A flat statement. "Any human who has chosen to become part of the Alliance knows *never* to breach BlackSea's territorial waters." Ice in his tone. "If you have evidence to the contrary, give it to me and I'll make sure the perpetrators are severely and immediately punished."

A shiver ran across Kaia's skin at the chill in his tone, at the implacability of it. But she wasn't about to be intimidated. "It's not my job to clean house for you." She dumped chopped butter into the mix. "You're cutting the walnuts too big."

"Kaia."

Thrusting the bowl under the mixer, she set the attachment spinning. "Yes, the Consortium has unquestionably taken some of our people," she said, "but as you said—humans cover the world. Your people are perfectly placed to hunt water changelings who get in the way of their illegal harvesting of the ocean's riches." She met his eyes, was stunned by the raw dominance in them. She'd never realized humans could interact with changelings on that primal a level. But hell if she'd look away.

"Is it possible?" he said, his cheekbones pushing against his skin and his shoulders taut. "Yes. But the missing have almost uniformly been healthy and young. BlackSea should've lost older people, too, if the vanishings were due to malicious kills by illegal fishers."

Malachai had said the same, but his features had been grim. He hadn't just brushed her off. Neither had he brushed off the information Hugo had compiled and given her for safekeeping. Her best friend had told her he wanted to undertake further investigation and confirm his data before he passed the dossier to Mal, but when Hugo disappeared, Kaia had known what she had to do.

On the data crystal she'd given Mal had been the names of a significant number of human fishing ships *and* how very close they'd been to the last seen locations of BlackSea's lost, the ships going to the very edge of BlackSea's boundaries and occasionally nudging over.

Also on the data crystal had been the damaging news that the Alliance was planning to set up its own shipping armada in competition with the mainly Psy conglomerates that currently controlled oceanic shipping. That, however, could be explained away as commercial aggressiveness. BlackSea had a fleet, too, but the clan wasn't interested in going after Psy-held contracts. The Alliance, in contrast, wanted to set itself up as a direct rival.

For that, they'd need BlackSea's cooperation.

And, as Hugo had pointed out, the only reason BlackSea had even considered the idea of friendship with humans was the vanishings. Yes, humans hadn't been the clan's first choice of ally when they realized they were being hunted, but a man who played a long game would be patient, would wait until BlackSea was desperate enough to stretch out a hand to humanity.

Bowen Knight struck her as that kind of a hunter.

That theory also perfectly explained the presence of ships from the tiny Alliance Fleet in BlackSea's territorial waters; the Fleet ships had been cunningly hidden among the fishing traffic, but Hugo was a comms expert. He'd tracked down beacons, gotten satellite locks, had *absolute* confirmation that Bowen Knight's ships had been in their waters when some of their people were taken.

The Alliance had played BlackSea for a fool.

The last and most painful item on the data crystal had been an image that showed the brutalized bodies of two of their vanished—on the deck of a vessel that bore the Alliance logo and was officially part of the Alliance Fleet.

She kept that damaging fact to herself because Mal had asked her to do so; he hadn't even informed the families of the victims about the Alliance involvement yet. Conscious that Kaia's anger was too hot a thing to be contained, he hadn't told her to keep Bowen in the dark about the allegations against the Fleet, just to not tell him the brutal extent of what they had.

"I want to be sure beyond any shadow of a doubt," he'd said, the pale, pale gold of his eyes like frozen sunlight. "We're talking about an act of war, Kaia. We *cannot* be wrong."

Kaia blinked back the burning at the backs of her eyes. "A large vessel wearing the Alliance Fleet logo was passing just beyond our territorial waters around the time Hugo was taken." Removing the creamed butter and sugar, she began to sift in the flour. "There are no records of any other vessels nearby. And it's not the first time Alliance vessels have been spotted near people who later disappeared, and a number of those vessels crept over BlackSea's border."

The fact that those incursions had been timed to avoid the clan's security sweeps added more fuel to the fire. That BlackSea had a traitor was an awful truth no one could ignore; Hugo's dossier made the link between that traitor and the Alliance as clear as glass. Luck couldn't explain the Fleet's faultless timing. "Hugo was the one who connected the dots between the vanishings and the Alliance Fleet—and now Hugo is gone."

A muscle pulsed along Bowen's jawline. "Do you have the data? I need to look at it myself, find out what the fuck is going on."

"You can ask Mal for it." Blood bubbling, she lifted a shoulder in a shrug. "Right now, you're just arguing with a cook."

"I don't think you're 'just' anything." Bowen was struggling to make sense of what Kaia had told him. If ships belonging to the small Alliance Fleet had truly skirted over BlackSea's territorial boundaries, then he had a serious problem—because *all* Fleet ships knew to give BlackSea space. The Fleet was also under the direct command of Heenali Roy, the Alliance's effective third in command and one of Bo's trusted knights.

His hand fisted on the counter. "Is there a comm I can use to contact Malachai?"

"The data panel in your room has a comm function." Picking up her organizer, she did something on the screen. "I've used my login to authorize you for full access." She put the organizer back down. "No point calling Mal right now, though."

"He still out searching for the vanished?"

"No." Her cousin and Miane had both come back furiously empty-handed. "He's gone for a swim."

Bowen had the feeling she wasn't talking about a few freestyle laps. "How do you know?" He glanced in the direction of the seaward wall, remembering how Malachai's eyes had gone from brown to an inhuman light gold, remembering, too, the sense of size around the other man. "Did you see him?"

"No, but one of the others did." Kaia had quickly rolled out the shortbread dough, now began to cut it into shapes with metal cookie cutters. "He'll probably be back in another two hours."

Containing his impatient frustration in a vicious grip, Bowen watched her competent yet graceful movements. "Is that what you think of me?" The realization hit him hard in the solar plexus, driving all the air from his lungs. "That I'm a monster who's behind the torture and deaths of your people?"

Her hand jerked, crushing the edge of the dough she'd been about to cut. She quickly nudged it back into shape and continued on. "You're a human stranger who's managed to create a relationship with BlackSea within two years of taking over the Alliance." She swapped the rectangle cutter for a circular one. "You also have a reputation for ruthless dedication to your goals."

Bowen clenched his jaw, tried to see things from her perspective. "You could say the same for Miane."

When she glanced up with lines marring her brow, he said, "Your alpha has managed to make an alliance with the two most powerful packs in the world despite BlackSea only recently breaking isolation. And I don't think either one of us will argue against her ruthlessness." Miane Levèque was a sleek, deadly predator.

Thrusting her prepared trays of shortbread into the oven, Kaia shut the door, then programmed the correct cooking temperature and time. The device started with a hum, the temperature racing from zero to the set number in a matter of seconds. "We didn't build a paramilitary army prior to seeking a relationship."

Bowen frowned. "Kaia, BlackSea has a massive number of men and women with military training. You also have armed submersibles, missile launchers capable of shooting down flying craft, jetboats, weaponized jet-choppers, hovercraft—the list is long and it's full of people and things that can kill."

Chapter 16

We will never again be prey.

—Tao Levèque, the founding First of BlackSea

BOWEN'S WORDS DIGGING into her brain and refusing to leave, Kaia began to throw together the ingredients for her second batch of cookies. And she kept thinking of Malachai and Armand, Teizo and Tevesi. All of them strong dominants. Mal as dangerous as Bowen Knight, the other three not far behind.

Armand was an expert at air defense, could pinpoint a target with laser accuracy, while Teizo and Tevesi were submersible experts—offensive and defensive.

"Our resources are necessary," she said at last. "Water changelings have been targeted and hurt through the centuries." Spread out as they were, they'd had no power and thus no one had respected their rights or territorial claims.

"Humans can't escape into water." Bowen's voice was hard. "We have to live on land where Psy can rape our minds and where strong changelings can take what's ours by force."

Horror uncurled in Kaia's gut. "To take forcibly from humans is against changeling law." Different rules applied between changeling groups—for a clan or pack wasn't meant to claim what it couldn't hold.

Bowen's lips tugged up in a humorless smile. "There are bad changelings just as there are bad humans." He rubbed at his face. "Two months before I was shot, I went in with our paramilitary team to protect an isolated human settlement against a violently aggressive group of changeling mountain lions. The fuckers had terrorized those people for days."

Staring frozen at him, Kaia whispered, "Did they hurt anyone?"

"Three men who went out to confront them." Bo got off the stool and began to pace, pressing his weight down on the cane with each jagged step. "All three were still in the hospital by the time I went off the bridge in Venice."

Kaia lifted trembling fingers to her mouth.

But Bowen wasn't done yet. "We tranqued the hell out of the bastards—should've shot them, but we're trying to build bonds, not break them. Took days to track down their pack, and when we did, their alpha told us the group had been made outclan." Shifting to face her, he said, "Because their alpha couldn't bring himself to execute members of his pack after they first committed crimes punishable by death, humans paid the price."

Dropping her hand, Kaia looked unseeing at the jar of raisins. "You need the fighters." It seemed so self-evident a truth when Bowen laid it out—but Hugo had seen a monstrous hunger for power in the Alliance's quiet increase in military capabilities. "Why so many?"

Bowen shoved a hand roughly through his hair. "We only have *one* main unit. The Alliance isn't big enough to spread out our might—we have to mobilize to multiple parts of the world as needed."

Meanwhile, BlackSea had a massive security presence on both Cifica and Lantia, as well as units on the smaller floating cities around the world. Kaia's inherent sense of fairness saw nothing wrong with humans having knives against a world that would otherwise step on them.

But . . . why would Hugo skew his report to make it sound as if the

Alliance was gathering a vast army that could overwhelm BlackSea? All she could think was that he'd misunderstood what he was seeing—her friend was a comms and computronics expert, not well versed in security.

Maybe that was why Mal was being so careful; he must've realized that particular part of Hugo's dossier made no sense. Frowning, the ground no longer so solid beneath her feet, she removed Bowen's now-cold plate of food and slid the leftovers into the organic recycler. She got a fresh plate afterward, dished out an extra serving of the casserole he'd scraped off his plate.

"Eat," she said, putting the plate on the counter.

He glared at her. "We're having an argument."

"It's over." She needed time alone to think, couldn't do it with him in the room. "Eat or all you're getting from now on is gruel." Putting her hands on her hips, she dug up her sternest expression. "And no coconut walnut snowballs, either."

Bowen Knight stood unmoving, his gaze dark on her—but Kaia wasn't afraid. Neither was she in the grip of the black anger that had driven her to throw Hugo's evidence in his face. Confusion had fractured her certainty; the wrenching shift left a gap, and in that instant she felt something else rise up to fill it, a sudden madness fueled by a primal and visceral response she didn't want to acknowledge. Her blood surged, the other half of her diving agitatedly in the sea that was her soul, and her heart pumped.

Holding his gaze, she picked up a handful of walnuts and began to eat them one by one.

"Kaia." Fury continued to hum under his skin.

She crunched another walnut in deliberate provocation.

Eyes narrowed, he began to move . . . but he didn't go to his stool. No, he came around to her counter. And though she could've easily evaded him in his current state, she stood her ground. Even when he came so close that her breasts brushed his chest with every inhale.

His body heat kissed her skin, his chin dark with stubble. "You need to shave," she murmured, her fingers rising almost of their own volition to brush against the roughness.

Cane clattering to the floor, Bowen gripped her chin in one hand without warning and pressed his lips to her own.

Kaia stumbled back, her hands reaching behind her to land on the counter. He came with her. His body was a hard press against her front, his hand still gripping her jaw. But his lips, they were soft, coaxing. And where Kaia could've withstood harsh demand, she found herself sweet-talked by the luscious charm of his invitation of a kiss.

His scent infused her senses, warm and with a hint of the soap he'd used for his shower earlier, but mostly just Bowen. She didn't remember raising her hand again, but her fingers were fisted in his hair, and oh, it was as pettable as it looked. She wanted to—

A shriek of laughter.

Kaia jerked away from the kiss, glancing over her shoulder with her heart booming thunder. They remained alone—but from the noises getting closer, that wouldn't last much longer. Putting one hand on Bowen's chest and trying not to sense the living heat of him under the thin barrier of his shirt, she pushed.

He'd already braced one hand on the counter, didn't lose his balance. His hair was tumbled, his lips wet from their kiss, and his eyes . . . She wondered if her pupils were as hugely dilated.

Smoothing back her hair, she said, "Your food's getting cold."

BOWEN didn't trust himself to move. He'd kissed Kaia in a fit of temper, but that temper had died a quick death at the taste of her, at the feel of her. She was so sweetly curved and silky warm, and she tasted like walnuts and pure, provocative woman.

He wanted to sink into her, wanted to worship her with his mouth, his hands.

No kiss, no woman, had ever before made him lose it. Bo was fucking renowned for his control. More than one lover had left him after screaming that he might as well be Psy himself, he was such a cold bastard. Not even that had truly pricked his temper. He'd been annoyed and a little aggravated at what he'd seen as an unfair accusation, but fury so hot it made him see red?

No woman had ever aroused that kind of passion.

No woman but Kaia.

Back away, said the cold and analytical part of him that had been born in the gush of blood that hit his face after he drove a thin black pen into a telepath's carotid. That part had learned that emotional choices got a man nowhere when he was fighting a battle against an emotionless psychic race.

But even the Psy, another part of him whispered, *have given up their chilly Silence.* Kaleb Krychek, the most violently powerful telekinetic in the world, had a woman he adored so openly that there could be no doubt of his devotion. Silver Mercant was mated to a *bear.* The world was changing on a fundamental level . . . while Bo remained stuck in amber.

Chapter 17

I worry about you, Bo. You deserve a life beyond this fight for humanity. You deserve to fall in love and to travel the world with a carefree heart. You deserve to be more than an eternal soldier.

—Leah Knight (50) in a letter to her son, Bowen (19)

"I'LL GET IT," he said when Kaia moved to retrieve the cane for him. "I need to retrain all muscle groups."

Broken out of the loop of memory, he bent with care for his balance and picked up the cane. He didn't look at Kaia as he walked around the counter, but that did nothing to break the electric connection between them. And it did nothing to erase the cold, hard fact that in fourteen more days' time, Bowen Knight might cease to exist without ever having moved beyond the panicked terror of the thirteen-year-old boy he'd once been.

High-pitched giggles infiltrated the area almost two minutes after Kaia had pushed him away, the sound accompanied by more laconic voices. He looked over to see four teenagers entering the kitchen area. All four shot him quick, curious glances, but they were more interested in their own conversations.

"*Aloha*, Kaia!" they called out before wandering over to a corner of the kitchen proper and pulling on aprons.

Bo had meant to leave, give himself time to clear his head, decide what the fuck he was going to do about Kaia's accusation regarding the Alliance Fleet. As for Kaia herself . . . His abdomen clenched, his gaze going to her without his conscious volition. She'd just finished pulling both large trays of shortbread out of the oven.

The teens swarmed, but though she warned them off with swats of a tea towel, she also said, "Give the cookies five minutes to cool. After that, it's two each. Any more missing and I'll feed you cauliflower stew three days running."

A boy with pale, pale skin and a shock of blond hair twisted up his face, his forehead scrunched. "Might be worth it," he said slowly.

"I know you like cauliflower." Kaia tweaked his nose. "For you, it'd be a special meal of wilted kale."

Shuddering, the blond kid backed off—and Kaia slipped four cookies onto a saucer, then placed that saucer beside the food she'd dished out for Bowen. Unknowable dark eyes caught his. "I'll heat up the casserole for you."

And Bowen didn't—*couldn't*—leave. Not even to save himself from the chaos churning in his blood and in his brain. Retaking his seat across from her, he inhaled the food she gave him, drank the coffee she poured, and ate the cookies she'd set aside for him.

Things deep inside his chest ached.

A RIPPLE in the air currents against Kaia's skin, like the kiss of water, followed by the sonic awareness of a familiar presence entering the kitchen. *Atalina.* She barely stopped herself from putting her hands on the counter and shuddering, her calf muscles threatening to knot from the sudden release of tension.

The juveniles' chatter had helped, but the four were involved in their own talk as they worked on their set tasks and paid little attention to Bowen and Kaia. It left them in a bubble of privacy that wanted to wrench things out of her she wasn't ready to see, to confront.

Reminding herself that he was the enemy was doing nothing to block her memory of that kiss that shouldn't have happened, or her awareness of his quiet, intense presence. Not after he'd so categorically negated one of Hugo's conclusions.

And he hadn't done it with pretty justifications but with facts she could check.

Hugo would've warned her that Bowen was putting on an act, manipulating her, but every part of her rebelled against the idea of it. Bowen Knight had consigned himself to a ninety-five percent chance of a living death in order to find even the *possibility* of an answer for the people he most loved.

Kaia couldn't believe a man with that much courage and honor would stain his soul with the ugliness of lies upon lies upon lies. Because if she believed he was a liar, then she had to believe their kiss had been a lie from start to finish. A kiss in which she'd felt his body harden against hers, had heard the thudding beat of his pulse, felt the voracious hunger of his mouth.

"Good, you're up." Atalina's face was flushed with health, her eyes bright. "It's time for a complete evaluation, starting with a comprehensive scan."

Bowen had cleared his plate and eaten two of the cookies. He threw the third into his mouth and grabbed the fourth before rising from the stool. "Thank you for feeding me, Kaia."

The words had been ordinary, but the reserved tone made her skin prickle as if she wore an itchy coat. She shrugged to get rid of the sensation and glared in his direction to warn him not to think he could just shut down whenever he felt like it—but he'd already turned away, wasn't looking.

Able to watch him without being watched in return, she traced the outline of his profile with her gaze, trying to see beneath his skin, trying to find out what it was about Bowen Knight that activated the crazy gene in her blood and made her act so impetuously and with such unthinking emotion.

Because while Hugo might've been wrong in one conclusion, that didn't mean his entire dossier was a mistake. The horrific photo of their battered dead flashed across her irises—an echo of pain and torture caught forever in color, smashing up against the remembered feel of Bowen's mouth on her own.

Her gorge threatened to rise.

"Wait," she said, reaching back to undo her apron and pull it off. "I'll come with you." She had to know more of this man, had to understand if she was seeing what she wanted to see, if she was being led by a primitive response that knew nothing of conscience or honor—or if there was more here than a pitiless human out to win even if it meant murder.

She made sure her kitchen hands had enough work to keep on with before she joined Atalina and Bowen in their slow walk out of the kitchen. Hex ran in partway. Picking him up, she carried him cupped in one hand.

It was as they exited into the atrium that she caught the faint glow in the water beyond the seaward wall. Wonder bloomed. "Look to the right and into the black." Someone had already dimmed the external habitat lights.

Kaia knew the instant Bowen saw the bloom of bioluminescent Medusozoa, their fragile tentacles hauntingly beautiful in the water and their bodies pulsing with light. Like living stars caught in a sky that moved.

He went motionless, didn't exhale until the family had passed.

The external lights glowed back up to full strength, just enough to penetrate the deep nearest the station so friends could look in and they could look out.

"I love it when they visit." The Ushijimas lived in the city above Ryūjin Station.

"They're changeling?" Bowen's question was directed at her, though his eyes still searched the deep for another glimpse.

"As changeling as me and Attie."

Hand pressing down on his cane, Bowen leaned down to whisper, "I thought jellyfish didn't have brains."

"Things get murky with certain water changelings," she managed to say as his warmth rubbed against her like an affectionate cat. "Impossible transitions are possible."

"I was lucky enough to be invited to take scans of their brains in their aquatic form." Atalina tugged off a hair tie from around her wrist to pull back her bob into a short tail. "Their neural structures aren't anything like those of their natural brethren. Along with a complex nerve net, they have a fully functional central nervous system—brain included. That's why they can control their movements instead of being reliant on the ocean currents."

"Are you *sure* I'm awake?" Bowen sounded less distant and more like the man who'd become absorbed in *Wild Woman* and talked to her about bears and walnuts. "I'm talking about jellyfish brains."

"They don't like the term 'jellyfish,'" Kaia warned, not about to have her friends inadvertently insulted—and Bowen Knight stung in retaliation; Mary Ushijima did not hold back when it came to protecting the hearts of her family. "Always use 'Medusozoa' in direct conversation."

Bitter chocolate eyes searching hers, so damn alive that it made her want to scream at the injustice of the choice he'd been offered. "BlackSea faux pas?"

Swallowing back the roiling wave of anger, she nodded. And told herself to take a step back, to be sensible, rational until she figured out the truth or lie of Bowen Knight. But that wild gene in her blood, it wasn't only awake, it was in control. And it made her eyes dip to his mouth again.

"Kaia." A rough whisper of sound.

Chapter 18

If you become as cold as the Psy, haven't they won?

—Leah Knight (54) to her son, Bowen (23)

"COME ON, TIME'S wasting." Dr. Kahananui's voice was absentminded, her attention on the slim organizer she'd pulled out of her pocket, but it was like a rock thrown into a mirror-still pond.

The moment broke.

Red kissing her skin, Kaia walked around Bowen to join Dr. Kahananui. "You had a good sleep?" he heard her asking.

He couldn't hear the doctor's answer past the roaring in his ears. He'd thought he'd gotten a handle on his response to Kaia, enough to think past it, but he'd been lying to himself. All he'd done was shut down the part of him that felt far too much, but one look from her and his shields had blown wide open.

Gut tight, he followed her and Dr. Kahananui out of the atrium and away from the magic of that wall that looked out at "the black," as Kaia had called it. He liked that description, because infinite blackness lay at the heart of the ocean. A place so deep and mysterious that there was no way to see through it unless you'd been born for it.

Kaia was like that, a mystery that swirled with dark currents.

"What do you shift into?" The words left his mouth before he was consciously aware of what he was about to ask, his hunger to know her a craving.

No time. He had no time to learn the mystery of her second by second, kiss by kiss.

The look she shot him over her shoulder was a challenge. "You'll know if I decide to show you."

At that moment, he'd have sold his soul for the answer.

"Here we go." Dr. Kahananui put her hand on the scanpad outside the door he'd seen on his way out of this same corridor only ninety minutes earlier.

It felt like a lifetime ago and in that lifetime, a massive earthquake had shaken his world to its foundations. Bowen was used to standing on solid ground, but this ground kept shifting, kept asking him to make new choices, kept whispering at him to *live.*

Kaia looked back at him after entering the lab behind Dr. Kahananui, her gaze going to his legs. Checking his balance. "You're not really relying on the cane anymore."

Bowen hadn't realized the truth of that until she pointed it out. "I love these bugs." Delighted at the slow but notable improvement in his mobility, he leaned the cane up against a nearby table and took in the rest of the lab.

It covered a significant area.

His room, he realized, must be on the other side of the far wall.

The space was clean and white with plenty of glass beakers and gleaming machinery that hummed while completing arcane tasks. In short, it looked like every other laboratory he'd ever been in. Except for the mouse currently running along one counter.

He hadn't seen Kaia put down her pet, but he watched as Hex ran into a maze at the far end of the counter that appeared to be created of stiff cardboard cut, bent, and taped neatly together so as to eliminate all external light and sightlines.

When he walked over to look down into that maze, he was astonished at the complexity of it—it went up in multiple levels and had any number of dead ends, as well as slides that would drop Hex right back in the heart of the maze. "Is he genetically engineered?" It was a serious question.

"No, he's just a mouse genius," Kaia said from where she was helping Dr. Kahananui with a large device centered on a chair that glittered with hundreds of lines of the same sensor wire that lay against his skull. "He kept solving the other puzzles too quickly so I made him this one."

Bowen thought of Toric again, of the simple joy of having a friend who asked nothing from him but his companionship. "What do you do when he just keeps going around in circles?" At this instant, Hex's nose was twitching as he debated between turning right or heading left.

"He's too smart to do that. When he's had enough, he rings one of the bells placed throughout the maze and I pick him up."

Dr. Kahananui waved Bo over. "Take a seat."

A tall and almost cadaverously thin man walked into the room before Bo could take a step. He was probably around Bo's age, though the total lack of fat or muscle on his frame made him appear at least a decade older. His skin was around the same shade as Lily's, but his eyes were a pale hazel and his hair a lightish brown.

"Dr. Kahananui," he said. "I went to ensure the med-panel was correctly recording all data and found your subject gone." A stern look aimed in Bowen's direction. "It's inconvenient having a subject who goes for walks."

Bowen saw Kaia's lips twitch and felt warmth uncurl within his own stomach. "Just consider me a brain on legs," he said, feeling oddly young.

Coughing loudly, Kaia turned away.

"Bowen," Dr. Kahananui said after a concerned glance at Kaia, "this is my assistant, George." She patted Kaia's back. "Did you swallow your own saliva the wrong way?"

Bowen saw Kaia's shoulders jerk, decided to rescue her. "Good to meet you, George." He held out a hand.

Shooting him a wide-eyed look, George shook it so delicately that it was as if he was afraid to break Bo. For an instant, Bo wondered if George was one of the clumsy orcas who kept breaking things, but he couldn't bring himself to believe it. The man looked like a twig Bo could snap in half.

"I have this, George." Dr. Kahananui patted Kaia's back one last time before returning her attention to the scanner. "Could you drop by habitat three and help Tansy move across a hydro processor? It's a bit big for her to manage on her own."

"I'll go over now." George looked again at Bo, his thin lips pressed tightly together before he spoke. "Consider staying put. Dr. Kahananui can't go around chasing her experiments."

"I'm guessing you didn't hire George for his charming personality," Bo said after the door closed behind the other man.

"No, for his brain. The same reason I want you."

Kaia had been wiping at her eyes, her lips curved . . . but her smile faded to nothing in front of Bowen's gaze as he stepped up onto the podium that held the large diagnostic chair.

"Kaia, help me calibrate."

Jerking at the doctor's voice, Kaia walked to the chair and took one of his forearms, lifting to position it exactly against the arm of the diagnostic chair. When she would've done the same with his right, he cupped her cheek with his palm. She leaned into the touch for a stunning heartbeat before pulling his hand off her cheek and positioning him as needed, his fingertips directly on top of five small sensors.

Her hands were strong and capable—and boasted small nicks and scars that probably came from the kitchen. Warmth lingered everywhere she touched, the sensation deeper and far more wrenching than the lightning that had struck him in the kitchen.

The cells of his body thirsted.

More. More.

Bo could've lied, could've told himself his response was a result of the coma. But this violent storm inside him, it had nothing to do with anything as ordinary as attraction or desire. In a short ninety minutes, Kaia had smashed his defenses open, aroused him to boiling point and to fury, and made him act the rash youth he'd never been.

Kaia was his reckoning.

And she was the greatest challenge of his life.

His muscles locked at the memory of her allegations, but the cold that seared his mind to razor clarity wasn't aimed at her. Kaia was fire and love and devotion. Her rage came from losing the people she loved.

What iced his senses was the possibility of evil among his own. Because in one thing, she was right: humans *had* benefited from BlackSea beginning to look outward.

Chapter 19

Bo, you don't have to ask. You know I'd walk into hell itself beside you.

—Heenali Roy to Bowen Knight (2079)

MALACHAI HAD NEVER specifically stated that it was the vanishings that had driven the change in BlackSea's isolationist policy, but the connection hadn't been difficult to make once Bo learned of the people BlackSea had lost.

It was a dagger in the back to think he might've been manipulated and lied to, nasty things going on behind an illusion of fidelity, but that didn't mean he was about to close his eyes to the possibility. But neither was he ready to write off Heenali. Small and fierce and marked by psychic scars that caused her to wake screaming in the night, she'd walked beside him into danger year after year.

Her loyalty to the Alliance was a force of nature.

He'd speak to Malachai, then contact Lily and Cassius. Lily was incapable of hiding anything from him, and the bond that tied him and Cassius together was too primal to be fractured by anything less than death. He couldn't go to the surface, but they would be his hands and his eyes. However, the ultimate responsibility was and would always be his: Bo had never believed in false truths, in saying he had clean hands simply because he hadn't had advance knowledge of an action.

If it was committed under the Alliance banner, he owned it.

And should Kaia's allegations prove true?

Bowen's hands tightened over the ends of the chair arms. If Heenali *had* helped commit the atrocities of abduction, torture, and murder, then there was only one suitable punishment—and Bowen would mete it out himself. It'd break his fucking heart, but he'd do it.

Heenali would die in a prison cell anyway.

In front of him, Kaia closed black straps over his forearms and wrists. Bo didn't protest. Of a soft fabric, they'd be effortless to break.

"These are to keep your hands from moving out of alignment," she said, her head bent as she nudged his fingertips back into position. "Try to remain as still as you can."

The cinnamon and exotic bloom of her scent swirled around Bo as she reached over and behind him to pull down a part of the machine that fit over his head, with a particular rectangular piece sliding in front of his eyes.

It was cold, metallic, a harsh contrast to the soft warmth of this woman who wasn't certain whether he was a monster. And yeah, the blow landed exactly as hard the second time around. "Eyes open or closed?" he asked from behind the metal that turned his world black.

"Open." Kaia seemed to brush her fingers over his hair, but that was probably wishful thinking on his part. "But it doesn't matter if you blink. This is going to be an intensive scan; if you try to keep from blinking that long, you'll probably burst an eyeball."

Bo had heard that some changelings bit their mates during sex, or just for fun, or when they were mad. He'd never been a biter, but he was starting to reconsider his stand on the matter where Kaia was concerned. They could call it foreplay. Of course, he'd probably have a kitchen knife embedded in his gut before he ever got close enough.

His lips tugged up.

"And in three," Atalina began, "two . . . one."

A soft hum entered his ears while multicolored lasers danced across his eyes—or that was what it felt like. "I'm in the middle of a kaleidoscope."

"Is it disorienting?"

"No, it's incredible." As if he were at a desert rave, the beat of his pulse the bass beat of the dance.

Except that Bo had never attended a rave. Never kissed a pretty woman while music boomed and lights crashed over their heads. Now, when he imagined it, he saw only one face in front of his: Kaia's.

Laughing and contrary and softhearted Kaia who thought he was the enemy and whose turbulent confusion over their kiss was an intruder between them.

Despite his decision to live in the moment, in the now, he felt the sharp spear of regret after all.

"Your brain is very active." Dr. Kahananui's no-nonsense tone. "Can you stop thinking for a minute?"

Bo took a deep breath and banished the images of a life he'd never have. "How?"

"Have you ever meditated, done yoga?"

"No."

"Mal says he goes into a meditative state when he moves through a martial arts kata." Kaia's voice, like dark water swirling around him. "Do that in your mind using your preferred form of physical combat."

The regret stabbed again. Kaia, water changeling and scientist-turned-cook, already understood him better than any lover he'd ever had. Someone up above had a hellish sense of humor to bring her into his path at this time and in this place—and with such horror in the world.

"Bowen."

"Working on it, Doc." Gripping the regret in a granite fist, he began to run through a mixed martial arts sequence in his head, concentrating on creating perfect angles with his body and nothing else.

Chapter 20

> Fixed the computronic fault in your oven before work today. I demand mocha cupcakes with chocolate icing as payment.
>
> —Message from Hugo Sorensen to Kaia Luna

"YOUR SUBJECT'S FALLEN asleep," Kaia murmured to Attie, her gaze on Bowen's face. Not relaxed, even now. But perhaps a touch less hard. "Do you want me to wake him?" It was a reluctant question; he needed the rest.

Day one out of a coma and Bowen Knight already made more demands on himself than any man she'd ever met. Even asleep, he had a drive and an unrelenting focus to him that was a silent storm.

"No," Atalina said absently. "I have the scans I needed with his eyes open. The rest will go more smoothly while he's asleep."

"He won't be happy when he wakes." A stark rush of unexpected affection had her brushing her fingers over his hair again. She wondered if he ever truly rested when at full strength, or if he rode himself brutally hard day in and day out.

Kaia knew the answer, had read it in the relentless lines of his face. "I think I'll make some blackberry pies," she murmured as Attie continued to stare at the large screen on the wall beyond which lay Bowen's room, her attention on the intricate mapping of his brain.

"You know that's not my favorite," her cousin muttered five minutes later. "I like cherry."

But Kaia was still going to make blackberry. Bowen's sister had thrust the list of Bowen's favorite foods into Kaia's hand on the day of the kidnapping, a hopeful desperation in her eyes.

And though Hugo's assertions had been loud in her head, Kaia had carefully saved the list. Just in case Lily's brother woke up. Only he wasn't simply that any longer. He was Bowen Knight, a dangerously compelling man and security chief in forced exile.

"Attie."

"Hmm?"

"Do you ever think about what Hugo said?" Kaia's mind remained in tumult, caught between the evidence gathered by her closest childhood friend—and the reality of a man who burned with honor. "The things I told you." Atalina and Hugo weren't close, never spent any time together except when Kaia was holding a get-together and had invited them both.

Attie took a minute to set up the next scan before she sighed and came to sit in her computer chair, turning it so she faced Kaia. "You know what I think of Hugo."

"I agree he's not the most reliable person." Hugo wasn't the friend you'd call if you needed someone around at a particular time. "But he's always been very clever with comms."

"Yes," Atalina agreed. "He's capable of having hacked into the information exactly as he said, but . . . Kaia, I know you adore Hugo, but why would he make the effort? He's one of the most self-centered people I've had the misfortune to meet."

"He is *not*." Kaia folded her arms. "He spent hours searching for the exact spice I wanted that time he went to the markets in Mumbai. And he built three different mazes for Hex." Those were just two recent examples of his generosity—Hugo had been there for her since they'd first met as children.

Even while traveling with her parents, Kaia had commed with Hugo regularly.

Atalina rubbed her hand over the hard curve of her belly. "You're right—he's different with you. You bring out the best in him." She got up, stretched out her back. "Which is why I *do* think about the dossier." A lingering glance at Bowen. "Hugo might be a poker-addicted screwup, but he's never involved you in anything questionable."

Though Atalina wasn't the most empathic of people, her brain more scientifically wired, she met Kaia's gaze and said, "I can't tell you if you can trust a word out of Bowen's mouth, Cookie." The old childhood nickname fell easily from her lips. "What I can tell you is that any decision you make, you need to make quickly."

Because the countdown in Bowen's brain wouldn't pause to give her time to sort through her confusion. "I hate this." It came out harsh, rough. "Why now? Why him?"

Atalina smiled softly at her, not misunderstanding her questions. "Even I know we don't get to choose." Smile fading, she said, "But take care of that soft heart of yours, Kaia. Right now, Bowen can guarantee you nothing but fourteen more days."

Hearing the ring of a tinny bell, Kaia went over and rescued Hex from the maze. His little heart was thumping, but she knew it wasn't in fear. He was a stubborn mouse determined to figure out the maze.

As stubborn as the man who'd thrown Kaia's world into chaos.

After taking a minute to pet Hex, she slipped him into a pocket of her dress . . . and returned to stand near Bowen.

Chapter 21

"I feel like I died in there. I'm a ghost now."

"No, you're a new Cassius. But you're still my best friend."

—Cassius Drake (13) and Bowen Knight (13)

BOWEN SNAPPED AWAKE in the scanning chair when Kaia shook his shoulder, and though he'd planned to call Malachai, Cassius, and Lily, he barely managed to make it to his room before his body shut down again. His last thought wasn't that he might never wake again should the chip or compound suffer a catastrophic failure, but that he wished he had Kaia's curves snug against him.

The next time he woke it was to find he'd slept for fifteen hours. The part of him used to getting up at four a.m. and working eighteen-hour days was aghast, but he knew there wasn't much he could do about the whole coma-and-implant situation. His body had suffered a terrible insult and it'd take time to return to full speed.

The one thing he *could* do was make those calls.

First, however, he had a shower and changed into a clean pair of jeans and a dark brown shirt with epaulets on the shoulders.

Shoving a hand through his hair, he ignored the gnawing in his stomach as he walked out of the bathroom. Food could—"Kaia." A strange and painful warmth bloomed inside his chest at seeing the covered tray beside his bed; it had appeared while he'd been in the shower.

Lifting the cover, he found a glass of orange juice, a banana sliced over a small bowl of cereal, and a shallow glass dish full of walnuts. Snacks to tide him over until he made it to the kitchen. She must've been keeping an eye on the feed from the data panel, been alerted when his readings altered. Even the cold, hard security chief part of him was disarmed by what she'd done with the information: taken care of him.

He ate and drank all of it before going to the panel and attempting to contact Malachai. The call went through but it was audio only—and even then, the connection was spotty. Bowen had the feeling it wasn't because of the station's location, not when his phone had a better connection. The BlackSea security chief must be in a place that interfered with a clean line.

"Malachai," he said. "I'm sure you know by now that I've arisen from the dead."

". . . news." Malachai's voice came through only in pieces. ". . . talk . . . back."

Bo tried to clean up the comm signal by boosting it on his end. "You hear me?"

"Yes, but it'll probably break again soon." The other man's tone was difficult to read.

"Dangerous allegations are being made against the Alliance," Bowen said, cutting right to the chase. "I need to know the details so I can hunt down the truth."

Malachai's next words had Bo's shoulders tensing. "You didn't tell me the Alliance wants to set up its own shipping line through BlackSea-controlled regions."

"New relationship," he replied. "Seemed bad form to bring that up when we'd barely begun talking." The line crackled again. "Why did you let Dr. Kahananui bring me on the station if you distrust the Alliance?"

"The information came to light after the initial arrangements had been made. If I pulled the plug prior to a full investigation, I killed you."

It was exactly the decision Bo would have made. "When was Hugo taken?"

“Three weeks ago. One week after I contacted your sister about the experiment, and two days before we brought you down.”

More static on the line.

“Will you send through the suspicious Fleet movements so I can track them on our end?”

“. . . the city.” Heavy static. “. . . tomorrow.”

The line went dead a second later and wouldn’t reconnect.

Bo thought about trying to touch base with Miane Levèque instead but discarded that option after a moment’s thought. It was Malachai who’d be in charge of this investigation, and it was Malachai with whom Bo had a relationship. He’d find out tomorrow if the other man intended to share the Fleet data—and it’d tell him how bad this was, whether BlackSea had already made its call for or against humanity.

He used his phone for the next call; if he’d been a security chief with a possible threat in his territory, he’d damn well have made sure to tap this comm line so he could monitor any calls that threat might make.

Cassius’s grin cracked the pale gold skin of his angular face when he laid eyes on Bowen. “Damn it, you asshole. Took you long enough to get in touch.”

“I keep falling asleep,” Bo admitted. “Which is why I’m going to talk fast now. I tried to loop Lily in but her line is busy, so you’ll have to fill her in.” Not bothering to pull any punches, he told his second-in-command about BlackSea’s belief of Alliance Fleet involvement in the vanishings; Malachai’s cool responses had made it clear Kaia wasn’t the only one who thought Bo and his people might have something to do with stealing and harming BlackSea changelings.

“Well, fuck.” Cassius put his hands on his hips, his strikingly clear gray eyes as piercing as a wolf’s. “Do we need to get you out of there?”

“No—I have to see this experiment through.”

“You really think they’d give us a solution if they think we’re killing their people?”

“The allegations came to light after they’d already offered us the experimental treatment, and Malachai is suspicious but not rushing to conclusions.” The timing of Hugo’s abduction, so close to the start of the experiment, niggled at Bo. "Dr. Kahananui, she's too much the scientist to allow politics to mess with her work—I think the questions about whether to give us any solution will come after the experiment is complete. We have to figure out the truth before then."

Cassius nodded. "Yeah, I follow." His hair glinted in the sunlight that hit him, the strands so closely buzzcut to his skull that you could barely tell they were blond. "What do you want me to do?"

That was the thing with Cassius—he'd follow Bowen's lead without hesitation. It made him the best lieutenant Bo would ever have, but they both knew Cassius couldn't take hold of the reins should Bo fall.

"I'm a damn good soldier," he'd once said to Bo. "But I'm not a general."

For succession, Bo had looked initially to his third-in-command, but while Heenali was an independent thinker, she was also angry on the innermost level. "Fleet is under Heenali's control," he said, the words crushed stones coming out of his throat. "I need you and Lily to get into Heenali's comms and into all records of Fleet movements."

"I'll feel like a fucking asshole doing it," Cassius said, "but it has to be done." Spoken in the flat tone of a soldier.

Bo felt worse than an asshole; he owed Heenali his life many times over. "We do this, we find nothing, it goes no further than the three of us and we can protect her against any accusations." Bo would never sacrifice one of his people for political expediency.

Cassius's eyes held his. "We all know Heenali hates the Psy, but she's never said anything against changelings."

"Hate" was too mild a word for Heenali's repugnance of the psychic race. The major reason Bowen had never been able to point to her as his official successor was that her psychological scars made her hatred of the Psy so violent that it turned into a critical weakness. She couldn't think rationally enough to forge the political alliances necessary to position humanity for the future.

Cassius's own thinking wasn't far from Heenali's—but regardless of his animosity toward the Psy, he had always backed Bo's decisions. In a drunken state during a dark time, he'd told Bo that he *had* to back him because it kept Cassius from acting on his most savage instincts and becoming a monster.

If Cassius did ever become monstrous, the Psy had no one to blame but themselves.

Prior to the attack that had forever changed both their lives, the other man had been shy and laid-back, more inclined to smile than not. That Cassius had died a lifetime ago, and Bo knew he'd never return; Cassius had had to become a new person to stay sane.

"That's exactly why I can't figure this out," Bo said, folding his arms across his chest. "The vanishings have been linked conclusively to the Consortium, and the Consortium includes Psy."

"Right. Heenali wouldn't touch those fuckers with a ten-foot pole while wearing a hazmat suit." Cassius's expressionless soldier mode gave way to a frown that barely moved his facial muscles. "I can't see it, Bo."

"Neither can I, but we have to look." A harsh exhale. "It might be someone under her who's fallen for Consortium lies or promises of wealth." Bo trusted his knights without question, but the Alliance was a large organization and plenty of its members had fucked-up psyches as a result of run-ins with Psy.

Those run-ins had led them to the Alliance, but every so often, Bo would hear whispers that he was breaching the stated goals of the Alliance by doing business with "outsiders." The rumblings were generally very small; the vast majority of the Alliance membership understood that humanity couldn't thrive in isolation. It had to find a way to stand on equal ground with changelings and Psy—and to do that, they needed to build bonds with myriad groups across the world.

But if one of those disgruntled people had ended up with enough power to cause trouble . . . "Ask Lily to tag every possible suspect order or route with the name of the person who gave the order."

"I'll make sure Heenali doesn't find out we're looking into her," Cassius promised. "You know what it'd do to her."

"Yes." Heenali Roy had no other family—the knights were her brothers and sisters. "Protect her as much as you can, Cassius. I'm trying to get BlackSea to share the suspicious Fleet movements they've detected so you have specifics to work with."

Chest tight, Bo then made another difficult decision. "Tell Lily to hack communications if she has to, but I need you to make sure *none* of our people are talking to unexpected contacts."

Cassius's expression went impossibly flatter. "You're not putting Lily in such a tough spot on the basis of rumors of Fleet movements alone."

"Malachai knows about our proposed shipping line." Bo hadn't mentioned it right off the bat because he'd needed time to process the implications of BlackSea's security chief having that information.

"Jesus fucking Christ." White lines bracketed Cassius's mouth. "*No one* outside of the knights knows about that."

"No." It was a long-term ambition intended to bolster the Alliance's economic power while making it possible for humans to do business without dealing with Psy.

The latter would no longer be relevant if they got the implants to work, but in the current climate—where ninety-nine percent of human minds were vulnerable to telepathic coercion—business dealings with Psy remained fraught with the possibility of psychic manipulation.

A human was *always* in a vulnerable position in a negotiation with a Psy because they had to rely on the Psy having enough honor not to attempt to influence the negotiation via psychic means.

"Whoever leaked that information either did it accidentally," Bo said, "or the BlackSea male who vanished was right in fingering us." And someone had taken Hugo out for it. "We have to look at all the knights." Saying that was like thrusting a dagger into his own heart.

Chapter 22

Kaia remains badly wounded inside. Food is the only language she finds safe, and so you must learn to understand what it means to her.

—BlackSea's senior healer to Natia and Eijirō Kahananui (2063)

ENDING THE CALL with Cassius without good-byes, Bowen made his way to the kitchen area, drawn by a compulsion toward a woman who remained unsure about his capacity for the ugliest kind of betrayal. And yet who made sure he was warm and had food when he woke.

Bowen had the feeling he'd never understand Kaia.

The skinny teenager with the black curls and the starburst birthmark high on his left cheekbone—*Scott, that was his name*—was topping up the bread tray when he arrived. "Can you really not swim in the deep?" the kid asked.

"Not unless I want to drown." The idea of exploring the blackness beyond the seaward wall in just his skin was an exhilarating one regardless. "You sound like you've never met a human before." The idea brought him up short. Most changeling packs and clans had humans in the group—but BlackSea had sequestered itself for a long time. Maybe they *didn't* have human clanmates.

"What are humans?" It was the glint in the boy's eyes that gave him away.

Apparently teens were likable assholes regardless of race.

"And what about you?" Bo asked, having scanned the entire kitchen area without spotting Kaia. "Some kind of a winged jumping sea frog?"

Scott bristled. "There's no such thing as a winged jumping sea frog!" Heavy eyebrows drawing together into a vee over the deep green of his eyes. "I'm a *shark*. A hammerhead."

"I bet every teenage boy I meet is going to be a shark."

"Scott, why are you telling lies during your lunch shift?" The tone was female and severe.

Cheeks going a hot pink, Scott ducked his head. "He thinks winged jumping sea frogs are real."

The woman who'd spoken, a gray-haired matron with a solid body, her gilt-colored hair pulled tightly back into a ponytail and a prominent beauty spot just below her right eye, raised an eyebrow. "I'm sure he believes you're a shark, too." Tumbling the boy's curls, she said, "Be proud of who you are, my love. For you are a being of patience and grace."

The boy's smile turned unexpectedly sweet. "I was just messing with him, Grandma." After turning to hug the older woman and get a kiss on the cheek, he limped off toward the back of the kitchen, where a middle-aged man appeared to be running things.

Definitely no Kaia, though. Could be her day off. Or she'd gone swimming, and if he waited long enough by the seaward wall, he'd see a brown-eyed siren swimming out of the black, her hair streaming behind her like living water. "Scott," he said when he realized the older woman was watching him, "what type of changeling is he?"

It was his turn to get a stern look down an aquiline nose. "That's a very rude question, young man." Pursed lips. "If my grandchild wants to reveal himself to you, that's his choice—and if you ask me what I am, I'll clip you about the ears. Now, pass me a roll."

Set firmly in his place and reminded of his paternal grandmother—the indomitable Cece—Bowen did as ordered, then set about filling his plate while considering how best to track down Kaia. He told himself it was so he could find out if she knew anything further about the Alliance

Fleet encroaching into BlackSea territory, but the truth was he just craved her.

He didn't feel like a man racing a clock counting down to oblivion when he was with her; he felt young, alive, more himself than he'd been his entire adult life. There were no shields with Kaia, no walls. He was Bowen and she was Kaia and what they had between them was a turbulent fire that threatened to burn them both.

Walking out into the atrium with his food and a mug of coffee, he nearly ran into a short and lithely muscular man with reddish blond hair. He'd been on edge ever since he left his room, expecting another reaction like that from the mustachioed man yesterday. But Hugo had apparently not shared his theories with all his clanmates because this one grinned at him.

"Good to see you up, dude." It was the heavily gritty voice that told him the other male's identity.

Bowen grinned back. "KJ. Thanks for not barging in while I was in the shower."

"No tentacles, only two arms, not even worth it to look." Laughter danced in his eyes. "Catch you later—I'm just grabbing my caffeine fix before I head over for my shift at the infirmary."

"Wait." Bowen angled his head as KJ went past. "The station has an infirmary?"

"Six hundred folks and guests—and a whole bunch of them full-time blackers who think racing sharks and diving with orca is a funtime activity." KJ threw up his hands as he walked backward toward the coffee station. "Infirmary's never empty is all I'm saying. I got job security for *life*."

The words caused a pang of homesickness deep within Bowen. The Alliance's head medic often muttered about his job security while patching up yet another injured soldier.

And it struck Bo out of nowhere that he might never see home again. That he'd go into oblivion without ever experiencing the glory of another Venetian sunset, or the quiet sound of water lapping at the building where he had an apartment. No more mornings listening to a busker outside his favorite bakery. No more runs through Venice's narrow cobbled streets dodging wide-eyed tourists clustered about with their cameras.

Bowen Knight might end forever in the black that was full of wonder and beauty and danger . . . but that wasn't his home.

The knot in his throat thick, he nonetheless forced himself to continue moving forward. He could not freeze. To do that would be to give up.

Scott's grandmother was already seated at a small table beside the seaward wall and beckoned him with an imperious wave of her hand. Bowen's heart hurt too fucking badly to want to make conversation, but the ruthlessly pragmatic part of his nature saw in the older woman a possible source of information on Kaia. "Name's Bowen," he said after putting his plate and mug on the table.

"Carlotta," she replied as he took the chair across from her. "Scott's grandmother and best friend to Kaia's grandmother on her father's side." She forked up a bite of quiche before continuing. "So, you're the experimental subject Atalina's brought down from the surface."

"That's me." Bowen ate a bite of peanut butter toast, his mind filling once more with images of Kaia provoking him, then giving him cookies. It eased the knot, softened the piercing sense of loss that speared through him. If this was to be the last place he saw before he ended, at least it had her in it.

"You should be proud," Carlotta said. "Atalina wouldn't accept just any subject."

The skin on the back of his neck prickled, the tiny hairs there rising. Even as he turned, he knew what he'd see: Kaia walking toward them.

His mechanical heart kicked. *Hard.*

She wore a sleeveless dress that flirted around her ankles and hugged her curves each time the fabric settled against her before moving again. The color was stoplight red and the top part a halter cinched below her breasts by a wide band of fabric and tied at the back of her neck.

Her hair, she'd brushed into a sheet of gleaming dark filled with myriad shades from black to brown to strands of copper. It went all the way to the flaring curve of her rear.

A wolf whistle pierced the air.

Bo didn't realize he was the one who'd done it until Kaia gave him a narrow-eyed look that could strip paint off a wall. Around him, a number of others whooped and clapped. Carlotta, however, was staring at him with a distinctly assessing expression on her face. "She's the best cook across five oceans." It was a mild rebuke. "I hope you enjoy gruel."

Sauntering over, Kaia leaned down to kiss the older woman on the cheek. "Good morning, Carlotta." The bloom tucked over her right ear was a creamy white and wafted an intoxicating wave of scent. "Would you like a piece of blackberry pie? I made it this morning."

"Blackberry pie?" Homesickness crashed over him again in a breaking wave. "My mom makes blackberry pie every summer." He tried to get back to his parents' farm at least once each summer, often ended up with scratched arms and juice-stained lips from his hunt for the lush, juicy berries that grew wild around their home.

KAIA was caught by the haunting poignancy of Bowen's voice, the sense of loss in the air so heavy that it made her want to rub the heel of her palm over her heart. "Don't expect to get a piece," she said, but it came out husky.

His lips curved at the edges, the hard-eyed security chief returning with a vengeance. "What if I say 'please'?"

Snorting, she fought the violent urge to go to him, touch him, give him the comfort of clan.

He's not clan, he's the enemy, cried the echo of Hugo's voice.

"You know I'd never turn down a piece of your pie." Carlotta's voice entered the moment without breaking it, as if Kaia and Bowen existed out of time.

Turning on her heel before she could surrender to the urge to touch him, Kaia sauntered into the kitchen as if she had not a care in the world. As if she hadn't spent the night tossing and turning, tormented alternately by dreams of tender caresses and kisses full of primal need, and the chilling screams of their vanished.

She still didn't have an answer to the question of whether Bowen

Knight was the enemy, but what she did know was that there was more to him than the ruthless leader of the Alliance. "Thank you for holding the fort," she said to Naz, who often took a shift so she could have time off.

Today, her clanmate—an experienced cook who now made his living as a mystery novelist but who continued to love food and the kitchen—had taken the midmorning-to-midafternoon shift.

"Any problems?"

"Aside from Scott's bottomless pit of a stomach? No, we're humming. Shoo, enjoy your break."

"I'm just grabbing some pie." She sliced out Carlotta's piece. After placing it on the plate, she picked up a bottle of raspberry syrup and did a bit of decoration on a second plate before heading back out.

"Here you go." She put a huge slice in front of Carlotta, then put Bowen's empty plate in front of him.

He took one look at the message she'd written on the plate and threw back his head, laughing so hard that several clanmates rushed over to see what was happening. They snickered at reading: *Wolf whistle the cook = no pie for you.*

And somehow in the melee, Kaia ended up beside him with her hand on the back of his chair. Her fingers brushed through the silken thickness of his hair to touch his skin. He went motionless . . . then leaned deeper into the contact.

Chapter 23

We cannot forget joy. No matter how deep our rage and pain.

—Miane Levèque to BlackSea

"WHAT IF I beg?" Bowen looked up at her, the piercing sadness she'd felt erased by a youthful playfulness that spoke to the heart of her nature.

His whistle had done the same—wolf-whistling might not be the acceptable thing in human culture, but Kaia didn't only have a human side; her other self *loved* whistles and loved that Bowen was good at them.

Playmate, it thought again.

"Your fate is in Carlotta's hands," she said, never stopping her covert touch. "If she wants to share, that's up to her."

"Hmm." Carlotta's censorious tone had them both looking at her. "I don't hold with wolf-whistling."

"Coma-brain," Bowen said. "I should get to use that as a free pass at least once a day."

"Not even my grandchildren have managed to come up with that particular excuse, so I suppose you deserve some pie for the outlandishness of it alone." Carlotta picked up a knife she hadn't used for her lunch and neatly cut the large slice in two.

As the other woman put one slice on Bowen's plate, Kaia made herself break skin contact before she fell into a sensory coma of her own. Because while she'd stroked him in an effort to ease his hurts, give him the comfort of clan in a place where he was far from his own clan, the touch threatened to turn her into an addict.

The sudden disconnection caused a stutter inside her, and she saw Bowen's shoulders tighten, but he said nothing, just forked up a bite of his pie. Instead of walking away as she'd intended, Kaia hesitated long enough that she saw his eyes close as a deep groan formed in his chest.

Her toes curled.

BO opened his eyes to see Kaia walking away, a luscious woman in scarlet who could cook like a goddess. "No more wolf-whistling," he said firmly. "This pie . . ." He forked up another bite even as he continued to watch Kaia.

"She has a flair." Carlotta ate a bite of her own pie. "And you can't take your eyes off her."

Bo didn't look away from the gifted, frustrating, tender mystery of Kaia. She'd stopped at another table and was chatting with a clanmate. "Do you blame me?"

Carlotta's smile was thin. "No, but has anyone told you about Hugo?"

Instincts sharpening, Bowen snapped his attention to the older woman. "I know he's her friend."

"They've been two peas in a pod since babyhood. It's generally believed they'll end up mates."

Bowen leaned back deliberately in his chair, his shoulders relaxed. "I don't think Kaia's the kind of woman who'll do the expected."

Taking a sip of her coffee, Carlotta continued to watch him. "No, and it's interesting you know that."

"You don't sound particularly concerned about Hugo," Bowen said just as Kaia began to move again, heading out of the atrium.

Carlotta went eerily immobile. "I mourn for all our lost," she said in a tone that held the darkness of the ocean.

In the distance, Kaia's red dress disappeared into a large opening that he guessed led to a connecting bridge to another habitat.

"You got balls, coma-guy." A dark-skinned man with long dreads punched him lightly on the shoulder as he passed their table. "No one messes with Kaia."

"I heard she threatened to fillet, then fry the gonads of the last guy who tried to court her!" another voice called out from a table behind Bo.

"Or that might've been because you tried to court her with dead clams, you numbnut," came a third contribution.

"Hey! They could've had pearls inside!" the numbnut protested. "It was *romantic.* I asked Aunt Rita in *Wild Woman* magazine about courtship. She said be unique but romantic. So I thought, why give jewelry when I could give mysterious clams?"

"And that is why you shall die a single, forty-year-old virgin!"

Laughter rippled through the atrium before people began to disperse. Across from him, Carlotta's expression grew softer. "It's good to hear my clan laugh."

Bo's own smile faded. "It must be hard to stay positive with the vanishings."

"Yes, but our children can't grow up in a people drenched in sorrow. It'd ruin an entire generation." She put down her fork. "Our First has made it clear we must not permit our anguish to shatter the childhood of our young."

"I get it." Bowen caught a glimpse of the mustachioed walrus-seeming man out of the corner of his eye. "Human families still have to raise their children with love and affection and joy despite the shadow of psychic violation." He'd seen the struggle firsthand on the faces of countless parents—but they kept on trying because their children deserved to know happiness and hope.

Carlotta's nod was slow. "Yes. We all have battles to fight." Picking up her fork again, she ate a little more of her meal while Bowen continued to keep an eye on the aggressive blond male Kaia had referred to as Alden.

The big man was staying on the far side of the atrium, but he'd shot at least three simmering glances in Bowen's direction in the last minute alone.

Picking up her coffee again, Carlotta took a long drink. "As for Hugo and Kaia," she murmured after placing her cup back on the table, "if there's one thing I've learned in my hundred years on this planet, it's that plans have a way of being derailed by this thing called life."

Her words rippled a shiver across Bowen's skin just as a large whale swept by on the other side of the seaward wall. Face crinkling into a smile, Carlotta waved. "There's my darling Filipe. He always grumps that he's spent half his life waiting for me to get myself ready." A laugh, another wave as the whale swam by again. "I'm coming, dear."

Bowen's mouth fell open. "I know I'm not supposed to ask . . ."

Carlotta gave an exasperated shake of her head. "Yes, I am a whale. Satisfied now?"

"No." Bowen was never going to be satisfied on this point. "Leopards and wolves, I can almost make sense of that matter differential, but how can you *possibly* have enough mass to become a whale?" He chugged down his coffee, put the mug on the table with exaggerated care. "No. Nope. Never."

Carlotta laughed and it was big and husky and gorgeous. When she finally stopped laughing and stood, apparently finished with her meal, she leaned down to kiss him on the cheek. "Dear boy, I do think I like you."

She left the atrium moments later.

That was when the mustachioed possible-walrus rose from his table and charged through the nearly empty atrium toward Bowen.

Well, fuck.

Chapter 24

Always move with purpose.

—Yamato Sensei to Bowen (17)

KAIA BREATHED A silent sigh of relief when she saw Carlotta step onto the bridge to habitat two. She'd been stuck in the spot ever since she left the atrium—courtesy of a clanmate who was one of the sweetest people on Ryūjin, but oh how she could talk. And talk. And *talk*.

"What an astonishing story," Kaia interrupted when Lori paused for a breath in between rapid-fire sentences. "But I've—"

"Oh, but I haven't told you the best part!" Lori put her hand on Kaia's forearm, her bright blue eyes twinkling. "That was when—"

"Kaia?" Carlotta's stern voice. "What are you still doing here? I had the impression you were off to meet your friends for your weekly lunch." She frowned at Lori. "And you, Loribeth, aren't you supposed to be teaching a swarm of young ones?"

Glancing at the large watch face she wore on a chain hanging from her neck, Lori squealed. "Oh, my God!" She began to run down the bridge. "I'll tell you the rest of the story later!"

"*Mahalo*, Carlotta." Kaia's ears were still ringing with the sound of Loribeth's squeaky voice. It was cute but extremely difficult to halt.

Shaking her head, the older woman said, "You have to cut her off before she gets going, Kaia. You know how guppies are—budgies of the sea, I call them."

"I know. But she's so sweet and—" Kaia froze at a surge of shouts from the direction of the atrium, so loud it threatened to overwhelm her sensitive hearing.

It was difficult to separate out the words until she heard Dex's voice roar, "Alden!"

Kaia kicked off her slippers and ran, arriving just in time to see the enraged walrus close the final inches to Bowen—who was on his feet. She wasn't going to get to the two in time and Alden's arm was rising, his huge hammer of a fist heading straight for Bowen's face. One blow and he could crumple bone, thrusting shards into Bowen's brain and ending his life.

Still running, she went to scream at the others to stop him, but Alden had mowed down clanmates like bowling pins. Dex was getting up, his craggy face a creation of harsh lines and solid bone, but he wasn't going to make it, either. *No one* was going to make it.

Kaia's breath rasped painfully in her lungs, her blood a roar in her ears. Then came an almighty crash. Horror shrieked through her system. She'd flinched and closed her eyes instinctively at the moment of impact, but when she flicked them open immediately afterward, she came to a halt, unable to comprehend quite what she was seeing.

Alden was on his back on the floor with an upside-down table flat on his face. Splatters of blackberry filling and coffee and what might've been scrambled eggs turned his body into a bad expressionist painting. He was attempting to push the table off, but as he lay there like a stunned beetle, Bowen calmly picked up a chair and slammed it down so the point of one leg came within a hairsbreadth of Alden's privates.

Alden froze.

Lungs burning, Kaia finally looked at Bowen's face. *"No."* She closed the distance between them in a heartbeat and grabbed his jaw. "He hit you."

"Just a split lip." Bowen scowled. "I'm slower than I'm used to being, miscalculated a fraction. He got in a glancing blow."

Kaia scanned his face, searching for any other signs of injury. But his eyes were clear, his nose unbroken. Scarlet liquid welled in only the soft curve of his lower lip. "I—" she began when Dex reached them. His face was white under the tan of his skin, blood vessels sticking out on his temples.

"Atalina's on her way to meet me for lunch." He stomped a foot onto Alden's chest when the walrus finally succeeded in thrusting off the table. "I swear, Alden, if you so much as fucking twitch, I will tear your stupid fucking head off your stupid fucking body."

Alden went motionless. Hard-faced and formerly hard-living Dex was the station commander because he remained calm even when the world went to hell—but he was also a great white shark capable of doing exactly what he'd threatened.

Wide and soulfully dark eyes stared at Kaia, Alden pleading for help. But she had exactly zero sympathy for him right now. "How far away is she?"

"She messaged two minutes ago." Dex looked at the time on his phone screen, a kind of painful desperation to him. "She'll be here in another two."

Kaia grabbed Bowen's hand. "Come on!" Avoiding Alden's sprawled form, she tugged Bowen out of the mess of fallen furniture that Dex was roaring at nearby clanmates to straighten up *now*.

Atalina wouldn't be surprised at the mess, not with Alden around. But Kaia's cousin couldn't be permitted to see Bowen's face. Going as fast as she thought Bowen could handle, she managed to make it to her quarters without running into Attie. She put her hand on the scanpad and pushed Bowen through as the door slid back.

And Atalina appeared around the corner. "Kaia." A beaming smile. "I thought you were planning to have lunch with Tansy and Seraphina?"

"I forgot something." She pressed a hand to the rapid tattoo of her heart and hoped Bowen would have the good sense to stay inside. "Just ran back to get it."

"Did you see Dex in the atrium?"

"He was making people straighten up the furniture." Kaia rolled her eyes. "Alden."

"When will that boy-man grow up?" Brow furrowing, Atalina waved good-bye and continued on her way.

BO could hear the two women outside the door, but though his lip throbbed, he was far more interested in Kaia's personal space. The room was open-plan, with the facilities tucked to the back left, a large and comfortable-looking bed in the middle, and a delicate chair set in front of a writing desk against the wall nearest the door.

The back wall was a transparent window into the black.

The bed was bracketed by tall and narrow white shelves that held physical books as well as small treasures. On the right shelf sat a ragged doll wearing a chef's hat that must've come from Kaia's childhood. Also there was a badly made mug painted with her name, and two computronic frames. One appeared to be glitching, the image on it heavily pixelated and unmoving, but the other displayed photographs of two people: a tall and lanky man with a playfulness in his smile that reminded Bowen of Kaia, and a dark-eyed and dark-haired woman of extraordinary beauty.

He was walking over to look more carefully at the images when Kaia's bedroom door shut and she strode over to push on his chest until he sat down on the bed. "Let me see that cut." First, however, she bustled into the bathroom and returned with a wet washcloth and a small first-aid kit.

Bowen wasn't used to being bossed around, but if it meant experiencing Kaia's touch, he'd do exactly what she demanded. He winced when she gently dabbed the blood away from his cut. Frowning, she said, "How bad is it?"

"Fucker made me sacrifice my pie." Bowen's stomach rumbled on cue. "And I'd barely gotten started on my breakfast-as-lunch."

Gripping his jaw, Kaia glared into his eyes. "Be serious."

"I am." He put his hand on the curve of her hip, wasn't sure she felt it, she was so focused on his face. "Lip's nothing. It's only cut because he was wearing a big-ass ring. My head didn't get rattled—I'm hungry and pissed, but the experiment's fine."

She ran her fingers through his hair. "We have to come up with an innocent explanation for the swelling and the cut."

Thinking of her panic and that of the rawboned man with the work boot on Alden's chest, Bowen put the pieces together. "Dr. Kahananui's a doctor. She'll know at a glance that this isn't serious." He'd come along with Kaia because, honestly, she'd had her hand linked to his and he'd have followed her anywhere, but he saw no reason for the extreme reaction.

Continuing to run her fingers through his hair, the rhythmic motion soothing on a bone-deep level, she said, "Did you ever wonder how my cousin got permission to bring a human test subject down into a secret research station in the first place? A subject who, if he woke up, would then know about this place?"

"I figured it was an act of good faith because of the growing relationship between BlackSea and the Alliance." After all, it had been prior to Hugo's allegations.

"That relationship is far too new." Kaia finished dabbing away the blood around his lip and, opening the first-aid kit, put the washcloth on the back of the lid. She picked up a small tube of ointment from inside the kit before returning her attention to Bo. "And it's not as if we were talking about bringing an ordinary human down here."

No, they'd been discussing the human who posed the biggest security risk of them all. "So why am I here?" It had something to do with Dr. Kahananui and the dread on Kaia's face when she'd realized her cousin was about to walk into carnage, that much was now clear.

"Attie grew up in a big family." Kaia dabbed the ointment over his cut. "Five younger brothers and me." She didn't explain why she'd been raised with her cousins. "And Mal's family was just down the way, so it was like having six brothers really."

Bowen had the family connections straight in his head now. Eight cousins, six of them in one family, Malachai and Kaia from separate families. But it sounded as if they'd all grown up together. "Changelings generally have small families." It wasn't a secret that they had lower levels of fertility than humans or Psy.

"Auntie Natia and Uncle Eijirō are *serious* outliers." Her finger gentle on his lip, Kaia continued to speak when he didn't interrupt. "I know Attie comes across as scientific and pragmatic, but she's the oldest of us all, and we grew up knowing that if we needed help with anything, Attie would step in without hesitation. She's ferociously maternal."

Bowen watched her put away the ointment.

Picking up the washcloth, she shut the lid on the first-aid kit, then walked silently into the bathroom. He heard water run in there, and when she came back out, it was with nothing in her hands but sadness in her eyes.

He rose, went to take her hand. It was cool from having just been washed. Tugging her over to the window that looked out into the black, he said, "Do you shut this when you sleep?"

A hard nod. "I love the deep, but half the time I think my clanmates treat those inside the habitats as their personal zoo exhibits." Exhaling softly after that dry statement, she said, "Attie is gifted, one of our most brilliant scientists. That's why it nearly broke her when she couldn't 'fix' herself. She said that to me—*Why can't I fix myself, Kaia?*"

Kaia swallowed hard. "It didn't matter what the healers or we said to her, how Dex tried to make her see that she was beloved and wonderful and perfect. This is her fourth pregnancy. She miscarried the first three."

"Ah, hell." Weaving his fingers even tighter through hers, he said, "That's why you're so scared of giving her any reason to worry?"

"She was anxious beyond belief before we brought you down here. All her attention was on not miscarrying and it was causing so much stress on her system that the healer worried she'd give herself a heart attack." Kaia looked up at him. "Atalina is so well loved that Miane authorized the experiment because it was the only thing that seemed to stop her from obsessing over the baby."

"I'm a distraction." Bowen nodded. "I'm fine with that—it doesn't make the work she's doing any less important to my people."

Kaia's expression softened. "She's been herself—cool, calm, centered, and practical—since the instant the experiment began."

Shifting position, Bowen raised his free hand to cradle her face and jaw. "You love fiercely, Kaia Luna."

Shadows streaked across her face, but she didn't break contact. And Bo could no more stop his head from dipping toward her own than he could stop the sun from rising or the moon from shining.

Chapter 25

I had a bad dream that I woke up and you were all gone and I was alone.

—Kaia Luna (10) to Natia Kahananui

"OUCH."

Kaia's eyes widened, her fingers rising to his mouth but not touching his lip as he broke the kiss before it had truly begun. He half expected her to laugh at the foolishness of the moment, of the security chief being brought down low by a stupid cut lip. But she didn't laugh.

"Bend down." Her voice husky, her fingers releasing his own to curve around the side of his neck.

Surrendering to her siren call with his heart a drumbeat and his own hand moving to the flare of her hip, Bo held his breath. It punched out of him a second later as she placed a soft, wet kiss against the side of his throat. His body grew hard, his muscles rigid, and the air in his lungs, it came in shallow bursts.

Another kiss, as deliberate and as sensual. Her fingers petted his nape as she kissed him, and her breasts, they pushed lush and tempting against his chest. Flexing his hand on her hip, he moved his other hand to under her hair . . . and found himself with his palm on warm, bare skin.

Her dress had no back.

"Kaia." Groaning, he nuzzled her throat, drinking in the scent that haunted him. He picked up another opulent thread now that he was so close to the source: coconut infused the tropical flowers, or perhaps it was the other way around. He didn't care; he just knew he could breathe it in for eternity.

She shivered, didn't push him away when he slid one hand up her rib cage to gently cup the erotic weight of her breast. He could feel the lines of a built-in bra, but her nipple was taut through it, and when he ran his thumb over the pebbled nub, she rose on tiptoe and let out a sound that was pure, pleasured female.

Skin hot, Bo went to caress her again when something vibrated against his thigh.

Releasing him with a jerk, Kaia scrambled at the side of her dress to pull out a phone from a pocket hidden among the folds. "It's Tansy," she said, her lips plump and slightly parted—as if he'd kissed the life out of her when she was the one who'd brought him to his knees with her kisses. "I'm supposed to be having lunch with her and another friend."

She coughed, cleared her voice, then answered the call. After telling Tansy she'd been delayed but would be there soon, she hung up and looked at him. "I shouldn't be kissing you."

He could almost see the battle within her. As he'd said, Kaia loved fiercely. Nothing in her behavior said she loved Hugo the way a woman loved a man, but that she loved the vanished male as a friend wasn't in question. Now, her loyalty to Hugo was in a hard collision with the potent beauty of what burned between her and Bowen.

"This isn't lust," he said softly, and it was an admission to himself as well as a statement to her. "It goes too deep." He thumped the flat of his fisted hand over the mechanical beat of his heart. "I feel it here when you touch me, when you smile at me. I listen for your voice and I've memorized your scent." That it had happened at brutal speed changed nothing. Some things just *were.*

And this broken, fleeting fragment of time, it was theirs.

Kaia took a step back, closed her eyes. When she opened them again, she'd raised a shield he could almost see, her gaze impossible to read.

"Will you tell Attie you stumbled into a doorway? Say you tripped on your duffel after you left it in the wrong place."

"Won't a clanmate tell her the truth?"

Kaia shook her head. "We all love her too much." Turning on her heel, she flowed to the door. "You need to go finish eating and I have friends waiting on me."

BOWEN got the explanation to Dr. Kahananui over with first, finding her at a table in the atrium with the man who'd ripped Alden a new one. "My own fault," he said with a scowl after explaining the lip. "My mother was always telling me to clean up the mess in my room."

"You're certain you didn't hit your head?" the doctor asked with a frown.

"Yes. I'd tell you if I did." He didn't have to add the rest—that he knew exactly what was on the line and would do nothing to sabotage it.

Muscles relaxing, she nodded at the man across from her. "Have you met my mate, Dex? He's the station commander." Pride glowed in every word.

It was so unexpectedly sweet that it cut through the heaviness in Bowen's gut. "Bowen," he said, holding out his hand to the other man. "Good to meet you."

"Likewise." Dex's handshake was firm. "You want to join us?"

"Thanks, but I could do with some alone time."

"Yeah, I get that—I'd lose it if I couldn't escape into the black now and then."

Bo had the thought that Dex could become a friend; the rough-hewn male reminded him of Cassius. Bo's best friend, too, didn't mince words. "I'll leave you two to enjoy your lunch."

Getting himself a fresh plate of food and a mug of coffee, he'd just sat down right next to the seaward wall when Scott limped over with a plate holding a generous slice of blackberry pie. "Kaia messaged and said this was for you." The boy lowered his voice to a whisper even though Bowen had chosen a seat far from Dr. Kahananui and Dex. "How did you *do* that to Alden? He's so big and you were sick and everything."

"Being big isn't an advantage if you don't use your brains." Scott, he sensed, had plenty of the latter—the boy's deep green eyes burned with a thirst to learn. "Intelligence and strategy have won far more fights than might."

Scott's expression turned quietly thoughtful but he didn't ask more questions, leaving Bo to his meal. And to the slice of pie to replace the one that had splattered on Alden's body. The ache in his chest expanded to encompass everything he was. "You'll drive me crazy, Kaia Luna," he whispered before taking a bite of the pie.

He didn't know what made him glance into the deep five minutes later, when the pie was only a memory entangled with the scent of his siren. Two large shapes moved beyond, flowing closer and closer . . . until they formed into the shape of humpback whales. One came to swim right alongside the seaward wall, seemed to be looking straight at him. It had different markings from the one who'd swum by earlier . . . including a small patch under the eye right where Carlotta's beauty spot had been.

Wonder a glow under his skin, Bowen pressed his palm to the glass. "Good swimming, Carlotta."

He watched after her until she disappeared back into the black with her mate, then searched the water for more glimpses into wonder until he had no more time. Going back to his room, he opened up the window, then went to borrow a chair from Dr. Kahananui's lab to place by it. She examined his cut again before she'd let him leave, seemed satisfied with what she saw.

He'd just put the chair down by the window when he looked up to find a bunch of obviously juvenile-sized sea creatures pressing their noses to the transparent wall. After laughingly waving at them, he took a seat and waited until the kids had swum off before he pulled out his phone and began to read the files Lily had sent through. He focused first on the file to do with the assassination attempt that was the reason his heart was now a high-tech construct instead of flesh and blood.

The Mercants, it turned out, had dealt with the problem because the same individual had also targeted their scion, Silver. Then they'd forwarded all relevant data. It appeared the Alliance now owed the Mercants a favor, but it'd be worth it to have a strong line of communication with the influential Psy family.

Word from Bowen's spies was that the Mercants were considered the most powerful information brokers in the PsyNet. If you needed information, it was the Mercants who either had it—or knew how to get it. But, oddly for a Psy family, they'd remained a cohesive and tight-knit unit throughout Silence. Mercants, it seemed, didn't let go of their own.

The final file in the packet was titled *Krychek*. He opened it to read that the cardinal telekinetic had been in touch after the shooting. He'd told Lily she had access to the resources of the Ruling Coalition of the Psy should she need those resources.

Your brother is critical to the Alliance, Krychek had written, *and the Alliance is critical to the success of Trinity. We can only outmaneuver and crush the Consortium if we stand as an unbreakable triumvirate.*

As Bo had expected, Lily hadn't taken Krychek up on his offer, but that the other man had made it had Bowen wondering. Since he was officially dead, he couldn't reach out to Krychek, but Lily could. He sent her a message: *Ask Krychek if he's thought about what I asked him during our last meeting.* To help create a psychic shield for humanity for nothing in return, simply because it was the right thing to do.

I'll do it now, Lily replied. *He gave me his direct contact details.*

Sliding away the phone, Bo decided to walk this habitat, stretch out his muscles further while seeing if he could discover more about the wider station. He'd reached the atrium and was in the process of figuring out whether to go in the direction Kaia had headed, or take the opposite way, when he caught a sense of movement with his peripheral vision.

A rather large sea turtle, its greenish skin tightly wrinkled, was walking purposefully—if in slow motion—across the carpeting toward him. And it *was* walking, not dragging itself on flippers. He couldn't see enough below its shell to figure out how. A semi-shift?

As he watched, it came to a halt two feet from him, openly judging him with its pitch-black eyes. “Good morning,” he said.

He could swear the turtle snorted at his polite attempt at communication before it turned around and walked back the way it had come.

“Don’t mind Bebe,” Oleanna whispered as she passed. “Been in a bad mood since 2032.”

“What happened in 2032?”

“She turned two hundred and decided that gave her leave to be crotchety. I swear she yells ‘Get off my lawn!’ to the other turtles who try to swim up onto her island.”

Bowen’s mind rocketed back to a conversation he’d had with Malachai. He scowled. “Is she seriously over two hundred or are you messing with the gullible human?”

Giggling, the changeling who’d made suggestive promises to him across the kitchen shrugged. “You should ask Bebe. I’ll nurse your wounds afterward—I have *lots* of tentacles to soothe your brow and massage your aches.”

Bowen’s increasingly dark scowl had no effect. Laughing, she winked at him before heading off in a wave of musky perfume that was perfectly fine except that it wasn’t tropical flowers and coconut and Kaia.

As for Bebe the crotchety turtle, she was still making her laborious way out of the atrium, but at least she’d turned her beady eyes on two teenagers who were studying industriously at a table. Or they were now. They’d been throwing spitballs at each other before Bebe’s arrival.

“Crotchety turtles who are apparently over two hundred,” Bowen murmured. “Tiny old ladies who turn into whales. And a cook with a mouse for a pet who turns me inside out. I’m still in a coma and dreaming.”

And yet he wouldn’t give up the dream of his siren with her tender kiss and a hidden sadness he’d glimpsed when she’d walked away—after seducing him so thoroughly that he felt tied to her with an invisible thread.

“Bowen.” It was George’s cadaverous form. “Dr. Kahananui needs to take blood samples to confirm your readings are within the acceptable limits as we prepare for the second injection of the compound tomorrow.”

Bo went motionless. “So soon?”

“Yes, the timeline is uneven.” George pulled out an organizer. “I have it here, the number of days you’ll have before the final injection, not counting tomorrow.”

“Twelve,” Bo murmured. “I’ll have twelve days.”

And a five percent chance of success.

A ninety-five percent chance of oblivion.

Chapter 26

Thanks for sticking up for me. I always know you'll be there, that you won't let me fall.

—Hugo Sorensen (18) to Kaia Luna (18)

KAIA ARRIVED AT the small Japanese garden in habitat two shaken and with the lingering imprint of Bowen's hands on her body, his roughly masculine scent in her nostrils. She couldn't understand how he'd gotten under her skin so quickly, until she couldn't not think about him.

"Kaia!" Tansy waved from the table she and Seraphina had snagged next to a miniature Japanese maple with leaves of gold and orange.

Like all the green spaces in the station, these delicately pruned plants provided not only a way to cleanse the air, but also food for their souls. Because to be a water changeling was to have two sides to your nature. One part lived for the ocean, the other craved green and earth.

Kaia had no desire to go upside and walk on land, but—aside from her kitchen—the green areas in the habitats were her favorite spaces. "Sorry I'm late," she said, taking a seat, Tansy to her left and Sera to her right. A large thermal carrier sat in the center of the table—food one of the teens would've run over from the main kitchen. Sera had probably bribed said teen with a favor only the assistant station commander could grant. "Alden wanted to go for Bowen Knight's throat."

Tansy and Seraphina groaned in concert.

"Here." Tansy opened up a sleek black thermos and poured a frothy coffee into the third mug on the table, the gray-blue wool of her top a perfect contrast to the cool white of her skin. "I made it in my new machine." She sank her teeth into her lower lip, her sharply pointed face anxious.

And though Kaia's heart still trembled from the encounter with Bo, she cupped her hands around the mug and lifted it to take a deep breath. Coffee, chocolate, cinnamon, the decadent scents swirled around her, but did nothing to erase the taste of Bowen from her lips.

Hesitant to take that step, she nonetheless made herself sip the coffee. And shuddered inside when Bowen's scent continued to cling to her, as if he'd sunk into the cells of her body itself. "It's perfect, Tansy." Creamy and rich and hot.

Tansy's face lit up. "Sera liked it, too."

Seraphina, generously curved and as generous of heart, tapped the side of her mug with one boldly red nail. "I could do with a refill." Her deep brown skin glowed with health, her springy curls so glossy and shiny that Kaia guessed she'd had the morning off—it took serious time and patience and a lot of conditioner to separate out each curl so beautifully.

"So," Seraphina said, "the human." She pursed her lips together, the color on them a perfect match to her nails. "Is he what Hugo said he was?" As Dex's second-in-command, she'd been fully briefed on Hugo's dossier, while Hugo had told Tansy himself.

Kaia put her mug down on the table with care, but kept her hands wrapped around it. "I kissed him." The words simply fell out, too huge to keep inside.

Tansy's hand flew to her mouth, while Seraphina released a quiet whistle.

Squeezing the mug, Kaia shook her head. "I know Hugo would never lie to me," she said, "but he got certain things wrong." She told her friends about Bowen's justification for the Alliance's military might. "I called Armand and asked about our own military numbers and capability." Her cousin had been amused by her sudden interest but happy to answer her question. "It's easily *twenty* times that of the Alliance."

"Dex and I did wonder about that part of it, figured Hugo just didn't have the military knowledge to properly judge things," Seraphina murmured. "Mal hasn't said anything else?"

"No, not yet." Kaia blew on the heated surface of her coffee. "I have that crazy gene in my blood." Bowen had been vehement in his denials of having taken or hurt BlackSea's people, passionately angry at being accused of such horror, but how could Kaia trust her reading of him?

Tansy's small hand on Kaia's forearm. "You say that, Kaia, but you always see through the men who try to spin you a tale." She bit down on her lower lip again, the action a nervous habit she'd never been able to break, and then Tansy said, "You love Hugo but you saw it even with him."

Kaia's eyes burned at the thought of her feckless but loyal friend. She'd never been in denial of Hugo's faults—he gambled too much, broke promises as easily as he made them, borrowed money he never returned, and juggled multiple women at the same time—but he also made her laugh and was there when she really needed him. "I feel like I'm betraying Hugo with Bowen."

"No." Seraphina's voice was firm. "Tansy's right—you have laser-sharp instincts. And if they're telling you Bowen Knight is a man you can trust, you have to go with that—you can't start second-guessing yourself. Could be he has someone in his organization who's betraying the ideals of the group."

"Like with us." Tansy's big blue eyes welled up with tears. "One of us is betraying our clanmates. Otherwise the hunters would never find them."

Silence fell, broken only by the sounds of the small birds that lived in this green space. BlackSea brought in only tiny birds for whom the area provided was a massive territory akin to a forest. They trapped no eagles, no birds who flew on long migratory routes. The birds in the habitats were homebodies who enjoyed a small forest to roam in, complete with insects and worms for them to find and eat.

"I have to make a choice," Kaia said quietly. "I can't stay stuck in the middle."

Both her friends nodded. But it was Seraphina who spoke. "Kaia, hon, you're not a woman who lets just any man kiss her. I think you've made your choice."

Seraphina was right; Kaia had made her choice the first time she played with Bowen Knight. "He drives me insane," she muttered. "I baked him a pie." It came out a growl.

Tansy giggled. "In that case, why are we even discussing this? You haven't even baked *me* a pie." Her giggle was silly and high-pitched and as infectious as when they'd been teenagers.

Kaia crumbled first, followed by Seraphina. Their laughter attracted a phalanx of curious birds, their tiny heads jerking from one of them to the next, which only made them laugh harder.

"I have to say," Seraphina said afterward, her voice a touch breathless, "you do have good taste. I saw the man yesterday when you left the kitchen with Attie and he's bitable. A little skinny from being sick but he's got that sexy dominant thing going on." She shivered.

Tansy, meanwhile, made a face. "I don't know why you like dominants. They're always so pushy and aggressive. Give me a gentle submissive any day."

"Water changelings don't have dominants and submissives," Kaia pointed out.

"Tell that to Miane," was Seraphina's riposte. "We might not be blatant about it like the wolves, but we have a hierarchy of power. You know I want to bite Edison, too."

"Stop that right now." Kaia pointed a finger at her unrepentant friend. "Changing the subject," she said with a glare at both grinning women, "have you seen Hex? He ran off while I was dressing."

"I hope for your sake that he's not in George's quarters." Seraphina's curls bounced as she shook her head, her lips pursed together. "You know he still hasn't forgiven you for the last time that mouse of yours jumped down on his head."

"He wouldn't mind if you jumped on him, though, Sera," Tansy said in her sweet, shy voice that hid the heart of a vixen. "Naked."

"Have you been smoking the herbs you grow?" Seraphina snorted. "George is adorable in that awkward, gangly way but I'd eat him alive. Not only that, but I don't think I've ever known him to date anyone."

Tansy scrunched up her nose. "Believe me or not, he has a crush on you. I've seen him making big heart eyes at you."

"More like *you* were making big heart eyes at Armand." Seraphina waggled her eyebrows. "I thought you didn't like dominants and their pushy, aggressive, grrrrrrowly ways."

Blushing red-hot, Tansy ducked her head. "He's different."

"I can't believe you are *both* talking about my cousins," Kaia moaned. "I cannot have sex discussions with you if it involves Edison and Armand."

"Who said anything about Edison and Armand?" Seraphina made a puzzled face. "We're talking about Bedison and Laymond."

Laughter erupted around the table again, and at that instant, Kaia didn't feel the aloneness deep inside her heart that nothing had ever been able to budge. Not since she was seven years old and watching her parents' chests rise and fall in breaths pumped by machines. The healers hadn't had to tell her that her beloved mama and playful papa were gone. She'd felt it. Felt the bond that had tied the three of them together break days earlier—but she hadn't said anything. Hadn't been ready.

Late at night, her only companion the dark, she often wondered if she'd die with that seed of aloneness inside her, that hole that had never closed. People had tried. Her aunts and uncles and grandparents, Bebe, Edison and Attie and Mal and the others, they'd wrapped her in protective affection. But Kaia had lost the two people who knew her inside out, who not only understood her quirks but didn't think them quirks at all. She'd lost the only two people who shared memories carried by no one else. And she couldn't forget.

"Come on, let's eat." Tansy's sweet voice broke into her thoughts, followed by the spicy scent of today's lunch.

Forcing herself to step out of the past, Kaia ate, drank, laughed with her friends . . . and hoped Hugo would forgive her the choice she'd made.

Her wrist unit buzzed some time later. Checking the message flowing across the tiny screen, she found it was from Atalina: *Are you free to oversee Bowen for an hour or two after your lunch? He wants to exercise and I think he should. But I don't want him alone—and I've got George double-checking my analyses.*

Kaia thought again of the ugly beep of hospital machines, the mechanical rise and fall of chests . . . and of a man who had a life expectancy so short it was measured in days. And then she thought of the warmth of his hand against her cheek, the violently alive sense of him, and the raw depth of their unexpected connection.

Not just lust.

Not just passion.

More.

Dangerously more.

And she said, *Yes. Ask him if he knows how to swim.*

Chapter 27

You'll be awake for the procedure. I'll remove a small piece of your skull, inject the compound directly into the same part of your brain that holds the implanted chip, then seal your skull back up. You'll have a slight tenderness at the site but should suffer no other ill effects.

—Dr. Atalina Kahananui to Bowen Knight

WHEN KAIA, DRESSED in a floaty black cover-up, her hair unbound over her back and her feet bare, poked her head into the lab, Bo had to fight not to tumble her into his lap and just hold her. It would be like trying to cage the ocean.

"You're ready?" she asked, taking in his casual white shirt with short sleeves, and blue board shorts—both items he'd been issued out of the station's stockpile of new clothes. That stockpile wasn't huge, but it was enough to add a few more choices to his wardrobe, including the trainers currently on his feet. As a bonus, he'd gotten to spend a little time with Dex, who'd come over to personally show him to the storeroom.

"Thanks for going along with the story about the lip," the station commander had said quietly when they were alone. "I used to be this wild daredevil—no fear, no regrets. Then I fell in love and fuck, fear's hell."

Bo hadn't needed the other man to say anything further. He'd never forget the instant he'd seen the red dot centered on Lily's forehead. That gut-wrenching panic, that rage to protect.

Now, he rose and said, "Yes," to another woman who was becoming intimately entwined with his heart. He knew it was selfish to keep on moving forward with Kaia when his life hung so precariously in the balance, but he—a man renowned for his control—had none where she was concerned.

"Here, take this." Dr. Kahananui passed Kaia a scanner that she dropped into the tote she carried over one shoulder.

It was after they were in the corridor that Bo said, "Is the pool in another habitat?" He hadn't actually made it out of this habitat yet. First, he'd had to give blood, then cooperate with Dr. Kahananui while she ran multiple tests, and then it turned out the storeroom was in this same habitat.

Kaia nodded. "Habitat four." The shine of her hair caught his eye, had his hand rising to run down it before his conscious mind could overrule his need.

Kaia stilled for a moment but didn't reprimand him for the contact. The silken feel of her hair lingered on his fingertips as the scent of her infused his every breath.

She took him toward the left exit out of this habitat and onto a wide connecting bridge that was transparent on all sides and surrounded by water. He couldn't help craning his head, trying to see everything at once.

Sleek and fast and mysterious creatures unlike any he'd ever before seen swam beyond, some only suggestions of a shape in the black, others huge behemoths who sailed above the bridge like majestic ocean liners. Below his feet, streamers of tiny bioluminescent fish passed in a silver river.

"What's that?" He was pointing to a creature on the seabed that glowed a haunting blue when he caught a sense of movement out of the corner of his eye and—

"Damn it, Oleanna!" A large octopus had whooshed over at manic speed to slam onto the glass, causing him to fucking jump.

Kaia's startled laugh was a caress. "How did you know it's her?"

"She's the only woman who's ever propositioned me by whispering *I have tentacles* across the room." Scowling at the octopus when she peeled away her suckers to slide into the water, he continued on with Kaia.

"As an octopus, she actually has arms, not tentacles," Kaia told him.

"Yeah, somehow I can't see Oleanna giving up tentacles for something as prosaic as arms," Bowen muttered.

Laughing, Kaia said, "No, definitely not."

They had to cross another habitat to get to habitat four, and from what he saw, it had the quiet feel of mostly living quarters. Going over the second bridge was no less fascinating than the first—even if a certain octopus did insist on swimming alongside them, delicately waving a tentacle just as they were about to head out of view.

Bo had been expecting a lap pool for those sea changelings who wanted to get exercise but didn't want to go out into the ocean. What he got was a massive pool on an unexpected lower level of this habitat. Roughly circular—though the edges were uneven—it hugged the seaward wall. Not only that, it wasn't the blue of an ordinary pool. No, this water was the greenish-blue hue of the ocean under sunlight, complete with seaweeds waving gently below, tiny fish darting through the clarity in silvery flashes, and what might've been coral in the far corner.

"Don't damage the coral." Kaia's soft voice sang with an open love for the water. "We mostly don't go in that corner so it can grow without being hurt."

Amazed by the beauty of this piece of ocean inside the habitat walls, Bo crouched down to dip his fingers in the cool but not icy liquid. "Why do you have this when you can swim outside?"

"Not everyone has long periods to head off into the black. This pool allows for short dips when clanmates have a half hour in the day." She raised her cover-up off over her head in such a quick movement that Bo sucked in a breath, half expecting smooth, naked flesh underneath. But she was wearing a simple autumn-brown swimsuit that hugged her body with a lover's possessiveness.

Throwing the cover-up on a nearby recliner, she dived into the water, a wild and enigmatic creature whose long hair danced in the air for a fraction of time before she disappeared under the rippling surface and came back up to sleek the water over her head. "Don't waste time." An imperious order. "I have to get back to supervise the dinner prep."

That got Bo moving. He didn't want to waste a single moment he had with this complicated, intriguing, astonishing woman. It took him only seconds to toe off his trainers and pull off his shirt.

Dex had insisted on issuing him a pair of goggles.

Not wanting to miss out on what might lie beneath the surface of the pool, Bowen took a minute to open the small case he'd slipped into his pocket and—using the mirror on the back of the lid—slipped the protective lenses over his eyes. Larger than ordinary contacts and reusable, they'd give him clear vision even in salt water.

Setting aside the case, he walked to the edge of the pool and dived in.

The water was an exhilarating shock to his system. It told him he was alive, that his heart was beating, his lungs pumping. Breaking the surface after his dive, he saw Kaia waiting for him, brown eyes unreadable and droplets running down her neck and into the soft valley between her breasts.

He wanted to touch her, wanted to taste her. When she came toward him, his heart turned to thunder. He was just beginning to reach for her when she jumped up without warning and pushed him under the water.

As he came up spluttering, the first thing he heard was the sound of her laughter. She sounded as young as he suddenly felt. He grinned and took off after her. She swam like a fish, which was unsurprising. What *was* surprising was her incredible playfulness, as if the touch of salt water had awakened a hidden part of her nature.

She'd disappear beneath the water and then he'd feel a grip on his ankle taking him down or she'd taunt him by staying mere inches out of reach, pure delight in her expression. He let her tug him under, just so he could hear her laugh when they both came up for air.

And though he was far slower than her in the water, he'd been born with an acute understanding of strategy. He managed to trap her against a corner at one point, but instead of pushing her under, he stole a kiss that made her gasp. Not giving her time to think about it and maybe talk herself out of her instinctive response, he lifted her up—*thank God for the metal bugs*—and threw her toward another part of the pool. She gave a little scream as she went under, was grinning when she came back up.

Swimming over, she said, “Do that again.”

So he did and she arced through the air in a twisting dive that should’ve been impossible. This time when she came up, she said, “You’re fun to play with.” Unhidden joy, no edginess, no distance.

“Your eyes,” he whispered, realizing her irises weren’t brown any longer but a vivid black that was nothing human.

Tiny droplets of water hung off her eyelashes. “Do you see me?”

“Yes,” he said, feeling sucker-punched by the gift she’d given him. “I see all of you.” The wild and the woman, the creature of the deep and the cook who fashioned magic with her hands.

“Here, take my hand.” A smile that held *so much* joy. “I’ll show you the bottom. If you start to lose your breath, just let go and swim back up.”

At that instant, Bowen would’ve followed her anywhere.

Closing his hand around her own, he took a deep breath and they dived under the water. Tiny colorful fish swam past their bodies, seaweed fronds waved, the world cocooned in a living silence.

He wondered if this was what it was like for Kaia and her people when they went into the ocean. She tugged him. Kicking his feet, he went. The bottom of the pool—of the habitat itself—was glass, or whatever engineered material it was that they’d used to build. Thanks to the lights that speared softly downward from the edges of the pool, he could see straight through to the sand of the seabed, while in front of him, the lights of the habitat lit up the ocean.

Schools of fish swam by on the other side, their slight bioluminescence when they danced out of the light telling him they were creatures of the black. Something else went by and it crackled as if it burned with electricity. The mysteries here would never fully be known, he thought. Because, as Kaia had said, the deep was never static.

He could’ve stayed below for hours, but his lungs protested and so, reluctantly releasing Kaia's hand, he swam his way back up to the air he needed for life. But even as he left, he kept his eyes open; he saw her watching the fish on the other side while her hair floated behind her, and he saw the slits open in her neck.

Erupting to the golden warmth of "daylight," he gulped in a breath and waited for Kaia to join him. When she did, he saw that the slits had disappeared as if they'd never existed. "You had gills." Wonder had him reaching his fingers to the smooth line of her neck.

Kaia allowed the touch but gave him a watchful look. "I've been told humans find that disturbing."

"If I could have gills, I would." He'd be able to swim with her in the deep, would be able to glimpse more of its mysteries. "How do you do it?"

She shrugged. "I don't know. A lot of us in BlackSea just can."

"Is it what the wolves and cats call a semi-shift?" Bowen had witnessed the predatory changelings release their claws, their eyes going inhuman while the rest of them stayed unchanged.

But Kaia shook her head. "No. Carlotta can do it even though she's an air breather. Maybe Atalina should study that next." Dancing eyes. "Gills on aqua-mammals: a treatise."

She splashed water at him without warning.

Any defenses he might've had in ruins, he splashed back.

They were having the water fight to end all water fights when the doors to the pool opened.

"Kaia's here!" cried more than one voice before at least five teenagers cannonballed into the water, causing the pool to erupt into smashing waves. What happened next was so extraordinary that Bo hauled himself to the side so he could just watch.

Chapter 28

I miss them and it hurts my heart.

—Kaia to Bebe (2068)

IT SEEMED TO be a game, with Kaia playing the prey and the teens attempting to catch her. Except that she was so fast and so clever that they stood no chance. Even when they got smart and attempted to surround her by working as a group, she was gone moments before they arrived.

Shouts bounced off the walls, followed by groans and laughter.

There was no such cheerful noise at Alliance HQ. None of his knights had kids—but he decided at that instant that when they did, those children would have a place at the HQ. He'd build a nursery inside the HQ, make it a place of family. They'd be a clan, a pack.

When Kaia came up next to him at last, telling the children to chase each other instead, her chest was heaving—hell, her breasts were gorgeous—and her cheeks flushed with color. "They never catch me." Pure adorable smugness.

Bo knew then and there that he was talking to both sides of her nature, talking to *her*. No shields. No walls. "You are the most complex, beautiful, extraordinary woman I have ever met."

. . .

A BEAM of simulated sunlight kissed the side of Bowen's face as he spoke, highlighting a small blue stain on his temple . . . and a cold blade of fear thrust itself through Kaia's heart. "Attie's been running tests." She knew the exact device that left that mark—the mark itself was nothing, just a dot of ink to help position the device, but it told a story.

Bowen's smile faded. "Second injection's tomorrow."

Sucking in a breath, Kaia tightened her abdomen. "You're about to get your head cut open and you just got out of a coma." It took vicious self-control to keep her tone dry. "You'll excuse me if I don't take your declarations about my beauteous presence seriously."

He locked his hand around her wrist. "You know this isn't anything ordinary." There it was, the dominance that hummed under his skin. "You *know*."

Slipping out of his grasp when a ball splashed in between them, distracting him for a split second, Kaia made for the side and got out of the pool. Once in the shower in the changing area, she pressed her palms to the tiled wall and tried to breathe, tried *not* to think of hospital rooms and bodies wrapped in biodegradable shrouds being sent into the black from whence they'd come.

"Stop, stop, stop." She squeezed her eyes shut against the cascade of memory and pretended the hot water that trickled down her cheeks all came from the showerhead. Even when it tasted of salt and a child's anguish.

She spent too long under the water.

Afterward, she rubbed herself dry using one of the towels provided, then pulled on her cover-up over bare skin. She'd brought underwear in her tote, but her other self was very much at the surface of her mind and it didn't agree with the concept of clothes. The cover-up was about as far as it was willing to go.

Black and shapeless and reaching to just below midthigh, the cover-up wouldn't scandalize even Bebe. For a turtle rumored to have thrown primal orgies in her youth, Bebe could be a definite prude. But Kaia loved her with all her heart. Bebe's wrinkled arms had cuddled a heartbroken Kaia so many times after the deaths of her mama and papa.

Kaia had been able to grieve on Bebe's little island when she couldn't anywhere else. She'd often fallen asleep curled against Bebe's shell, the sun beating down on them and the sand gritty under her naked body.

Since she'd forgotten to put a comb in her tote, she twisted her hair into a rough bun. Then she rinsed out her swimsuit and hung it to dry on one of the lines provided for that. She'd pick it up tomorrow or a clanmate would grab it for her while retrieving their own gear.

The towel went in the large basket nearby; it was another station team's job to handle laundry, as Kaia and her team took care of Ryūjin's food needs.

A well-run station needed everyone to do their part.

Unable to delay any longer, she stepped out, her heart searching for the man who was going to ruin her. He sat on a poolside bench created of stone, watching the teenagers in the water. She could tell he hadn't showered, just pulled on his shirt over damp board shorts that exposed thighs in far too good a shape for a man who'd been in a coma.

Kaia, whispered the alone, sad, lost part of her soul, *he's about to have a second dose of a test compound injected into his brain. The clock is ticking faster and faster.*

Despite the desperate warning, Kaia's fingers itched to weave through his heavily damp hair as she came to stand beside him. The other part of her nature wasn't always in agreement with the human side of her—and it *loved* playing with Bowen—but it didn't fight her this time when she curled her fingers into a white-knuckled fist.

It, too, bore scars of grief that would never fade.

It, too, watched for Hugo to swim back into the habitat.

It, too, swam silently through waters she'd first explored with her parents, their bigger bodies keeping her safe.

And it, too, knew that falling for Bowen Knight was a terrible, terrible mistake.

"They're fast, except for Scott," Bowen said, his tone thoughtful. "But even with the gammy leg, he has more endurance."

Even though she really needed to get to the kitchen, Kaia stayed and watched the children. "Scott's also the most patient of the lot." He was the one she trusted to watch dishes that needed a careful eye. "He never rushes."

Bowen nodded and pulled on his trainers. "The others zig and zag and dive and jump, but he thinks about every move. He's the one who'll catch you one day."

"No, he doesn't have the speed." And Kaia was nearly as fast as Edison. "But, if the others listen to him, he could use *them* to catch me."

"You're right. The kid will make an excellent security chief one day." His gaze, when it turned to her, was primal in its intensity. "I'm not about to give up, Kaia."

The soft promise raised every tiny hair on her body.

"You can't control the universe," she said, her eyes on the tendrils drying against his forehead, one kissing the dot of blue.

"I won't know until I try." He rose to his feet on that uncompromising statement.

Throat dry, Kaia led him out of the pool area. It was as they were crossing the final connecting bridge that the heavy mass of her hair unraveled from her bun to slam onto her back. "Damn it. I'll have to spend ten minutes brushing and drying this before I can head into the kitchen." It wouldn't totally dry that quickly even under her high-strength dryer, but she could manage enough that she could scrape it back and out of her way.

It would be more practical if she just cut it, but Kaia had her vanities.

And her father had loved her hair. The same hair as her mother.

When they'd lived on the island, she'd used to sneak out of bed at night sometimes and peek out onto the sea-facing porch to see her parents sitting there, laughing and talking. Often, her father would have a brush and he'd be running it through her mother's long hair, detangling and smoothing and loving.

"I could brush it for you," Bowen offered.

Kaia's heart skidded, today and yesterday colliding, a crash that was an earthquake.

Chapter 29

Love can alter the fabric of the universe, my heart.

—Iosef Luna to his only daughter, Kaia (4)

KAIA KNEW EXACTLY what she should do: walk away right this moment. Bowen Knight might be a man of honor according to every instinct she possessed, but he was still going to wound her unbearably.

Be safe, Kaia, whispered the scared child inside her. *Push him away.*

But the thing was, whether she did or not, Bowen's path was set. The compound *would* be injected into his brain twice more and the dice *would* be rolled. The five percent chance wouldn't alter whether or not she surrendered to the craving low in her body, the ache deep in her heart.

All that would change was her level of pain.

She slipped her hand into his and closed her fingers around his palm.

His own fingers wrapping warm and strong over hers, he walked with her in silence. She saw more than one pair of eyes widen at the sight of their linked hands, several mouths purse tight, but no one called out and none of those Hugo had trusted with his thoughts attempted to get in her way.

She opaqued the window into the black the instant they were in the privacy of her room, then went and sat down in the chair in front of the white writing desk with curved legs that also functioned as her vanity. Pulling open one small desk drawer, she got out a brush and a jar of leave-in deep conditioning treatment.

The mirror she'd mounted on the opposite wall, its silvery surface surrounded by white curlicues, reflected back her stark eyes. But behind her, Bowen's face as he lifted up her hair to run it through his fingers, it held devotion.

Her hands fisted on her thighs.

She wanted to disbelieve what she saw, wanted to tell herself it was all happening too fast to be real. Hugo would be horrified; he'd probably say Bowen had created an illusion and Kaia had fallen for it. But Kaia *knew*. The creature inside her skin knew. Bowen Knight was no black villain and this was a beautiful and terrifying and once-in-a-lifetime thing.

Not a thing you chose. A thing that chose you.

Unable to look that truth too deeply in the eye, she opened the jar. "Work this through my hair," she said in a husky voice. "It'll make it easier to smooth out the tangles."

Bowen began the task, his every action intent. It made her want to smile. She had the foolish thought that he'd probably build a crib or plan a family outing with that same military attention to detail.

She let the thought pass before it could lodge in her throat and, picking up the phone she'd left on one side of the writing desk, sent a message through to her scheduled kitchen team. "Tacos for dinner," she told Bo afterward, her eyes meeting his in the mirror. "My crew can handle that on their own." Kaia always taught each team one dish they could create from scratch and without her oversight.

Bo's hand paused in the act of working in the conditioner. "We have time, then."

Such an paradoxical statement. "Yes," she said. "Today, we have time."

The familiar scent of coconut oil fused with tiare flowers rose into the air as Bowen continued to work the conditioner into her hair, and in her mind ran the ghost of a sand-covered little girl kissed by tropical sunlight. She watched him in the mirror, watched the fierce concentration with which he did the task and thought she could become very used to being the nucleus of Bowen Knight's attention.

The security chief of the Human Alliance would have endless calls on his time, of that she had no doubt. But Kaia also knew that were she his, she'd have direct access to him anytime she wished. Bowen Knight wasn't the kind of man to push aside his promises or discount the bonds he'd forged: he would love with the same intense concentration he did everything else.

"Is that enough?"

Kaia nodded and closed the lid on the jar before she gave him the brush. His fingers grazed her own as he took it and her stomach clenched, a tight curl of sensation.

Holding her gaze in the mirror, he bent down to press a kiss to the curve of her neck. She shivered, raised her hand to run her fingertips over his cheek and jaw. "Your lip."

"Magic ointment. Can barely feel it." His breath whispered over her skin like a warm wind shaped for her alone.

She could see his lips in the mirror and the swelling was gone, the cut barely visible. "All right," she said with a smile that came from the wild heart of her. "In that case, you're permitted to use your mouth."

His smile was so bright and so young that she knew without asking that this was a smile only she would ever see. It was too innocent for the security chief or the older brother or the trusted son. Too vulnerable for the world.

As if his shell had cracked, allowing her a glimpse of the naked core of this man.

"Tell me if I tug too hard," he said before beginning to run the brush through her hair.

He almost immediately hit a snag. Stopping at once, he began to work to loosen it up with far more patience than Kaia; where she would have hit at the knot impatiently, he unraveled it with a care that caused no tension on her scalp.

"I used to braid Lily's hair when she was small," he said unexpectedly.

"My cousin Edison did it for me." Kaia smiled. "Your sister's hair was probably less trouble than mine." She loved her hair, but a tiny part of her could still be jealous of the heavy silk of Lily's, so slick that it would fall smoothly back in place no matter how turbulent the wind.

"To brush, sure," Bowen confirmed. "But man, it was like the strands were coated in silicone—or possessed little devil minds of their own. Every time I tried to fix a braid, it'd fall apart." He shook his head. "The only good thing was that it'd make her laugh when I tried not to swear."

Kaia's thoughts rolled back in time. "Before I came to live with my aunt and uncle, my mama helped me wash and oil my hair, and my papa used to do my braids." Maybe if she'd grown into a teenager with her parents, she'd have started calling them Mom and Dad, but she'd lost them as a young girl and they were frozen in time as Mama and Papa.

Two brilliant young people whose lights had burned incandescent in their souls. They'd wanted to change the world, share that light, and they'd brought up their daughter to believe in hope, in passion, in the power of love to alter a universe.

But then the very world they'd loved had snuffed out their lights and Kaia had lost her way in fear. Shame might've twisted her up at the choices she'd made except that her parents had left her with a gift neither time nor death could erase, a promise that "We will love you, no matter what. Always, Kaia. *Always.*"

"My father was a lyricist by training and inclination, but he also loved to create other forms of art," she told Bowen as echoes of her father's voice filled her head. "It was never enough for him to do a simple braid. He'd do hundreds of fine braids, or a big braid across my head like an ancient queen, or a bun with a braid around it."

"I'm starting to feel braid envy." Light words, but his eyes were gentle in the mirror. "He's gone?"

"They're both gone." It was so hard to say that even now, admit it. "I wouldn't let my aunt or anyone else touch my hair for months after I lost my parents. I washed it and brushed it as well as I could, but I still looked half-feral."

Bowen bent to press a kiss to her temple. "A little warrior princess."

The bloom of warmth inside her was nothing erotic and devastatingly intimate. "I finally went up to Edison one day, brush in hand." She laughed softly at the memory of the look on his face. "He was fifteen and had Atalina for a sister—she's had a no-fuss bob since the day she got a voice and could make her wishes known. He had no idea what to do."

"But he did it."

"Yes." Because that was what brothers did and Edison was her brother, no matter their official relationship. "He slowly got better at it and these days he tells me it helped with his hand-eye coordination."

Bowen hit another snag, worked at it. "This beautiful hair, I dream about it."

The deep rumble of his voice shivered through her, her breasts swelling under the airy fabric of the cover-up. But she didn't rush him, the pleasure she received from watching him behind her, his chiseled face set in focused lines, a deeply visceral thing.

And though she had childhood memories of her father brushing her hair, that sepia-toned memory faded under the reality of today.

That had been a childhood sweetness.

This was a very adult moment, honey richness in her blood. "Bowen?"

"Hmm."

"Give me your arm."

Halting his smooth strokes, he stretched forward his left arm. When she put her fingers on his skin and pressed down on the muscle trainers, he gave her a curious half smile. "Testing my muscles? Trust me, I have enough to brush your hair."

"Does it hurt if I apply pressure?"

"The bugs?" He withdrew his arm and continued with her hair. "I barely remember they're there. Things are fucking incredible."

His brush stopped partway. His eyes blazed at her in the mirror. "You thinking about putting pressure on my skin?"

Her own eyes dark pools of fire, Kaia said, "I think the knots are out."

"But if I don't dry it, it'll get messed up when I do this." Fisting one hand in her hair, he leaned down to kiss her neck again. It was hot and wet, the slight pull on her scalp an exquisite spice to the mix of sensation.

She twisted around and wove her own fingers into his hair, her mouth meeting his in a kiss that devoured. Kaia didn't know who was the hunter and who the prey; the reins passed from one to the other breath by breath. Bowen slid his free hand to her throat as she bit down softly, so softly on his lower lip, a caress of teeth that came from her other side.

She wasn't aware of rising, but she gasped a breath into the kiss when their bodies came into heated contact. His hard and lean. Hers softer and curvier. Every cell in her body sighed. Sliding her arms around his neck, she tried to get even closer, her tongue licking his and her breasts crushed against the plane of his chest.

He ran his hands down her back, gripping her hips to hold her so tight not even a molecule of air could get between them. It was only Kaia and Bowen in the here and the now. A man and a woman.

A desperate hunger in her, she tore at his shirt.

Bowen didn't break the kiss, but he raised his hands between them and began to unbutton it. His knuckles brushed her breasts with every move until she couldn't take the excruciating sensation of fabric tugging over needy flesh. Wrenching back, she put her hands at the bottom of her cover-up and pulled it off.

"Fuck." Bowen halted with his shirt partly open, the pale brown of his skin exposed in a triangle against the white of his shirt.

He came at her the next moment, his mouth voracious and his hands possessive.

She was still trying to tear open his shirt, but his kiss was driving her mad and she couldn't focus.

When the mattress hit her back, Bowen's weight coming down on her, she wrapped her legs around him and ran her hands down his chest. The muscle trainers broke the smoothness of his skin, but she could feel the heated life of him and that was all that mattered.

He stroked her with a roughness that betrayed his own desperation, his mouth demanding kiss after kiss. Breathless, aching, she finally managed to undo the last two buttons on his shirt and shove it off. He helped her get rid of it. "Kaia. Siren. *Mine*." Harsh, hot breaths against her ear before he kissed his way down her throat, his hand plumping her breast.

Dipping his head without warning, he sucked her nipple into his mouth.

Kaia arched on a moan so deep it was nearly silent. Pulling at his hair, she said, "Bowen, I want skin." She pressed an openmouthed kiss to his shoulder, tasted salt from his swim. *"Bowen."* It was an order this time, imperious and wanting and on the edge of madness.

He kissed his way back to her mouth. "You are so fucking beautiful." A hard kiss before he pulled back just long enough to kick off his board shorts. His shoes were already long gone.

She entangled herself around him the instant he returned, this human who burned with life, his inner light so hot it scalded.

When he reached down to see if she was ready, she said, "Yes." Another kiss. "I want you."

Shuddering, he stroked her with his fingers regardless, that fierce concentration on his face that she'd already started to adore.

Her body was his, melting on his fingers. She orgasmed on a silent scream, her inner muscles clenching in hard pulses. She was yet humming from it, her blood as thick as lava, when he began to push into her. And the hum deep inside her began again, building and building with each rigid inch.

Their eyes met, held.

What passed between them was an unspoken and heartbreaking promise that resonated in the air, held them locked in time as they swam in a sea that belonged to them alone.

Chapter 30

> Belief can move mountains. I never, not for a second, allowed myself to believe that I would fail in the peace negotiations. To start there is to not start at all. You *must* start with an absolute belief in success.
>
> —From the private diaries of Adrian Kenner, peace negotiator, Territorial Wars (18th century)

BOWEN LAY ON his back with Kaia tucked up against him, his arm around her shoulders. The muscle trainers had to be irritating her skin but she seemed not to mind, and he couldn't make himself let her go.

Contentment turned his muscles heavy, his eyelids lowering. "I don't think I've ever felt this good." As if he'd had a Kaia-shaped hole inside him his entire life, and now, *at last*, here she was.

"Hmm." Kaia stroked his chest, stopping over his heart.

He waited for her to say something else, but she stayed silent after that lazy sound. Bowen played with her hair, draping the damp strands across his chest. And he thought of what she'd told him about losing both parents as a child.

Then he thought of the ticking clock in his head.

That was when he realized she was feeling the beat of his heart with her palm. Guilt was a metal claw around that mechanical organ, twisting and tearing.

Lifting his hand, he closed it gently over her wrist. "I'm sorry."

She snapped up her head, shoving her hair back from her face. "This wasn't your decision." Furious eyes. "It was mine."

God, she was magnificent. "Ours," he said. "It was ours."

A taut pause before she inclined her head and came back down against him.

He felt whole again. His body warm. Kaia's skin under his touch.

Sleep came softly, a warm, lazy wind.

HAVING woken in Kaia's bed after an hour when Dr. Kahananui tagged him to come in for another test, Bowen had forced himself to move—and after the test, he'd eaten dinner with Kaia, then made himself sleep in the clinic bed that monitored all his stats.

The doctor would need those stats prior to his surgery.

He'd slept fourteen hours, waking at ten—but the frustration of losing so much time was balanced out by his increased sense of stamina and strength.

An hour after waking, he took a seat in a surgical chair and permitted George to put his head in a vise. It was to stop him from moving it—even a fractional shift could cause catastrophic problems.

Minutes after that, Dr. Kahananui said, "This shouldn't hurt. Alert me by raising your hand at the first indication of trouble. Pain means something is wrong."

"Understood."

The surgical saw was far quieter than the horror show he'd been expecting. As for his hair, it turned out he already had a small—hidden—shaved patch where she'd injected him the first time. It was currently exposed courtesy of the glittery yellow and pink bobby pins that held the rest of his hair out of the way.

Cassius would bust a gut laughing at the idea of it; Bowen would have to share the details with his friend after he came through this. Because he *would* fucking come through this.

Belief can move mountains.

Words written by Adrian Kenner, a man who had turned the impossible into reality. Bowen had found a copy of his famous ancestor's diaries in the family archives when he was fifteen; he'd ended up reading every single page. Adrian Kenner had been a man of peace while Bowen was fighting for the survival of the human race, but in many ways, they were the same—each determined to forge a path through infinite darkness.

"George, the injector I prepared." Dr. Kahananui's cool voice.

Her assistant passed over the instrument.

Bo braced himself for it . . . but he felt nothing, exactly as the doctor had promised. Far quicker than he'd expected, she was sealing the bone back up using a small device she'd told him effectively "blended" the cut part of his skull with the rest.

He felt fine when released from the vise, but the doctor insisted he go to his room and lie down. "I need the readings," she said, "and this'll knock you out soon. Trust me." She glanced at George. "Can I leave you to tidy up? I'm going to escort Bowen to his room."

"Of course, Doctor."

"I'm not going to faint walking a few feet," Bo said after they'd exited the lab; he hadn't wanted to criticize the doctor's choice in front of her assistant.

Dr. Kahananui didn't say anything until they'd reached his room and he'd changed into a pair of sweatpants. "Lie down."

Having begun to feel a pounding at the back of his head, Bo did as directed. Dr. Kahananui worked at the data panel before looking up, and her dark brown eyes saw far too much. "She is loved." Quiet words that hit like a punch. "Deeply and by so many."

"You don't need to tell me that." He'd sensed it in the air around Kaia, seen the way her clanmates' faces lit up when she neared.

"But," Dr. Kahananui continued, "though she gives her love and affection freely, none of us have ever been able to reach the part of her she locked away as a child." The doctor began to move to the door. "If she honors you with that secret piece of herself, protect it like the treasure that it is."

"Why aren't you warning me off?" Bowen asked roughly.

"Kaia is like a sea storm. She'll pick her own path."

"Wait," he said as the doctor reached the door, but the word slurred and then there was only sweet nothingness colored by the rich aroma of coconut oil and the fleeting scent of a creamy tropical flower.

KAIA undid her apron. She was the last one in the kitchen, as she always liked to be; there was peace in having ten minutes to herself in her domain after the chaos of the dinner rush. That dinner was long over, her crew had put the leftovers in the cooler where night owls could access them, taken care of the dishes, and wiped down all the counters.

As was her tradition, Kaia had made a special dessert for this rotation of kitchen hands—a yogurt passion fruit cake, by their choice. They'd be rotating out of kitchen duty in another three days. After eating the cake down to the crumbs, they'd begged her to put in a good word with Seraphina to get them back on the kitchen roster as fast as possible.

"Someone has to scrub the toilets," she'd said, and received a round of groans.

"You don't," Scott, smart and patient and a sweet troublemaker, had pointed out. "How come?"

"Because I did my time with the toilet scrubber and in the laundry and with the window washing crew when I was your age." It was a rite of passage in the clan: to pull your own weight and at the same time, be shown that even the smallest of them had value. The clan's minnows could often be seen industriously "helping" at various tasks, mostly with toy tools created for just that purpose.

Now the children had all gone and she was alone except for Hex—who slept curled up in a pocket she'd sewn into this dress for him—but for the first time, she found no peace in lingering here. She'd blocked out what was happening in the lab while it was occurring, but Attie knew her well enough to have sent her a message when it was over: *Successful, no complications. He's asleep, will probably stay that way into tomorrow.*

Kaia had been able to breathe after that, had been able to pretend to be her normal self, but she wasn't and would never be again. "Just go," she said to herself, the whisper harsh.

Leaving the kitchen, she skirted the muted lighting of the atrium to make her way toward Atalina's lab and Bowen's room. The door to the lab was open, and when she peeked in, she saw George working at the computer as he so often did till late into the night hours.

Not interrupting, she padded her way to Bowen's room. Her breath came in shallow pants, her heart thundering. But she put her hand on the scanpad and the door whooshed open. And though Kaia hated hospitals, hated the machines and the sounds and the antiseptic cold of knowing life hung in the balance, she walked inside.

Chapter 31

Papa! Look! Lion! Grr, lion, grr!

—Kaia Luna (3) to her petrified father, Iosef

BOWEN WOKE TO a sense of warmth and softness all along one side of his body. He was groggy with the vestiges of a heavy sleep, but he knew Kaia's touch, her scent. Snuggling her closer with the arm he must've put around her in sleep, he felt her go suddenly motionless . . . and he realized the wet on his chest was from her tears.

About to turn to face her, he became aware of a far smaller source of warmth curled up on his breastbone. Cracking open his eyes, he saw Hex's peacefully sleeping form. So he turned his head instead, to look down at where Kaia lay with her head on his chest, her hair a dark waterfall over him.

His body told him he'd been asleep for hours, and when he glanced at one of the slumbering machines, he glimpsed the timecode: 5:57. He'd lost all of yesterday after the operation. More importantly, he'd lost time with Kaia.

"*Tesoro mio*," he said, the endearment falling off his tongue as if he'd been waiting a lifetime to say it to her. "Why are you crying?"

Fingers flexing on his chest, a shaky exhale, but she didn't speak. He stroked her hair, trying to think of what would drive his strong and fierce Kaia to tears.

"I hate hospitals," she said at last, the words a rasp.

Bowen pressed a kiss to the top of her hair, the strands luxuriantly soft under his lips. "Were you in one as a child?" Cassius had a hatred for hospitals, too, and the roots of his hate lay in the same incident that had ended with a dead telepath and a blood-soaked thirteen-year-old boy.

"Not as a patient." She took a deep breath, her fingers rising to gently stroke Hex's sleeping body. "My mother was a doctor who worked in struggling clinics all over the world, places that couldn't really pay and were often funded by charities."

He heard no fear or hate in those words, only a soul-deep sadness. "Did you ever go with her?"

"Our whole family traveled as a group." She placed her hand flat over his heart again. "The three Lunatics. From Africa to the Pacific to the Americas to the heart of Asia." Her lips curving against him. "When I was an infant, then a toddler, my father would keep me with him through the day and—after I outgrew the crib—I'd spend it splattering paint on canvases while he wrote lyrics or painted."

He could see her now, a bright-eyed child gleefully splashing in paint as the world changed around her. "Palm trees one day, giraffes the next?"

She laughed. "I met a lion once. He prowled out of the forest while I was toddling about outside after climbing out of the playpen when my poor father left me alone for one minute to use the outdoor toilet—from that point on, he started putting a leash on me and hooking the leash to something immovable if he had to step out to use the facilities."

Bo whistled. "Jesus, I wouldn't want to walk out of the john and see my daughter facing a lion."

"I had my hand fisted in the lion's mane and was kissing his face."

Bo choked. "Changeling?" he guessed.

"Alpha changeling." Kaia rose up on her elbow to look down at him, her gaze lit with an inner glow. "He'd come to check us out. We had permission to be in the area, but he wanted us aware that we were in lion territory."

"Yet he let a baby kiss his face." Bowen smiled at the image that formed in his mind, of a plump toddler clutching at the golden mane of a large, patient lion. "A good alpha, then."

"Yes. A very good alpha, I later found out. His pride is one of the most stable on the African continent." She brushed strands of hair off Bo's forehead. "When I grew a bit bigger, my mother would sometimes take me into work with her. Only when it was a small clinic and she was doing routine work. The people who came didn't mind—they used to bring along their own children and I'd play outside with them."

Running his hand over her back, Bo said, "What happened?"

And the light in her, it dimmed, flickered, faded. "My parents got sick and died," she said baldly. "And I began to hate hospitals."

A tiny scrabble of feet, Hex coming awake. After going to Kaia for a stroke, he ran down the bed and off along one of the legs.

"I'll need to open the door for him," Kaia murmured.

"After a second." Bowen wrapped his arms around her and held her close. "I'm going to get out of this place," he told her. "You won't have to watch me die."

"You have a powerful will, Bo." Her lips kissing his jaw. "But even your will can't change hard medical facts."

Bowen's hand fisted on her back. "Maybe not," he said, "but I don't plan to go without a fight." And if the result was to be oblivion, he'd leave Kaia with memories of joy; he wasn't a man who knew how to play, how to court a woman, but he'd figure it out because leaving her with only sorrow was fucking unacceptable. "You are the greatest gift of my life."

Kaia's breath broke before she pushed away from him and got off the bed. Scooping up her pet, she walked to the door, opened it. When she paused and looked back at him, it was with eyes so dark that he knew he was talking to both sides of her nature. "I don't know if I can." The words seemed torn out of her. "I don't know if I have that much courage."

She had so much courage, he thought as the door closed behind her. She might have shut away a part of herself, but she loved with such generous warmth that it was a luminous light around her. He'd seen how the teenagers came to her for hugs, spotted how clanmates tugged her aside for advice or conversation, heard it in the steel of Dr. Kahananui's voice when she'd told him to treasure Kaia.

He hadn't needed the instruction; Bowen would do everything in his power to build memories so beautiful that even if it all went wrong, she couldn't look back in regret. They might only have a fragment of an instant in time, but he'd make that fragment extraordinary.

Chapter 32

"You have no romance in your soul! It's solid steel! I'm out!"
"Does your heart even beat? Is there a flesh-and-blood man under the stone?"
"Oh, look, you forgot Valentine's Day. This is my shocked face. Don't call me again."
"Why do you have to be so fucking sexy and so terrible at being a boyfriend? You should date the Alliance. She's the only thing you care about anyway."

—Compilation of words spoken by women to Bowen Knight

BOWEN LOOKED AT Dr. Kahananui after that morning's round of scans, the two of them in her lab. One of Kaia's kitchen hands—a heavily muscled blond kid named Jayson—had turned up with breakfast trays soon after Bowen entered the lab. He'd also brought a pitcher of coffee for Bo and a pot of what looked like herbal tea for the doctor. Bo poured refills for both himself and the doctor as they got ready to discuss the results. "So?"

"Progress is as per the computer model." She bit off a piece of toast but she wasn't paying attention to the food, her eyes on the large screen on the wall.

She stood staring at it.

Walking over with the drinks, Bo handed her the mug of tea and took a sip of his coffee. He tried to make sense of the scans on the screen, but the only thing he could say for certain was that the computer had created a facsimile of his brain in 3D. "Then why have you been scowling at this for the past ten minutes?"

She gulped down half the mug before setting it aside and finishing off her toast. "It's possible the compound might alter the effectiveness of the chip."

Bowen braced his feet as his world shuddered. "My course is set." He'd see it through to the end. "But if that is the result—and assuming no brain damage—it'll be a major problem for the others." Bowen would have no choice but to stand down as Alliance security chief—and yeah, even the thought of that hurt—but he couldn't trust himself in a position where Psy might be able to influence his thoughts and decisions.

But Cassius, Lily, Heenali, the other knights, they'd also have to make a choice and he knew the choice they'd make: to die in freedom. What was the point of living longer when your mind could be taken at any moment, when fear of such a violation was a constant horrified whisper in the back of your head?

"When will you know for certain?" he asked Dr. Kahananui, even as ice crystals formed in his blood. Surviving but being wide open to telepathic interference would destroy him in the end, as effectively as acid dripping on his bones.

"I'm not certain. We're navigating in the dark without lights." She returned her attention to the screen. "Come back in four hours. I have to remove the muscle trainers."

Having already made plans for his day, Bowen left without argument. It was as he was walking down the corridor that Hex ran over and stopped in front of him.

Bending down, Bowen held out his hand.

Kaia's pet took a moment to think about the offer before deciding to accept it.

Putting the mouse in the front pocket of his navy blue shirt, Bo continued toward his destination. KJ was walking in his direction, dressed in the same blue scrubs that Bowen had spotted him in the other day. "Yo, man!" He held up a hand for a high five.

After slapping his palm to the shorter man's, Bowen said, "You got a minute?"

"Sure. I was just going to ask Dr. K if she wanted me to do anything for her before I head over to the infirmary."

The orderly's eyes brightened when Bowen told him what he needed. "There's one righteous spot," he said at last. "It's not real flash, but it's the least used. Good chance you can find it empty, especially at night."

Quickly memorizing the instructions on how to reach the location, Bowen asked a couple more questions, then said, "Thanks. And keep it under your hat."

"Total word of honor," the other man drawled. "Good luck."

Bowen bumped fists with him and carried on ahead, hoping the luck would stick. It wasn't like he knew what he was doing. According to the last woman he'd dated, he was about "as romantic as a block of wood." She'd suggested he read some romance how-to books before "foisting" himself on another "unfortunate" woman.

"I should've made time to read them," Bo muttered to Hex.

The mouse twitched his nose in response.

Bo's next step was to locate Seraphina or Tansy, the two women Dr. Kahananui had told him were Kaia's closest friends after Hugo. He was wondering who to approach for their whereabouts without his questions getting back to Kaia when he spotted Oleanna.

She waggled her eyebrows at his request. "No tentacles," she whispered. "Either of them."

His lips twitched; she was so joyously open about her sensuality that he could do nothing but like her. "I'm already very happily taken." It felt damn good to say that; he wasn't certain what Kaia's response would be to his declaration, but she'd walked hand in hand with him through Ryūjin.

As far as Bowen was concerned, she'd claimed him.

"Talk about no tentacles!" Oleanna scowled and put her hands on her hips. "But I love Kaia, so I *suppose* I'll allow her to have you." She dipped her head toward him, eyes narrowed. "Why are you looking for other women if you're with Kaia?"

Realizing he'd have to confess if he wanted her help, he gave in. She clasped her hands in front of her chest afterward, bouncing on her feet. "Oh, oh, please let me help. I'm really good at sneaking things."

"As long as you can keep it secret."

"Puh-leeese." She snorted. "If you only knew the people I've had in my bed." Patting his cheek, she said, "What do you need, handsome?"

Not long afterward, he tracked Seraphina down to the assistant station commander's office. He didn't get a warm welcome.

"Hurt Kaia and I'll kneecap you." Hands on her hips, jaw set, and her purple lipstick a perfect match to her purple nails.

"I'll stand still for it if that ever becomes necessary." Bo knew he'd drive Kaia crazy in the future he was determined they'd share, but he'd never purposefully cause her pain.

"Hmm." Seraphina tapped one skyscraper-high heel on the carpet of her office. "What do you want?"

A faint softening in her face when he told her. "Well, I guess it's better than dead clams," she said, putting him firmly in his place. But she gave him what he needed—and added an unexpected extra. "I can close out the location for you. It'll say *Closed for Maintenance* on the panel. Input this code and you'll be able to get in."

"How about a no-swim zone above the transparent area?"

Seraphina gave him a *you're pushing it* look but said, "Doable. I'll turn the external lighting from white to blue in that spot—that's a sign to our people that we're working there and they should steer clear."

Tansy was softer and sweeter, and had giant garden shears in her hand when he found her in an internal garden that was apparently also a lab where she worked on plants genetically engineered to thrive under the simulated sunlight. She snapped those shears menacingly after telling him to "Take care of Kaia."

He found himself grinning on the inside, imagining what implement

Kaia would use to warn off any suitors Seraphina or Tansy might have. "I will," he said. "Thank you for the help."

It was all going well until he ran into Alden the Walrus—no way in hell was the man anything else—in a dark and silent corner of the station. When Alden's face began to go a blotchy red, his hands bunching, Bo had had enough. "Stop," he said very quietly. "Or I will be forced to dislocate your arm, break your femur, and crack three ribs."

The extremely specific list had Alden freezing. When the changeling found his voice at last, he said, "How're you going to do that, bug man?" He curled his lip.

Bowen smiled at Alden and it was what Lily called his "scary" smile. Alden stumbled back a step.

Deciding to give the man an out so he wouldn't feel compelled to follow through on his implied threat in order to save face, Bo said, "You should also know that Dex is still so angry he wants to take a sledgehammer to your bones." He shrugged. "I'd stay out of sight and out of mind unless you want to screw with him."

"Yeah, fine, whatever." Alden's voice came out a growl. "But you can't hide behind Attie forever. Soon as she's had her pup, you're mine." He thumped a fist into the open palm of his other hand. "Not that I'll have to hurt you when Hugo comes back. He'll crush you for touching his future mate."

Bowen didn't move until Alden's footsteps had faded far into the distance; Alden was the last person he wanted to know about his plans. "Pup," he murmured softly, ignoring the other part of Alden's threat. "What sea creature has pups?" Seals were the only ones he could think of; seals were also playful.

Was Kaia a seal, round dark eyes and inquisitive face?

Intrigued by the idea, but conscious that many things could alter genetic lines, he reminded himself that not only was Dr. Kahananui Kaia's cousin rather than sister, he had no idea of Dex's animal. He also needed to know what beings Kaia's parents had carried inside their skins before he could hazard a guess at her own.

Chewing on the mystery, he got on with what he needed to do; he was halfway through the physical prep when KJ poked his head into the doorway. He'd changed out of his scrubs into dark brown cargo pants and a short-sleeved white T-shirt.

"Hey, I'm off shift and don't need to get to my lessons for like two hours," the orderly said around the gum in his mouth. "Want some help?"

"Thanks, 'preciate it." The sooner he cleared this space, the sooner he could get to work on the second part of his plan—and *that*, he'd be doing on his own. "What're you studying?"

"Nursing, dude." He cracked his gum, the fresh scent of peppermint in the air. "I get teaching from our healers, but I'm also enrolled in a remote university to make sure I cover all the bases."

KJ whistled as he worked, his good nature so infectious that Bowen could see exactly why he'd gone into not one but two areas of medicine that meant constant patient contact. "You mated, KJ?" He nodded at the gold ring the BlackSea male wore on the ring finger of his left hand; it was rare to see that among changelings. They tended to rely on scent or other markers to tell if someone was single or not.

"Working on it—married three years now." The orderly grinned, his muscular arms bulging as he lifted a large box and carried it to the far left wall. "She's human, likes me to wear the ring." Another grin. "Says it's like her brand on me. I'm cool with that until our mating bond kicks in—'cause I know it will."

Bowen frowned. "I didn't realize there were any other humans on this station."

"Lis is the only one." He helped Bo move a particularly heavy box, his strength surprising for his size. "Solo round-the-world sailor. Had a wreck. I rescued her and she fell madly, passionately, forever in love with her heroic merman." His smile was wicked, his eyes dancing. "At the moment, she's holed up in our living unit working on a totally awesome yacht design. Once she needs to sail again, I'll switch shifts to the city upside."

The city upside.

Bo had known such a city must exist—Ryūjin would otherwise be too isolated, too difficult to service—but it was good to have confirmation. The security chief part of his mind automatically recalculated his situation but came to the same conclusion as before: Bowen couldn't leave unless he managed to commandeer a submersible, then outmaneuver BlackSea's security protocols.

He'd spotted a map at the back of Seraphina's office and his brain had automatically taken a snapshot. Now that snapshot came to the fore, and he understood the map was of oceanic routes around Ryūjin. The sea was a big place. If a man was careful about how he stole a submersible and he figured out the frequency on which to listen to security transmissions, he *could* thread the needle.

Chapter 33

There's nothing I wouldn't do for her. Nothing.

—Hugo Sorensen in a message to Alden Jones

BO SPENT MUCH of the afternoon being divested of the bugs.

He'd worried their removal would weaken him, but he felt the same. Obviously, the bugs had done their job and done it well.

The rest was up to him.

Hundreds of tiny pinpricks dotted his body where the bugs had hooked into his system, but Dr. Kahananui prescribed him a thin gel that sank into his skin and caused an immediate reduction of the redness. Another day and the pinpricks would be all but gone. Since Bo wasn't a man who went around moisturizing himself, it felt distinctively odd to slather the gel all over his body, but he told himself it was topical medication and got on with it.

When he realized he couldn't get to all the pricks on his back, he decided to use the opportunity to play with his siren. He hadn't seen her since she left his bed, the hunger inside him a throb.

Using the comm function on the data panel to access the station's list of public codes, he contacted the kitchen. It was postlunch and predinner, so hopefully, Kaia would be free. He kept it audio only until he got her on the line; he'd noted the location of the kitchen comm panel the first time he entered the room and knew no one else would see him if he turned on the visual.

"YES?" Kaia was *not* having a good day; she missed Bowen like he was a part of her she'd mislaid, and none of her rational arguments about how he'd inevitably break her already scarred heart seemed to be having any impact on the painful need deep within.

Even her exuberant other self was morose and sulking. Which was why she'd given all her kitchen staff the afternoon off and was personally making the vat of pasta sauce for tonight's dinner. Her clanmates shouldn't have to put up with her bad mood.

"What—" She cut off her impatient question when she saw the face of the man who'd called—and noticed his half-naked body.

Her thighs clenched, her nipples suddenly plump, hard points. "I'm sorry," she said aloud. "I didn't sign up for a porn show." Or for this man who'd thrown her world into chaos.

"So you think I could be on a porn show?"

Kaia's lips wanted to twitch. How could she have seen him as harsh and grim at the start? He was so wickedly playful, reaching the core of her nature. "For those with a hospital-patient fetish, maybe."

"Ouch." Making a downcast face, he said, "That's kind of why I called."

She folded her arms, refusing to soften . . . trying to keep her distance.

He held up a small jar of what she recognized as a healing gel created by Tansy. "I can't reach my back."

"Try using a shower scrubbing brush." She switched off the screen on those sharp words and told herself to concentrate on her work; dinner wasn't going to make itself. She had no time to go pet a man who was going to leave her, one way or another.

Oblivion or back to the surface, those were the only two choices open to the security chief of the Human Alliance.

Both were places Kaia couldn't go, couldn't follow.

It took her two short minutes to surrender to the compulsion to touch him, draw his scent into her lungs, take care of him. "Argh!" Leaving her ingredients spread out on the counter, she pulled off her apron before stalking out.

Hex was nowhere in sight; maybe her genius mouse had decided to avoid her temper, too.

"COME in," Bo called out when someone knocked on his door.

It slid open. He'd been expecting Dr. Kahananui, come to take another scan or reading, but the scent that whispered across on the air was of an exotic tropical flower fused with a hint of coconut. A creamy white bloom sat tucked over Kaia's right ear.

Bowen's gut clenched.

Striding over, she grabbed the jar and said, "Stay still."

He obeyed . . . but couldn't help the smile that spread across his face. At least until she slapped the gel onto his back hard enough to tell him she'd caught his response. His lack of a grin didn't last long—Kaia might still be wearing the flower over her right ear, but she had her hands on him and after that first rough touch, she'd turned gentle, caressing the gel onto his skin, where it sank in without a trace.

Bowen wanted to purr like a damn cat.

"What's this tattoo?" she asked as she worked.

"Which one?"

"This." She touched the design just below his left shoulder. "No, wait. I've seen this before . . ."

Wondering if she'd recognize it, Bo closed his eyes and surrendered to the bone-deep pleasure of her hands on his flesh, strong and competent, with the odd patch of roughness from her work in the kitchen.

"It's the emblem of the Peace Accord." She traced the lines with a fingertip.

Fighting back a shiver, he said, "My first tattoo—got it when I was fifteen." After reading all of Adrian Kenner's journals and earning enough money to pay for the tat himself; he'd known his parents wouldn't give him permission, but Cassius was friends with a guy who knew an artist who didn't ask for ID.

It had been stupid teenage luck for Bo that the artist was excellent at what he did.

"Why do you have it?" A wild curiosity in the question that told him he wasn't only talking to her human side, her body close enough that he could feel the lush warmth of her against him. "Humans don't often care about the Peace Accord."

Bowen knew it was mostly changeling blood that had drenched the land in red, changelings who'd fought so brutally that they'd ended clans and devastated packs. The Peace Accord had forever altered their history. "Do you remember the name of the peace negotiator?"

"Of course. Adrian Kenner is one of the most respected men in our history."

"He had a middle name."

"Adrian B. Kenner, yes." Her hand paused on his back. "Bowen? You were named after him?"

He nodded. "My full name is Bowen Adrian Knight." It was a heritage he wore with pride. "A lot of humans respect him as deeply as changelings do." Kenner had stopped a war that had caught nonpack humans and Psy in the crossfire, turned rivers red with blood; he'd left a legacy of peace that stood to this day. "He was my great-great-many-times-over grandfather."

"You have a proud history." Kaia began to smooth the gel into his skin once more. Bowen closed his eyes again, his focus on her touch alone. Only when he heard her screwing on the lid of the jar did he turn.

She stood her ground, though he was far too close, her breasts a bare inch from brushing his chest. Shoving the jar against his breastbone, she said, "I have to get back to the kitchen."

"A couple of your clanmates cornered me earlier." Bowen had listened politely to the older women while his muscles bunched one by one. "Said it was a disgrace I was taking advantage of you when your future mate wasn't here to protect you."

"I don't need protecting." Kaia scowled.

"Is he? Your mate?" Bowen had shrugged off Alden's comments and reasoned his way out of Carlotta's earlier ones, but the words had built silently inside him until he needed Kaia to tell him her heart didn't belong to another man. "Is that why you're pulling away?"

"If I had a mate," she gritted out, "if I felt that way about a man, I sure as hell wouldn't have shared intimate skin privileges with you!"

He'd insulted her honor, he realized too late. "Jesus, I'm a fool." Knowing he was playing with his life, he kissed his enraged siren and she went straight to his head.

Chapter 34

Lover.
Friend.
Laughter.
Mate.

—Unknown poet (circa 1763)

KAIA FELT THE punch of Bowen's kiss right down to the bone. She'd been tempted to lie about Hugo—she could fight her compulsion to go to Bowen if he was keeping a cold distance from her. It wasn't as if her clanmates wouldn't support her; half the station *and* the city thought she and Hugo were a meant-to-be pair.

But Kaia wasn't a liar.

And Hugo would only ever be a friend she thought of in the same breath as Mal and Edison and Armand and the others. A brother, even if they were unrelated by blood. He'd never terrified her as Bowen terrified her, never come close to smashing through the defenses she'd erected desperately as a young girl who'd watched her parents' chests rise and fall accompanied by the *hush, hush* of the machines.

It was as if Bowen had a key to her psyche he could use at will.

He had the key to her body, too. It had gone tight and hot the instant she walked into the room, and then she'd touched him, indulged herself in the living steel of him. Her breasts ached, threatening to overflow the confines of her peach lace bra, hunger a dark, glowing heat in the pit of her stomach.

Still furious with him, she bit down hard on his lower lip. He hissed out a breath but didn't pull away, giving her the pound of flesh she damn well deserved. Kaia dug her nails into his chest even as she laved her tongue over the hurt she'd caused.

With him, she had no reason, no logic, no walls.

When he grabbed the plas jar she held between them and threw it on the bed, she didn't resist. She swiveled with him when he backed her into the wall and sank his body against her own. Moving her hands up his chest, she luxuriated in his lean strength, her heart thumping in time with his.

Except . . . his heart wasn't like her own. It was mechanical. And it was inside him because he'd been shot. But that didn't matter, wasn't important. His heart would outlast hers. His brain, however, hung on a knife edge.

The being inside her cried in remembered sorrow.

Ripping away her lips, she deliberately didn't look at Bowen. He saw too deep, caught too much of her with those penetrating eyes. "Off." She pushed hard at his chest. "I don't have time to play tongue hockey with you."

"How about no tongue and all naked?" Bowen's voice was rough, his body a wall of luscious heat.

Kaia's toes curled. The other part of her, sad but as compelled by him as the human side of her, nudged at the inside of her skin, wanting to swim with this strong, intriguing man in deep water. It liked him. But it was hurt, too, so when Kaia pushed again then slid away from Bowen, she didn't have to fight it for control.

"Kaia."

She paused at the door, glanced back. A red flush kissed his cheekbones, his eyes glittering. "I'm supposed to put the gel on again tonight," he said with a slow smile that hit her right in the crazy "bad boy" gene.

The other side of her being laughed, delighted with him.

“The shower brush should be in the bathroom,” she said, the fight for control very much real now. “Or you can use the toilet brush.”

Deep and warm, his laughter followed her out the door.

Kaia braced herself with one hand against the corridor wall a second after the door closed; she hadn’t been prepared for Atalina to step out of her lab and catch her. Nudging her head, the white-streaked black of her hair gleaming in the simulated sunlight, Attie stepped back inside the lab.

Kaia followed, shutting the door behind herself. “Don’t ask.”

Of course, the cousin who was a big sister to her didn’t bother to listen. “You appear thoroughly kissed.” A pointed look. “In fact, I’ve never seen you so mussed.”

Kaia had never *felt* so mussed. Or so deeply scared. “Why do you look happy about that?” she asked, her heart yet racing and her palms damp.

“Because, Cookie”—Atalina cupped her face with warm and slender hands—“I see that he reaches you where no one else can.”

Kaia’s throat was dry; she couldn’t breathe. “He’ll *leave* me.” It came out a broken keen.

Immediately cradling her close, Attie rocked her. “I know you’re afraid. But I’m happy you’ve tasted this depth of joy.” A kiss on her temple. “Whatever happens, you know now what awaits on the other side.”

Attie didn’t understand.

She thought this was a passionate love affair, the loss of which would hurt but not permanently damage. But Kaia was feeling things that reached through her human skin to her wild heart. This wasn’t as simple as passion or attraction or even love. It held the whisper of a visceral bond that only came along once in a changeling lifetime.

Squeezing her eyes shut, Kaia locked herself in Attie’s embrace and tried to drown out her own mind, her own heart.

Chapter 35

You are my hunter, Mal. Hunt down the truth. Find out if the humans have been playing us for fools.

—Miane Levèque to Malachai Rhys

BO HAD TO take ten minutes to come down from the high of Kaia's kiss before he could pull on his shirt and call Lily and Cassius.

What they had to tell him erased any hint of a smile from his face.

"There are irregularities in the Fleet data." Lily tucked a wing of hair behind her ear, her eyes still smudged with purple bruises. "A few of our ships *have* strayed into BlackSea territory."

"One or two and I'd blame it on bad driving"—Cassius, his arms folded across his chest, his biceps bulging—"but it's more than that and Lily says the data was buried."

"Someone attempted to overwrite the reports sent in by the ships," Lily confirmed. "I was able to find the 'ghost' images of the originals."

Bo swore low and hard. "If the captains sent in undoctored reports, they didn't think they were doing anything wrong."

"Means they had orders," Cassius agreed. "This is coming from the top."

"Heenali?" Bo forced himself to ask.

"We can't pinpoint anyone yet." Lily glanced at Cassius, the two having been in the same office when Bowen called. "Cassius is handling the offline investigation."

"All I have so far is that Heenali and that guy she was dating broke up and she's in a shitty mood." His expression was flat, unreadable—the vagaries of the human heart had no claim on Cassius and he didn't understand how others were so broken by it.

Bowen knew the other man took lovers but his relationships were purely physical. He'd never had a girlfriend, never bonded with any woman past the shallow link forged by physical attraction devoid of liking or intellectual fascination or even just plain old interest.

"Heenali's not spending money beyond what she can afford," Cassius continued, "and she's not disappearing without warning. No mysterious meetings or shady contacts. Far as I can figure, she's just doing a little extra drinking."

"Post-breakup drinking." Lily made a sympathetic face. "I've been there."

"What about you?" Cassius asked. "Heard back from Malachai Rhys?"

"No." Bo had given Malachai extra time to get back to him because Mal wasn't the kind of man to play games; if he hadn't been in touch, it was because he had a damn good reason.

But Bo planned to follow up after this call regardless—he had to make sure BlackSea knew the Alliance wasn't ignoring the problem. The last thing humanity needed was for the water changelings to turn against them. "I'll deal with that side of things," he said when Cassius's jaw grew hard.

"Bo." Lily put down her organizer. "How are you?" A smile that was more in her eyes than on her lips. "You look good and you haven't got those silver things all over you."

"Head feels fine. No headaches, no diminished vision. I told Dr. Kahananui I feel better than I did before I went into the water." Which meant the slow breakdown of the chip had already begun to affect him on some level. "The only problem is that even if the compound works, it might neutralize the chip."

Cassius hissed out a breath. "Fuck."

"Yeah." Bo had to live with the outcome, whatever it might be; no use railing against it even if the lack of a functioning chip would be a death sentence of another kind. "I'll update you when I know more."

Lily suddenly leaned closer to the screen. "Bo? Is that a mouse peeking out from your pocket with his tiny paws on the edge?"

"Name's Hex." The mouse had hung out with him most of the day, had been dozing on his pillow while Bowen kissed a woman he wished he'd met a lifetime ago. "He's Kaia's."

The angular lines of Cassius's face cracked into a huge and rare grin. "Aren't you freaked out by mice? What did you say that time about their 'tiny beady eyes and long slithering tails'?"

Glaring at his best friend, Bo said, "You were supposed to be drunk that night." For some reason he'd never been able to figure out, mice had always made goose bumps break out over Bo's skin. He didn't "eep" and run when he saw one. Neither, however, did he usually walk around with one in his pocket.

"And Hex is a special case," he added while his sister wiggled her fingers at the mouse. "He's a mouse genius." The small creature mattered to Kaia, and so he mattered to Bowen. It was that simple and that complicated.

"Who the hell are you?" Cassius was full-out laughing now. "You have a fucking pocket mouse."

"You're an asshole," Bo said easily before hanging up, then moving to the data panel to make the call to Malachai. This time, he got an automated recording asking him to leave a message. He did, but forty minutes later there was still no response.

Bo considered going directly to Miane, but this was a conversation he needed to have with Malachai. The Alliance and BlackSea's entire relationship was through their respective security chiefs.

Interestingly, Miane Levèque *had* been in touch with the official head of the Alliance. Bo liked the alpha of BlackSea better for that—the leader of the water changelings was smart enough to know that Bo ran the Alliance, but she'd treated Giovanni Somme with the same respect that Bo always did. In taking the figurehead position as the Alliance's chairman, Giovanni left Bo free to work without having to deal with time-wasting politics.

Giovanni had been incredibly proud to be treated as a fellow alpha by Miane Levèque. "She's a dangerous one," he'd said afterward. "Beautiful but deadly as a stiletto across the throat. Good thing she's friendly or we'd be in trouble."

Bowen hoped Miane would still be friendly after this was all over.

He spent the next two hours on his personal project and was on his way to grab a mug of coffee from the kitchen when his eye caught on the silver shine in the water outside the atrium's seaward wall.

A massive school of fish darted in the habitat lights, their small bodies swirling and dancing in a froth of activity. "Is it me," he murmured to Dex, who'd come to stand next to him, "or does the wildlife look unusually agitated?"

"They always get that way when Mal visits." The broad-shouldered male offered Bowen the last peanut in his small bowl. "He's a big fucker."

No wonder Malachai hadn't responded to his call—he'd probably already been in the ocean. "When did he arrive?"

"He's not out of the wet yet."

Bowen gave the station commander an assessing glance. "I don't suppose you'd tell me where Mal will surface inside the habitat?" There had to be an airlock system to ensure the sea wouldn't shove into the habitats, causing catastrophic destruction.

Dex grinned, his blue eyes mixed with enough green that the shade was as changeable as the sea. "Anyone who doesn't know Mal is always trying to catch him midshift."

"His own fault." Bowen's instincts pricked, warning of an approaching predator—what he didn't yet know was whether there'd be blood spilled. "He's an expert at the inscrutable smirk."

"I don't think anyone's ever described me as smirky before," came a familiar voice from Bo's right.

He shifted to face the security chief of BlackSea—whose expression told him nothing about the current state of the Alliance-BlackSea relationship. “They probably usually do it behind your back.” Malachai Rhys was a big man who moved with deadly grace, not someone most people would want to antagonize.

A gleam in eyes Bo had first seen as brown, then as a pale gold so unusual they were eerie. Today, they held an in-between state, as if the creature inside Malachai’s human skin were swimming at the top of his consciousness.

“Atalina hasn’t popped yet?” Malachai asked his cousin-by-mating.

“I dare you to ask her exactly that to her face.” Dex leaned against the seaward wall, his tone bone dry. “And where in the hell do you get those suits? You’re the only man I know who comes out of the black dressed in a sharp suit—and I know we don’t stock your size on Ryūjin.”

It was true. Though Malachai’s dark hair was damp, he wore a black suit with a crisp white shirt underneath. No tie, the shirt open at the collar, the jacket unbuttoned.

“If I told you, I’d have to bury you in the deep,” Malachai responded without a hitch.

Something beeped right then and Dex checked a small computronic device wrapped around his wrist. “Duty calls.” He glanced at Mal. “You staying tonight? Dinner?”

“No, this is a flying visit. But I’ll come down again before Atalina’s due date so we can have one last party before you two turn into haggard, sleep-deprived zombies.”

Walking backward, Dex grinned. “Yeah, and who do you think is going to be babysitting for date night, *Uncle* Mal?”

Bo waited until the station commander had left before looking at Malachai. “You’re here to talk to me.”

Malachai’s expression changed, a cool-eyed predator replacing the warm affection of a man of family. “I—”

“Malachai!”

Turning, the other man caught the small teenage girl against his body. “Miss me, did you, Pania?”

The petite girl, one of the swimmers who’d cannonballed into the pool the other day, lifted up a face that shone with love. "You haven't visited for *ages*."

"Otherwise known as three weeks." Tugging on one of her curls before he released her, Malachai kept his hand on her shoulder. "Shouldn't you be in school?"

"School's out. I'm going to science club."

"Then you'd better get moving. You know how strict Mrs. Dempsey can be—she threatened me with a lichen beard last time I was late."

Pania giggled before racing off.

"Come on," Malachai said afterward. "We need to get out of here if we're going to talk. Where's your room?"

The other man didn't say anything else until they were behind the closed door of Bo's room. Bo had opened the window before he left, and they both walked naturally toward the view.

The water was a tangle of silver.

"Jesus, do you emit sea pheromones or something?" There were so many fish out there that it glittered.

"That's not for me." Malachai's lips curved slightly. "One of the schools must've come down. They always get the best reaction from the natural schools."

A sudden tightness in Bowen's gut. "Kaia told me humans ate sea changelings before." The idea of it made his gorge rise.

"In the dark past," Malachai confirmed, his eyes on the water. "We're no longer such easy prey—but we roam far and wide. I can't lay a security perimeter around the entire globe."

Bo blew out a breath. "I've always seen changelings as powerful in your packs and clans." Tight-knit units who hunkered down and fought together against any threat. "Before Ryūjin"—before the harsh truths laid bare by Kaia—"I never truly understood the risks faced by your people."

"And we didn't understand the battle humans fight each and every day to walk out into a world where Psy can penetrate your minds at will." Malachai's voice was deep, contemplative. "That takes as much courage as swimming alone in an endless ocean, perhaps more."

"I haven't betrayed you, Mal," Bo said bluntly after turning to face Malachai.

The other man echoed his position. And his response, when it came, was from the lethal predator that lived under his skin—because Malachai Rhys was nothing harmless, of that Bo was dead certain. "We've confirmed Alliance ships have helped steal our people."

Chapter 36

The only way to make our confidential data absolutely secure is to ring-fence it. No network connections of any kind. It will, however, make it impossible to work in the cloud or remotely.

—Excerpted from brief by Lily Knight to Human Alliance security

"I HAVE NO information on your vanished," Bo said, holding the other man's impenetrable gaze, "but I've had it verified that Alliance Fleet ships have gone where they shouldn't have gone."

Malachai raised an eyebrow. "It began before your coma, just took Hugo's detective work to put together all the scattered pieces of data."

"I'm not going to try to avoid the responsibility—it's mine." Bowen had accepted that duty when he took the reins of the Alliance. "I'm working on getting to the root of why the ships were in your waters. I won't condemn any of my people without irrefutable proof."

Malachai said nothing for long seconds, the two of them locked in a silent battle—not for supremacy, but for something deeper. "What do you know about Hugo's dossier?" Mal asked at last.

"He took aim at what he called our 'paramilitary arm.'" Kaia didn't speak like that, so it had been obvious to Bo that she was echoing Hugo's term. "You have to know that's bullshit."

"Rest of it isn't so easy to disregard."

"No, the Fleet movements happened. I can't tell you why yet, but I will."

"Kaia didn't tell you anything else? I've had reports you two have become close."

Stabbed by the cold blade of unexpected betrayal, Bo nonetheless kept his expression neutral. "No, that's all I have."

A slight shake of Malachai's head. "If you get angry at a woman who knows how to keep a promise, you're not worth her." Removing a small organizer from his pocket, he said, "I asked Kaia to keep quiet about this while I had our techs check its authenticity."

Bo shoved his hands through his hair. "You're right." That vivid punch of betrayal had been a knee-jerk reaction. It was the envy that ran deep. Malachai had Kaia's loyalty; Bo wanted the same . . . but loyalty took time to grow.

He could give her his devotion, but he couldn't demand her own.

"Show me."

Malachai turned the screen in his direction.

Horror curdled his stomach. "Confirmed as authentic?"

"Beyond any doubt. Two of our vanished."

Malachai didn't have to point out that the two badly beaten and bloody—likely dead—changelings were on the deck of an Alliance Fleet ship. The name was only partially obscured and the Alliance brand obvious. "This is the *Quiet Wind*." The smallest ship in the fleet, but one that could move like quicksilver. "Needs minimal crew and is normally used to transport delicate goods that require personal care."

"Minimal crew means fewer people who can talk."

Bo nodded before raising his eyes to Malachai's. "I need you to let me run this."

"My people are dying."

"Neither humanity nor BlackSea can afford to be in a war. We're stronger together, but apart and enemies, we'll devastate both our peoples."

Malachai slipped his organizer back into a pocket. "Agreed," he said, then gave a slight smile. "You have such passion in you, Bo. I truly hope I don't have to hurt you."

"I will clean my house." It was a promise to himself as much as a statement to Mal. "But to do that, I need to know certain things. Such as how Hugo got the information about our future plans for a major shipping line. Did one of my people pass it on?"

Malachai shook his head. "Hugo was in comms before he was taken. Brilliant, would probably be head of the team if he wasn't also a slacker when he could get away with it." Turning with Bo to face the water again, he continued on. "He's also addicted to poker, plays in dedicated high-stakes online clubs."

"He met someone through there."

"Didn't name that person, but said the individual was human. The last time Hugo was in Venice, they met up and ended up drunk together—and the human player said something about the shipping line." Malachai's eyes were translucent pale gold when he looked at Bowen again. "He got a bad feeling about it, began to dig, cross-referenced hundreds of minor reports about ship movements, and managed to hack into the Alliance's shipping records."

Bo stilled deep within. The Alliance's shipping records weren't on a hackable system—they were totally isolated from any outside network, with the backups kept in another isolated location. Hugo would've had to be in the data room *inside* Alliance HQ to get the information. "He did the hacking from here?"

Malachai took the question as Bowen had meant him to take it. "Signal to and from Ryūjin can get problematic. He did it from Lantia."

Lantia.

The massive BlackSea city located in the North Atlantic Ocean.

Whether it was the city above Ryūjin or not made no difference. Because nothing changed the fact that Hugo had told a lie. He couldn't have hacked the Alliance's shipping records from Lantia. It was a physical and computronic impossibility. So how had he gotten his hands on the data?

And if a man could tell one lie, was he capable of telling a far more brutal one?

Chapter 37

I need your help to pull off a covert operation.

—Bowen Knight to Scott Reineke

DINNER WAS ALL set up and under way, Malachai gone. He'd made time to visit Kaia and update her on the search for Hugo: "Nothing. No sign of him."

Smashing out her anger and worry on harmless avocados had gotten the clan an extra helping of guacamole, and then she'd gone ahead and made them fresh corn chips. She'd made so much food, in fact, that people were walking around groaning while trying to stuff in an extra bite of another dish.

The one man who hadn't appeared to fill a plate was the human who'd gotten under her skin and stuck like a burr. Even the news about Hugo hadn't dislodged that burr—she knew Bowen too well now, simply couldn't see him authorizing or taking part in the cowardly abduction of BlackSea's people.

"The man needs to eat," she muttered to Tansy when her friend walked in to get dinner.

"You know those dominant types." Tansy shook her head like a wise old owl. "Have you eaten?"

"No." Kaia couldn't eat if he was going hungry. "I'll take him a plate." Was it possible the meeting with Malachai had gone badly? Her cousin had said nothing to her on that point and she hadn't asked.

It had felt wrong.

She and Bowen, they owed each other truths now. She wouldn't go behind his back to get them; she'd ask *him* about the meeting.

"Oh." Tansy bit down on her lower lip. "Um, I don't think Bowen's in his room. I saw him . . . and Alden was there."

"What!" Dropping the empty plate on the counter, Kaia rounded on her friend.

Tansy blurted out the coordinates of a corridor outside a disused warehouse in habitat five. "I'm sorry! I d-didn't—"

But Kaia was already gone.

What was Bo doing there, she thought as she ran, skirting startled clanmates—including a disapproving Bebe—and pelting along the connecting bridge. Despite her physically fit state, she was out of breath and had a crashing heartbeat by the time she finally reached the corridor. Yes, he could defend himself, but Alden was a berserker when he fought. And Bowen had just had brain surgery!

She braced herself for bloodshed.

And found . . . nothing. The corridor was empty, no drops of blood, no dents in the walls. Pressing a hand over her heart, she walked farther down the otherwise vacant space.

What was that?

She bent down to pick up the delicate white petal, brought it to her nose.

Rose.

How odd. Ryūjin's gardener did grow rosebushes, but there was no growing area in this habitat. Maybe someone had carried a bouquet through here. Because there was another petal and another . . . She followed the trail of petals with a delighted curiosity that momentarily pushed aside the tumult of pain and anger and confusion that had twisted her up the entire day.

The last petal lay on a folded note with her name on it.

"Tansy," she said sternly to her absent friend, "no wonder you went bright red and started stuttering." But her lips were smiling and she was opening the note.

A bold and generous hand, the words shaped in deep blue ink: *There's a dress in the room with the red rose on the door.*

That door stood to the right of her.

Walking over on feet that felt winged, she slid it open and entered to discover herself in a small storage room that had been cleaned until it shone. A pretty little white table and chair sat to the right, a rectangular mirror standing on the table, while in solitary splendor in the center of the room stood a clothes rack. On it was a long blue dress from her own closet: one shoulder was formed of three strings of pearls that swooped down her back then up to join the other shoulder, the front a sharp vee and the shape of it slinky.

She'd fallen in love with the gorgeous creation online and bought it in a midnight shopping spree. But she'd never worn it—had been saving it for a mating ceremony when one of her single cousins finally fell and fell hard.

The idea of wearing it for her own lover . . . She sighed, her smile glowing. Because this depth of planning had a certain security chief's hands all over it.

She ran her fingers over the fabric before looking to the table she'd noticed when she walked in. Laid out on top was her hairbrush, her face cream, and a bottle of her moisturizing lotion, as well as the cosmetics and jewelry she might use when she wanted to dress up.

"Sera." Only her high school friend would know just what to choose.

The last item on the table, however, hadn't been chosen by Sera. A tiare flower sat in solitary splendor in an open blue velvet box; it looked like a glowing jewel, its scent a familiar kiss. Bowen must've done some fast-talking to get his hands on that. Or he'd used security chief skills to purloin it—because Bebe only gave flowers from her prized bushes to people she liked and who hadn't annoyed her in the past month.

Smiling with girlish abandon, she was glad she'd had to take a quick shower toward the end of the dinner prep. Scott had stumbled and spilled pasta sauce all over her. "Oh, Kaia"—she shook her head with a soft laugh—"that was your security chief's doing." She wondered what he'd said to Scott to get the boy to agree to act the klutz in front of his crush—and how he'd known she'd feel foolish putting on this beautiful dress after getting all sweaty in the kitchen.

"Because he listens, he watches, he cares."

And he was so, *so* dangerous to her. But Kaia didn't have it in her to turn away from a gift this sweet, this wonderful. Even if the future was a burn at the back of her eyes and the past a heavy weight on her shoulders, her worry thick with guilt.

She still couldn't step away. This moment would never come again.

Reaching back, she tugged down the zipper of her knee-length dress with its skirt just full enough to allow her to move with freedom and the fabric light and floral. It fell to the floor in airy grace. Now clothed in lace panties and a matching bra, she picked up her dress to hang it on the clothes stand, then went to the table.

The first thing she did was remove the beaded wooden bracelet from around her wrist. Pain speared her as she put it gently aside, but she thought Hugo with his laughing eyes and outgoing ways wouldn't begrudge her this—not if he knew Bowen as she knew him. Her friend was not a man who held grudges.

After inhaling a long, shaky breath, Kaia gently rubbed in her face cream, then stroked the tiare-scented lotion over her body. The bottle of foundation was the next thing she picked up. She took her time doing her makeup and brushing her hair until it shone. A man should wait for his lover. Bowen would wait for her.

The bra had to come off at the end—the dress didn't allow for it.

Skin soft from the moisturizing lotion, she pulled on the dress. It moved over her body like a lover's hands, hugging her curves and flowing in a fall as liquid as water.

That was when she realized: "No shoes." Laughing as the being inside her twisted in an exhilarated dive, she wondered what else the security chief had noticed.

The last thing she did was tuck the tiare flower behind her ear.

Ready, she opened the door and walked out barefoot.

The man who leaned on the wall on the other side was wearing an old-fashioned tuxedo, his hair neatly combed and his face lean. "Where did you get this?" She ran her hand covetously over his lapel, sensing the tensile strength of him.

"Dex borrowed it from another clanmate." He stood still as she stroked the smooth line of his jaw, then buried her nose in his throat and took a deep breath.

"I like the smell of you, Bowen Knight."

He shivered and raised his fingers to the tiare flower. "You're wearing it behind your left ear."

Kaia's lips curved. "I am."

His own smile was young and possessive and a little smug. Oh, he noticed everything, this man—even the silent language of flowers spoken by those on Ryūjin.

"Come on, Siren," he said with a touch of the flower that told the world she was taken. "I have plans for you."

Refusing to acknowledge the dark shadows that awaited in the corners on wings of night, Kaia took his elbow and he escorted her to the door of the old warehouse.

She thought she was ready, but she wasn't. *"Bowen."* Releasing his arm, she walked into a dream. She'd forgotten this warehouse was right at the top of the habitat and had a seaward wall above. The warehouse was currently unused because the station team was discussing how to turn it into living quarters.

Streamers of white fabric fell from the support beams below the seaward sky to pool on the floor. Those gauzy curtains were held back by ropes of tiny lights that glittered like stars under the simulated moonlight, turning this room into a cocooned piece of the night sky.

More rose petals covered the floor, and in the center of the splendor was a Persian rug in hues of midnight blue and gold. On that rug stood a table covered with a tablecloth as white as snow, and two upholstered chairs in white with black swirls. More streamers of twinkling golden lights ran across the tablecloth.

The only other thing on there was a metal bucket of ice that held a bottle of champagne.

Bowen's hand on her lower back, his mouth kissing the curve of her throat. "No tears," he whispered, kissing away the hot wet that rolled down her cheeks. "No sadness tonight."

He was breaking her heart with the gentleness with which he kissed her tears into his own mouth. "I know life can't stop," she found herself whispering, "but it feels wrong to experience any kind of joy while Hugo and the others are out there, lost and hurt."

"I get it, Siren." Bowen's cheekbones sliced into his skin. "I carry the same guilt inside me every single day." Hard words, a tender touch. "The chip protects my thoughts, but there are millions of humans who can't say the same. They wake up knowing that today might be the day an invisible hand reaches in and rapes their mind."

Her gut lurched at the idea of it. "I'm sorry." She couldn't imagine being so without moral boundaries that she'd violate another's mind. Her parents hadn't had to teach her that; she'd known right from wrong even as a small girl. Other people's minds were private places unless they invited you in.

"You have no reason to be sorry." He rubbed his thumbs gently over her cheeks to capture the final remnants of her tears. "Take this night with me, Kaia. Live this dream."

Unspoken was the bleak reality hanging over his head.

She held on to the passionate life of his eyes. "No tears tonight." It was a pact that shut out the world: the chip in his head, the compound, the inevitable end of this dance, the accusations against the Alliance, Hugo, the other vanished . . . all of it.

Tonight was their impossible dream.

Chapter 38

Love is a razored blade of glass.
Gleaming facets more brilliant than rubies and emeralds.
A jewel among jewels.

—Adina Mercant, poet (b. 1832, d. 1901)

"POUR ME CHAMPAGNE," she whispered, then took a kiss, her hand on the warm skin at the back of his neck, his overlong hair soft on her fingers.

His own hand on the curve of her hip, he let her lead. When she pushed playfully at his chest in an echo of their morning encounter, he smiled and walked to the champagne bucket. He'd had flutes tucked in there, pulled them out to place them on the table before he popped the champagne.

The liquid he poured out was a cool gold, the foam a delicate white.

Picking up a flute, he held it out. "For my lady."

Laughing, she took it, clinked it against his with a clear bell-like sound that was a delight to her senses. It bounced around the room, brought the shape of that room to her. "To us."

"To us."

Their second kiss tasted of the crisp bite of champagne.

Music filled the air in the aftermath, soft and romantic. She nuzzled his nose. "Magic?"

"Or a remote in my pocket." He put the flat black rectangle on the table, did the same with his champagne, and held out a hand. "Dance with me?"

Setting aside her flute, she placed her hand in his and they danced under the moonlight and the starlight.

No one swam above them and she knew he'd somehow arranged that, too. Tonight, they existed in a cocoon, in each other's arms, in each other's eyes.

It felt dreamy and wonderful and a gift.

They danced, they drank champagne, they whispered silly things that lovers say. Later, her security chief asked her to wait a moment, then, as she watched, he whisked the bucket to the floor before pulling out the chairs. Taking the ropes of lights off the table, he placed them behind the chairs.

As if the stars had fallen to earth to create a carpet just for them.

When he lifted his hand again, she took it, allowed him to seat her. Smiling, she sipped champagne as he ducked behind a curtain. Of course she'd made pasta today. But even the prosaic simplicity of the meal wouldn't change the romance of this night—Bowen had worked so hard to pull it all together.

He entered pushing a cart that held several covered dishes. "Don't judge me too harshly," he said before pulling off the lid on the first plate.

Her hands flew to her mouth. "Crepes? How did you know I love crepes?" Savory like these, sweet, experimental flavors, all kinds.

"I have sources." He slid the plate in front of her with a lopsided grin. "But I'm not the best cook."

Kaia's heart melted into a puddle. "You cooked?" There were small kitchens in all the other main residential habitats, for use by those clanmates who felt like cooking for themselves, but she'd never imagined that Bowen Knight, security chief and weapons specialist, would do that for her.

"Cooking is how you show care, affection, love," he murmured as he took his seat. "I want to speak your language."

He'd told her no tears tonight, but he was going to make her cry if he kept this up.

She ate every bite, and with pleasure. He'd created more than one course, even included dessert. It was strawberry ice cream.

"I ran out of cooking mojo."

Laughing and giddy as a schoolgirl with her first love, she lifted a spoonful of ice cream to his lips. He fed her in turn and it was silly and young and wonderful. She saw no tension in his face, no weight on his shoulders.

If she could, she would've lived this night forever, but time kept moving on.

The station was quiet when they snuck through like teenagers out too late. Once inside her room, they kissed slow and deep, undressed each other as slowly, stroked and touched with endless patience, found pleasure in every fragment of a moment.

But dawn, it still came, and the clock, it continued its inexorable countdown.

Chapter 39

Genetics is a game with an infinite number of possibilities. Every so often, the rarest of those possibilities combine in a single individual.

—From the draft of an unpublished paper titled "Recessive Gene Markers and the Rarity of True Genetic Death" by Dr. Natia Kahananui and Dr. Eijirō Kahananui

DR. KAHANANUI CALLED Bo in for a scan after breakfast. Lily had sent him more files overnight and he'd been sitting at the kitchen counter reading them while Kaia did her meal planning for the next few days.

"I'll come," she said, putting down her computronic pen.

Bo could still smell her on his skin, as if she'd become fused into his very cells. But it wasn't enough, would never be enough for him. He was like KJ's mate, who wanted the orderly to wear a wedding ring—Bo wanted Kaia to wear his brand and he wanted her to ask him to wear hers.

Ten more mornings.

He could make no promises before that, could ask for no loyalties. That would be a selfishness too far. So he took her hand and he took a kiss that made a passing Pania giggle behind her hand, while Scott gave him a thumbs-up. And he hoped his siren would forgive him if it was oblivion that waited on the other side of the door.

Dr. Kahananui was standing by her data display panel when they entered, her head on her mate's chest while Dex rubbed her back.

Bo and Kaia both froze on the doorstep, went to move back out, but the couple had seen them. "Come in," Dr. Kahananui said. "Dex has to get to work."

Rumbling in Dex's chest. "I told you I can take the time off."

"You'll spend it driving me crazy." Rising on tiptoe, the coolheaded scientist kissed her scowling mate's nose. "I'll see you at lunch."

"Count on it," Dex promised darkly before he left.

Bo got himself into the scanning chair, used to the procedure by now. Kaia silently strapped down his arms, then lowered the strip that went over his eyes. He was ready for the kaleidoscope in front of him, but what he saw in the back of his mind was Kaia's face . . . and the shadows that lived once more in her gaze.

He gripped the ends of the chair arms to keep from tearing away the straps so he could rise, wrap her up in his embrace.

When the kaleidoscope finally blinked out ten minutes later, Kaia lifted the top of the scanning equipment and pushed it back behind his chair. "I have to get back to the kitchen," she said with a glance at the time, "but I'll pop in again when Attie has the results—if you don't mind."

Bo caught her hand. "No secrets between us." He'd give her everything he had, even knowing that he had only a five percent chance of giving her freedom from the fear that ten more tomorrows was all they'd ever have.

Leaning in, Kaia ran her fingers through his hair, then kissed him with a wildness that left him shaken. He was still trying to catch his breath when she walked out the door. She'd never be an easy lover, his siren. But she'd love fiercely and she'd light up his fucking life.

"You adore her."

Bo looked at Dr. Kahananui. "I'd lay the world at her feet if I could." He wasn't about to play games or hide what he felt for Kaia. "Still five percent?"

"Unfortunately." She rose, arched her back, and winced.

Having gotten up, Bo hesitated. "Um, do you want me to do . . ." He held out his palms awkwardly.

She laughed. "My mate would sulk for days. You're not a cousin yet—and I did send him out."

Bo swallowed his sigh of relief; he'd have massaged her back if she'd said yes to his offer, but it wasn't exactly an area in which he could claim any expertise. "So, what's next?"

It took a further three hours to complete the full battalion of tests, with Kaia coming in with coffee, hot chocolate, and snacks about fifteen minutes before Dr. Kahananui was satisfied she had all the data she needed. Bo ended up standing with his hand on the back of Kaia's chair afterward, both of them focused on the results.

"As I told you," Dr. Kahananui began, "there's a risk the compound is altering the effectiveness of the chip in your head, but I can't be certain of that without running a test you'll no doubt find deeply uncomfortable."

Having drunk half his mug of coffee, Bo put it aside with a frown. "I haven't said no yet." This wasn't only about his future—no matter how fucking badly he wanted that future. Lily, Cassius, Heenali, Ajax, Zeb, Domenica, so many lives, so many brilliant minds, rode on the outcome of this study. "What's the test?"

Dr. Kahananui's next words were stark. "A telepathic attempt against your mind."

Every one of Bo's muscles bunched, his knuckles turning white from the force of his grip on the back of Kaia's chair. He was conscious of her turning to look up at him, her hand rising to touch his. "It won't be so bad," she said with a soft smile that hit him right in the solar plexus, it was so full of light.

He smiled back at her because he couldn't help it. Even when what her cousin was suggesting was his worst fucking nightmare. "Yeah?"

"Atalina has access to a telepath she trusts without question."

Bo felt an unexpected chill whisper across his skin. "I haven't heard of any Psy defecting into BlackSea."

"We don't need a Psy." Eyes dancing, Kaia got up and put her hands on his chest. "I can do it."

Time stood still, the world frozen in place. Bo could see every separate lash shading Kaia's eyes, the air coming out of his mouth a slow burst of particles and the beat inside his chest a bass of sound.

It all crashed in a massive boom inside his skull. "What?" The word came out harsh, rough as crushed granite.

Eyes of primal onyx locking with his own, the playfully secretive curve of her lips fading to be replaced by deep grooves between her brows.

"How can you be Psy?" He closed his hand over her wrist while his blood ran hot, then cold, then back again in a chaotic cycle that was a roar in his ears.

"I'm BlackSea." Kaia's response was firm, her expression guarded. "Both my great-great-grandmothers mated powerful telepaths. I also have multiple other Psy ancestors on both sides of the family tree." She shrugged, as if she hadn't just shattered Bowen's sense of reality. "I'm hardly unique. Plenty of changelings have Psy ancestry."

So did any number of human families, but this was very, *very* different. "You're talking about attempting to *hack my mind*." As another telepath had once done, shoving her cold mental fingers into Bowen's brain. "That's not a small genetic quirk."

"One of Kaia's direct ancestors was a cardinal, the other a hairsbreadth from cardinal-level power." Dr. Kahananui looked from Bo to Kaia, her eyebrows drawn together. "My parents did a gene map for Kaia when she turned sixteen—their idea of a birthday present." A slight smile. "While predicting psychic strength on the gene level remains a murky exercise, Kaia appears to have inherited every single Psy gene floating around in the familial gene pool."

Bowen's confusion crystalized into a single blinding thought.

Tightening his grip on her wrist, he said, "Are you sick, having headaches?" His heart might be bionic, but it felt as if it would explode from the pressure within. "The Psy have a psychic network that provides the biofeedback they need to survive. Are you in a network?"

"I'm fine. You don't have to play knight in shining armor." A pat of his chest with her free hand, her lips curving up a little.

Bo thought of the packs that did have Psy defectors. Those defectors were alive and thriving, so changelings—BlackSea included—must have some way of providing the energy needed by strongly psychic minds.

But now that he knew Kaia was safe, he could no longer ignore the crushing wave of betrayal that had slammed into his heart the instant he understood she was a telepath. "Why didn't you tell me?"

"It never came up." Her fingers curled into his chest. "It's a part of me. Like my arm or my leg. I don't go around telling people I have an arm—and there are no other telepaths on Ryūjin. My telepathy is a dormant limb nearly a hundred percent of the time."

He wanted to shake her. "You've listened to me talk about how defenseless humans feel against telepaths. You know *exactly* how I feel about the Psy. Yet you said nothing!" Bo had trusted her with his soul, and she'd held back this elemental piece of herself.

Wrenching her wrist out of his grasp, she stepped back, and her eyes, they were no longer in any way human. "Because it didn't apply!" Her chest rose and fell in jagged breaths. "I have ethical lines I will never cross! What does it matter if I'm a telepath when I would never, *never* enter another mind without permission?"

"That's not what this is about!" It was about him and Kaia and a bond they'd forged based on truth.

"No, it's about you thinking of me as a psychic *rapist*!" The brutal word was a verbal slap that made his head ring. "No, don't speak. I don't want to hear anything you have to say."

Bo wasn't about to be given the brush-off, not by his siren, but he caught a glimpse of Dr. Kahananui's face at that instant. Her shoulders were tense, her face pale, her eyes darting between him and Kaia. *Shit.* "Do it," he said to Kaia even as his stomach twisted. "Run the test." The rest of this conversation, they needed to have in private.

Hands fisted by her side and her eyes pools of black, she said, "Think of a five-number sequence as hard as you can and push the sequence out of your mind."

Bo took three seconds to put together the sequence. "I have it. Pushing now."

Kaia stared directly at him for at least a minute before shaking her head. "Nothing, not even a whisper. Your shield is rock solid." She folded her arms. "Since you think I'm a lying cheat—"

"I never said that," he began.

"—you should get a second opinion from a telepath you trust."

"Ashaya Aleine should be suitable, I think," Dr. Kahananui said, her expression deadly in its immobility. "I'll get in touch with her." She held Bowen's gaze. "You should go. I need to scrutinize the test results in more detail."

It was a clear dismissal, but Bo wasn't used to meekly following orders. "Come with me," he said to Kaia. "We have to talk."

"We have nothing to talk about." She turned her back to him, spine stiff and shoulders rigid.

Bo went to speak again when Dr. Kahananui winced and shifted restlessly in her chair. No way could he add any further stress to her system. Nodding curtly, he left—but this conversation wasn't over. Not by a long shot.

Chapter 40

I have to do this, find out what happened. I can't live with regrets.

—Heenali Roy to Domenica Bianchi

BO COULDN'T THINK. His head rang, his senses wrapped up in a black fog.

How could she not have told him?

How could she have kept such an integral part of herself from him?

Shoving both hands through his hair as the questions repeated over and over in an endless loop, he walked back to his room and grabbed his board shorts. When he got to the pool, he found it mercifully empty, the salt water motionless but for the silent movement of the small creatures that called it home.

He changed quickly before diving in. Haunted by memories of how Kaia had laughed when he'd thrown her, how she'd said he was "fun to play with" when he'd never known how to play aside from in his role as brother to Lily, he swam as hard and as fast as his body would permit.

Lap after lap after lap.

His muscles were feeling it by the time he pulled himself out of the pool, but the crushing blackness in his head hadn't let up and his thoughts ran on a tortured circuit. He could've blamed it on the experiment, but he knew this was very much him.

His sense of betrayal.

His anger.

His . . . hurt.

Bo's hand crushed the soft fabric of the towel he was using to rub his hair dry after a quick shower. He hadn't wanted to admit that, even to himself, but he was so fucking hurt that she hadn't told him. Had she not trusted him to react in the right way?

His mind flashed back to the image of her mischievous smile, and how it had wilted in the wake of his response.

He'd done that.

Gut churning, he got dressed and made his way back to his room. Then, despite the tumult in his mind, he folded up his shirtsleeves and got to work. His fucked-up emotional state didn't mean he was no longer the security chief of the Alliance; as long as his brain worked, he'd do everything he could for his people.

And when it came to any subject but Kaia, he could think clearly.

First, he finished reading the files Lily had forwarded to him. So far, she'd found no indication that one of the knights might be involved in the high-stakes poker world. Another dead fucking end. But it was her final update—sent while he'd been in the lab with Dr. Kahananui—that had him swearing a blue streak.

Calling Cassius rather than Lily because this wasn't a data matter, he said, "What the fuck is this about Heenali going AWOL?" He'd started the investigation on her because that was his duty and he couldn't turn his face from it, but he'd never truly expected to find evidence of conscious betrayal. However, for her to go missing now? It poured fuel onto the embers of suspicion.

Cassius made a face. "It's not what you think—or what we thought when Lily sent that report." Folding his arms, he braced his feet, his body swaying in a way that made it clear he was on a waterborne vessel. The wood paneling behind him told Bowen nothing further about his location.

"Turns out she told Domenica where she was going," Cassius continued. "After the ex-boyfriend. She wants to convince him to give the relationship another go."

"Oh, for Christ's sake!" And yet how the fuck could Bo say anything against Heenali's behavior when his head was a screwed-up mess and his heart bruised? "At least tell me she's keeping in touch with Domenica."

"Yeah. I also stuck a tracking dot on that knife she takes everywhere." Cassius didn't look happy about his decision. "I'm still feeling like an asshole, but at least my assholishness might help her out if she gets into a jam."

"Range on the dots isn't huge." Useful because they were all but undetectable, the devices had the concordant limited amount of tech and transmitting power. "Does Domenica have her general location?"

Cassius nodded. "She made Heenali promise to check in twice a day, said she was worried about how down Heenali was."

"I never understood what Heenali saw in that guy."

"All shine and smile and no grit," Cassius said bluntly. "But I figured he was her version of a pretty girl who didn't ask too many questions."

Bowen had made much the same assessment—that Heenali needed a lover who didn't challenge her; she'd spent her life fighting challenges. Maybe, he'd thought, she just wanted to hang out with a handsome man who found her attractive and treated her as if she were an ordinary girlfriend, not one who was never far from her favorite knife.

Trey Gunther had given her roses for Valentine's Day, sent chocolates during the long periods when he was away working his salesman route. It was witnessing Heenali's response to the romantic gifts that had made Bowen soften toward the other man—whatever Gunther's faults, he'd made Heenali smile and that was as rare a sight as with Cassius.

Wishing his knight well in her quest to heal her broken relationship, Bo said, "Have you got a staffing issue?"

Cassius shook his head. "Heenali briefed her deputy and got ahead on her work before she took off." Unfolding his arms, he put his roughly scarred hands on his hips. "But, with her gone, no one will blink if I step in to oversee the odd thing. I'm heading out to talk to the captain of one of the ships that breached BlackSea's territorial borders."

Bowen realized Cassius must be on a small vessel heading out to where the big ships anchored in far deeper water. "Brief me as soon as you're done," he told his best friend. "Malachai Rhys is letting me run this, but I don't know how long his patience will last."

His eyes on the blackness outside the window, he shared details of the brutal image Malachai had shown him. "I had an erratic signal at the time, couldn't complete the upload, but looks like I have a stronger signal today." Pausing for a second, he sent the image. "Fifty percent, seventy-five . . . you should have it."

Face as hard as stone after taking in the photo of the bloodied changelings on the deck of the *Quiet Wind*, Cassius said, "I don't care what the fuck evidence this Hugo has compiled, Heenali would never help butcher innocent people. Especially not water changelings. She's always asking to be allowed in on the BlackSea meetings—she's fascinated by them."

Bo didn't say it out loud, but Heenali's fascination could well be a cover for far darker aims. He ran up against a solid wall of disbelief seconds after the thought.

No, not Heenali.

But they had to collect evidence to prove that beyond any doubt—right now, everything pointed to her.

His mood even darker after he ended the conversation with Cassius, he decided to do what he should've done from the start: find out about Hugo. The question was, how did he do that without getting stonewalled? The other man was a clanmate, while Bo was a relative stranger.

But he was security chief for a reason: he knew there was more than one way to ask a question. Heading back out, he glanced at the closed door to the lab and knew Kaia couldn't still be inside. It'd be easy enough to swing by the kitchen if he wanted to track her down, but he remained too messed up to see her again, his feelings of betrayal raking bloody furrows inside his skin.

When he spotted Carlotta sitting at a seaward table with a big-boned man whose sailor-brown skin glowed with health, he walked over. "Mind if I join you?"

Carlotta waved a hand graciously at the empty chair at the table. It was across from her, her companion seated so he faced the seaward wall—and was by her side.

"Bowen," she said, "this is my mate, Filipe."

Bowen shook the other man's extended hand before sitting down. "I think we've already met in your other form." He nodded at the transparent wall that looked out into the ocean. "You were the reason I realized this was definitely *not* Venice."

Chuckling, Filipe ate the last bite of his cookie. "Carlotta's been telling me you think you have a chance with Kaia."

It was the perfect way in. "That's kind of why I came over." He shook his head when Carlotta offered him a cookie from the plate in the center of the table. "Everyone talks about Hugo, but I can't get a handle on who he is as a man."

He knew the other man liked poker a little too much, and that he was a comms expert, but Hugo was an empty silhouette beyond that vague sprinkling of facts. "My rival is a shadow, not a flesh-and-blood man."

Carlotta's pale green eyes held his over the rim of her coffee cup. "He is one of our vanished," she said softly. "He's no obstacle in your path."

Chapter 41

Hugo, you're late! We're going to miss the start of the show!

—Message from Kaia Luna (16) to Hugo Sorensen (16)

"LOVE ISN'T THAT simple," Bo replied, and using that word, it came easy. It felt *right*. And yet his mind continued to churn, his heart fucking aching with the hurt. "A man who isn't here has no faults, can't make Kaia angry."

Carlotta nodded after a long pause, a slight curve to her lips. "Absence does definitely make the heart grow fonder." She looked at Filipe and something unspoken passed between them, the communication so effortless that Bo thought of a distant future in which he and Kaia sat next to each other and spoke with their eyes.

Filipe's deep voice shattered the fragile daydream. "Hugo's a charmer, as my ma used to say. That boy can make Bebe herself laugh, and when he was younger, he could make anyone, even my Carly, forgive him his sins." Reaching out an age-spotted hand, he closed it over his mate's.

She turned hers upside down, wove her fingers through his. "Black-haired, with skin as dark as Filipe's and a smile like the sun, he's got the devil in him—but it's a charming, likable devil. There's no meanness in Hugo."

Bowen had never been called charming. "What's he like as a friend?"

"He can be fickle," Carlotta said with a smile. "But he's so joyously dismayed about being late or forgetting an appointment or not paying back a loan that you forgive him instantly." A glance at her mate. "He was careful with Kaia, though, always there when she needed him."

"She's special to him," Filipe confirmed. "He'd do anything for her, I think. They laughed together a lot."

Bo's shoulders knotted, his thoughts snapping back once again to the exchange in the lab and to Kaia stepping away, putting distance between them. "Did he have curiosity?" he asked past the rock that sat in his stomach. "Like Kaia." For the sake of the investigation, he needed to get a handle on why a poker-playing charmer would suddenly turn detective, but it was the man who adored Kaia who wanted to get to the core of this stranger who lived in her heart.

"Curious?" Carlotta pondered the question. "Not a word I'd choose to describe Hugo. He can find out information, yes. But it's usually because he's been told to find that information or because he needs it for a reason of his own."

The hairs stirred on the back of Bowen's neck.

Was it possible someone else had asked Hugo to look into the movements of the Alliance Fleet? It couldn't have been Malachai—it was obvious the news had come as a shock to both him and Miane. So either Hugo *had* been so struck by what he'd heard from his drunk friend that he'd begun digging, or someone else in BlackSea had pushed him to it after Hugo shared what he knew.

But if that was true, why had that unknown individual left Miane and Malachai out of the loop, not even coming forward after Hugo vanished? It wasn't as if Hugo and his hypothetical partner had been acting against BlackSea. They'd been doing the direct opposite.

The questions lingering on his mind, Bo took his leave from Carlotta and Filipe ten minutes later, then continued on in his attempts to understand Hugo. He was careful who he spoke to, and he didn't turn all conversations to the missing man. That would leave too wide a trail if clanmates got together and began talking.

"I love Hugo, don't get me wrong," Tansy said when he tracked her down to the large growing area in habitat three where she was pruning plants using a sharp pair of shears. "But I never saw him as Kaia's mate. I've always thought she needed someone stronger, someone who'd be her shield and her rock." She put her cuttings in a basket by her feet. "With Hugo, Kaia was the rock and the shield and the one who got him out of scrapes. Been that way since they were kids."

Bo still had more questions than answers by the time he called off the hunt, but he had begun to form a real picture of Hugo Sorensen. A charming and feckless friend, but one on whom Kaia could rely when it mattered. The man had a weakness for poker but was gifted with the comms, seeming to coax a signal from thin air sometimes.

He was also an accomplished hacker who'd once made every comm screen across BlackSea's entire network display a fight scene featuring two samurai cats.

He'd been fourteen at the time.

Bowen had to like the guy for his balls and ingenuity.

However, before the dossier—and his childhood pranks aside—Hugo didn't appear to have proactively done anything beyond the necessary that didn't relate either to Kaia or to himself. He'd once spent eight days sourcing a rare food item for Kaia, and he'd learned how to tile because he didn't like the tiles in his bathroom, but in general he seemed happy to grin and coast along.

Bo stopped on a connecting bridge, staring out into the black where nothing seemed to swim, the world beyond the lights of the habitat an endless darkness. Like the dark places in his soul, the scars on his psyche that meant no one would ever describe him as having a "smile like the sun."

Despite Hugo's faults, he was widely liked—and badly missed. Nearly all his clanmates had smiled when talking about Hugo. Others had frantically blinked back tears at the loss of him. Hugo could be careless, but he had the ability to make people love him.

Had their positions been reversed, Hugo would've already been a station favorite.

Bo didn't have that gift. It took him time to earn people's trust, time to build friendships . . . time to win a woman's heart.

"You keep your promises," he said quietly, even while knowing it was foolish to compare himself to a man who wasn't here and who might never return. "You don't forget to do the things you say you'll do."

Kaia, however, was the one person for whom Hugo had kept his promises.

Hugo had also made Kaia laugh. He hadn't hurt her.

Again and again, Bo saw the smile fading from her face, the playful mischief replaced by shock and pain. The anger had come later. First had come the terrible hurt.

Why hadn't she told him, he'd asked.

The real question was: why hadn't he told *her* the one thing she needed to know to understand who and what he was?

Because his reaction had nothing to do with fear that she'd violate his mind. "You're a fucking asshole, Bo." Kaia would *never* go where she wasn't invited. It wasn't in her nature to act in a mercenary and cruel way. She had a wild gentleness inside her that was all about caring for others.

A hard object poked him in the thigh. He jerked his gaze to the left, to find himself confronted by a woman with night-dark skin who stood under five feet tall and was so heavily wrinkled that her wrinkles had wrinkles. But her eyes were bright and hard and sharp, and though she held a cane, it didn't really look like she needed it. "What did you do to Kaia?" A querulous demand.

Bowen flinched inwardly at the wording of her question. "What business is that of yours?" He'd go to Kaia and he'd lay his worthless heart at her feet, and maybe she'd decide she didn't want it, but that was between him and his siren.

The wrinkled little woman poked him again with her cane.

Bo could've easily grabbed the cane from her, but if she did actually need it, he'd be consigning her to a painful tumble to the floor. He decided to simply move out of the way of her next salvo—she was spry but he'd surely regained enough muscle mass to have the edge over a woman who looked three hundred years old.

"It's my business because I say it's my business," she said, her beady eyes reminding him of—

"You're the turtle," he blurted.

She just snorted. "Well, whatever you did, you'd better fix it. Or I'll throw you out an exit pool myself." Lifting the cane, she shook it at him. "No one gets away with bruising a heart that soft—all that girl knows how to do is love. And she's not one to betray her pain, so whatever you did, it must've been awful. Go *fix it*." Pushing him out of the way on that command, the tiny turtle woman stomped off down the bridge.

Chapter 42

"He hasn't cried once."
"He's a tough kid."
"But holding all that pain and horror inside . . . I want him to cry. I want our boy to cry and I want to hold him and rock him and promise him nothing will ever hurt him again."
"That's not the world he has to live in."

—Leah and Jerard Knight (2065)

DR. KAHANANUI BLOCKED Bo's plan to go straight to Kaia and attempt to mend what he was afraid he'd broken; the doctor summoned him to the lab by flashing up his name on the public comm panels around the station. Spotting him after passing by a panel, Oleanna pointed him in the direction of the lab. "Attie's looking for you, handsome."

"I have to take another set of scans," Dr. Kahananui told him crisply when he entered. "Everything is balanced on a knife edge. I must have continuous data to check if I need to recalibrate the third dosage and the only choices are multiple scans or to ask you to stay in the monitoring bed all day."

"This is definitely the better option." Bo took position in the scanning chair, but this time, it wasn't Kaia's competent hands strapping down his arms, it wasn't the scent of coconut and tiare flowers in his nose.

Dr. Kahananui made no small talk, their interaction strictly subject and doctor.

Bo didn't attempt to bridge the cool divide. He'd hurt Kaia and he had to try to fix his fuckup first. Unfortunately, Dr. Kahananui told him she had to inject him with a sleeping agent as part of this round of scans. His muscles bunched in rebellion, but this was why he was here. This was a promise he'd made.

So he walked with her to his room and lay down in the bed. "How long will I be out?"

"Until about eleven thirty," the doctor told him. "I should be able to take all the readings I need during that time." She pushed up his sleeve and touched something cold and hard to his biceps.

Bo didn't remember falling asleep, but sometime later, he was aware of a presence in the room. A presence that was fiddling with the machines that surrounded him. *George.* He mumbled a groggy greeting and had the sense of Dr. Kahananui's assistant going preternaturally still.

The door swooshed shut only seconds later, leaving behind only a faint scent of something familiar. He frowned, tried to capture it . . . and fell into sleep once more.

THE time on the machine closest to his bed glowed a soft blue: 23:23.

Twenty-three minutes past eleven p.m.

His brain shaking off the last vestiges of sleep on that realization, Bo rose and went to splash some water on his face. He'd lain down fully dressed, so he was ready to find Kaia as soon as he'd dried off his face. Even if it meant waking her, he'd do this. He couldn't bear the idea of her believing he thought her capable of such a monstrous act.

The lab door down the corridor was open, George hunched in front of a computer inside, his bony shoulders poking up against his lab coat and his arms appearing too long for his body. "Do you know if Kaia's still awake?"

The other man jerked up his head, his eyes bulging for an instant before he recognized Bowen. Color streaked across his cheekbones in the aftermath. "I think she might've gone to the central habitat." It came out a mumble. "I saw her walking that way about fifteen minutes ago. You know where it is?"

"Yes." He'd memorized the map of Ryūjin at the back of the "Emergency Evacuation Procedures" manual that Kaia had made him read. It had been in the sweet, sensual aftermath of their dinner under the stars, when she realized he hadn't been briefed on the evac protocols.

"Most guests receive a briefing before they ever get here." She'd scowled as she grabbed her organizer to pull up the manual, a siren with long, love-tangled hair tumbling over bare breasts marked by his touch.

He could've watched her endlessly.

As it was, he'd been fascinated to discover that the small toe on her right foot overlapped her fourth toe. Such a small, intimate fascination, one that could only exist between lovers learning one another.

"Broke it as a teenager," she'd told him absently while she downloaded the manual. "Didn't really notice it till the healer would've had to rebreak it to fix it, and it made no difference to me physically, so . . ." She'd shrugged. "The nail never grew back, either. I had multicolored dots tattooed on it. I call it my diva nail."

Examining the tiny tattoo, her bare foot close to his hip and his hand around her ankle, he'd said, "The ink lasts through the shift?"

"Uh-huh. Special changeling formulation." That was when she'd thrust the manual at him, then quizzed him to make sure he knew what to do should the station suffer a catastrophic disaster. Taking care of him. As she did everyone else.

For those unable to survive underwater, the procedure was simple: *Get into a lifepod, close the seal by pushing the large green button above the entrance porthole, then eject the lifepod by pushing the red button. Beacon will activate automatically. You will be retrieved within the hour if not pulled up by station-mates who have the capacity to survive in the black.*

Bo didn't like the idea of floating helplessly in a sealed capsule, but he'd learned the locations of all the lifepods. Kaia had tested him on those, too, making up increasingly horrible disasters for him to escape—culminating in a "Godzilla-sized kraken" on a rampage.

His heart squeezed at the memory of how she'd giggled, snorting accidentally in the midst of it, then laughed so hard tears had gleamed wet in her eyes.

Leaving George to his solitary work, Bo forced himself to detour to the kitchen to wolf down a triple-layer sandwich. He thought of it as fuel necessary to keep his brain and body functional and the experiment stable. It was as he was walking out of the kitchen that he realized the lighting had been muted to silvery moonlight, the station settling in for deepest night.

Only a couple of people sat on the sofas in the atrium, both looking out at the water, cups of what might have been coffee or hot chocolate in hand. The connecting bridges he needed to take were empty, and when he looked out into the darkness this time, he saw huge creatures moving at the very edge of his vision.

He couldn't glean any details, just a sense of enormous size.

Kaia's kraken?

But even that mystery wasn't enough to distract him from his goal, his heart thundering with the need to find Kaia. However, when he finally entered what Kaia had told him was the recreational hub of the station, complete with a basketball court and a park filled with tall trees and myriad flowers, it appeared empty.

Desolate.

But he swore he could smell the lush tropical flower that lingered in the air when Kaia moved, twined with faint threads of coconut and . . . chocolate?

He'd seen remnants of chocolate cake in the cooler when he'd raided the kitchen. Kaia must've made it for tonight's dessert. His siren was somewhere in this huge habitat where trees whispered in the airflow currents and nocturnal insects made irritated sounds at the interruption of his presence.

Moonlight glimmered over his every step. There were also pathways lined with what appeared to be old-fashioned gas lamps but were more likely very cunningly camouflaged ecolights. The faux-lamps gave off a soft golden glow that didn't penetrate the shadows beneath the trees.

It should've taken him hours to find Kaia.

Five and a half minutes later, he walked up to where she sat on a carved stone bench in front of a pond. "Why would you need a pond in the middle of the ocean?"

Hex peeked over from where he sat on her left shoulder, but Kaia kept her eyes resolutely forward, her sleeveless and scoop-necked green dress flowing like water in the moonlight. She'd tied her hair into a bun at the back of her head, revealing the delicate skin of her nape, and he wanted nothing more than to bend and press his lips to that soft, warm spot.

But he'd given up that right when he did what he'd done. He'd have to earn it back. And he would, even if it meant splitting open his veins. "I'm sorry." Naked, primal, the words came from the equally primal heart of him.

Kaia ignored him with regal grace.

"Siren." Knowing he deserved nothing less, Bo went down on one knee in front of her. "I was a bastard." There was no other way to put it, no way to dress it up. "I reacted out of fear"—it twisted him up inside to admit that—"but I *never*, not for a single fucking second, believed that you would violate anyone's mind, much less mine."

Kaia spoke at last, her voice devoid of emotion. "Atalina's been in touch with Ashaya Aleine. She'll leave San Francisco for Ryūjin tomorrow morning."

He could've taken it if she'd yelled at him, but she'd shut down. Gone inside that protective shell Dr. Kahananui had warned him about—and he'd fucking pushed her into it. "Ashaya doesn't need to come." He'd contact Ashaya himself to call off the trip. "I trust you with every cell in my body."

Kaia still didn't look at him. He couldn't blame her.

Trembling inside, he flexed then curled his hand. Again and again. "There's something in my past not many people know about." His voice broke under the weight of the nightmare. "A Psy once forcibly breached my mind."

He didn't know if Kaia looked at him—because he couldn't look at her, couldn't bear for her to see the echo of the terrified boy he'd been.

He stared at the grass that grew so far underneath the sea, tried to focus on the wonder of that, but his mind was in an old barn eighteen years in the past.

"I was thirteen at the time." Sweat broke out along his spine. "The short story is, the telepath who had me succeeded. She shoved her psychic fingers into my mind and tore it wide open." It had felt like daggers of ice stabbing into his brain. "She didn't need to be that violent—human shields are agonizingly thin."

The Tp-Psy had been so brutal as a message. "The shock caused my spine to spasm. I also lost the ability to speak or to see for four point five seconds." Each instant of the terror had felt like a year. Bo would never ever forget those four point five seconds.

"Why?" A question stark with horror. "What could a boy know?"

"My father was Alliance." One of the good ones, already being nudged to the margins by a subtle corruption it had taken Bowen's generation to dig out. "I don't know if I was meant to be a warning, or if they wanted to twist me after breaking me, but the result was the same." Bo screaming while Cassius lay unconscious and bloody on the floor.

Bo took care not to mention Cassius—he'd made a promise to never speak of what had happened to his best friend. Cassius had locked the incident deep in his mind and preferred to pretend it never happened. "The worst of it was that I was led to slaughter by a Psy neighbor I considered a friend of sorts—she'd tutored me in chemistry, known me since I was an infant." Not many Psy lived outside the cities, but the ones who did learned to get along with their human and changeling neighbors.

"And the telepath who did it was a friend of hers I'd admired from afar—a boy's dreams." But the *very* worst was that Cassius had had a serious crush on the eighteen-year-old telepath, too compelled by her intelligence and ice-queen beauty to care that she was part of an emotionless race.

Kaia's fingers touching his jaw, her fingertips smoother than his as a result of handling heated pots. "How did you escape?"

He held on to the sensation of her touch to keep himself in this time and place. "Back then, the Psy used to think their minds made them invulnerable. The telepath didn't physically bind me." She'd violated Cassius first, stripping his mind bare and forever shattering his psyche.

"All it took was a single moment of distraction." Cassius rising to consciousness and attempting to get up even though his arms and legs wouldn't work right, the insult to his brain so violent that it had taken a year of rehabilitation for him to recover—physically at least. "I didn't think. I just drove a pen into the telepath's carotid and I was free." Drenched in hot, metallic arterial spray, with a badly wounded friend on the straw-covered floor and a possible enemy outside the barn, but free of the telepath's viciousness.

Kaia's penetrating gaze was absolute midnight that glowed at the edges, and only then did he realize he'd lifted his head, met her gaze.

Chapter 43

Fear is a thief that comes in the bright light of day, an intruder arrogant and assured.

—Unknown philosopher (18th century)

"YOU'RE HAUNTED BY what you did," she whispered, her night-glow eyes stunningly beautiful.

"Not by the killing. That was in self-defense." He'd never suffered any guilt over the actions of that thirteen-year-old boy, or over what had followed. His parents burning down the barn after burying the telepath where no one would ever find her, and the disappearance of the neighbor girl.

A Psy squad had responded to the telepath's sudden disconnection from the PsyNet, but they'd been hours too late. Either the telepath hadn't been important enough to rate an immediate response, or she'd been a disposable pawn. One who could be shrugged off while leaving her masters with plausible deniability.

As for the neighbor girl, nobody in Bowen's family had touched her; she'd come into the barn seconds after Bo drove the pen into his attacker's carotid. Whatever she'd seen on his blood-splattered face had made her run. Bo had a feeling she hadn't lived a very long life after that—the kind of people for whom she'd worked rewarded success, not failure.

"That feeling of being under someone's control," he said, "having a stranger's psychic touch forced into me—" He gripped his knee hard enough that the skin of his hand went bloodless. "I still wake with nightmares where I can feel her fingers crawling in my brain, in my memories, in *me*."

"Here." Kaia held Hex out to him after coaxing her mouse from his perch. "Pet Hex. It's good for stress and he likes you, so it won't stress him."

Feeling naked and vulnerable and fucking scraped raw, Bo lifted his hand, palm open.

"I'll ask Attie to tell Ashaya not to come," Kaia said after transferring over an agreeable Hex.

"It had nothing to do with you." Bowen needed her to understand the truth on a level that would forever erase the pain he'd inflicted. "I was angry because I thought you were deliberately keeping a secret from me, but the rest of it—"

"I know." Kaia's fingers on his cheek, her tenderness giving him a reprieve from once more acknowledging the fear that was a shadow he'd never been able to shed.

Shuddering, he sat down fully on the grass, his back against the bench. When Hex ran down his leg and onto the grass, he let the mouse explore. Hex stayed close, as if simply stretching out his tiny legs. "Don't you want to use it?" he asked after a while with a frown. "You said it's like an arm or a leg, but you never get to stretch those muscles. That doesn't seem right."

"You're a strange man, Bowen Knight." A touch on his hair, the caress featherlight. All his muscles bunched. The touch grew firmer, Kaia's fingers stroking through his hair in a way Bo wanted to see as possessive. He wasn't a man who touched often, and in the months before the assassination attempt, he hadn't really had contact with people beyond the hugs he gave Lily.

It hadn't been a conscious choice.

So many years and all his attention, all his focus, all his energy had gone into the Alliance. But when Kaia touched him, he knew he'd never again be satisfied living a monastic life devoid of her laughter, her caresses, her joyous playfulness.

"NOW you want me to use my telepathy?" Kaia asked with a tug at Bowen's hair.

"It's part of you." Unsaid was that he accepted all of her—even when her gift was entwined with his greatest nightmare.

Fury raced through her like a lightning storm at what the unscrupulous telepath had done, the damage she'd caused in the heart of the boy Bo had once been. "I suppose if I'd grown up using it and then suddenly had to stop, I'd miss it," she said, answering his question because she understood his hunger for knowledge now, maybe better than he did himself.

If he knew enough about telepathy, perhaps the fear would stop tormenting him deep in the night when he should be able to lower his shields and rest. "But I grew up around changelings with solid shields."

"What about your own shields? How did you learn to create them? I've heard telepaths can become overwhelmed by the noise of the world."

Kaia paused. "I've never thought about that." But the answer was obvious. "I must've learned by running up against changeling shields. Baby see, baby do, so to speak." She'd had a powerful shield against unwanted external input by the time her parents took her out into the wider world.

"It's also possible your brain works differently than a fully Psy brain and you were born with the shield."

"Yes, that's very possible." Kaia certainly couldn't remember ever being overwhelmed by psychic noise.

"If true, that gives you a psychic advantage."

He shifted his head slightly.

Heart swelling with an emotion she shouldn't be feeling for this man whose time was running out—except that it was far too late to step back—she restarted her petting of his hair.

"Have you *ever* used your telepathy to communicate?"

"I have a few clanmates with telepathic abilities." Nowhere near as strong as hers but enough to hold a conversation. "We mostly treat it as a game, to be honest. Like a parlor trick."

And at last, he broke out of the shadows with a laugh. "Only you would treat telepathy as a parlor trick."

"I have gills if I want them and I can swim in the black." She tugged playfully on his hair again. "What's telepathy next to that? I can open my mouth or change my expression and communicate as effectively."

Bowen looked over his shoulder at her, his smile a thing of beauty. She wanted to tumble him to the grass and kiss him and hold him and try to soothe the pain of the boy he'd once been. Because it existed still inside this powerful man. But he wasn't done with his questions.

Shifting position to lean against her legs so she had better access to his hair, he said, "Your clan knew about the Psy need for biofeedback long before Sascha Duncan defected into DarkRiver. Did you tell the cats?"

"We weren't allies then." She ran her fingers down to his neck, began to give him a gentle massage. "By the time we heard about the defection, the leopards had already figured out what they needed to do."

He dropped his head a little forward. Kaia massaged out the stiffness, giving him a soft end to a hard night. It had nearly destroyed him to tell her what he had—but he'd done it because he'd caused her pain and that wasn't acceptable to him. Even if it meant tearing open his greatest hurt.

She leaned down and kissed the skin of his nape.

A shiver ran through him.

Getting up onto his knees, he turned and braced his hands on either side of her on the bench. It was instinct to bend and press her mouth to his. He let her lead the kiss . . . until he wrapped his arms tight around her and pulled her right off the bench.

Landing on his back on the grass with an audible "oof," Kaia sprawled on top of him, he laughed and that laugh fell into the kiss. When she said, "Hex," in a worried voice, he shook his head. "He's a few feet to our right. We didn't crush him."

The sudden spike of worry flatlining, she returned to a kiss that was molten wetness and a dark demand. Bo gripped the back of her head with one hand, while his other arm was a steel band around her waist, but Kaia felt no fear, nothing but a sense of rightness that was liquid fire in her veins.

Breathless, needy, she demanded as much in turn. He gave without hesitation.

His body was big and warm and his heart pounded so powerful a beat that her blood thundered in time with it. *"Bo."*

Tightening his hold, he flicked his tongue at her own, teasing her with soft licks and sucks; it spoke to the other part of her nature as deeply as it did to the human side.

Kaia was seduced by playful and roughly real as she'd never be by smooth charm or practiced seduction.

A little nip of her lower lip that made her toes curl, then a groan that tore out of him as he kissed her deeper and deeper. Until she didn't want to break it even though she needed air, her lungs aching.

When he pulled up her dress to stroke one hand over her thighs, she moaned and said, "Hurry," driven by a visceral hunger to erase the darkness of what had come before with passion and sweetness and touch.

Bowen moved his hands to the sides of her panties and began to tug down the flimsy scrap of lace. The erotic brush of lace against flesh, the rough warmth of his hands, the way he kept becoming distracted by the damp heat between her legs . . . Kaia would go mad before he was done.

Scrambling back, she took care of the task herself, then got to work on his belt. He rose up on his elbows and watched her, the glittering heat of his eyes accompanied by a slight smile that made her crave another kiss. But she needed this most primal sense of connection with him even more. Belt undone, she flipped open the button on his jeans and pulled down his zipper, careful over the hard ridge of his body.

It didn't take her long to free him into her hands—to the hiss of his breath. She straddled him, her dress covering them both. "If we get caught," she whispered as she sank down into him, her nails digging into his chest through his shirt, "just pretend I'm sitting on you."

He laughed and it came out a groan. "You can sit on me anytime you like, Siren." He sounded like himself again, no fractures in his psyche from that long-ago attack, but Kaia knew that was an impossibility. The fractures might one day heal totally, but the scars would remain. She wondered if he'd ever spoken about the horrific attack to anyone—she'd ask him another time. They'd had enough darkness today, enough pain.

Today, she'd love him with her body and show him once again that there was more to this world than a fight for survival.

Flowing over him, she kissed him slow and deep as she rocked her body on his. He put his hands on her hips to help her maintain the rhythm and so she wouldn't have to do all the work. Kaia smiled against his mouth. "You're a keeper, Bowen Knight," she whispered. It was so quiet that she didn't know if he'd heard.

His fingers clenched on her hips, his body beginning to stiffen. She increased her pace, ready to watch him go over, but her lover was a master at strategy. He put his hands on her breasts and squeezed her nipples between his thumbs and forefingers, jolting her beyond the edge in the instant before he fell.

Chapter 44

Mama and Papa won't wake up.

—Kaia Luna (7) to Geraldine Rhys

KAIA LAY ON top of Bowen, their clothing set to rights but their hearts pumping and their breaths short. He had one arm around her back, the other folded under his head, a big warm male pillow with more than one hard edge.

Unbuttoning his shirt to expose the warmth of his skin, she spread her hand on him with a sigh. He didn't have any chest hair, though the last time they'd been in bed she'd discovered a trail lower down on his abdomen. As he'd discovered so many exquisitely sensitive places on her own body.

"Someone's coming," he murmured.

Kaia had already heard the low-voiced conversation of a couple on a walk, been lazily ignoring it. "They won't see us if we stay quiet and motionless." It helped that she'd chosen a bench in a pool of liquid night created by the dimmed lighting as Ryūjin settled into sleep.

Station dwellers all worked different shifts, but they tried not to lose complete touch with the surface world. It made meetings and research cooperation difficult if the Ryūjin scientists were on a divergent sleep cycle. As a result, the entire station went "dark" for about four hours a night.

She continued to pet Bo as they lay there. He didn't stop her exploration, not even when she traced the scars above his heart, where the surgeons had gone in. She'd seen the bullet scar on his back, too. The impact site had, ironically, suffered almost no damage; it was *inside* him that the designed-to-fragment bullet had devastated.

Those, however, were far from the only scars on his body. "What's this from?" She rubbed a faint ridge on his lower abdomen as Hex came over to curl up in the warm spot between Bowen's shoulder and neck.

"Security op when I was young. Stealing back data a Psy business had stolen from a human one. I didn't dodge a knife-wielding ninja fast enough."

Kaia laughed softly. "A knife-wielding ninja?"

"Fine, you've tortured the truth out of me," he grumbled. "An explosive detonated early, blew a piece of shrapnel into my gut—looks and sounds bad but it didn't perforate any internal organs, just my pride." Despite his scowling words, his eyes were closed and he lay boneless against the grass, akin to one of the changelings who liked being stroked. A cat, maybe. Or perhaps a wolf. Maybe even a creature like Kaia. Or maybe he was simply being human.

Kaia had known a great many humans as a child, her mother and father defiant adventurers who wanted to save the world. So foolish, so wonderfully hopeful. So deeply betrayed by the very people they'd fought to help. "If only my parents could've known I'd one day exchange skin privileges with a human under the moonlight."

Bowen ran his fingers through his hair. "Would you be struck from the family tree?"

Kaia smiled. "No. My parents were rebels—they didn't believe in BlackSea's isolationist policies. They'd be happy I no longer see humans as a monolithic group. My mama and papa taught me to judge each individual person on their own actions." But the child she'd been, scared and angry and grieving, had forgotten that lesson.

"Why were you so angry toward humanity?" Bowen asked softly. "It had to do with more than Hugo's dossier, didn't it?"

No smile on her face or in her heart now. "My parents fell ill from a virus running red-hot through a human township." Her mother had been working in the township's run-down clinic to stem the tide of illness, while her father had driven emergency supplies in and out—Kaia herself had been enrolled in the local school, but her father would pick her up after school and she'd ride with him.

"Why blame humanity for a virus?"

"I didn't blame them for the virus. I blamed them for not giving my parents the medicines they needed." Even so young, Kaia—the child of a doctor—had known Elenise and Iosef shouldn't be dumped in the corridor without even the most rudimentary line of fluids going into their bodies.

Bowen crushed her closer to the hard heat of him. "Corruption?"

"Certain people pulled strings to get their families seen to first, even though they weren't critical like Mama and Papa—and even though my parents had done more to help than any of them." Her face went all hot as it had done when she'd been a small girl afraid and suddenly without the voices of the two people who were her world. "They left my parents on stretchers in the corridor, on dirty sheets."

Scalding wet burned the backs of her eyes. "I ran back to our small home to get them blankets, but someone had broken in, taken everything."

"Ah, baby." Bowen's free hand coming around to cup the back of her head, his mouth pressing a kiss to her hair. "How old were you?"

"Seven." Scared and alone in a distant land. "We didn't have a built-in comm and the thieves took the organizers. My mother should've had a phone in her pocket, but it was gone by the time I found them on the stretchers—after my father didn't come to pick me up from school." She'd run over to the clinic with a friend who lived close to it, figuring he'd been held up and she'd sit in her mother's office.

"I want to kill the bastards who did that to you." Bowen's muscles rock hard under her, around her.

"I finally found a nurse who'd worked with my mother and she snuck me into the supervisor's room so I could use the clinic's single comm to call my aunt." Her parents had made sure she memorized a list of emergency call codes. "BlackSea airlifted my parents to one of our own clinics, but even with how fast the clan responded, it was too late. If they'd had the medicines in time . . ."

Kaia had sat and watched their chests rise and fall because of the machines and she'd willed them to wake up even knowing it was far too late. "I began to hate humans the day my mother and father stopped breathing."

"I'm sorry, Siren. I can't blame you for it." His exhale was rough, his hold warm and strong. "I ran on hate against the Psy for a long time."

That he understood and didn't judge her for her pain-fueled anger, it meant everything. "What changed?"

"A little Psy girl in the street who rushed to pull a kitten to safety when it would've tumbled into a canal, Ashaya working so hard to build a shield for humans, empaths helping to heal broken human minds, the old Psy woman at the grocery store who carefully adds up her purchases before going to pay . . ."

Another kiss pressed to her hair. "The adult me knows not all Psy are powerful or wealthy or ruthless. I see them struggling to survive same as humans and changelings. But even then, I can't forget what the Psy as a group have done to humanity over the centuries."

Kaia petted his chest. "It's hard, isn't it?" To forget. To forgive.

"You're stronger than me, Kaia. Thank you for not kicking this human to the curb."

She smiled, and it was shaky. "Some things are inevitable."

Even when they were the worst possible choice for a woman.

Kaia was a cook in an undersea station for a reason. It was *safe*. People didn't get shot going about their business. And because strangers couldn't easily come or go, the station wasn't exposed to potentially devastating diseases. As she'd learned as a child, while changelings were tough, they weren't immune to deadly pathogens. Should there be an outbreak on land or even in the floating city above, the station could be sealed; at least *some* of her friends and family would survive.

She wouldn't, once again, lose everyone she most loved in a single horrific event.

Bowen Knight wasn't safe, would never be safe. The woman who called him her own would have to accept that each and every day of her life. Kaia's scarred heart didn't have that capacity—it was as well that was a road she wouldn't be asked to travel . . . because Bowen would leave her one way or another.

To the surface, she thought fiercely, she'd lose him to the surface and to the land that was a nightmare she could never again face. Her world was the deep and the ocean close to Ryūjin, and, very rarely, Bebe's isolated little island with its five palm trees and two fruit trees amid rocks and sand.

Kaia hadn't walked on inhabited land since she was seven years old.

Chapter 45

We're heading to Ryūjin. Apply for leave.

—Edison Kahananui to his brothers Armand, Teizo, Tevesi, and Taji

"I HAVE TO go." Kaia's voice twined around Bo in the darkness, the sadness in it tempered by the warmth of who she was at the core: a caretaker.

. . . *all that girl knows how to do is love.*

Bebe was right; love was at the core of Kaia's psyche. Which made her terrible loss as a child even harder to think about. From "the three Lunatics" to a single lonely girl. Rolling them over so that she was below him, Bo nuzzled at her nose in the way she'd done to him when they were alone and in bed, and he silently called himself a selfish bastard for being unable to let her go even when he knew the scars that marked her.

"Are you sure?" he asked with another nuzzle.

Her smile was a glow. "I have to wake up in a few hours to bake pastries. I promised the children."

And his Kaia was a woman who kept her promises. "I'll walk you to your room." Rising to his feet, he held out a hand and tugged her up. Then, bending, he scooped up Hex and placed the mouse in his front pocket.

When Kaia slipped her hand in his and swung their clasped hands back and forth, Bowen's blood surged with a youthful joy he hadn't felt since before that bloody day in the barn. He felt old more often than not. A man burdened with a thousand worries, his entire adult life spent attempting to put humans on the chessboard on an equal footing.

No longer disposable pawns but opponents worthy of respect.

Bo didn't regret the choice. He'd taken on the task with open eyes and a passionate heart. He would split his veins to keep the Alliance strong. It was as much—*more*—a part of him as the mechanical heart that beat in his chest.

But every dream, every ambition, had a price. He'd become an adult too early. Had never chased girls or stolen a kiss in the rain or snuck out at night to throw pebbles at a crush's window. While other boys did exactly that, Bo and Cassius had hounded Bo's father for information about the Alliance and picked up after-school jobs so they could pay for hand-to-hand combat training. They'd also pitched in with hard physical chores around his parents' small farm far more than was expected, doing everything in their power to become stronger.

Neither one of them would ever again be an easy target.

But in all that drive, all that coldly burning anger, Bo had buried a part of himself so deep it had taken a siren to awaken it. That part was young and painfully hopeful and scared.

Bo could control many things, but not the chip or the compound.

"Why so quiet, Tall, Dark, and Handsome?" Kaia's smile was mischievous as they left the habitat, her onyx eyes dancing. "Plotting something nefarious?"

"Always." Bo rubbed at his jaw like a B-movie villain, felt the scrape of stubble against his skin.

Dropping his fingers from his jaw, he ran the back of his knuckles across Kaia's cheek and down her throat. "I need to shave," he murmured. "I've marked you."

A whistle sounded down the connecting bridge to habitat one.

Kaia's eyes jerked that way, as did Bo's.

It was Mr. Dead Clams—currently wearing gray coveralls with a station logo on one breast, and carrying what looked like an engineer's tool kit. "Putting the moves on our favorite chef," he said when he got closer, good-naturedly enough for someone who'd struck out with Kaia himself.

"Good luck, man." He slapped Bo on the back of one shoulder as he passed, his midnight skin gleaming blue-black under the simulated moonlight. "I wouldn't want to be you when Edison and the others find out." A glance at Kaia. "Did you warn him?"

"About what?" Kaia said with a scowl.

Walking backward down the corridor, Dead Clams called back, "You're a cruel woman, Kaia Luna, but you make the best pierogi in the universe." And to Bowen, "Watch your back. They hunt as a pack."

Bo hadn't needed the warning; he knew what it was to be a protective older brother—he'd run a background check on every single man Lily had ever dated. He'd also had more than one talk with said men. The last time Lily had found out about the latter—back when she was sixteen—she'd threatened to brain Bo with her softball bat. Not that it had stopped him. He'd just gotten sneakier about checking up on the men who wanted to lay hands on his baby sister.

Kaia had grown up with her cousins; they might as well be her brothers.

She rolled her eyes now. "I don't know what Junji is going on about. Mal, Eddie, and the others wouldn't dare interfere in my private life. It's hardly as if they're monks."

Oh, shit. Mal and the others clearly had sneaky down pat.

Junji was right: Bo had better watch his back.

DESPITE the warning, Bo was still taken by surprise midmorning on the fifth day following Junji's caution. He was running on the track in the central habitat when he found himself surrounded by five sleekly muscled men with brown eyes that ran the gamut from a near-hazel to close to black, brown skin both darker and lighter than his, and damp black hair that went from slick straight to thick and curling.

The odd droplet of water gleamed on the skin of more than one. All five wore blue jeans, and T-shirts of various shades that stuck to the dampness of their bodies, their feet bare.

"Kaia's cousins, I presume." The family resemblance with Dr. Kahananui was startling despite the range of their looks. "Where's Mal?"

"Busy," said the biggest one, his voice quiet. "He gave me his blessing to beat you twice if necessary. Once for me. Once for him."

"Nothing political, you understand," said the one in the tight black T-shirt whose hair was actually combed rather than just towel-dried and left at that. "This is about family."

The five of them began to herd him toward a quiet part of the habitat; the section was drenched in shadow as a result of the trees that shaded it. All five Kahananui males moved with a predatory grace that said they'd had training, but Bo was a security specialist—he could've extricated himself ten times over. However, he decided to allow this to run its course. If the roulette wheel in his brain stopped at the thin five percent wedge, then he'd have to deal with Kaia's cousins the rest of his life.

Might as well start things off on a good footing if he could.

Having been backed into a corner, he leaned up against the transparent wall. "Bowen." He held out a hand. "And I happen to think your cousin is the most fascinating woman I've ever met."

All he got in return were gimlet stares and folded arms.

Dropping his hand, he attempted another tactic. "I have a sister, too," he said, in case Malachai hadn't already shared that information. "I understand the protective instinct, but it's not necessary here."

A kind of a rumbling sound from the cousin closest to him, one of two in white T-shirts. "Kaia doesn't know how to protect herself from men like you."

"Men like me?"

"A human who sees her as a trophy or a curiosity. A notch on his bedpost to boast about—that time I bedded a mermaid. A fucking human fantasy."

Bo straightened up from his relaxed position, his shoulders squared. "First of all, Kaia's too fucking smart to be taken in by the kind of asshole you're describing. And secondly, speak like that about her again and I'll rearrange your nose until you forget it was ever straight."

The cousin in question took a step forward, his feet pressed up against Bowen's shoes. "Do you really believe you can take me, human?"

Bo slipped past the other man, twisted his arm behind his back, and kicked out his knees to send him slamming into a kneeling position before the dark-haired male knew what was happening. "I could've twisted your head back to snap your neck," he said quietly, "but Kaia likes you."

He released the man. "You are *not* getting in the way of my courtship." The continued hunt for the traitor within the Alliance combined with Dr. Kahananui's tests and scans and recalibrations sucked up most of his time, but he'd talked Kaia into a dance in the kitchen late last night, after which they'd gone swimming in the otherwise deserted pool.

He'd been her sous chef one day, learned why her cousins called her Cookie.

Another day, he'd joined in while she babysat the "minnows."

She went swimming in the black while he was in the lab, so they'd have as much time together as possible. But she still mischievously refused to confirm her animal, laughing and telling him he had to figure it out from the clues. "I have faith in you, security chief."

Her playful words had hurt him—because he couldn't honor the deeper faith she showed in him, not in the way he wanted to honor it. He couldn't make any promises until he knew if he'd be whole at the end of the experiment, but he could show Kaia what she meant to him. She'd have that if nothing else. She'd *know* it hadn't been a waste or a mistake but a brilliant, blinding moment of joy.

He'd permit no one to obstruct the memories of happiness he wanted for her.

Not even the five men who stared at him with eyes gone obsidian. Inhuman.

The one he'd taken down reached up to massage his abused shoulder, but it was the quiet and watchful one with a scar along his jaw and the pale brownish-hazel eyes who said, "He could look after Kaia."

Bowen's blood cooled. "Are you worried about a specific threat? Give me the details."

Kaia's cousins grinned.

A second later, he was being hugged, the back of his shoulder slapped—a little too hard by the cousin he'd taken down—and his hand shaken.

"Kaia has a soft heart," the quiet one said afterward.

"Marshmallow soft," added the one with the combed hair as straight as Lily's and the black T-shirt. "Don't bruise it."

"Or we'll beat you dead," the remaining three said in concert.

Bo knew Kaia was far stronger than her cousins realized. The same no doubt applied to Bowen and Lily. But Bo would be running security checks until he was dead—and Kaia's cousins would protect her to their last breath. "Did you just swim down?" he asked now that the formalities were over.

One of the younger three thrust his fingers through hair that was straight and thick except for a curl at the edges. "Had to. We got word that you were putting the moves on Kaia."

"I'm starving," another added. "Let's go raid the kitchen."

Bo finally got their names on the way to the kitchen: Edison, Armand, Teizo, Tevesi, and Taji. Last name Kahananui. Middle name Suzuki. The latter came out when they commented on the genesis of his name and asked about Adrian Kenner—Mal had apparently mentioned that connection at some point.

Because of course the other security chief had ferreted out the information.

"Mal's not big into signs and omens," Edison said in a measured way that was already becoming familiar. "But it meant something to him and Miane and the rest of us that you were a direct descendant of Kenner's."

Bowen hadn't known until right then that his ancestry had helped BlackSea decide to trust him. It made the current state of suspicion and dangerous doubt even more troubling. Bowen silently reaffirmed his vow to fix what was fractured, returning the Alliance and BlackSea to the path they'd been following before Hugo's dossier and Bowen's chilling realization that Alliance Fleet ships had indeed breached BlackSea's borders.

Setting aside that deeply problematic truth for this moment when he was getting to know more of Kaia's family, he said, "Suzuki a family name?" He was curious of everything about his siren.

"Dad's surname," Armand shared. "He took Mom's surname since one of her sisters decided to be a Lunatic and the other a Rhys."

"Kahananui is way more awesome," Tevesi said. "Suzuki Kahananui is even better—both names go all the way back to the founding of BlackSea. Girls are always like, wow, that's such a cool name, tell me more. And boom, I'm in."

All five brothers grinned in agreement.

"We have Suzuki cousins, too," Armand added. "All much older than us, since Dad's the baby of his family. Seven brothers and sisters."

"Is he the one who brought in the fertile gene?" Bowen joked.

"He takes total credit," Teizo confirmed with a grin. "Mom keeps pointing out he couldn't exactly reproduce by himself, but Dad's all 'La-la-la, I can't hear you, I'm the *maaaaan*.'"

The five cracked up in a booming bass of laughter.

By now, Bo had them all separated in his head.

Edison had the scar on his jaw and a presence that shouted his big-brother status.

Armand was the one who'd found a comb and the time to fold up the short sleeves of his black T-shirt to better show off his biceps and the intricate tribal tattoo that circled his upper left arm. He was also the one with razor-blade cheekbones fit for a catwalk model.

Teizo, Taji, and Tevesi were each unique in personality, but had faces and bodies so similar that . . . "Triplets?"

"Identical." Tevesi bumped fists with the other two.

Bo looked from one to the other. "You have a freckle on your left cheekbone below your eye." He switched his attention to Teizo. "You have a tooth that's just slightly out of alignment." Last was Taji. "And you have a small mark on the side of your neck that's probably a childhood scar."

"Fuck it," Taji muttered. "You're just like Mal." A glare.

Armand shrugged. "He's always been Kaia's favorite."

"Speak for yourself, asshole," one of the triplets muttered. "*I'm* her favorite."

The entire atrium went dead silent when Bo walked in with the five brothers. Clearly, they'd all expected him to end up at least a little bloody. He was happy to see that, Alden aside, the others looked relieved—Oleanna and KJ even sent him discreet thumbs-ups.

An odd twisting in his chest.

It was good to know Ryūjin's residents liked him enough to worry about him—and respected him enough to leave him to deal with the Kahananui brothers on his own.

"Sera, my darling, my delicious cupcake, where are Attie and Kaia?" Armand lifted Seraphina off her feet to her shriek of outrage.

One of her emerald green heels fell to the floor.

Slapping him on the chest, her nails polished a matching green, the assistant station commander said, "Attie's in her lab and Kaia's making a very sensitive soufflé, you pest. Wait thirty minutes before bothering her or she'll serve you deflated soufflé as punishment." But Seraphina couldn't keep up the stern tone when brother after brother picked her up for a cuddle and a kiss on the cheek.

It was as obvious as the nose on his face that the six had a relationship that permitted such familiarity. Changelings, he'd come to see, were more careful about skin privileges than the outside world realized—they never took physical contact for granted or treated it as anything but a cherished gift.

Seraphina's laughter was husky and as open as her affection for the Kahananui brothers. "Menaces, all five of you," she said. Then she grabbed Edison's face and planted a kiss on his lips that had steam coming out of the man's ears.

Other clanmates hooted and hollered, while his brothers stamped their feet and let out a set of piercing whistles that sounded strangely familiar to Bowen's ears.

Sliding her foot back into her lost high heel afterward, while quiet, intense Edison stared at her like he'd never before seen her, Seraphina turned her formidable attention on Bowen. "Since you survived them, I'm beginning to believe that you, too, are a menace."

Bo smiled slowly. *"Mahalo."*

Scowling when Edison rumbled a question at her, Seraphina turned to respond. But Bo didn't hear either question or answer: his head throbbed.

Once.

Twice.

Sharp spears of electric sensation down his arms.

Sudden numbness in his fingertips.

Chapter 46

I can't see any damage, but there are indications that the compound is beginning to crystallize around the implanted chip. If the process continues as modeled, the final injection should complete the crystallization and freeze the chip in place—and in its current state.

The symptoms you've described are most probably a side effect of the crystallization process. The models do show an eighteen percent chance of some discomfort during this phase of the project. Alert me at once if the symptoms return. Now, let's get back before my brothers come searching.

—Dr. Atalina Suzuki Kahananui to Bowen Knight

KAIA REMOVED HER noise-canceling earplugs; everyone in the clan loved these soufflés and she enjoyed the challenge of making them, but concentration was a must. A single mistake and she'd end up with sad-looking sunken abominations. But the hard work was now done; all she had to do was take them out of the oven in exactly twenty-one minutes.

Hearing a commotion out in the atrium, she wondered if Junji had started up a dance-off. A fan of late twentieth-century breakdancing, the air-systems engineer had delusions of his own skill, but he was fun to watch. A few more months' practice and he might actually become as good as he thought he already was.

Then laughter erupted, big and bold and brash.

Kaia's heart bloomed. She knew the tones of that laughter, as she knew the sound of the deep male voice that answered whatever had been said.

Temper licked at her a second later, but it did nothing to lessen her searing joy. She did miss the idiots.

Walking out of the kitchen after pulling off her apron, she came face-to-face with a scene she'd never expected: all six of her Kahananui cousins, Attie included, at a table with Bowen, eating and drinking, and not killing him.

Dex leaned on his forearms on the back of Attie's chair, listening to something habitually-grumpy-but-always-ready-to-hug Taji was saying.

Inside her, her other self dived and splashed.

So many of her pod here!

It was Bo who spotted her first, though he wasn't facing her way. Looking back, he began to rise. But Kaia was already closing the distance to the group, came to a halt beside his chair with her hands on her hips. "What," she said to her smirking male cousins, "are you five doing down here?"

Armand, to the left of her, snaked out an arm and tumbled her into his lap. "Hello, Cookie. We just missed you."

"Do you think I was born yesterday?" She poked a finger into his left pectoral muscle. "This is ridiculous. The five of you have jobs."

"We took a day off," Teizo said from the other side of the table before shoving his mouth full of scrambled eggs and toast that a beaming Oleanna had just carried over from the kitchen.

When Tevesi and Taji complained, she winked. "Down, boys. I have enough tentacles for all of you."

Leaving the triplets to fend for themselves against Oleanna's attentions, Kaia pulled Armand's perfectly combed hair. "You do realize Bowen can break your heads with his little pinky finger?"

"*Hey!*" came the cry from several throats.

Rolling her eyes at the insult in their tones while Atalina laughed, she finally managed to get off Armand's lap. "How long are you idiots down here?"

"Only a couple of hours," Taji said around a mouthful of food another clanmate had delivered. Oleanna, meanwhile, was whispering in Tevesi's ear.

Bowen's hand curled around hers. A slight tug. A request. She went into his lap, frowned at the lines flaring out from his eyes, but she knew him well enough not to ask what was wrong in public. "So," she said to her cousins, "what's happening up above?"

Their stories were as wickedly amusing as always and she was sorry to disappear even for a minute when it was time to take the soufflés from the oven, but Bowen came along to help her, which gave her time to brush her fingers over his cheekbone and say, "You're in pain?"

"No, but I was," he said after checking to ensure they were alone. "Dr. Kahananui says the models predicted the likelihood of pain during this stage of the process." He put a tray of the miniature soufflés where she indicated. "It means we're on track."

Gut twisting, Kaia put down her own tray. "You're sure?"

He pulled another tray out of the oven. "I'd never lie to you, Siren." Leaning in, he kissed her. "It hurt like a bitch, but it's gone. As if my brain misfired for a second, like it didn't know quite how to direct the signals, then figured it out."

Tugging off her oven mitts, Kaia walked into his arms after he'd put down the final tray. She held him fiercely tight, holding off the future. She wanted to live a little longer in this impossible, extraordinary dream. Nuzzling the side of his face against her temple, he said, "Seraphina kissed Edison and I'm pretty sure he's still on fire."

Her lower lip trembled at how he was attempting to distract her, and inside her, the creature who was her other half slid along her skin. It wanted his touch, wanted him to swim with her in the sea. "You're making that up," she said, pulling back to look up into a face that held far too much life to be on the edge of oblivion.

"Cross my heart." That too-long hair sliding over his forehead, he took a kiss of his own that left her breathless. "Come on, Siren. The men want to spend time with you."

It was a party out there now, complete with dance music across the atrium's system, and Junji and KJ having a dance-off while KJ's wife egged him on. The mini soufflés disappeared at the speed of light, were replaced by bowls of tortilla chips and dip, along with thick sandwiches, and plates of chocolate cookies from Kaia's emergency party stash.

"It's always like this," she murmured to Bowen while they danced and Armand flirted with a blushing Tansy, having backed her extremely willing friend up against the seaward wall. "Everywhere the five of them go, they attract people to them."

Bowen, his arms around her, bent to press his forehead to her own. "I'm not like them." His eyes were fathomless. "It takes me time."

"I know." Bowen was like water on rock, a slow, relentless, determined pressure. "I like your patience, Bowen Knight." Such an understatement when she adored each and every part of him.

His honor.

His commitment to the Alliance.

His courage in walking into the unknown.

The way he'd never, not once, hesitated in looking into the terrible darkness that might exist in the heart of his own organization.

And most of all . . . the way he looked at her. As if she were a dream come to life.

Her stomach clenched. *Only a moment*, she reminded herself. *Only the now.*

KAIA wasn't the least surprised when Edison found her an hour into the gathering and, wrapping his arm around her shoulders, gently walked her away from the crowd. Kaia was aware of Bowen watching them go, but he didn't interfere.

She and her second oldest cousin walked in silence to the connecting bridge between habitat one and habitat five, then stood there looking out at the water. Schools of wild fish swam beyond, their bodies giving off a faint luminous glow. A bigger body would swim past every so often, usually a clanmate from Ryūjin.

They were drawn by the activity in the atrium and as soon as they spotted one of her cousins, nearly all headed for an entry pool. While Atalina was deeply respected and loved, her brothers were flat-out adored by clanmates as well as by Attie herself.

The boys even had the ability to make Malachai unbend.

Last time the five had taken their lone Rhys cousin for a night out at one of the bars on the closest inhabited island, all six had come back three sheets to the wind. Kaia had never before seen Malachai drunk, but that day, he'd scooped her up in his arms and swung her around in a zigzagging dance he'd insisted was a waltz.

Big as Mal was, she could do nothing but laugh and hang on until he got dizzy and decided "the waltz was fucking hard."

"Kaia, you know what I'm going to say." Edison's body was warm next to her own, his arm a heavily protective weight around her shoulders.

She wrapped one of her own arms around his back. "I can take care of myself." All her older cousins—Attie, Mal, Edison, and Armand—still saw her as the shattered, broken girl who'd come to them at seven years of age, but that had been a long time ago.

As an adult, Kaia had never wanted to live in a bubble.

Which, of course, was the irony of ironies. Because she *did* literally live in a bubble. But it was a bubble of her own choosing. A bubble she could leave at will. And oh, how well she lied even to herself. Big words didn't prove the measure of a woman. It was what she did that proved that.

"I'm such a fake," she whispered before Edison could respond. "Hiding down here and pretending I'm a big, tough, independent changeling." None of her family would ever say that, would ever confront her with her cowardice, but no matter the justifications she sold herself, Kaia knew.

Edison squeezed her closer. "I wouldn't mess with you."

She snuggled into the comfort of him. He'd been fifteen the day her world ended, and he'd hugged her then, too. His scent was familiar and of family and she could let down her walls with him. "I heard Sera laid one on you." It was easier to talk about that than the terrors that kept her swimming range limited to the areas around Ryūjin and Lantia. *Never* beyond the patrolled borders.

He blew out a breath. "Where has she been all my life?"

"Right under your nose." It tickled both parts of her that one of her best friends might end up her sister-in-law. Because she'd never before heard that tone in Edison's voice when he spoke about a woman.

It happened that way at times with changelings. Two people who'd known each other all their lives suddenly realizing they were never meant to be just friends. Kaia had always thought it was when both reached a point in their lives where they were ready for one another.

Sera was younger than Edison, couldn't have handled his intensity even a couple of years ago. Now, however, her friend was well bedded into her role as assistant station commander and could go toe-to-toe with anyone. Including a certain Kahananui male.

"We'll get back to my future mate," he said in that quiet Edison way, "but first things first. Have you told him?"

She should've known better than to try to distract Edison. "I'll tell him once the experiment is complete." Not telling Bowen about the telepathy had truly been an oversight, but this was a conscious choice. "There's no point bringing it up now."

But she was talking to the cousin who, as a youth, had taught a fearless five-year-old Kaia to swim beyond the clan's boundaries, the cousin who'd helped her jump fences so they could escape out into the great blue. He'd always watched over her when they played outside the fences, but she'd felt so free, so wild and dangerous even though they were only meters from the safe zone for the minnows of BlackSea.

Kaia felt a keening pang for that small girl who'd swum without fear. Who hadn't understood the pain and death that awaited. That girl had *lived*.

"You have to tell him." Edison cupped her face. "You have to give him the freedom to make that choice while he *can* make it." She knew then that he'd spoken to Atalina about her experiment, understood that Bowen might not make it out of this whole. "I trust your instincts when it comes to people, so I know he must be a good man; he deserves the truth."

"I don't want him to see me as permanently damaged goods."

Edison's face tightened at her shaken whisper. "If he doesn't see you for the gift that you are, then he doesn't deserve you. Don't sell yourself short, little sister."

When Kaia didn't answer, he said, "And what about you?" A kiss pressed to her forehead in that big-brother way of his that made her feel profoundly rooted. "You love so deeply, Kaia, that your heart breaks into a million pieces when you lose someone. How will you survive him if the experiment fails?"

Kaia laid her head against her cousin's chest, allowed herself to be enveloped in the warm comfort of his arms. "I don't know." It came out a broken sound. "I don't know if I will survive him."

Bo wasn't simply a lover.

He was Kaia's.

And she was his.

Chapter 47

Life cuts us. A million bloody slices.

—Adina Mercant, poet (b. 1832, d. 1901)

BO TUGGED KAIA away from the atrium an hour later to steal a kiss . . . and to try to erase the faint sadness that had lingered in the back of her eyes since she'd returned from speaking with Edison. "What's the matter?" he asked.

Huge brown eyes looked up at him. "I have a secret." It was a bald statement. "It's a bad one and I'm scared to tell you."

He didn't misread what she meant. "Nothing you say could ever change how I feel about you."

Swallowing hard, his tough Kaia with the marshmallow heart said, "Give me a little more time?"

"Take all the time you need," he whispered.

Her eyes shone wet for an instant but she blinked away the tears and they danced in their quiet, secret place as if time weren't racing forward toward an unknown future.

Her cousins were gone by the time they got back to the atrium.

"Damn it." Bo looked around, spotted a distinctly ruffled-looking

Seraphina—her curls were a mess and she didn't appear to have much lipstick left. "How long ago did they leave?"

The assistant station commander blinked. "A couple of minutes maybe." Breathy voice, her hand pressed to her chest.

"Which exit pool?"

"Um"—Seraphina smiled dreamily—"I think he said three."

Dropping Kaia's hand, Bo began to run. "Back soon!" he yelled over his shoulder and, from the burst of laughter that washed over his senses, his siren knew exactly why he was running like a madman.

He was glad for his foolishness if it had made her forget the sadness.

His heart pounded, that mechanical piece of him keeping exact time as he dodged around the startled changelings in his path. And the coolly strategic part of him thought—*this heart is better than my old one*. It could last longer at higher rates of activity. It'd give him a physical advantage once he was back to full strength.

But it remained a heart. His heart. A *human* heart.

The mechanics didn't change the blood that ran through it, or the mind of the man in whose body it was integrated.

Now it pumped with smooth efficiency as he pelted down the bridge to habitat two, the sea flashing by on either side. A large being swam alongside him for a while, its eye appearing intensely curious. Before Ryūjin, he'd have thought it impossible to read the gaze of a creature of the deep. Now he knew nosy fish who liked to poke about outside the window to his room and who he swore laughed when they startled him by appearing without warning. As for his current companion . . .

A fucking hammerhead shark! Who here was a shark? Or was it someone from the city above?

He ignored the extraneous thoughts as he crossed the bridge to habitat three and exploded into the habitat proper. Kaia and the Kahananui men were cousins, not siblings, but they all displayed a similar mischievous playfulness. Even Taji, the acknowledged grump of the group, had gleefully snuggled Seraphina, then informed Oleanna—with utmost solemnity—that he didn't stir out of bed for anything less than ten tentacles.

It solidified Bowen's suspicions about Kaia's animal, but he needed proof.

However, the doors to the exit pool had already closed by the time he arrived. A red light flashed above to alert him that the doors had locked and wouldn't open until exit was achieved. He pressed his face to the transparent material. Though the water of the pool lapped strongly against the edges, there was no sign of the men.

Discarded jeans and T-shirts littered the benches to the left of the pool.

Since those clothes had all fit the men, they'd either had them in storage on Ryūjin all along—or they'd somehow swum down with them. BlackSea changelings had to have come up with ways to carry a change or other items; otherwise, they'd have to build clothes-and-money caches along every shoreline.

Spinning away from the pool, Bo ran to the closest seaward wall, having calculated exactly where the men would come out once they exited the habitat. But he was too late. Water rippled in the lights from the habitat and he caught the silvery flash of a sleekly powerful creature moving up above, but it was only the slightest glimpse and nowhere near enough to confirm or deny his guess.

Groaning, he leaned down with his hands on his thighs and tried to catch his breath. His heart thundered, but it was holding strong. It was the rest of his post-coma body that wasn't impressed with his sudden headlong run.

"They'll drive you crazy," a male voice said.

Bo wasn't startled, having sensed George walking up to him. "I'm starting to get that feeling," he said before rising to his full height and turning to face the thin male.

For once, the dour-faced man was smiling. "It's a game the Kahananuis play," he said, "not telling people their other self. They do it to unfamiliar clanmates, too."

Bo took in George's face and body and could come up with no creature he might resemble. "Will you answer about your own other self if I ask?"

A sly smile. "No, I like it to be a secret, too." Something in the way he spoke made Bowen pause, but when George simply stared out at the water with a half smile that shouted wonder, he shook off the sensation. Clearly, Dr. Kahananui's assistant enjoyed being inscrutable as much as Kaia liked being mischievous.

BlackSea's motto should be: *Secretive R Us.*

EXACTLY forty-four hours later and Bo was sick to the pit of his stomach. "You're sure?" he said to Cassius and Lily.

They both nodded. "Orders definitely came from Heenali." Cassius's grim voice. "Lily was able to track the calls the Fleet captains say they received. All were from her direct line."

"Any chance a skilled hacker could have hacked her codes?" Bo struggled to believe that Heenali would scupper their alliance with BlackSea—what possible reason could she have for such a massive betrayal?

And the missing Hugo was a hacker who'd lied once already.

Bowen felt disloyal to Kaia for considering that option, but he *had* to consider it. Hugo was an unknown to him, while Heenali was a trusted friend and compatriot.

"The captains were adamant it was her voice on the line, her way of speaking." Cassius folded his arms across his chest. "We have to find her, ask her."

"Yes." It was the least she deserved. "You lost track of her in Ireland?"

"Last fix was a place called Cork. She must've discovered the tracker and gotten rid of it."

"And she's too smart to give herself away by using electronics that can be tracked, or tapping her accounts," Lily pointed out. "She might have cash but it's more likely she's using an unregistered card."

The latter wasn't a problem in itself—they *all* had unregistered cards, a safety feature that had sprung up in the aftermath of the previous leadership's betrayal. Lily herself had helped Bowen and the knights skirt the registration system, but she was scrupulous about never knowing any details that could be used to track those cards.

Their whole point was to turn the runner into a ghost.

"Track her ex," Bo ordered. "Only reason Heenali probably hasn't already found him is because she's trying to do it on her own." Heenali had many skills, but she was no expert in Lily's field. "We find him, we find her."

Lily picked up an organizer. "I know where he stayed while in Venice. I should be able to unearth a financial trail."

After ending the troubling conversation with Lily and Cassius, Bo went directly to his scheduled appointment with Dr. Kahananui. She proved to be cautiously optimistic. "The changes are progressing exactly as modeled. I feel comfortable in saying the third injection will permanently stabilize the chip."

"What about my brain?"

"It could still go either way."

Bo shoved his hands through his hair and stared at the ground before getting to his feet. "Thank you, Doctor." There was only one place to go, only one person he wanted to see.

Kaia took one look at him and tugged him into a quiet corner of her busy kitchen. "What did Attie say?"

He told her, then said, "I haven't spoken to my parents yet." A lack that tore at him. "I figured they'd already mourned me once. Why give them hope when it could all be over in three more days? Two, since I won't have much time on that last day."

The lack of time was a freight train rushing at him.

Kaia searched his face. "Talk to them," she said softly. "Last time, it was an act of violence that brought you to the edge of death. This time around, you've taken hold of your own destiny—and your parents know their son, will understand the choice you've made." Her hand, warm and strong, pressing against his cheek. "If I could speak to my parents again, even if only for a single minute, I'd take it."

The raw hunger in her voice shattered Bo. Enfolding her in his arms, he held her until one of her assistants called for her.

Kaia told her younger clanmate she'd be there in a moment, then kissed Bo sweet and infinite. "You need this, too. Go, talk to them."

Bo contacted Lily first, so she could warn Leah and Jerard Knight. Five minutes later, he took a deep breath and placed his call. Smiles cracked two grief-worn faces. Their joy was piercing, their sadness a punishing heartbreak, and their pride in his choice to be used as an experiment an open thing.

Bo was who he was because of these two people who'd raised him to honor his commitments and fulfill his promises. He should've known they'd stand with him in this as they'd stood with him for every other choice he'd made.

That done, he spent most of the day going over everything Lily and Cassius had found to date, and comparing it against the dossier that Malachai had quietly sent him. He had to admit it—Hugo had been right in what he'd pointed out about the Fleet movements. There were too many incursions for it to be accidental, and at least two lined up with vanishings.

Fuck.

He had no answers by the time night fell in the habitat, but he talked over what he did have with Kaia, without mentioning Heenali's name. If she didn't know, she couldn't be torn between her loyalty to BlackSea and what she felt for Bowen.

"It's so hard, isn't it?" she said, a black anger in her eyes. "When the betrayal comes from within?"

"Fucking hurts more than any bullet I've ever taken."

A raised eyebrow. "How many bullets have you taken?"

He told her, relating the story behind each one. In return, she shared how, as a trainee chef, she once gave herself third-degree burns on the insides of her forearms because she refused to drop a perfectly baked cake. After that, they moved on to other memories, other pieces of themselves, desperately trying to fit a lifetime within the screamingly short time left to them.

ELEVEN a.m. the next day and very conscious he had only forty-five hours before the third injection and an uncertain future, Bowen went looking for Kaia again. Up since five a.m., he'd already spoken with Lily and Cassius not only about Heenali but about contingency plans should the experiment fail.

He'd written out a step-by-step strategy for the two.

After grudgingly agreeing to step into the breach, Cassius had said, "I'll fuck it up. Doesn't matter how many notes you give me. I've got the subtlety of a hammer when it comes to politics."

"You just need to hold the Alliance together until the knights find a viable replacement."

"I'll fight to the bitter end, but we both know the Alliance will fragment without you." The clear gray of his friend's eyes held no judgment, only hardheaded reality. "You're the glue, Bo. You've always been the glue."

The idea of all their brutally hard work crumbling to dust, leaving humanity without any champion, it was crushed gravel in his lungs. Refusing to believe that it was the only possible outcome, he'd spent three hours talking Cassius through the most critical of the myriad things his friend would need to know should the worst come to pass.

Now, his time was his own and he wanted to spend it with Kaia. She wasn't in the kitchen, but he spotted Seraphina in the atrium. "Have you seen Kaia?"

"Sorry, can't help." A narrow-eyed glance. "But you're doing good, Security Chief. Keep on looking after my girl and we'll get along fine."

Holding those words close after the assistant station commander walked off, Bowen was considering in which direction to mount his search when he found himself the focus of a familiar set of hazel eyes. "George."

The other man bristled. "You and Seraphina? I thought you had respect for Kaia."

"What?" Bo frowned. "She's Kaia's friend and she almost-maybe likes me, that's it." He took in George's blotchy face and raised shoulders. "You have feelings for her?" If so, he'd left his pursuit too late—Kaia had mentioned Edison meeting Sera out in the deep yesterday. The other man had been in full courting mode.

Flushing, George shook his head. "Seraphina is too much woman for me." Utter puppy-love adoration in his tone.

"Women," Bo said, "they twist a man up."

George turned to stare out into the black. "Everyone's saying she kissed Edison Kahananui. Is it true?"

"Yeah." Bo figured the man might as well have all the information. "I'm sorry."

Face falling, George sat down at a table. Bo wasn't sure quite what to do, but he couldn't leave the dejected changeling alone. He grabbed a couple of coffees from the kitchen, then came to sit with George. They didn't speak, but neither did George tell him to get lost. It was maybe half an hour later that Dr. Kahananui's assistant stirred. "I have to go do . . . something."

Bo watched him leave, lines furrowing his brow. "Does George have many friends on the station?" he asked KJ a minute later, when the other man sauntered over to say hi.

"I totally tried, man, but George is a lone-wolf type." The orderly shrugged. "He's welcome to join any table at dinner or to turn up to group swims and walks, whatever—I mean, you joined the basketball game in the central habitat—no stress, right, but George mostly, like, holes up in the lab."

That was all true. Bo hadn't realized a game was about to begin when he went to the central habitat for a run, had been cheerfully assigned to a team when he stopped on the edge of the court.

"I figure he's just one of us who likes to be alone." Finishing up his coffee, KJ reached in his pocket and pulled out a stick of gum. "Duty calls. Catch you later."

Bo raised a hand in reply, then restarted his hunt for Kaia. Fate was laughing at him—he eventually backtracked to find her in the lab, having an early lunch with her cousin.

When a tiny bell rang just as he entered, he detoured to scoop Hex up from the maze. Stroking the mouse's silky white fur, he carried Kaia's pet over to where Dr. Kahananui and Kaia sat on opposite sides of a lab bench.

The doctor had a large organizer beside her, data scrolling through it.

Angry at the gods for all the things he couldn't yet say to his siren, he went around the counter and murmured, "Hi, Kaia." Then he stole a kiss that was all tongue and possession and need.

Breath short, she smiled against his lips. "Have some respect. Hex is watching."

"He's a worldly mouse." Wrapping his arms around her from behind after putting Hex into her pocket, he held her close and tried not to crush her with his possessive need.

Something buzzed into the silence.

Throwing a quick glance at her mobile comm, Dr. Kahananui touched the answer key. "Tansy? I have you on speak—"

"Atalina, someone's smashed all our Beta Seventeen samples!" a distraught female voice interrupted.

Chapter 48

> This isn't personal and it says nothing of my admiration for you. I'm also sorry that Bowen Knight will pay a deadly price for this—no human has ever harmed me, and Bowen has always treated me with respect. But it must be done. The debt must be paid.
>
> —Note slipped under the door to Dr. Atalina Kahananui's personal quarters

KAIA COULDN'T BELIEVE the carnage she saw inside the massive lab in habitat three. Unlike Atalina's lab, this larger one was built against a seaward wall; it had been decided that as the people who worked here had to stay inside for hours at a time, with no quick access to an atrium, it was too much to ask them to do so devoid of the visible presence of the ocean.

To the right side of the huge space, beyond a transparent but hermetically sealed wall, were growing bins, many of which supplied the fresh-goods needs of those who lived on Ryūjin. The area even boasted dwarf fruit trees that thrived under the light of the artificial sun.

But Kaia's attention wasn't on the growing area, a place that was often a calm and contemplative retreat for her fellow clanmates. Run by Tansy in her role as the station's chief agri-scientist, the lush, green space was a stark contrast to the antiseptic whiteness of the lab that occupied the left half of the area.

This was where the station's scientists ran experiments on materials recovered from the sea, all of it designed to teach BlackSea about the properties of those unknown compounds. Unusual seaweeds, exoskeletons discarded during a molt, secretions found on rocks, those were the types of things that made it to this lab.

Atalina did grow a few cultures in her own lab, but for the most part, she used the communal facilities here. Tansy stood on this end of a large rectangular table clearly marked with the title *Beta Seventeen*, the two women's names beneath that.

Kaia's friend was crying.

She went to move toward her, but Tansy's pain seemed to jolt Attie out of her own shock. Walking over, she wrapped the other woman in a maternal embrace. "We have the data," she said in a firm voice. "This is only a small setback."

Astounded at her cousin's courage in being able to say that when this represented the destruction of *years* of painstaking work, Kaia took a quick moment to send off a message to Dex. Atalina would need her mate in the minutes and hours to come.

Then Kaia just stared at the damage. It was as if an enraged attacker had taken a hammer to the curved glass jars—miniature habitats—in which Atalina and Tansy had nurtured various items. Invisible bacteria. More solid seaweed. Each in an enclosed glass environment that mimicked nature or provided an acceptable alternative.

The Beta Seventeen experiment offered the hope of a cure for a disease even the most advanced medicine and their own healers couldn't fix. A rare disease suffered by only a tiny percentage of the world's population, and nothing, *nothing* that could cause such hostility.

Yet shards of glass glinted on the surface of the table, sand and water and soil and agar having spilled across it to drip down to the floor. "This is five years of work," Kaia murmured to Bowen. "Five years of excruciatingly complex and delicate work. Atalina came up with the idea, but Tansy's been in from the ground up."

"Does it have anything to do with this?" He tapped the side of his head.

"No. It's a secondary project for both of them—they spent hours of their free time on it, including weekends and holidays."

"Careful." Bowen snapped out his arm to stop the three of them from moving forward any further. "There's glass all over the floor."

Only then did Kaia look down and notice the danger. She was wearing shoes today, but they weren't hard-soled. The same applied to Tansy and Attie.

"The data's backed up?" Bowen asked, his hard gaze taking in everything around them.

"Yes, but this is a continuous project. It took time to get each of these environments, cultures, and plants to the stage that they were. Tansy can't make them grow faster without compromising the study."

Tansy sniffed back her tears. "But we'll start again, won't we, Attie? This is too important to abandon."

"We'll ask Eddie to bring in new samples of the things he found for us."

"And Greta." Wiping away the wet on her face, Tansy stuck her hands into the pockets of the large gray cardigan she wore instead of a lab coat. "She's in the area."

As the two women continued to discuss how to restart the project, Kaia gritted her teeth, her blood hot. "We need to find out who did this," she muttered to Bo. "There are no strangers on Ryūjin. We are *ohana*!" *Family.* "But what possible motive could drive one of us to such malicious destruction?"

Bo knew what it meant to work hard—to have all that work so callously wiped out was an insult and a crime. Unlike Kaia, however, he thought not about the why but about the how. The only access was through the door—Dr. Kahananui had scanned him and Kaia in. People couldn't just walk inside anytime they pleased. "Where do you store the records from your entry systems?"

Kaia's eyebrows drew together over her eyes. "What?"

Realizing he was asking the wrong person, he said, "I need to talk to Malachai." He took out his phone, input Malachai's direct code.

The BlackSea security chief's voice was curt when he answered. "You're calling from an unidentified number."

"It's Bo. I've got Kaia, Dr. Kahananui, and Tansy with me."

"What's happened?"

Soon as Bo told him, the other man knew exactly why Bo had called. "Ryūjin is too far down for the security data to be automatically backed up in the city," Malachai said. "We do the data transfer manually week by week. All information for today's entries will be in the security station in habitat four."

"Thank you." For trusting Bo to watch out for BlackSea.

"Don't thank me yet." A grim tone. "It's not as if you even know where you are in the ocean—not much of a risk on my part to give you the information, and with Dex needing to be with Attie, you're the most qualified to handle this. Ryūjin's not exactly a hotbed of crime—no reason for me to station a security team there."

Despite Mal's pragmatic words, Bo knew they both understood the importance of this.

He hung up half a minute later, after memorizing Mal's instructions on how to access the security station. When he informed Kaia about his next step, she put her hands on her hips. "I didn't even know we *had* a security station."

"It's a security chief's job to be sneaky." He tapped a finger on her nose just to see her scrunch it up and scowl at him, sadness no longer a dark whisper in her expression. "I'm going to look at the footage. Want to come with me?" Three others had just entered the laboratory—and all three were walking over to Dr. Kahananui and Tansy, their eyes huge and their faces pale.

"I'll stay." Tansy had stabilized after the discussion with Dr. Kahananui, revealing a steely backbone underneath her fragile exterior—not a woman who'd run headlong into danger, but Bowen wouldn't count her out if anyone threatened people she cared about.

Tansy might cry as she did it, but she'd shoot an attacker dead all the same. And she'd definitely help Kaia bury bodies if required.

Bo liked her.

"I'll put on protective gear," she said now, "and start cleaning up this mess."

"I'll help."

Tansy shook her head at Dr. Kahananui. "I'll only worry about the baby if you do. Let me handle it—and here come Bettina, Piri, and Kianmei. You know they'll pitch in."

The door opened again before the doctor could answer, Dex rushing in. Only once in his arms did Dr. Kahananui allow herself to release a shaky breath and surrender to someone else's strength.

Deciding the lab was safe enough at present—whoever had done this had wanted to damage things, not people, plus Dex had a vicious look in his eye that said he'd butcher anyone who came near his mate and her friend—Bo led Kaia outside, then over the bridge into habitat four.

She stayed unusually quiet throughout. Hex had scrambled up to her shoulder in the lab and now rubbed his nose against the side of her neck, as if sensing her turbulent emotions.

Bo couldn't help it. He lifted her hand to his mouth, pressed a kiss on her soft skin. "I know it's bad," he said. "But your cousin's tough and determined and now that she's past the first shock, Tansy's looking to how they can salvage the experiment."

"It's not actually the destruction that's the worst thing." Kaia closed her fingers around his own. "Attie and Tansy are too focused on the work to see it, but they will. It'll make the whole situation a million times worse."

"You—and they—must know the person who did it." It was the only possible scenario, taking into account Ryūjin's isolation and the security features of the lab.

"Yes." Kaia's voice shook. "We are who we are because we are *one*. We are BlackSea."

Bo's cold rage grew even colder at her distress. "We'll find the culprit. I bet he or she has no idea Ryūjin has a surveillance system."

The security station was located in an unassuming little room that said *Maintenance* on the door.

Kaia narrowed her eyes at the sign. "Why is Mal hiding the security station from us?"

"For exactly this reason." Bo took a quick glance around to make sure they weren't being observed before he opened the door and ushered Kaia in, then followed. "If no one knows it exists," he said, shutting them inside what seemed to be a fairly standard maintenance room, with brooms, repair kits, and other supplies stacked up neatly on metal shelves, "no one can come erase or compromise the data."

"I assume that data isn't stored in a broom."

Grinning at the arch question, Bo used a screwdriver from a maintenance kit to unscrew a specific panel on the floor. A small keypad glowed up at him, the light a thick, hazy green that wouldn't penetrate the panel.

He input the override code Malachai had given him and, when prompted, a second code that confirmed his authorization to enter. That done, he closed the panel back up so it appeared to be just another part of the floor. One of the walls unlatched five seconds later, complete with the shelving unit attached to it.

A small tug and the space was wide enough for Bowen to slip through, Kaia at his back. She gasped at the tech within, all of it humming and bright with lights. "Who in Ryūjin runs this? Is *everyone* keeping secrets?" A furious whisper. "We're meant to be a family!"

"Entire thing is autonomous," Bo told his fiery siren. "It's only here in case of an emergency—like if one of you lost your mind and committed a murder. The person who came in to investigate would have a starting point."

Kaia's glower didn't appreciably decrease. "Security chiefs have suspicious minds."

"Hazard of the job." He found the log he needed. "Here we go—today's list of entries into the lab." Entry was via a retinal scan paired to a palm print, with the resulting scan cross-referenced to an individual on Ryūjin. Each of those individuals was represented by a four-digit ID number rather than their name. Pretty standard for a backend system like this.

Skimming the list, he pointed to the screen. "See that entry that's the fifth from the end? That should coincide with Dr. Kahananui's personnel number." Four others had entered after them and each of the scientists had come in alone, the door closing at their backs before anyone else could slip in. To enter, every one of them would've needed to place their palms on the scanpad and pass the retinal scan.

Last had been Dex, who, as station supervisor, must have an override to every room on Ryūjin—including this one. The station commander had to know the security station was here; Malachai wouldn't be doing his job if he kept Dex in the dark. Which likely meant Seraphina also knew.

Bo decided not to mention that to Kaia right then. He'd wait until her blood wasn't so hot and she could accept that Sera's position on Ryūjin meant she had to keep certain things confidential, even from her closest friends.

"Yes, that's Attie's Ryūjin ID number," Kaia said now. "3333, hard number to forget." A frown in her voice when she added, "But we went in with her and the system has no way of tracking that."

"I don't think that'll matter with our saboteur—one traitor I can accept, but a pair working in concert pushes things." After printing out the list, he pulled up the master list of personnel ID numbers and put a name next to each entry.

Dex's, appropriately enough, was 1111.

"There's Tansy five hours ago," Kaia murmured. "She usually takes a quick ten-minute peek each morning at how things are progressing before heading over to the growing bins. That's her entering again just before she called Atalina."

There were only three entries after Tansy's morning inspection and before her recent reentry. "Anyone who doesn't belong?" he asked Kaia.

"I don't know what George was doing there—he's not involved in that study. He must've been looking for Atalina or Tansy. The other two are the most senior scientists on the station. Atalina's their protégée and they're like proud papas. They'd never harm her work."

Bo didn't have as much faith in human nature, but what he did have was evidence. "Those two also entered and exited within seconds of one another. And they would've noticed the damage if it had been there when they arrived." Which left only one possibility. "We need to talk to George."

Chapter 49

Demons, monsters, nightmares.
Three dread horsemen of the abyss.

—Adina Mercant, poet (b. 1832, d. 1901)

"GEORGE?" KAIA SHOOK her head. "No, he wouldn't do that to us."

Us. Family. Ohana.

"It's possible someone slipped in behind him and managed to stay concealed until after he left," Bo said, though that was stretching the realm of possibility. The lab was open-plan, with no useful pools of shadow.

"Do you have any idea where he is now?" Bo was already scanning the security system in case it held the answer to his question, but the surveillance cameras only covered a limited number of critical areas. Likely because the station was home to hundreds of people and Malachai hadn't wanted to spy on them.

There was a fine line between protection and autocratic control.

Arms folded, Kaia said, "If it *was* George and he's decided to destroy Attie's research work, then the next step would be her personal lab."

They left the security station with the same stealth they'd used to enter it, and made their way quickly to Dr. Kahananui's laboratory. The door had locked automatically when they left, and Kaia scanned them in. "Who has access to this lab?" Bo asked.

"Other than Dex and Sera—Atalina, George, Tansy, and me." Kaia glanced around the lab. "I have entry privileges because Attie forgets to eat. Makes it easier if I can just walk in with a tray for her."

Bo took in the scene.

Nothing had been smashed up, nothing destroyed.

Going to the back of the lab, Kaia placed her palm against a scanpad. "It runs on the same security protocol as the door," she explained.

Which meant the same people had access.

The scanpad went green, was followed by a small snick of sound. Bending, Kaia opened the door to the medical cooler in which Bo assumed Dr. Kahananui kept samples or chemicals.

"It's all gone." Kaia shut the door on those oddly toneless words.

"What?"

She strode to the computer instead of answering. "I have access," she muttered. "Attie wanted me to be able to get her any data she needed if she was put on bedrest for the last part of her pregnancy. In-station connections can get iffy at times."

"Why not ask George?"

"Even Attie isn't pragmatic enough to want any man but Dex in her bedroom while she's in her pj's."

The screen cleared and Kaia began to work.

The blood drained from her face moments later. "The data's been erased." Fisted hands, white lines bracketing her mouth. "We have to fix this."

"She'll have backups," Bo reminded her. "Mal told me about the weekly manual backups. Dr. Kahananui will only have lost a few days' worth of data."

"*George* was the one in charge of the manual backups." Gritting her teeth, she drew in a short, hard breath. "He could've filled the data packets with anything he wanted. No one upside would have any idea. They don't look at the information—they just check to make sure it hasn't been corrupted."

Shit.

"How long has George been working for Dr. Kahananui?"

"Three years. Attie trusted him with everything. She had no reason *not* to trust him."

Right now, Bo didn't care about George's motives. "He can't have gotten far." Not with data crystals and whatever he'd taken from the cooler—and Bo had a bad feeling about exactly what the other man had stolen. "He took the compound?"

"Every last ounce."

Brain already running with ice-cold precision, Bo put his hands on his hips. "The submersibles come up and down on a regular schedule. If he's caught one, he'll be stuck inside. Or, he's still on the station."

But Kaia was shaking her head. "George is extremely comfortable in the black—I think he'd live there permanently if he could do his scientific work in the wet. All he would've had to do was put everything into a pressure-proof container and swim out."

"Dr. Kahananui was able to flash all the screens around the station with my name when she was looking for me," he said. "Do you know how to activate that system?"

Kaia showed him a symbol on her cousin's computer. "All senior personnel have access to it, including me." Logging out her cousin, she logged herself in so that her profile image would show up alongside the text. "What should I say?"

"Ask if anyone's seen George." People liked being helpful if your query was a neutral request that didn't force them to take sides. "Say it's critical you find him and pass on some news."

Kaia's phone buzzed only seconds after she sent the message. "Oleanna, you've seen George?" she said, putting the call on speaker so Bo could hear the other woman's answer.

"You'll have to wait for him to surface—I spotted him at one of the exit pools. He had a case with him, like he was going up to the city. I hope the news isn't too bad."

"He's not going to surface on Lantia," Kaia said after Oleanna hung up; she gripped the back of Dr. Kahananui's chair with one hand, her bones pushing up against the warm hue of her skin. "I don't want to believe it, but for whatever reason, George has deliberately sabotaged years of work."

Bo zeroed in on the most important fact. "I know the compound is rare, but can BlackSea source enough for the final injection?" At least the third injection gave him a chance at life, even if that chance was a mere five percent—a chance to take the Alliance into the future, to be there for his friends and family, but most of all to love his siren and find out who he could become with her laughter in his life.

Without the compound, the likelihood of death was a hundred percent.

Pressing her palm to his chest, Kaia curled her fingers into his shirt. "Even if we could source the compound, George has erased the complex distillation process it took Attie weeks to work out."

Bo closed his hand over hers, and he wondered if she'd always have that habit of listening to his heartbeat with her palm. "I thought it was a wholly natural product."

"It is, but only part of it is active. Attie had to figure out a way to separate that active ingredient from the rest—undistilled, the compound is a glowing blue sludge so thick it'd overwhelm your brain." She pushed back a lock of his hair that had fallen across his forehead. "It took Attie something like two hundred iterations to find the solution."

"How much of that will she have in her head? Could she reconstruct it?"

"Attie's brilliant, but we're talking minor changes in temperature, measurements in micrograms, times down to the second." Nails digging into his chest. "No one could repeat that entire process in under two days—but she'll break herself trying if she finds out what's happened."

And Dr. Atalina Kahananui had already miscarried three babies, was only days away from delivering a healthy child. *Fuck.* "Then we find George," Bo said flatly. "Dex will have to cover for us, make sure Dr. Kahananui doesn't learn the truth."

Kaia got a gleam in her eye. "I'll tell him to loop in our healer, get *him* to put her on strict bedrest, no work permitted. It'll drive her stir-crazy, but she'll be safe."

"What about the scans she's been taking of my brain? Won't it concern her to not have those prior to the final op?"

"No, she has all the data she actually needs—she told me she was being overcautious with monitoring you because you're the first recipient of the compound."

"Good. Let's figure out how to fix this."

Her hand trembled. *"Bo."*

Shaking his head, he squeezed her hand. "We can't think about anything but success." Even if the clock was counting down louder and louder with every second that passed.

Kaia's jaw worked, but she nodded.

"Is there a financial value to what George stole?" They needed a starting place, a way to track the thin man with pale hazel eyes. "Could George sell the research to an unscrupulous pharmaceutical company, for example?"

"I wouldn't think so. Attie and Tansy's research is in the early stages and the reason the disease hasn't really been studied is that not enough people have it. No possibility of mass-market profits."

Taking Hex out of her pocket, she absently stroked her pet. "But, having said that, the disease affects proportionately more humans than Psy or changelings." No accusation in her tone, just thoughtfulness. "Do you think it might be the same person who told your ships to breach our waters and take our people?"

"Two weeks ago, I'd have said a categorical no, but now I have no idea what the fuck is going on." He rubbed both hands over his face, trying to figure out why Heenali or anyone else would want to steal an incomplete cure to a rare disease and coming up blank.

"It doesn't make sense, does it?" Kaia leaned the side of her body against his, the heat of her soaking through his clothing to caress him deep within. "The same applies to the compound. Attie was already giving it to you—what use is it to anyone before the experiment is complete and we know the outcome?"

Weaving his fingers into her hair, the scent of coconut and tiare flowers teasing his nose, Bo went to press his lips to her temple in an act of need as much as an attempt to comfort, when the door opened and Seraphina walked in. The assistant station supervisor held a piece of notepaper. "You're looking for George?" she asked Kaia, deep grooves forming on her forehead.

"He's gone out an exit pool." Kaia put Hex in her pocket but didn't move from Bowen's side. "Why?"

"I just found this exceptionally odd note slipped under the door to my quarters—went back to grab a forgotten organizer and it was lying there."

Bowen's mind flashed to those silent minutes with George this morning as he ran his eyes over the note Seraphina passed across to Kaia.

Dear Seraphina,

I'm conscious this is an unexpected message, but I hope you know it's from the heart. You're the most extraordinary, beautiful, and intelligent woman I've ever met. I wish I could've been a different man, a man who was good enough for you. But I'm not. And so I could never bring myself to approach you. Now there's no more time but I can't go without telling you.

I love you and I always will.

You'll hear terrible things about me after I'm gone, and some of them will be true. I've betrayed us all, but BlackSea betrayed me first. I was never protected as a clan always promises to protect. I was left to suffer on my own. Why is BlackSea helping the Alliance when it can't even help its own people?

What I'm doing, it's for our benefit. BlackSea needs to focus on itself instead of extending the hand of friendship to another race.

I never meant to be a traitor, but BlackSea made me into one. I don't know if I'll ever get to come home again, but then, I've never had a home. At least with the money I'm going to be paid for what I've taken, I'll be able to have a good life somewhere else, in a faraway ocean where I can keep my distance from those who would call themselves my people and yet have never supported me.

I'll watch for you, Seraphina. If you can forgive me, then perhaps one day we'll meet again.

Your servant,
George

Beside Bo, Kaia stared wide-eyed at her friend. "Tansy was right about George having a thing for you."

Seraphina threw up her hands. "He's barely spoken two words to me since he first set foot on Ryūjin!" Blowing a curl out of her eye, she jerked her head at the note. "What's he talking about when he says he's betraying BlackSea? What's he done?"

"Stolen things," Kaia said simply. "Can we keep this letter?"

Her friend nodded. "You need any assistance from me or Dex?"

"I think this is Malachai's domain—there doesn't appear to be any risk to Ryūjin itself." Bo had no doubts that BlackSea's security chief would brief Dex and Seraphina on what was going on, but Bo had some things he needed to say to the other man first.

Seraphina raised an eyebrow. "Careful, or I'll start to think you want my job."

"I already have the job I was born to do." He felt Kaia stiffen beside him, ran his hand down her spine in a gentling caress.

His siren was a creature of the deep, Bowen a man bound to land.

Even if he won that five percent chance at life, where would they find common ground?

Chapter 50

> "I like your island, Bebe."
> "That's because it's safe and warm. But it's not home for you, child. You're meant to fly free, a wild and laughing creature."
>
> —Bebe to Kaia (10)

FOCUSING ON THE here and now to deal with her visceral rejection of losing Bowen to the land that was his natural ecosystem, Kaia said, "Something is very wrong with George," after Sera left the room.

Bowen continued to pet her back in slow, warm strokes that made her want to cry. "That letter definitely wasn't from a cold-blooded saboteur. This sounds personal."

"I only know bits and pieces about him." Kaia had tried with George, learning the foods he liked and providing those for him as she did with all her clanmates, but he'd always maintained a wall of remoteness she couldn't cross. "The most personal thing he ever told me was that he was an orphan, too—he grew up with his mother's family as I did with mine."

Bo frowned. "Your father's family?"

"Oh, my paternal grandparents are wonderful." Kaia loved them to pieces and it had nothing to do with the fact that they'd paid for her training as a chef—no, it was because they deeply understood the artistic heart of her, the same heart as had lived in their son. "But they're older, and my father was their only child. The entire extended family decided I'd be better off growing up in an active young family."

Bo nodded. "George said nothing else?"

"I have a feeling I'm forgetting something," Kaia murmured, "but I can't put my finger on it." A frustrating will-o'-the-wisp just out of reach. "Malachai might know more. He would've run a security check before George came to work on Ryūjin."

But her cousin scowled when she told him what George had done, then read out his note to Sera. "There's nothing in George's records to hint that he might have an issue with the clan," he said, his eyes the clear sunlight of his other self and his body swaying.

Kaia didn't have to ask to know he was on a ship caught in a heavy swell.

"There's been another vanishing," Bowen said without warning.

Malachai's mouth tightened before he gave a curt nod.

Fingers trembling, Kaia lifted her hand to her mouth. She never forgot Hugo and the others, not even when she smiled, but she'd hoped they'd lose no more people to this evil. "Who?" she whispered.

"Not a clanmate you know," Mal said gently, but his next words were far harder. "They made a mistake this time around and left a witness. We have a scent."

"I don't think that's a coincidence." Bowen folded his arms, his feet set apart and his voice holding the same hard edge. "And I don't think they made a mistake."

Malachai braced himself against a swell as his eyes became even less human, his pupils nearly as light as his irises. "The ones behind this wanted me out of the way so I couldn't go after George." His shoulder muscles bunched. "Their fucking timing was perfect. I'm fast but even if I was willing to abandon our taken clanmate"—an act of which Kaia knew Malachai was incapable—"I'm not fast enough to get back to Ryūjin in time to follow George."

"Do you have anyone else who can track him through water?" Bowen asked Mal, and in that moment, they were two sides of the same coin.

One human. One changeling. Both with minds that could think with cold clarity even when in the grip of furious anger.

"Tracking through water is difficult at the best of times. It'll be impossible if George is determined not to be found. The ocean is in constant flux and water holds no footprints, keeps no traces."

"Then this is mine, Mal." Bowen held Kaia's cousin's eyes, the space between them humming with a dark masculine power. "I won't touch George if I find him, but he's holding my life and the lives of my people hostage. Even if I have to steal a fucking submersible, I won't be sitting on my hands."

Forty-three and a half hours.

Kaia's brain kept counting down, relentless and unwavering. "I'm going with Bo," she said before she could surrender to the fear that lurked always at the back of her mind.

"Kaia." Malachai shook his head. "You—"

"I'm *going.*" With her tone, she told him not to say another word, not to betray the secret she couldn't bring herself to tell Bowen. "And Bo is right—this is his *life.* If you use BlackSea's power to keep him trapped on Ryūjin, you're no better than those who are stealing our people."

Malachai flinched. "We have no confirmation he wasn't involved with the movements of the Alliance Fleet."

"You have *my word.*" She knew the truth deep inside in a way that was painful to look at, the promise there one that would never be fulfilled. But she could use that knowledge to make sure Bowen got out of Ryūjin.

Unlike most members of BlackSea, Kaia had an advantage with Malachai—she could stand up to his dominance because he let her. Older than her by three years, he was used to treating her as a younger sibling . . . and he'd been there when she'd come in, broken and lost.

He'd never hurt her.

"Kaia." It came out a growl from two male throats.

Turning, she glared at Bowen. "Stop it."

"This is my fight." His eyes flashed fire at her.

Narrowing her own, Kaia poked him in the chest. "No. It's ours."

"Shit." Wrapping an arm around her shoulders, he hauled her close. "Ours then, Siren." His next words were to Malachai. "We're going to do this with or without your authorization." Not a challenge, simple fact.

But Mal wasn't a man to back down easily. "I can get together a team that knows how to move in the water."

"Will they fight as hard to retrieve what George has taken?" Bowen demanded. "Will it mean as much to them?" Each word was a gauntlet thrown down between them.

Malachai's body jerked violently again.

"Why are you on a ship?" Kaia asked. "You're so fast in the water." *Nothing* got in Mal's way when he swam, which made him the perfect playmate for a little girl who wanted to swim to Bebe's island but was afraid to go out alone.

"Ship's a quick one and the witness is wounded and on a damaged vessel." His eyes took in the way Kaia had her hand over Bowen's heart, returned to her face.

And she saw him realize the truth, realize how she knew Bowen was no liar beyond any shadow of a doubt.

Those sunlight eyes darkened. "Lunatic," he murmured.

"It's in the genes."

Switching his attention to Bowen, Mal said, "Are you healthy enough to undertake the chase? George might look like a stick but he's very strong."

"I'm up to ninety percent of normal," Bowen answered with security chief practicality. "It'll be enough—George might be strong, but he's still a scientist."

"Do it." Mal's form swayed with increasing intensity. "I'll alert my people in Lantia that you have my authorization. Use what resources you need—and bring George back alive," he said, and it was an uncompromising demand. "He's Miane's, not yours."

"Understood."

Mal's strange, beautiful, golden eyes landed on Kaia once again. "You sure, Cookie?" An unspoken question, a hidden worry.

Though her gut churned, Kaia nodded. "Bo will need someone with him who understands how to handle the compound once we retrieve it from George."

"Will it survive outside the fridge?"

"Long enough." Because if it took them longer than just over forty-three hours to find George, the experiment was over, Bowen's life forfeit.

Chapter 51

Lily, I need this photo sent out across the Alliance network. No one is to approach this man or do him any harm. Report his location only.

—Bowen Knight to Lily Knight

"I HATE THIS, that we're hunting a friend," Kaia said after Malachai hung up and Bo had spoken to Lily about sending out an alert on George. He knew Malachai would be giving the same order to his own people.

"I know." Enfolding her in his arms, he whispered Heenali's name in her ear—Kaia had made her loyalties clear by standing with him against Mal *even knowing Bowen might soon be lost forever*, and it left Bowen shaken down to the soul.

He had to honor her faith with his own. "Heenali deserves happiness and peace after all the horror in her past," he said. "I don't want it to be her, but I won't turn my face from it if it is."

"Oh, Bo." A soft breath against his neck. "Thank you for trusting me with her."

Pulling back so he could see her face, he pressed his forehead to hers. "Forgive me, Kaia, if it all goes wrong." The bond between them might be forged of stubborn hope, but the realist part of his nature knew too well that hope alone couldn't alter fate.

"There is *nothing* to forgive." Fierce words.

Cupping her face in one hand, he just held her, held his siren with her marshmallow heart and her courage in loving him when he was her worst nightmare.

She turned, pressed her lips to his palm. "We have to get up to the surface."

"Yes." They had to be ready to move the instant George was spotted. "When's the next scheduled submersible?"

"Four hours," she said. "That's a long time for George to disappear."

Bo considered ejecting himself using an emergency capsule and asking to be hauled up, but not only would that take a lifepod out of commission, it'd shatter Ryūjin's peace—and alert Dr. Kahananui that something very bad was going on.

"I'm guessing we have time," he said after calculating all the possibilities. "If I were George, I'd swim as far as I could before coming up on shore. He's going to be counting on the fact that Malachai will be running the search—and while your people are good, they're limited to areas near oceans and other waterways."

"So is George," Kaia pointed out. "He won't be able to go too far into the dry."

"But he might deliberately head that way to shake off the scent, then swing back toward the water." He ran his hands down the sides of Kaia's body, her lightweight dress airy under his palms. "We'll both need changes of clothes. No knowing if George will head to warmth or to cold."

"I'll go pack a small bag."

Returning to his room after reluctantly releasing her, Bo did the same. As for money, he had access to his accounts via the phone.

It all took far too short a time.

With the hours ironically heavy on his hands, he strode to the window and looked out at the endless black that was his quarry's domain. Bo couldn't hunt him in the ocean. He'd have to wait for George to surface. And hope the other man didn't simply stay in the silken wet darkness.

In the Deep

GEORGE SWEPT OUT his tentacles as he moved through the water with smooth grace. Here, he could be a dancer, could be as athletic as he wanted. In human form, he was awkward and gangly and without confidence. But in the cold blackness of the water that was his true home, he was a powerful being who made others scurry away.

He smiled inside his other self, feeling whole and strong and not damaged as he was in human form. Not scarred and used up and broken.

His tentacles thrashed.

He nearly lost his grip on the case he held so tightly.

Calm, be calm, his human self whispered. *No one can touch us here.*

It was difficult at times. The most primal part of his changeling nature occasionally wanted to take over. He knew that was dangerous. But part of him *wanted* the wildness in control. The others in the clan, when he heard them talking, they all spoke about how both sides of their nature were in balance, how it was never a fight between one or the other. They didn't worry about shifting and becoming lost in the shift.

George never said anything when they talked like that; he'd learned his lesson as a child when he dared tell a long-ago friend about his fight for control. That friend had immediately told his own mother, who'd told George's mother. She'd then made him go to extra lessons meant to teach him how to manage the powerful creature inside him.

Her voice had been soft and warm as she explained it wasn't a punishment but only a thing he needed to learn for his future. Like math and science. He'd gone quietly because that was what he did, that was what made her happy.

George had loved his mother. He hadn't liked it when she cried.

But though he'd gone to the lessons, he'd tried not to learn anything the adults wanted to teach him. He'd pretended he did, but inside, he stayed the same. Because if he ever learned how to control this self, he couldn't lose himself in the black and forget the horrors that had been done to his human body.

In the water, he was free and strong and no one's victim.

In the water, he was the predator and everything else quailed in front of him.

In the water, nothing could harm him.

He smiled again, the human part of him curled up happily within the wildness of his other side. And he thought about just giving in, taking that extra step and losing himself to the wildness forever. But no, he was a scientist and he'd read enough reports to know that changelings who did that, the "rogues," inevitably went mad and began hunting their clanmates.

The latter didn't worry George. He felt very little loyalty toward those who were meant to be his clan.

Except for Seraphina and Dr. Kahananui and Kaia.

Dr. Kahananui had always treated him as an equal even though he was less qualified. She'd even given him the position of responsibility that allowed him to take his vengeance. He'd never want to hurt her or the innocent child she carried in her womb.

The same with Kaia. She always made a special effort to bake his favorite cake at least once every month. She didn't have to do that—there were a lot of people on the station and carrot cake wasn't as popular as chocolate or red velvet. But Kaia always said he had just as much right to her skills as anyone else. He never felt bad asking her for a burger on a day when that wasn't on the menu. She'd scowl and tell him she was busy, but then a little later, the burger would turn up on his desk.

Kaia was nice in a deep-inside way. He wouldn't want to kill Kaia in his madness, either.

As for Seraphina . . .

He thrashed again, unable to stand the idea that he might hurt her in his insanity.

So no, he couldn't give in to his primal heart. Not today, anyway.

Because the pain, it was growing inside him. Each year it felt as if it grew stronger, huger. Until he could no longer escape it. Maybe when that happened, he'd stop fighting. Maybe he'd forget Seraphina and Kaia and Dr. Kahananui.

Maybe he'd become this creature, magnificent and dangerous.

And because he didn't want to be human again, he kept on swimming. The ones to whom he'd sold his spoils could wait. They could all wait.

He would come up in his own good time.

Chapter 52

Fear is an intruder in your life, child. You must cast him out.

—Bebe to Kaia (17)

KAIA'S HEART THUNDERED when the submersible finally docked with Ryūjin. "I'm only going up to Lantia," she told herself silently, but her mind knew this was the first step on the road to a nightmare.

"Hey." Bowen's hand closing around hers, warm and strong. "The doc is doing fine. I just spoke to Dex."

Kaia smiled tightly and nodded, not ready to tell him that her fear was her own and that it was an aged and knotted thing with roots sunk into her soul. Waiting until the passengers from Lantia had disembarked—and after exchanging hugs with more than one—Kaia forced herself over the threshold.

Bowen prowled in behind her; the stronger he got, the more he reminded her of some sleek hunting creature. This man would always be a demanding lover—but oh, his capacity to give was a vastness that enfolded her in affection and an emotion to which she wasn't ready to give a name.

"Where's Hex?" he asked, settling down beside her.

"With Tansy." She'd kissed Hex good-bye and told him to be good for her friend. "I moved his house to her quarters. That's how he knows he's supposed to stay with her until I get back."

"Mouse genius."

Kaia couldn't smile, but it was all right. Bowen was distracted by watching their departure from the station, his attention on the procedure so acute that she knew he was storing it all away in his brain just in case he ever needed the information.

They were the only two in the autonomous submersible, but Kaia knew they weren't the only station dwellers heading cityward. When she spotted movement through the windows on the other side, she touched Bowen's shoulder and said, "Look."

His muscles moved under her hand as he turned. Bowen was fascinated by everything in the deep, laughed when an octopus touched its suction pads against a window for a second. "Oleanna?"

"Yes. She told me she's swimming up to surprise Tevesi." Kaia wasn't sure her cousin had any idea what he was in for.

Bowen kept watch for other visitors, but stayed pressed up alongside her, his body thrumming with tension.

Thirty-nine hours.

Fighting to shut down that voice with its ominous countdown, Kaia leaned her head against his shoulder. "Tell me a story about your childhood," she said. "A happy one."

"I've got nothing that can top kissing a lion." He laughed and it was a big, warm, *alive* thing. "But I did get chased by an angry cow once."

Kaia couldn't help but smile as he told the story, just able to imagine a wild little boy running amuck in a muddy field full of normally lazy cows. Deep inside her, however, fear continued to curl outward with tendrils as black as night.

THEY arrived in darkness, the sky above dotted with stars. Stepping onto the sprawling floating city of Lantia, Bo felt a chill wind against his skin, a taste of the winter that held this hemisphere of the planet in thrall. And though he had a hundred questions, the first thing he did was look to his phone to see if Lily had sent through any updates about George.

Nothing. No sightings.

He and Kaia headed directly toward a grim-faced woman who stood with the bearing of a soldier; this had to be the commander Malachai had said would be waiting for him. Miane was with Malachai, a sleek and dark shadow in the water.

"Have you found your people?" he asked the commander, who reminded him strongly of someone, though he couldn't put his finger on whom.

"The wounded witness, yes," she said shortly, though her face softened when she turned her attention toward Kaia. "*Aloha*, Cookie. It's good to see you—you need to come up more often."

"*Aloha*, Aunt Geraldine." Giving Bo the lightweight box she'd carried onto the submersible along with her overnight bag, Kaia leaned forward to hug the tall and sober-faced woman.

The resemblance clicked.

The commander's dark eyes had an edge of sunlight to them.

"I had just enough time to bake your favorite muffins." Kaia took the box from Bo, held it out.

Commander Geraldine Rhys smiled and shook her head before pressing a kiss to Kaia's forehead, her hands rising to cup Kaia's face. "The same old Cookie." Afterward, she set the box of muffins carefully aside on a nearby stack of small shipping containers that were still wet on the sides—either from being recently offloaded, or because a rogue wave had crashed onto the massive deck that jutted out from the city.

Bo couldn't see all of Lantia from his current position, but he could tell there were sharp towers within, not quite high-rises but not exactly small family homes, either. Material that appeared to be glass dominated, though he guessed it was apt to be the same thing BlackSea had used to build Ryūjin.

There was no wood or brick, the deck under his feet apparently metal. The same type of material was incorporated into the buildings he could see—but there were no signs of rust, which told him this was another

BlackSea-developed solution to the salt water. Greenery cascaded from various balconies and on the roofs he could spot, this city supporting a thriving internal ecosystem in the middle of the ocean.

In front of him, Geraldine Rhys returned her attention to Bo. "This is BlackSea business." No trace of maternal softness in her face now. "I don't know why Malachai is letting you run it, but I promised him that I'd help. What do you need?"

"Have any of your people spotted George?"

"No." Chilly dark eyes in a face full of angular contours that made her striking. "We have excellent lines of communication, but we can't reach those who are swimming in the deep. If they see him, we'll only find out once they surface."

"Then we wait." He might be running out of time, but rushing off half-cocked would achieve exactly nothing.

"We should eat," Kaia murmured, and though she didn't say it, he knew she was thinking about his continued recovery.

He had the piercing knowledge that were she his, he'd never again miss dinner. Kaia would make sure he ate. That was what Kaia did—look after the people who mattered to her.

Her aunt nodded at her. "You know where everything is."

"Your mother was the youngest?" he asked Kaia after they were alone.

"By quite a few years. It hurt her sisters a lot when she died." Weaving her fingers through his, she smiled sadly. "Aunt Natia cried but Aunt Geri got angry. I think part of her is still angry."

"She protects her own."

"Yes, just like Mal and his father. All three of them are the same."

"She and Mal don't look alike, not really, but there's something in the presence."

"He looks more like his dad." Leading him inside, Kaia took him to what appeared to be a small break room. "Because the city's so big," she said, "it's divided into grids. Each grid has a central kitchen, but there are smaller eating and lounge areas like this scattered around."

"Communities within a community."

A true smile, one that lit up her eyes. "Exactly. The whole point of BlackSea is being one. We don't want anyone feeling isolated from the group." Her smile faded. "George did, though."

"George often chose his isolation." KJ was right in that. Even Bo, a stranger, had walked out into the atrium and grabbed a seat with different people. George, he'd noticed, had always taken his food into the lab—even when invited to join a table.

Kaia didn't reply, her expression pensive.

"Let's sit outside," he said after they'd made sandwiches and grabbed bottles of water. Kaia was a creature of the deep; he had the sense she'd feel better if she could see the ocean. "It's not every day I visit a floating city in the middle of the ocean." Lantia moved under him, the motion slight but ever-present, as if BlackSea eschewed too much physical stability. "Does this city float away at times?"

"No, it's very strongly anchored." Kaia looked around the outer deck to which they'd returned. "No chairs."

"I don't mind sitting on the ground."

Without a word, she sat down beside him, their backs to the wall and their eyes on the black stretch of open water. They ate in silence, protected from the view of any others up this late by another pile of small shipping containers. Waves crashed against the edge of the city, throwing up bits of foam, the ocean in competition with the star-studded sky.

Putting aside her plate and his, the half-drunk bottles of water beside them, Kaia shifted to kneel between his legs. And in her eyes, he saw an infinite darkness. But she didn't give him a chance to speak, to ask about the terrible sadness within. Her kiss was an invitation . . . and it was a request.

Need crashed into him, as primal and untamed as the ocean.

He could no more deny her than he could stop breathing. Weaving the fingers of one hand into her hair, he kissed his siren with the sad eyes and the lush curves and the marshmallow heart, giving her everything. They kissed until his heart pounded and his lungs protested and she was breathless.

She sat back on her haunches, her hands on his raised knees. "I still don't want to tell you my secret." A pained whisper.

The wind blew her hair forward, surrounding him in a silken wave of deepest brown threaded with black. He closed his eyes, drew in her scent. "I can wait," he said when he opened his eyes. "For you, Kaia Luna, I'll wait an eternity."

Her throat moved as she swallowed. "You don't mind?"

Bo's lips kicked up. "How could I mind?" She might not be ready to share whatever it was that she held inside, but she'd done nothing to hide its existence. "And security chiefs learn patience. It's a prerequisite for the job."

Crawling up close to him, Kaia undid the buttons of his shirt, then slid her arms around him and cuddled in, the side of her face pressed to his bare skin.

Heart an ache, he wrapped her in his embrace, her hair a warm weight over his skin. "I love your hair." The heaviness of it, its coconut and tropical flower scent, the way it fell down her back in a dark waterfall.

She traced a pattern on his chest with her finger and they sat quietly for long, still minutes while the sea crashed beyond. Nuzzling at her when he heard the distant tread of a boot, he said, "Someone's coming this way."

A soft breath, a puff of warmth. "Will you stay with me tonight?"

"Try to drag me away."

Shifting, they buttoned up enough of his shirt that he was decent, then rose and slipped away into the sleeping city. Kaia knew exactly which rooms they'd been assigned. Bo was glad to see they were side by side.

They went into hers.

As he turned after locking the door, his breath rushed out of him, his knees going week. Kaia had already stripped down to the glowing warmth of her skin, strands of her hair brushing the lush heaviness of her breasts, her nipples dark and the curls between her legs even darker.

Naked, his siren walked to him on silent feet. He stood, her prisoner, while she undid the buttons again and this time, pushed his shirt off his shoulders to crumple onto the floor. Stroking her hands up over his shoulders once more, she pressed herself against him. "Love me, Bowen."

His hands on her hips, he buried his nose in her neck, just breathed her in as he lifted without thought and turned to pin her against the door. She wrapped her legs around his waist, her hands shaping his body, her touch caressing and possessive and a branding.

"I'm yours," he said against her mouth, the wrenching he felt inside him a violent thing, as if part of him wanted to tear away and lay itself at her feet.

"Bowen." Her eyes shimmered.

It was inevitable that he'd kiss her, that he'd surrender to the need. She didn't shy. Arms locked around him, she met him kiss for kiss, a sleek, strong creature who was nothing he'd ever dared dream.

Walking backward away from the door, her body held safe against his, he managed to stumble into the bed. He fell back on it with her on top. She laughed in a sudden delight that eased the knot in his heart, before nipping at his lips and kissing her way down his throat.

Bo managed to kick off his shoes, but it was Kaia's fingers that went to his jeans. "You look uncomfortable," she said with a solemn solicitousness belied by the mischief in her eyes. "I think you'll feel better if I undo this."

Beguiled, enslaved, hers, Bo ran his hand over the smooth skin of her thigh, felt her shiver. "How about you come closer first?"

Abandoning his jeans, she leaned in, her hands braced on his shoulders. When he clasped the back of her neck and held her to him for a kiss followed by a soft bite, she melted voluptuously into his body. He moved his hands down the curves of her in a slow exploration, stopping to caress and squeeze and delicately tease every few inches.

Her breath catching, she sucked soft and wet at his throat before demanding another kiss.

Drunk on her, Bo was more than willing to give Kaia everything she wanted. Her nipples rubbed against his chest, the musk of her arousal rising to scent the air. Groaning, and knowing his control was on a razor-thin edge, he flipped their positions so she was on the bottom. And began to kiss his way down the sweet curves of her body.

"Kaia." It was a song in his heart, her name, her scent, *her.* "My beautiful Kaia."

He gave himself permission to suck on her nipples, having learned exactly what made her back bow and her skin shimmer. But he couldn't linger today; he wanted to drench her in pleasure, wanted to take a little more of the sorrow from her. Because one thing he knew: his greatest weakness now had human form.

He couldn't bear it when Kaia lost her smile.

The curve of her belly quivered under his kiss, her voice a whisper as she said his name. Determined to drown his lover in erotic sensation before his control went up in flame, he licked his way through her delicate folds, one of his hands on her inner thigh to hold her wide open for him.

Her body arched, her hands pulling on his hair. He felt her muscles clench as she came apart for him, and her trust, it was a gift he'd never take for granted.

It was as he was rising up over her, his need as frantic as hers, that the comm panel on the wall began to buzz in an urgent beat.

Chapter 53

Unusual activity spotted in quadrant delta-4. Going to investigate.

—Call-in by Rina Monaghan, DarkRiver leopards

BO HAD TO force himself from Kaia to answer the comm. He did so audio-only. "Has George been spotted?"

"Long way away," was the answer from a familiar male voice. "We have a jet waiting for you on shore." A slight pause. "I'm going to pretend I didn't have to buzz *Kaia's* room to get you."

Bo told Armand they'd be there soon, then hung up.

Returning to the bed, he brushed tangled strands of hair off Kaia's face. "We're going to have to finish this another time," he said, though his whole body ached.

Eyes stark, she tugged him down onto her. "We'll be quick."

Bowen didn't argue. He sank into her, she wrapped herself around him, and they shut out the deadly countdown for a fraction of time.

GEORGE had surfaced over four thousand miles from Lantia. It was an almost unimaginable distance for him to have traveled so quickly. He *must've* surfaced at some point to take a high-speed jet to cross over from the North Atlantic to the Pacific, though no one had spotted him. But even if he was extraordinarily fast and relentless in the ocean, on land, he became a man. And the land was Bo's hunting ground.

"San Francisco?" He couldn't believe it. "Why would he emerge anywhere near allies you might contact to capture him?"

"Because they *are* allies," Armand said, his hair tumbled by the sea breezes today but his black T-shirt perfectly fitted to his body. "The leopards won't react violently if they spot him—they might give him a pointed warning that he's meant to alert them before entering their territory, but they won't harm him."

Bo nodded, frowning. "Could also be that if he *does* have a buyer for what he's stolen, he doesn't quite trust that buyer."

"Yeah, cats would step in to help him if he asked for it, or if he appeared in distress." Armand folded his arms. "I know you want to bring him in but we can ask the cats to do it."

Bo went to agree; none of this was about ego. "I'll take whatever help I—"

"No." Kaia stepped forward. "George gets frightened easily and he's already emotionally unstable. He could destroy everything if he's scared or startled." Kaia had scared him once, quite by accident, and the resulting carnage had taken the two of them an intense hour to clean up.

Kaia had never said a word about his lack of control, getting rid of the evidence by throwing it in the kitchen recyclers, and she thought maybe that was why he'd become a touch more comfortable with her—enough to ask for a burger every so often. "All he'd have to do was shift form," she explained to Bowen and Armand. "His tentacles are capable of massive amounts of crush pressure." He'd almost wiped her out with one when he shifted so suddenly that time.

"The DarkRiver leopards are deadly, Kaia." Bowen put his hands on his hips, his eyes wholly focused on her in that way he had of doing. "They can take him."

"But will they try to take him alive if he's hurting their people?" Kaia knew the answer and so did Bowen and Armand. "He's one of ours. We have to give him a chance." George was wounded in some terrible way and Kaia understood wounds, understood that the deepest ones never stopped hurting.

The ruthless and bloodthirsty leader of the Human Alliance gave her a lopsided smile. "I bet you're going to rescue stray cats and dogs and ferrets and fill our house with them."

"Don't forget the mice," she said, playing the game, imagining the impossible dream.

He tugged lightly on her hair in punishment before turning to Armand—who wasn't doing a very good job of hiding a smirk. "How about asking DarkRiver to keep an eye on George as he moves through their territory? No approach, nothing to tip him off." The leopards were stealthy hunters while George was a scientist out of his depth.

"The commander will have to make the contact—strict protocols." Armand stepped out to find their aunt, who happened to be Lantia's commander even when Malachai and Miane were in residence. Each member of the clan had different duties, different responsibilities.

"Are all your male cousins in BlackSea's security forces?"

Kaia shook her head. "Eddie is an explorer. His job is to update our maps of the ocean floor, find interesting new things for our scientists to study, mark any spots that might provide valuable salvage." She smiled. "He found a centuries-old sunken ship full of gold bullion once. Miane's always said he can take a percentage of what he finds because of how risky his job can be, but he usually never does—that time, though, he brought each one of us a coin."

Bowen's eyes gleamed as men's always did when they found out what Edison did for a living. "He ever find any other treasure?"

"New deep-sea life forms, including a bioluminescent shrimp." Laughing at his face, both parts of her happy to simply be in his presence, she said, "Two of the triplets are in security with Armand, but Taji's an architect."

"He moves like he has training in how to fight."

"He started off in the same job as Teizo and Tevesi—I think it's the first time the triplets have diverged on something that really matters."

Bowen's eyes held hers, a sudden intensity in them. "You want children, Siren?"

Stomach clenching, Kaia dared admit one truth. "Yes. Lots of them."

"Cats are on it." Armand walked back into the room on those words, froze. "New rule. No meaningful looks across the room while I'm in the vicinity. Have some respect for those of us who are hopelessly single."

Grinning at his aggrieved tone, Kaia went over to press a kiss to his modelesque jaw. "Single, yes. Hopelessly? I don't think so." Armand's face would fit perfectly under the dictionary definition of "player." Kaia might've worried about Tansy's heart if her friend hadn't already been well aware of Armand's love-'em-and-leave-'em ways.

Regardless, Kaia had still raised the subject with her friend. She adored both Armand and Tansy too much to see either hurt.

Tansy's answer had been simple. "Sometimes, a woman has to walk on the wild side."

Bowen stirred, his lips curved, as Armand pretended to strangle her with one arm around her neck. "Cats agree to the commander's request?"

Armand gave a short nod. "They'd already spotted him by the time we called and were planning to ask him what the hell he was doing in their territory without notice, but the sentinel the commander spoke to has given the order for their people to fall back."

Running his fingers through the relentlessly straight strands of his hair after releasing Kaia, Armand carried on. "I didn't have Bo's contact details, so the commander gave them yours," he said to Kaia. "DarkRiver will keep an eye on George and send updates directly to your phone." Nothing but grimness on his face as he added, "But if George threatens to hurt anyone, all bets are off. Sentinel was very clear about that."

Bo had expected nothing less. The cats hadn't held their territory against all comers—including the lethal SnowDancer wolves—because they were in any way weak. Bo had made one of the worst mistakes of his life in their territory and he was still fixing the damage from that mess, but he had nothing but respect for both the cats and the wolves.

"According to the cats," Armand added, "George is fully dressed and carrying a large pack."

"He only left the station with a small pressure-proof case." Bo had spoken to Oleanna while waiting for the submersible, gotten the dimensions of the case George had been carrying. "Means he must've cached the other gear elsewhere."

"He's been planning this for a long time." Kaia hugged her arms around herself. "I feel like I never knew him at all, that none of us did."

Closing his hand over her nape, Bo ran his thumb in a gentle, soothing motion across her skin. "We'll find the truth soon enough."

Her pulse jumped erratically under his touch.

"Jetboat's ready," Armand said before Bo could ask Kaia if she was still worrying about Dr. Kahananui. "I sent someone to retrieve your gear." His eyes flicked to Kaia. "You ready, Cookie?"

The question seemed natural enough, but the tone . . . Bo watched Kaia's face as she answered, saw the sudden lack of color in it even as she nodded firmly. The tension beneath the surface, he realized, had nothing to do with Dr. Kahananui. This was Kaia's secret, the shape of which his brain had just barely begun to glimpse.

THE sleek silver boat cut through the water like a knife. There was *just* enough light in the very early morning sky that Bowen clearly saw an orca rise up in the distance. It dived back in in a smash of droplets.

His heart thudded. "Was that one of you?"

Kaia, her eyes focused resolutely forward and her hands fisted to bone whiteness, nodded.

Closing his arms around her from behind, Bo didn't ask probing questions, didn't demand as was his nature. Kaia had told him she wasn't ready to share her secret and he'd honor that wish, but that didn't mean he had to stop looking after her.

Her spine stayed stiff, but she lifted a hand to wrap it over his wrist, and they sliced through the water together, bodies braced against the rolling waves. Armand was piloting the boat while Teizo and Tevesi had jumped in for the ride. All three kept shooting Kaia careful looks that she studiously ignored.

Land appeared on the horizon.

Chapter 54

What I wish for you, my curious little monkey, is adventure, freedom, love. All these things and more. I want the stars for you.

—Elenise Luna to her daughter, Kaia (3)

NAUSEA THREATENED TO steal Kaia's faltering courage as she stepped out of the boat Armand had coasted all the way to shore. Her boots sank into the sand, the water close enough that she could cling to the illusion that she wasn't leaving the blue.

"You have everything?" her cousin asked, but what he was actually asking was: *You really want to do this, Cookie?*

She nodded and tightened the straps of the little pack that held two changes of clothing, a few toiletries, and a first-aid kit packed with the anti-anxiety medication Ryūjin's healer had prescribed her. "Yes," she said simply, because if she turned back now, she'd never again be able to look at herself in the mirror. "Go."

Bowen took her hand into the rough warmth of his. "I'll take care of her," he said. "I'll bring her home."

Kaia could've told all four males she was quite capable of getting home—*that* wasn't the problem—but Bowen's words made her cousins' shoulders ease, the strain disappear from their faces, so she left it.

"Good luck," Armand said before the three of them pushed out the lightweight craft, then jumped in and started up the engine.

They headed off into an ocean still shrouded in the dark gray of early morning.

While she stood on land.

Far from the safe cocoon of Ryūjin.

Swallowing hard, Kaia looked at Bowen. "Our ride will be waiting."

He nodded but took a moment to touch his fingers to her jaw. "Just hold on to me. Whatever it is that's put that look in your eyes, I'll fight it beside you every step of the way."

Kaia squeezed his hand tight.

He never let go of her as she took another step onto land, then another, and another. The thread that tied her to the ocean stretched tauter and tauter and tauter. Her stomach, it threatened to lurch. And her mind, it wanted to drown her in the horror of the last time she'd set foot on land.

It had been beside her parents' dying bodies, Kaia running to the jet-chopper as BlackSea paramedics carried her mother and father to the same gleaming machine while a healer worked frantically on them. Dust had swirled in the air, her hand locked safely in Aunt Geraldine's and her dirty summer dress twisting around her knees.

The medication stopped the nausea from becoming sickening reality, but the healer had been very strict in saying she could only take that medication for just over twenty-four hours before her system would begin to violently reject it. "It's powerful stuff, Kaia." Concern in the soft blue of eyes that had known her since she was an infant. "You shouldn't be using it to suppress your emotional hurt. You have a phobia and you need to work through it with counseling and—"

"I don't have the time." Kaia accepted the truth of the healer's words; she also knew that once Bowen left her, she'd have no more reason to ever again step on land or venture beyond the safe seas around Ryūjin and Lantia. "I just need to be able to function until we find George."

Adding to the strain on her already stretched psyche was the countdown that continued to tick in the back of her mind.

Twenty-eight hours.

But though it was his life on the line, Bowen kept on going, his concentration a laser.

So would she, Kaia vowed. Never would she give up. Never would she surrender. And never *ever* would she permit fear to steal her time with Bowen.

THE BlackSea changeling who waited for them beside a beat-up truck had skin the color of strong black coffee and nearly as many wrinkles as Bebe. He also drove like a bat out of hell, rocketing them down the potholed road that looked as if it had come straight out of the nineteenth century.

A surprisingly gleeful Kaia held on to the side of the open-topped vehicle, while Bowen fought his instinct to reach over and grab the steering wheel. The cool air whipped across his face, the weather here not exactly tropical despite the palm trees zipping past the truck.

He was almost startled to discover they were still alive when they skidded into the parking lot of an airport so tiny, it didn't even have an air traffic control tower. From what he could see, all it had was a tin-roofed shed that functioned as the administration building, snug up against a large hangar.

Bo was certain the place had far more tech than was visible to the naked eye. Teizo had let it drop that this was Lantia's preferred airfield. "Too much wear and tear on the city with the heat from the jets," the younger male had said. "Lantia's strip can accommodate all aircraft, but mostly everyone uses the island."

"Safe journey," the driver said after Bo jumped out.

"I think I've survived the most dangerous part already," Bo pointed out as he swung Kaia down to solid ground.

The driver was still cackling at Bo's response when he drove off in a whirl of dust.

Glancing at Kaia, Bowen raised an eyebrow. "He's Bebe's boyfriend, isn't he?"

Her eyes sparkled as she looked around, her face full of color once more and the stiffness gone from her spine. "It's been a long time since I was on this island. I'd forgotten how beautiful it is."

"Oh?" From what Armand had said at the start of the journey, BlackSea visitors and residents powered the island's entire economy. The only reason the roads were potholed was that repairs hadn't yet been completed after a storm a week earlier.

Lifting her face to the sky just kissed by the edge of dawn, Kaia said, "I tend to stay in the black." She took a long breath of the island air. "But I think I'll come up more often now. Sit at the bar my cousins talk about, have a cocktail or five." A kind of taut desperation in her.

And Bo wondered if she was thinking about the hours racing past.

"I'll buy you those cocktails." He kept his tone deliberately light. "And when you're drunk, I'll carry you home and tuck you in."

"Deal," she said huskily, her eyes no longer human brown but an inky black.

"I see you," he murmured.

Convulsively squeezing the hand she once more held, she nodded to the runway. "Is that our ride?"

Bowen crushed his own desperation under the weight of grim determination and took in the sleek black jet that looked as out of place on the two-lane runway as a tuxedo would in a village where everyone else dressed in shorts and Hawaiian shirts. "Fits Armand's description," he said as they entered the administration building.

A man and a woman Bo immediately tagged as pilots were hanging out inside, shooting the breeze. Another woman, this one round-faced and matronly, stood behind the counter. "Kaia!" Her hands flew to her mouth. "Girl, you could've warned me!"

Grinning in delight, Kaia dropped his hand to run over and hug the other woman.

A scruffy-jawed male leaning up against the counter a few feet from the pilots grinned along with the two of them. Dressed in grease-stained blue coveralls, he might as well have had "mechanic" painted on his forehead.

The final occupant was a good-looking young male who stood in a large doorway that had to lead to the hangar. For some reason, he made the back of Bo's neck prickle, agitated his instincts.

Dressed in blue coveralls identical to the mechanic's, he was currently frowning at a piece of metal in his hand. "Hey, Rick," he called out, his rich auburn hair streaked with grease. "I can see a crack in this. On the underside, hidden by the charring."

"Well, thank bloody Poseidon I finally have a competent apprentice. You're the first one who's passed the bloomin' test!"

Smile sharp and brilliant, the young man turned to walk back into the hangar. There was something about the way he moved that told Bo he was a changeling—but not BlackSea. No one in BlackSea moved with such distinctly *feline* grace.

His eyes narrowed. But the unknown male wasn't his concern right now. "We ready to go?" he asked the pilots.

"Just waiting for an update on the winds," the older of the two replied. "They can be a touch unpredictable here."

Kaia's friend handed over a thin organizer a bare two seconds later. "You're good to go. Clear skies."

Twenty-seven hours and twenty-eight minutes until it was too late.

Chapter 55

> She won't talk to me, just shuts down no matter how I approach the topic. We should consider alternative methods of reaching her.
>
> —Note from Counselor Mei Shi to Natia and Eijirō Kahananui regarding Kaia Luna (9)

SHIVERS RIPPLED INSIDE Kaia's skin as the jet came in to land a long eight hours from takeoff, the response driven by her visceral and irrational fear that this landscape was inimical to her survival.

The second dose of the medication was wearing off.

She glanced at her watch. Another hour until she could safely take the next dose.

Her heart skipped a beat, two. Her skin flushed.

Falling back on the breathing exercise her counselor had taught her as a child, she somehow managed to hold herself together as they left the jet. Bo had taken her hand inside the plane and she clung to his warmth, his strength.

"You should've told me you were afraid of flying." It was a scowling statement.

"I'm not." An honest answer that only made his scowl deepen.

But they had no more time for private conversation; waiting at the bottom of the disembarkation steps was a red-haired woman with brown eyes and creamy skin kissed with sun-gold. Her hair scraped back in a high ponytail and her body clad in blue jeans, work boots, and a zipped-up black leather jacket, she fairly pulsed with dominance.

Kaia didn't have to be told she was facing one of the DarkRiver sentinels.

Shooting Bowen a deadly glance, the redhead said, "Fair warning—I'm fighting the urge to shoot you."

Kaia bristled. "That's rude in any language and for any clan, I don't care how dominant you are."

The redhead narrowed her eyes at Kaia . . . before groaning and throwing up her hands. "Sweet insanity, you brought a maternal with you?" The words were directed at Bowen. "I just got away from a whole cabal of them."

Maternal.

What an odd thing to hear herself described as; BlackSea had no such position in the hierarchy—and Kaia didn't have children.

Bowen blew out a breath, his expression drawn. "Mercy has reason to want to shoot me." Open regret in his tone. "I did something unforgivable the first time I entered this territory." He shifted his attention back to the sentinel. "How are they?"

"Fine. *Now.*" Calm words but her eyes had gone the dangerous gold of a large hunting cat. "The family and the pack appreciated your personal apology—but the rest will take time." Turning her attention back to Kaia, the sentinel held out her hand. "Mercy, and I'm scared of maternals."

Kaia's lips twitched; the other woman might be holding a serious grudge against Bowen, but she had a lethal charm it was difficult to ignore. "Kaia, and I'm protective when it comes to my people."

"What did I say? Maternal." Her handshake was firm without being a display in aggression. "We have your man in our sights."

Kaia's heart twisted at the thought of George alone and emotionally lost in unfamiliar territory. "How is he?"

"Appears stable enough, though obviously you'd be a better judge of that." Shifting on her heel, Mercy began to lead them to a heavy-duty all-terrain vehicle. "He's working his way toward SnowDancer territory—way inland for a sea creature. Hitchhiking."

"No plan, movements that can't be predicted." Bowen nodded slowly. "Smart if he doesn't want to make it easy for anyone to find him."

"Except that he's in DarkRiver territory and sticks out like a fish out of water—pun intended." Mercy got into the driver's seat, with Bowen jumping in the back and nodding at Kaia to take the passenger seat.

Though her stomach wasn't exactly settled, Kaia took a deep breath and accepted the offer.

"This have anything to do with the Consortium?" Mercy asked once they were away. "Or is it just a clanmate gone AWOL?"

"We're not sure yet," Bowen said. "I heard you had triplets. Congratulations."

Kaia momentarily forgot her nausea. She couldn't imagine this sleek and deadly woman having given birth—it was like trying to imagine Miane doing the same. "Do you have photos?" she asked, and when Mercy shot her a cat-curious look, felt compelled to explain. "I have triplet cousins. They once booby-trapped my room with *extremely* realistic rubber spiders."

Laughing with a deep warmth that made Kaia certain she could come to like this lethal woman very much, Mercy slid out her phone and passed it over. On the home screen was a shot of three naked babies against the wide chest of a heavily muscled brown-eyed man. His smile made it obvious he was hopelessly besotted with both the photographer and their babies.

Kaia sighed, her anxiety not proof against such gorgeous sweetness. "Your mate is wonderful."

"No argument." Tapping her finger on the steering wheel after putting away her phone, Mercy began to go through George's movements to date. "He's not very good at being stealthy, but he mostly seems to be trying to avoid DarkRiver. One of our people got close enough to sniff out his pack and caught chemical scents she couldn't identify, but she was able to confirm no trace of explosives."

Though the DarkRiver sentinel kept her eyes on the road, her attention was a scythe against Kaia's senses. "You two know anything about those scents? Your commander assured us this guy isn't carrying a deadly pathogen or disease."

"He isn't," Bowen confirmed before pausing. "Kaia?"

Realizing what he needed to know, she said, "Atalina's been in touch with Ashaya Aleine. DarkRiver knows about the project."

Mercy's gaze connected with hers for a heartbeat, a powerful understanding in them. "Brain chip?"

And at that second, Kaia realized Mercy wasn't as hardhearted toward Bowen as she appeared. "Yes." That was all she could say before her throat dried up, the fear this time having nothing to do with being on land and everything to do with the clock that continued to count down in her head.

Nineteen hours.

"How long to get to George after you leave us?" Bowen asked from the back, his tone as pragmatic as always.

Bowen Adrian Knight would never surrender, Kaia thought. He'd never slide silently into the forever black. He'd fight to the end. And yet, in an effort to save those he loved, he'd agreed to be part of an experiment that wrenched control from him.

Clenching her hand against the side of her thigh, Kaia spoke to the gods she'd broken with the same day her parents' bodies were consigned to the ocean that had been their home through all cycles of life: *You do* not *take his life. You do not punish his courage and honor by consigning him to an existence where he's a mindless ghost of himself. You don't do that!*

"I'll get an update as we go"—Mercy's voice, breaking into her furious thoughts—"but currently, he's three hours from our present location."

That wasn't so bad. Until you factored in that Atalina was in the deep, far, *far* from here and she was the only one Kaia would trust to inject the compound into Bowen's brain. Others might attempt to follow her notes, but only Attie *knew* exactly where to inject and how to do it. And no one would want Atalina putting her body through the strain of surfacing to Lantia, not with her due date so close.

Don't panic, another part of her brain said, reminding her that Mal could pull down the submersible, increasing its speed to the level of madness. That was true, but they had *no* margin for error. A single lost hour could end Bowen's life.

Kaia's heart thumped double time. Her skin flushed. And her hands began to tremble, her anxiety about being on land colliding with her anxiety about Bowen to create a toxic stew that threatened to overwhelm her.

She'd slipped a preloaded injector into her pocket, knew she had to use it before she curled up and began to whimper like a trapped animal. Clearing her throat, she said, "Could we stop for a quick bathroom break?"

"Oh yeah, sure. I should have asked earlier." Nothing in Mercy's tone betrayed whether she'd picked up the scent of Kaia's fear.

She must have, was simply being polite in the changeling way in not drawing attention to it.

Not long afterward, the sentinel pulled to a stop in front of a small café on the road out of the city. Backed up against tall green firs and painted pink and white, then decorated with strings of tiny white lights that glinted against the fading light, it looked like a fairy-tale cottage.

"Belongs to a packmate." Mercy opened her door to the icily crisp air. "Restroom's through the back."

Avoiding Bowen's incisive gaze, Kaia slipped inside the café. She knew she had to tell him, but every time she thought about it, she couldn't make her mouth work; all she could think was that she should've gotten over this fear long ago. It was childish and stupid and oh God, it *hurt.*

A sob caught in her throat.

Her hands began to tremble.

She barely made it inside a private stall before shudders racked her body so hard that her bones rattled.

Chapter 56

I've had a financial ping from Heenali's ex. He's crossed over from Ireland to France. She can't be far behind.

—Message from Lily to Cassius

BO KNEW THERE was something seriously wrong with Kaia, wrong enough that he had to find a way to break through her reticence. He couldn't let her keep on suffering this torment in silence.

But no matter his need to go after her, hold her, he didn't move. Kaia wouldn't thank him for confronting her now. This was a private thing. Gut tight, he pasted a casual expression on his face as he glanced at Mercy. "Buy you a coffee?"

The DarkRiver sentinel's responding look—all golden leopard eyes—made it clear he remained on probation. "No, but I'll take a lime milkshake."

Bo followed her inside the café without making any attempt to defend himself. Two and a half years ago, he'd made a decision driven by desperation—his motives had been pure, his intent never to harm, but that didn't change that he *had* done harm. He'd traumatized an innocent little girl and he'd never forgive himself for it; he didn't expect Mercy or the rest of her pack to forgive him, either.

It was enough that DarkRiver didn't blame the entire Alliance for his mistake.

Bo kept an eye out for Kaia as he and Mercy walked up to the counter. The young teen who came over to take their order had a nametag that identified him as Charlie; he smiled at Mercy with unexpected sweetness—until you caught the nefarious glint in eyes the color of sea glass. "Hi, Merce. Can I come play with the pupcubs tonight?"

"Talk to Riley. He's on triplet duty today." Mercy reached over to ruffle the boy's dark curls. "You were over only the other day. My packmates will get jealous if wolves get more turns than leopards."

"I'll just sneak up later," the boy said, totally unrepentant. "After the cats have slinked away."

Bo placed the order for Mercy's milkshake to the accompaniment of her laughter. He also ordered a latte with two caramel shots for Kaia, and a lemonade for himself. His head had begun to ache a little, but he was trying not to think about what that might mean. "Your pupcubs are popular," he said to Mercy after Charlie moved away to make their drinks.

"Are you kidding me? We've got *two* packs' worth of nosy parkers swinging by every five seconds—it'll be even worse with today being Saturday." She shook her head. "The wolves are categorically worse than cats. Yesterday, six of them sat on our lawn in wolf form and howled out a lullaby." Her lips twitched. "The babies loved it."

Bo couldn't see any sign of Kaia; his skin stretched taut over his body as his muscles bunched. "Talking of DarkRiver young," he said with a conscious effort at keeping things on a normal footing. "Do you have an auburn-haired male off roaming the world?" It was something the cats did in their youth. "Maybe twenty, twenty-one? Gives off an oddly dangerous vibe?" The boy was a power, but one who hadn't quite matured.

"You've seen Kit?" Mercy's face lit up. "Where?"

Tense with worry inside, Bo nonetheless managed to spin a tale about the tiny island airport and the mechanic's apprentice and the driver who drove like a maniac.

Kaia appeared at last, her hair—which she wore in a single braid down her back—wet around the edges of her face, and her smile so ferociously bright that it hurt. "Sorry I took so long," she said. "Decided to freshen up."

Charlie returned with their drinks before Bo could reply. Picking up Kaia's, he handed it over. "Latte, two shots of caramel."

Wide eyes. "How did you know?"

"Security chief."

It twisted him up deep inside to see her determined smile soften into reality, the mask slipping to reveal the lines at the corners of her eyes, the lack of color in her skin. An unnamed intruder was stealing the life out of his Kaia.

MERCY hopped out of the car soon after they began to hit patches of snow. "Keep heading up," she said, pointing along the road lined with fir trees on either side. "You're still in DarkRiver territory and our sentries will make sure you turn where you're meant to turn. If your boy keeps going, however, he's going to end up in wolf lands."

Normally, that would've meant a quick and bloody end for George—the SnowDancer wolves were not renowned for their hospitality toward strangers who breached their boundaries. *Shoot first and ask questions of the corpses* was their motto.

"The wolves know?" Bo asked.

"Yep. But they'll take him down if he makes any attempt to go places he shouldn't." Mercy pushed back from the door. "Good luck."

Kaia arched her neck to watch as Mercy disappeared into the snow-dusted woods. "Where's she going? I don't see any houses."

"I'm guessing she's planning to shift." Bowen began to drive.

"I wish I could see her. I've never seen a changeling leopard before."

But Bo had other things on his mind. "Kaia, what's wrong?" It came out more than a little rough. "Whatever it is, it's hurting you."

"I'll tell you." A husky but firm promise. "But we have to find George first."

"Kaia." Stopping the vehicle on the otherwise deserted road, he turned to face her.

Huge eyes, the irises pure black with the slightest reflective glow against the falling night. "Let me finish this, then I'll tell you. I have to do this. I have to go all the way."

The pain in her, it fucking broke his heart. "Then we finish it." If that was the only way to ease her suffering, he'd hunt George to the ends of the Earth.

He would *not* fucking die while Kaia was in pain.

Driving faster than he should, he nonetheless spotted the leopard waiting on the side of the road fifteen minutes later. Bo slowed . . . and the leopard crossed the road to stand by a left turn. Getting the hint, he turned and carried on into the increasingly snow-draped landscape, the ground a gentle but constant slope. "We must be at the foothills of the Sierras."

"George will be scared here." Kaia took in the white and green landscape around them, majestic and alien and not of her home. "He's free in the ocean, but he knows the ocean. He's not built to deal with this much change."

And even though George might have stolen his chance at life, Bowen felt for the other man; he couldn't forget George's dejection when he'd realized Seraphina was seeing another man. Whatever else drove Dr. Kahananui's assistant, part of it was a broken heart. "We'll find him," he said to Kaia. "Mercy would've contacted us if he was in trouble."

Nodding, Kaia shifted in her seat to angle her body toward him. "Your head's hurting, isn't it?"

"Slight headache," he admitted. "But that could just be the interrupted sleep I had on the flight." He'd been too amped up to really rest.

"Only Atalina knows how to do the operation."

Bo tugged gently on the end of her braid. "One step at a time." He couldn't be a hostage to the loudly ticking clock; he had to go forward, had to fight for his future. "It's possible George may hunker down to rest." The man had been on the move since he left Ryūjin, had to be exhausted. "That should give us enough time to catch up to him."

"I don't want to lose him." Kaia tucked escaped strands of hair behind her ears, her attention on Bo rather than the now pitch-black road lit only with the headlights of their vehicle. "He's burned his bridges with Black-Sea, exposed himself. That means he's probably of no use to these Consortium people—if they even played a part in any of this in the first place."

"What will happen to him if we manage to bring him back alive?"

"He is *ohana*," Kaia murmured. "We have punishments, yes, but we don't shun or execute clan unless there's no other choice. If all he's done is stolen things, he'll be expected to pay for his actions, but he'll still be *ohana*, still be ours." Her voice trembled. "No one should be left all alone in the ocean."

Bowen hadn't thought of it in those terms, but she was right; such cruel aloneness killed or twisted or poisoned. "I'll do everything I can to make sure we don't lose him in the capture." Physically and tactically, he was far more skilled than George, but the stakes could change in a heartbeat if the other man shifted. "Help me make sure he doesn't shift." Thanks to Kaia, Bo knew what he was facing—George would be a formidable opponent in his nonhuman form.

"Try not to frighten him," Kaia said, thinking back to that time when she'd so badly startled George. "He reacts like a child might—morphing into the form in which he feels most powerful." It made her wonder what scars he bore, what had frozen him in childhood as far as his control was concerned.

"Even though he's on land, not in water?"

Kaia's eye caught on the pulsing vein in Bowen's temple, and her lungs emptied of air. It was beginning, the ultimate countdown. If they didn't get him the third injection in less than sixteen and a half hours, his chance at a full lifetime could end in this snowy forested landscape so very far from the canals of Venice and the place he called home.

Squeezing her eyes shut, Kaia took a hard mental step back to the now. Not the future that hadn't happened and *wouldn't* happen. If Bowen was to leave her, it would be to the surface and to decades of life. That was the only future she'd accept.

"Kaia?"

She flicked open her eyes, thought back to the question he'd asked. "I don't think it's a conscious choice with George. He shifts in reaction, like a hermit crab retreats into its shell." For George, his other self was the shell, the safe place.

"Got it." Bowen turned the wheel to follow the curve of the road. "For your people to be hunted, especially the ones who swim in remote parts of the world, someone had to have given the hunters their coordinates."

The thought was a crushing weight on her lungs, as heavy now as the first time she'd realized the inescapable truth. "George wouldn't do that." Kaia folded her arms. "Yes, he's stolen things, but to set up our people for murder? That would be an act of evil." Of a person devoid of conscience and empathy. "He doesn't like mice, but the one time Hex ended up in his quarters, he carried him back to me cupped gently in one hand."

"People aren't always simple, Kaia." Bowen's voice was quiet. "A man who hesitates to harm animals could well believe they are innocents but sentient creatures aren't." He blew out a breath. "George knew I'd die in a matter of weeks without the third injection."

It was true. The injection couldn't be given later. It *had* to be given by the quickly looming deadline. And God, she couldn't think about that.

"Whatever happens, I'll make sure George has a chance to explain why he did what he did." Taking her hand, Bowen pressed a soft, tender kiss to her palm before placing her hand on his thigh.

And they drove on through the snow-blanketed night.

Kaia began to feel her heartbeat quicken in an erratic pattern soon afterward, her gut churn. Taking an injector from the small bag at her feet, she injected herself in front of Bo. "After," she reminded him when his jaw set in a brutally hard line.

"After." A promise—and a demand.

Chapter 57

They've just crossed our border.

—Message from border sentry to the alpha of the SnowDancer wolves

IT WAS A bare five minutes later that the vehicle's lights glanced off silvery eyes on the side of the road. "We've got wolves," Bowen murmured, bringing the car to a halt.

A man appeared out of the falling snow. His hair was a stunning silver-gold, his eyes a strikingly pale blue. All Kaia could see of his body through the window were bare shoulders and a bare chest that gleamed with a slick of heat.

He looked like a wolf in human form.

She knew exactly who he was; a man that distinctive tended to be spoken of, especially among women—she was looking at the alpha of the SnowDancer wolves. And what she saw was that while he might be the stuff of female fantasies, his real-life presence was a crash of violent power. Her blood chilled at his presence, the tiny hairs rising on her arms.

His mate clearly had an iron constitution—and was maybe a little insane. No sane woman would consider this man anything but a deadly predator.

"Hawke." Bowen nodded. "I didn't expect to see you."

"I like to keep an eye on what's happening in my territory." Icy blue eyes landed on Kaia as snow dusted his shoulders and caught on his hair. "You smell afraid," he said softly.

Kaia's entire body grew tight. "I'm fine." Folding her arms, she told the lethal wolf alpha to "shut up" with her eyes, because the fear he'd scented wasn't because of him—and she didn't need Bowen reminded of her small madness.

Hawke's lips tugged up in a slight smile—and even then, she was glad he was all the way on the other side of the vehicle. "Your clanmate's taken shelter for the night with a family that lives down the drive you'll see about a hundred meters along on your right."

"Wolves?" Kaia couldn't imagine George asking such dangerous predators for sanctuary. "He has an acute sense of smell."

"Not wolves, but SnowDancers all the same," said the wolf in human form. "Go get your boy." He drew back into the falling snow. "We'll stay far enough off that he doesn't scent or spot us."

Raising a hand in silent thanks, Bowen pulled away to continue on down the road.

Kaia saw a shower of light beyond the windows, caught the merest glimpse of a huge silver-gold wolf in the rearview mirror. Exhaling quietly, she said, "He is the scariest person I've ever met in my entire life." She stared at Bowen's jaw. "How can you just talk to him like he's an ordinary person?"

"That's how you deal with alpha predators." He shot her an unexpected grin. "Never show fear. And Hawke's not that bad if you don't pull shit in his territory or against his people."

"No," she murmured, "you deal with him alpha to alpha." Bowen didn't wear his power in as primal a way as Hawke, but it was drenched into his bones. An alpha's power grew with the trust of the people who gave him or her their loyalty—and Bowen had the loyalty of humans across the globe.

He ran the back of his hand over her cheek. "I'm glad you're not scared of me."

"Never." Part of her had always known who he would become to her. "There, that's the turn."

They had no problem finding the house—it was lit up from within, a glowing beacon in the night. The land beyond was devoid of trees and, from what Kaia could sense through the snowfall when they pulled on their jackets and stepped outside, appeared to drop off into a gully or ravine.

Alerted by the lights of their vehicle, a bearded male stepped out to tell them that George wasn't inside. "Went for a walk to the lookout even though the snow was coming down. Said he'd be fine. Took all his gear with him, too." The man squinted his eyes against the snow that fell onto his lashes. "Not sure how helpful flashlights will be, but here's one." He passed it to Bo. "Give me a sec and I'll get another."

"I don't need a flashlight." Kaia began to walk through the snow in the direction the SnowDancer had pointed, Bowen beside her.

"Your night vision's that good?" he asked in a quiet murmur.

"No, I'm using echolocation." As natural to her as breathing. "There's enough ambient noise for me to hear it bounce off objects or people." The rustle of the trees, the movement of small creatures in the calf-length grass that defied the snow. If the noise fell and she needed an extra directional marker, she clicked gently with her tongue to send out a wave of sound.

It wasn't the call she used in the ocean, was far more subtle—and less likely to alarm George.

She sensed her lost clanmate while she and Bowen were still some distance away. The snow stopped falling halfway to his location, making him visible to the eye. When the moon slipped out from behind the clouds moments later, it was as if a silvery flashlight had been turned on the world.

The snow, glittering like crushed glass, reflected back the light.

In all that glory, George was sitting with his legs hanging over the edge of what was actually a sharp drop into a steep ravine, his pack beside him and his hair lifting in the breeze.

It was fairly flat from the edge of the house to the lookout, with no trees or outbuildings to hide behind, so when George glanced back over his shoulder, she expected to see him scramble to grab his pack and run. But he stayed in position, turning his face back toward the ravine and the jagged rocks that lined it.

Even the snow couldn't soften their lethally sharp edges.

George's shoulders were slumped and she thought she'd caught a glimmer of wet in his eyes before he'd turned away.

Kaia's heart clenched. "I'll speak to him."

"Don't get too close. That's a dangerous drop."

Nodding, Kaia continued on through the snowbent grass. Until she was only two meters away and George looked around and said, "That's far enough." He gripped the pack. "If you come any closer, I'll throw this entire pack and the compound over the cliffs."

Kaia held up her hands palms-out, then slowly took a seat on the snow. The cold seeped through her jeans to sear her skin. She was aware of Bowen remaining in a standing position to her left. "You look tired, George." Scanning his face, she noted the shadows and the hollows. "Tell me what's making you hurt."

His smile was tremulous. "That's the thing I always liked about you, Kaia. You pretend to be tough, but you care. Thank you for the burgers and the carrot cake."

It made her terribly sad that such small gestures of care had meant so much to him. "I'm furious with you," she admitted, because George was far too intelligent to fall for a lie—and because he deserved the truth. "But that doesn't mean you're still not *ohana*. I don't let go of family that easily. We can go home. We can fix this."

George shook his head. "I've done terrible things," he rasped out. "I've leaked all kinds of information. Miane would never again trust me in the clan."

"We are *one*." Kaia held the eye contact with steadfast honesty. "Yes, you'll be punished. But we don't abandon our own." They'd fought too long and too hard to come together to shove people away now. "Our laws are not the laws of those who live on land, or even of our fellow changelings."

His thin, long-fingered hand tensed on the pack. "Your clan isn't my clan," he said, his voice harder. "Where was BlackSea when I needed them? When I was a child screaming and bloody?"

Kaia thought back to what little she knew of George's family history. His father had died first, she remembered, causing his devastated mother to move George and herself to a small family compound founded by her uncle.

But she, too, had died only months later.

During that one conversation they'd had, George had seemed so curious about how Kaia had felt joining a settled family, and Kaia had been happy to talk to him about it—her pain had never centered on the loving and affectionate family that had embraced her brokenhearted presence. Both sets of grandparents, Bebe, her aunt Geraldine and her small family, and of course, Aunt Natia and the rest of the Kahananuis.

Kaia had been cocooned in love.

Unlike her own family, however, George's extended kin were only peripherally part of BlackSea; they preferred to keep mostly to themselves. In the course of their conversation on the topic of being adopted into extended family, George had said, "The Kahananuis treated you like their own?"

When she'd nodded and asked if he'd had a different experience, he'd changed the topic of the conversation so smoothly that she'd followed without realizing he'd never answered.

"What did they do to you?" She dug her hand into the snow. "People hurt you."

"He used to use an electrical cord or sometimes a switch cut from the tree outside. A few times, he used his belt." A single tear trickled down George's face. "I screamed so hard, but no one came. He was the boss."

"Your mother's uncle."

A jerky nod. "He told me not to tell my mom or he'd kick us out. But she found out and she was going to take me away. Then she got sick." Wet eyes holding Kaia's. "I still have the scars on my back—the belt was the worst because he used the buckle end."

Kaia's heart broke for the child George had been and for the man he'd become. She understood now why she'd never once seen him in the internal pool, or in human form in the sea. To do so would've been to expose his scars and his past as a brutalized child.

The vast majority of changelings adored children, treating them as precious gifts. The only reason BlackSea's minnows weren't awfully spoiled was that the whole clan raised a child—and the elders taught the younger generation. Many believed no changeling would *ever* harm a child. But changelings were people, and just like any other race there were good people and bad people. "We'll go to Malachai and Miane." Kaia couldn't keep the heat out of her tone. "We'll tell them what happened—"

"It won't matter," George interrupted bleakly. "He's dead. I killed him." The confession might've been flat and blunt, but she glimpsed a painful vulnerability in the eyes that clung to hers.

"Good." Kaia wasn't a bloodthirsty person, didn't ever get violent, but should anyone hurt the people she cared about, she'd use every knife in her collection to claim lethal vengeance. "You did what you had to do to survive. No one will judge you for that—least of all our First." Miane was ruthless when it came to protecting their vulnerable, a woman who took no prisoners.

George shook his head. "No, she'll look at me and see only a traitor."

And though Kaia didn't want to ask this next question, she had to or it would remain a cancer between them. "Our vanished, George. Do you know anything about them?"

Chapter 58

Pick up the phone. Just once! You owe me that!

—Message left by Heenali Roy for Trey Gunther

GEORGE'S SHOULDERS SHOOK, a sob breaking out of his mouth. "I swear I didn't know." He wiped his nose on the back of his arm, the checked shirt he wore woefully inadequate for this weather. "I thought it was about money and stealing scientific breakthroughs. Things that would hurt BlackSea but not any person. I didn't know they were the ones taking and killing our own."

Agony gripped Kaia's heart. "How did you find out?"

"I never betrayed anyone." He stared desperately at her. "I never gave my contact any coordinates or even spoke to him about specific people in the clan. I just passed on tech data and they put money into a hidden account."

Blood cold, Kaia somehow managed to keep her voice soft, gentle. "Then why do you think your buyers are behind the vanishings?"

"Someone made a mistake." George swallowed hard. "I got paid twenty times what I should've been, and when I queried it because I didn't want to end up hounded for it, my contact slipped up and said my payment had been confused with that of another informant in BlackSea."

Hugging the pack, he carried on. "It was two months ago, right after we lost a swimmer in the Arctic. I knew, I *knew* what it must mean, that one of us was selling out clanmates, but I didn't know how to tell anyone. And I had no details."

Just confirmation of what they'd all begun to suspect. That in itself was enough. It backed their decision to look within, dig out the poison that threatened their family. Kaia was trying to find a way to say that to George without making him feel bad about having withheld the information—she knew what it was to be frozen by fear, would never judge him—when Bowen spoke.

"But you don't consider BlackSea clan." His voice was quiet, the question in it devastating.

George's head jerked toward Bo before he returned his frantic gaze to Kaia. "I would *never* allow anyone's family to be targeted. I would *never* leave a child without his parents, without safety." His voice sang with anguish. "I just wanted to make BlackSea hurt in other ways. I wanted to destroy the cooperation agreement with the humans and the alliance with the leopards and wolves. Make everyone feel alone and powerless as I felt alone and powerless."

"Who is your contact?" Kaia was having a difficult time keeping her distance. Every part of her strained to go closer and grab hold of George, give him the comfort of clan.

"All the information is in a file on the organizer inside here." He tapped his pack. "I thought I was dealing with a conglomerate tied to a pharmaceuticals company, people who wanted to co-opt our research." Fingers trembling, he moved his hands from the pack. "I didn't know it was the Consortium."

Kaia's breath caught, her body bunching almost before her brain processed the meaning of his actions, but George was already turning toward the rocky danger of the ravine—even a small jump would send him crashing onto the lethal edges and sharp corners of those rocks, his body gaining momentum as it careened down.

He'd be dead long before he hit the bottom.

"I'm sorry, Kaia. I never intended for anyone to die."

Even as Kaia screamed and attempted to move fast enough to grab him, George jumped—or he tried to. Because, at the end, he'd forgotten about Bowen and that Bowen Knight wasn't a scientist or a cook. He was the security chief of the Human Alliance and it turned out he could move a lot faster than a cerebral sea creature stranded on land.

He wrenched George from the edge, dragging the crying, screaming man back until there was no chance George could escape and make another suicide attempt. Ignoring the pack that held the data and the precious compound, Kaia all but jumped on top of her clanmate at the first glimmer of a shift. "How dare you try to end your life?" she yelled, successfully startling him into staying human. "You're part of my family, George! You don't get to just give up!"

George's sobs turned even harsher and he tried to curl into himself, but Kaia was having none of that. Dragging him to her, she let him bury his face against her neck, his arms locked tight around her, and then she rocked him as he cried, a broken child in a man's body.

Her own tears fell above his head as she watched Bowen walk to the edge of the drop-off and retrieve the pack.

Sixteen hours to go.

Chapter 59

Financial trail's turned ice-cold. Either Trey's wised up that someone's tracking him, or something's wrong.

—Message from Lily Knight to Cassius Drake

THIS HADN'T GONE anything like Bowen had expected.

There was no way he couldn't believe every word George had said; there were no more lies left in the man. George wasn't even holding himself together. It was Kaia who was doing that, Kaia who was stopping him from crawling into himself and never coming back out.

A glimmer of light along the edges of George's form.

Bo had seen the same fracture of light with Hawke. And he realized what the BlackSea male was about to do. It had nothing to do with violence and everything to do with being a creature designed for the ocean on dry land—if KJ's story about the colossal squid scared of needles was true, George could probably survive a certain time out of the water once in his other form, but it was unlikely to be a long period unless George semi-shifted to breathe air.

Regardless, once in his powerful wild form, he could propel himself over the edge, shifting back into his more vulnerable human body as he fell.

Bo reacted instinctively. "No," he ordered using the most dominant tone in his arsenal.

He saw George flinch and the glimmer faded . . . only to reappear a second later.

This time, Bo went down on one knee beside the other man and clamped him hard on the shoulder. "*No*," he ordered again. "You owe the children of those lost swimmers answers." George had mentioned those children only by implication, but it was obvious he felt bad that a number of them had lost a parent and at least two were now orphans. "Pay your debts to them, even if you don't believe you owe a debt to anyone else."

Kaia pressed a kiss to George's hair, her palm firm against the side of his face. "Don't you dare, George," she said, her own voice harder than he'd ever heard it. "You do and so will I."

The last edges of the oncoming shift faded, George's body slumping against Kaia's. "You shouldn't be on land," he said, his voice a rasp. "You know you shouldn't be on land. You're so afraid on land."

Kaia stroked her hand through the other man's hair. "Did you really think I'd just give up on a member of my *ohana*?" Kaia shook her head. "We'll figure this out together. Even if I have to go toe to toe with cousin Mal."

She was magnificent, Bowen thought. Loving and strong and fierce.

It took fifteen more minutes of time they didn't have for George to get up. His legs were shaky, his face white—but though he looked longingly toward the drop-off, he didn't attempt to run in that direction. Pulling on the pack, Bo walked on the man's left, while Kaia wrapped an arm around him from the right.

Hawke appeared out of the trees at that instant. He was wearing only a pair of jeans, his feet bare against the snow. When Bo went over to talk to him, the SnowDancer alpha offered them lodging and food. "Thank you," Bo said, "but what I really need is a jet-chopper that can get us to our plane. We have to get back to Lantia as fast as possible."

A large black chopper landed on the snowy grass only seven minutes later, the wind generated by its blades causing the snow to ripple in a dramatic pattern. Bo made sure George bent his head and that Kaia, too, was safe from the blades as he ushered them into the craft. As the pilot took off, Bo looked down and saw a pack of wolves looking up. Including a big one with fur of silver-gold.

After noting that Kaia had George in hand, the other man slumped on her shoulder with his eyes closed, Bo made contact with Malachai. As he didn't want the SnowDancer pilot to overhear their conversation, he sent a written message, outlining the basic facts of what George had confessed and what he'd accused his mother's uncle of doing to him.

Malachai's response came back ten minutes later: *His great-uncle was before my and Miane's time in the leadership, but I just spent the past ten minutes talking to those older than us who knew the bastard. The general consensus is that he was a nasty man, one who preferred to keep his family isolated. We'll talk more when you arrive. Miane and I will be back by then.*

We have a timing problem, Bo wrote back. *We'll reach Lantia with a few hours to spare but it won't be enough to reach Ryūjin by the injection deadline.* The station was too far in the deep.

I can haul you down, Mal replied. *We have aerodynamic shells made for that purpose. Just get to Lantia, then we'll figure out the rest.*

Sliding away the phone, Bo looked over at Kaia. His siren was murmuring to George, trying to keep the other man from slipping into shock. And in her worry about him, she'd lost her own fear—a fear the shape of which Bo now understood. His gut clenched, his skin hot. He wanted to shake her for doing this to herself.

KAIA could feel Bowen's coiled intensity, but he said nothing when they reached the airport, simply helped her get George onboard. Then, while she continued to try to comfort her shattered clanmate, he went and conferred with the pilots. Kaia was desperate to talk to him, but George was barely holding himself together right now, the psychic damage inside him a bomb that had finally exploded with destructive force.

It was two hours later that George finally fell asleep, his head in Kaia's lap and her hand stroking through the light brown strands of his hair as the jet cut through the clouds. Bowen, seated across from her, his forearms braced on his thighs, watched George with inscrutable focus. "Do you think Miane will permit an empath onto one of your cities?"

"I thought you didn't like Psy?"

"I make an exception for empaths"—that dark gaze shifted to her, held her prisoner—"and for a telepathic siren."

The rough gentleness of his voice as he spoke those final words twisted her up. "I think if it was an empath associated with an ally, then Miane wouldn't have a problem with it." BlackSea's First had spoken about the empaths to Kaia the last time Mianc had been on Ryūjin, the conversation part of a wider one they'd had on the fall of Silence.

Miane had sat at the counter in Kaia's kitchen, drinking the strong Turkish coffee she adored and chatting with Kaia in between visits from other clanmates. "Miane admires what it takes to be an empath, the courage it requires to take terrible, painful emotions into themselves, but their very softness makes them suspect."

Bowen nodded. "Be pretty easy to break an E if you were cruel enough, get them to act for certain interests." He leaned back in his seat. "Good thing they've got some very dangerous protectors."

"The Arrows." Kaia didn't know much about the deadly Psy squad, but Mal had mentioned the squad siding very publicly with the empaths—and that the Arrows and BlackSea were building a strong working relationship. "I still don't think Miane would accept just any E."

"Sascha Duncan? She's part of DarkRiver."

"Yes. Or—there's an Arrow teleporter who helped find several of our vanished. I think he might be mated to an empath." She looked down at George. "You should talk to Mal, see if he can arrange for an E to be waiting when we land." Kaia wasn't sure how much of George was left to save but she damn well wasn't about to give up on him.

"I'll do it now." Not wanting to inadvertently wake George, Bo went to the back of the plane to have that conversation.

It turned out the BlackSea security chief's thoughts had been running on a parallel track. "I've already spoken to Miane about arranging for empathic help."

On the tiny screen of the phone, Malachai shoved a hand through his hair, his eyes that eerie pale, *pale* gold that was nothing human. "It all depends on whether I can get one of the Es we trust." Glancing offscreen at that moment, he seemed to be listening to someone else.

When he turned back to Bowen, he said, "We have an empath."

"It's bad, Mal." Bo looked over at where Kaia continued to gently stroke George's hair, keeping him linked to the present and to his clan. "I'm not sure the E is going to have a whole person to work with."

"I'll pass on the warning."

"What will you do with him?" Regardless of all else, George had broken his vows to the clan, had turned traitor.

Malachai went motionless in a way a human never could. "What would you do if you were in Miane's shoes?"

"As long as he truly wasn't responsible for the capture or deaths of any of the vanished, I'd give him another chance." George had never had a real chance, had been twisted up inside since childhood.

And yet, despite it all, the other man hadn't been able to sell out BlackSea. "I've had a look at the organizer on which George loaded his data. He was supposed to meet his contact on a beach in the Caribbean, but he couldn't take that final step, couldn't bring himself to ally with those who had so badly hurt his clanmates."

Bo leaned up against the bulkhead. "Give him another shot, get him help, and you might be able to save him." Somewhere in his fractured psyche, George *did* have the capacity to build connections and to feel loyalty.

Malachai's golden eyes turned almost translucent in the sunlight where he stood. "When I met you, I didn't think you were anything like Miane—but you both put your people first, ambition second." He paused for a moment, his expression difficult to read. "I don't believe you'd send Alliance Fleet ships to harm our own, but someone in your organization did."

"I don't have any answers for you yet," Bo said. "But it does look like we have a traitor in the ranks." It was tough to say that, to admit Heenali might've done things that went against everything Bo believed.

"Who?"

"I won't give up the name until I know beyond any doubt."

Malachai's lips curved slightly. "Yes, you and Miane will never get along. You're too much alike."

Hanging up soon afterward, Bo turned his attention to the woman whose scent was embedded into his skin, a kiss he never wanted to escape. A woman who'd had to inject herself with drugs to survive on land.

He squeezed his phone so hard that the screen cracked.

Chapter 60

It is our mandate to do no harm and to heal psychic and emotional wounds. By now, we have all seen that some wounds are too deep to heal without leaving lifelong scars, but don't allow that to crush your spirit. Remember this: if we can take away even a small percentage of a wounded person's pain, we give them freedom to live a life free of horror and suffering. It may only be for a minute or an hour, but all healing begins with a single moment.

—Letter from Ivy Jane Zen, president of the Empathic Collective, to its membership

KAIA KEPT GEORGE'S hand in hers as they stepped off the boat that had ferried them to Lantia in the heavy dark of a world wrapped in sleep. He was so distraught at this point that he'd stopped crying, his head hanging low, but his hand clutched hers like a lifeline. And when he looked at her, his eyes were those of a child. "Please don't leave me."

"You couldn't get me to go," Kaia assured him, though her mind continued to count down. They *had* to get Bowen to Atalina within the next seven hours or it would be far too late. Bowen had told her of Malachai's offer, but her chest remained tight. Mal was fast in the water, but they were still cutting it dangerously close.

"No, you should go into the deep," George said without warning. "You shouldn't have come on land—I know it hurts you."

"How do you know?" Kaia asked softly, very aware of Bowen listening with silent concentration. "I don't speak about it."

"I heard Dr. Kahananui talking to her mate once." Another pause. "Has she had her baby? I'm sorry if you missed that."

Her heart, it expanded all over again. "Let's talk to Ivy before we decide anything," she said after drawing a deep breath of the salt-laced air; she'd already told George that an empath would be waiting for them on the city.

According to what Bowen had told her after speaking to Malachai late into the flight, Ivy Jane Zen was the empath mated to the teleporter who'd helped BlackSea. She also happened to be the president of the Empathic Collective and part of the Psy Ruling Council. A very powerful woman.

Yet the small stranger with soft ebony curls who stood on the deck not far from them, bathed in the glow of the external lights, had no sense of dominance or aggression to her. A deep warmth uncurled in Kaia's stomach, her urge to befriend the woman coming from both sides of her nature.

"I'd heard that about empaths," she said to George. "That they have a magic about them that makes people want to trust." Nothing coercive, just a sense of innate goodness, a deep inner radiance.

"They could do terrible things with that trust," George whispered, his gaze having finally lifted—to settle on Ivy Jane Zen.

"That's true. Just like Attie could do terrible things with the chemicals she handles." Kaia didn't know if George was mentally present enough to understand what she was trying to tell him, but he swallowed and continued to walk toward the empath.

The wind played with Ivy's hair, tugged at the bottom of her deep magenta coat with white detailing, her jeans and boots as prosaic as the coat was cheerful. "I'm Ivy," she said with a smile when they reached her.

Kaia shook her proffered hand, and though the empath offered the same greeting to George, she didn't seem to take it badly when he stayed mute and motionless.

A woof sounded from a short distance away, the sound soon followed by a small white dog of indeterminate breed who came to sniff around Kaia's ankles. Smiling, she bent to pet him.

He stood patiently for her, but his nose twitched inquisitively the entire time. "Who's this?" Kaia asked, wondering if the little guy had met Mal's dog yet; born and raised on Lantia, the big German shepherd was a pro swimmer.

"His name's Rabbit." At the sound of his name, the dog looked at Ivy. "This is his first time on an oceanic city. He's pretty suspicious about it." Warm affection in her tone. "When we got here, he kept barking at the waves as if they were intruders trying to take over the city."

Rabbit slipped out from under Kaia's touch to run over and sniff around George's legs. Releasing Kaia's hand at last, George went down onto his knees with broken stiffness, then began to pet the dog, his hands hesitant but gentle. Where Rabbit had been all energy and quivering flesh under Kaia's hand, he was quiescent under George's touch, almost as if this small creature knew the man couldn't take anything else.

Though they were standing outside, in the open air, the cold sea winds whispering across their skin, Ivy didn't motion for them to go inside. Instead, she sat down directly on the deck, and she began to talk to Kaia about the city and how she hoped she'd be permitted a tour.

Following her lead because Ivy was an expert in her field as Kaia was in hers, Kaia took a crosslegged position across from her—George to her left—and responded as if this were just an ordinary conversation, not one taking place at three a.m. in the middle of the ocean. At one point, she was aware of Ivy's eyes—an unexpected copper ringed by a rim of gold—flicking up in Bowen's direction, the look accompanied by a faint shake of her head.

Kaia looked up, too, telling him with her gaze that it was all right. George would do nothing here. He was too hurt inside, had given up. As for their limited time to reach Ryūjin, she could see the aerodynamic "shell" ready to go and she'd also spotted Mal. They'd make it.

She could believe nothing else.

Bowen gave a curt nod after taking another look at George. Then, running his fingers over her hair, he bent to press a kiss to her temple.

“I’ve got one of those, you know,” Ivy whispered after he’d left.

When Kaia tilted her head in a silent question, Ivy grinned. “A tall, silent, and handsome.” Her eyes sparkled as she angled her body to point out a black-clad man who stood talking to Malachai in the distance.

As they watched, Bowen joined them in the hazy light thrown by the external lamps. Kaia wished she could claim Bowen as hers as the empath had assumed, but he was only hers for a stolen instant in time. But all she said to Ivy was, “We have excellent taste.”

Ivy laughed.

Rabbit turned over onto his back at the same instant so that George could scratch his belly, and the man beside Kaia finally began to speak. At first, he talked only about Ivy’s dog, asking questions about what Rabbit liked to do, his favorite games, his favorite things to eat. Kaia didn’t know how long it took for him to even approach anything else and when he did, it was in the most indirect way.

Ivy didn’t push him, simply followed his lead—and slowly, George began to relax until he was no longer poised for flight.

“You should go into the deep,” he said again ten minutes later, his voice raw. “Time’s running out.” A glance over at where Bowen stood with Mal and Ivy’s mate. “He’s a good person. He deserves a chance at a long life. Take him to Dr. Kahananui so she can finish the experiment.”

Finish the experiment.

Spin the roulette wheel one last time . . . and hope Bowen would make it through to the other side.

Chapter 61

Choices, we tell ourselves we have choices.
So foolish are mortals.
An amusement to the Fates.

—Adina Mercant, poet (b. 1832, d. 1901)

BO STOOD WITH Malachai and the Arrow, Vasic Zen. The BlackSea security chief had confirmed they could make it to Ryūjin with two hours' breathing room. An hour for the op, a little more time on Lantia to talk through the implications of recent events while Bo was still Bo.

A few hours, he thought grimly, could alter everything.

In front of him, Malachai was still going over the data on the organizer George had provided. Dr. Kahananui's assistant appeared to have been clinically precise, to the extent of recording minute details of every conversation he'd had with his contact.

"Can't say George wasn't thorough"—Malachai's gaze went to where the man sat with Kaia and Ivy—"but his contact only made that single slip."

It didn't surprise Bo that Malachai made no effort to hide the data from Vasic. The Arrows were at the forefront of the fight against the Consortium, and Vasic Zen was their rumored second-in-command.

"We'll run the data through our systems," Vasic said in the cool voice of a man who'd come of age in Silence. "It's possible the computers may pick up a hidden clue."

"We can do the same," Bo said, half his attention on Kaia and her emotional state.

"I'm most interested in the identity of the traitor selling out our people." Malachai's fury was a darkening storm.

That was when Miane Levèque pulled herself out of the water not far from them. Black hair sleek against her skull, she wasn't naked, as Bo had half expected. Changelings came out of the shift in their skin. But Miane wore a sleeveless black wetsuit that went from neck to ankles.

Bypassing them, she went straight to where Kaia and Ivy sat with George.

Fear flickered across the man's face, but he made no attempt to escape his alpha's anger. Miane hunkered down in front of him and began to speak, her voice too quiet to reach Bo. Swallowing hard, George just listened. Miane spoke for several more minutes before gripping George's face between her hands.

Eye to eye, she leaned in and pressed a kiss to his lips.

George was crying when she left him, but it seemed a catharsis rather than a result of shame or fear. When Ivy reached out her hand, he took it, his other hand locked with Kaia's.

"Gentlemen." Miane stopped beside Bowen, her eyes a shade of hazel that appeared green in this light. "Thank you for bringing back one of mine." That was directed at Bowen. "And thank you, Vasic, for bringing your mate into the heart of our territory."

The words were calm, controlled . . . and her anger a cold burn against Bowen's skin. She reminded him very strongly of Hawke. Both alphas who could be perfectly polite and civilized—and who'd tear out your throat if they considered you a threat.

"Mal told me you were able to save the clanmate who was attacked," Bo said.

"Unfortunately, he may choose death when he rises to consciousness and realizes we couldn't retrieve his mate." Miane's eyes went an eerie obsidian that was somehow less "human" than the midnight of Kaia's other self. "We'll take care of things from here."

Bo hadn't been expecting any other response; this was Miane's kingdom and her people who'd been hurt. He'd have made the same call. "If you'll excuse me. I have to speak to Kaia."

Miane and Malachai exchanged a look before Miane said, "Walk with me." It held the command of an alpha.

Certain enough in his own skin and his own power not to bristle, Bo went without argument. Miane shot him a narrow-eyed glance. "Never follow another alpha's orders."

"I will if it's in my own best interest," Bo said in a tone as unbending.

Pausing on the edge of the deck, Miane stared at him before a small smile lit her inhuman eyes. "Interesting. Humans have an advantage there. No changeling alpha would ever do the same, *even* if it was in his best interest."

"That's why it took a human to end the Territorial Wars."

"Your ancestor."

Of course Miane would know; she wasn't alpha because of brute strength alone. Like most changeling alphas Bowen had met, she had a razor-sharp mind. "Yes."

"I'd do well to remember that." Turning to face the ocean, she nodded. "This is Kaia's home and where she's at peace. Attempt to take her from it and you may permanently break her."

Bowen knew Miane was doing only what came naturally to any alpha—protecting her own. If only she knew that Bo would cut off his arm if it would save Kaia from hurt. "The decision will be hers." He shoved his hair back from his forehead, watched a wave come in to crash against the edge of the deck. "But first, we have to run another gauntlet."

Miane's eyes were a strange in-between shade when she turned to face him. She held out a hand. "Good luck, Bowen Knight. You are far more intriguing a man than I first understood."

He shook the sleek strength of her hand, but his attention was on another woman getting closer, the scent of her whispering to him on the breeze. "And you, Miane Levèque, are a far more lethal predator than the world realizes."

Her laugh was dangerous but the arms she opened to Kaia affectionate. "The shell is waiting," she said to Kaia. "Go, fight this battle. Surrender is not for the likes of us, Kaia Luna."

MALACHAI was already in the water when Bo and Kaia got into the windowless shell and sealed it behind them. Bo had spotted the "straps" with which Malachai would pull them, but there was no sign of what Mal might become when he shed his human skin.

The shell began to move through the water.

"Fuck." The ride was smooth, the speed insane.

"I used to hold on to him as a child and go racing through the sea." Kaia's smile faded as their eyes met. "You know."

Tugging her into his lap, Bo gloried in the warm weight of her, his siren with her marshmallow heart. "You find it so horrifically painful to be on land that you have to medicate yourself to get through it."

"It's a child's fear," Kaia said starkly. "Yet it feels like a clawed grip around my lungs. Squeezing and squeezing until I can't breathe and my face is all hot and my gut churns."

Bo hated the idea of her in such anguish. "Have you spoken to anyone about it?"

"The clan and my family tried when I was younger, but I refused to cooperate." She kneaded his shoulder in a restless movement. "I was so *angry*. I didn't want to go to land and I didn't understand why they couldn't accept I was quite content to stay in the blue near Lantia."

Bowen could see her, a furious little girl with a spine of steel and the grit to withstand the desires of the adults around her. "Are you still angry?" It came out husky, his heart right there for her to see.

A single tear rolled down her face. "Oh, Bowen." Pressing her cheek to his stubbled jaw, she whispered, "It's too late. The fear is rooted in my soul."

Wet against his skin. "Six months after my parents' deaths, I agreed to at least swim in the wider ocean. I went out with my aunt and uncle and an hour into the swim, I swam ahead a little and into an illegal net cast by poachers—I panicked and shifted and nearly drowned. It didn't matter that my aunt and uncle got me out in under a minute, I never wanted to swim wide again. I just wanted to be safe in the heart of BlackSea."

Bo's own soul raged, wanting to reach out and capture her, this luminous creature who had never been meant to be his and yet was. He might be human, but he'd been around enough changelings to understand the primal tug of the mating bond. It was a gift. One he couldn't accept when his future was a black unknown and when taking Kaia from Ryūjin would be to destroy her.

But he had to tell her, had to do what he could to make sure the future wouldn't further scar her. "I love you, Kaia Luna." Never had he spoken those three words to a lover. "With all of the man I am, the good and the bad, the mistakes and the glories. I love you to the depths of my being, and if tomorrow I don't wake as me—"

She pressed her fingers against his lips. "Don't." A shaken word, a fresh wave of tears streaking down her cheeks.

Kissing those fingers, he tugged them gently away. "No matter what tomorrow brings," he said, "know that I, Bowen Adrian Knight, belong to you for however long I exist as myself." It was his turn to press his fingers to her lips when she parted them to speak. "If the worst happens, please don't feel obligated to me. Even if a glimmer of my mind remains, knowing I'm a burden to you will torture me for eternity."

"You could *never* be a burden!" Scalding heat in her voice.

"Promise me." He grabbed her hand, pressed it to his cutting-edge mechanical heart that would keep going long after he fell. "If it goes wrong, you'll walk away. *Promise me.*"

"How can you ask that?" She shoved at his shoulders with angry hands. "You're my mate!"

Bo shuddered under the emotional blow. "I know." He'd found the one person who sang to his heart and he'd found her at the worst possible moment in his life. "And your mate asks this one promise from you.

Don't live your life loving a shell—I won't be in there, Kaia. I'll be dead. Mourn me, but please don't bury yourself with me. *Promise.*"

A mutinous look. "I'll decide tomorrow, after you wake."

"No." He shook her with furious gentleness. "We decide now, when we're both whole." Kissing her hard, devouring her, he broke away on a gasp of air—and admitted his deepest horror. "I can't go into this knowing I might be consigning you to a living death."

"Mates are forever, Bowen! Forever!" Her face set in dangerous lines. "You'd *never* walk away from me if our positions were reversed."

No, he wouldn't, but that wasn't the point and *oh fuck!* Bowen's instincts blared a screaming warning. "Don't you dare!" he yelled. "Kaia, don't you fucking—"

But it was too late. She dropped her defenses and the primal fury of the mating bond did the rest, whiplashing into his own wide-open heart. Because, as a changeling had once told him, when a man and a woman mated, it was the woman of the pair who made the final choice—and Kaia Luna had chosen Bowen Knight.

He felt the joy and sorrow and wildness and endless ocean of her smash into his soul in crashing waves, and in the onyx of her eyes, he saw the creature who was her other half and he felt it swimming in his own bloodstream.

"Kaia." Arms locking around her, he drowned in the wonder of it.

She had her own arms around him just as tight, the two of them holding on for dear life. "You're mine. Whatever happens after the third injection, you will *always* be mine."

Kissing her in a rage that turned into piercing tenderness, Bo didn't remember stripping off her clothes or his, but there, hidden in the deep, far beyond either the denizens of the surface or those who swam in the blackness below, they loved each other as only two mates could love. It was disorienting at times—he could feel her pleasure and her need as well as his own, the mating bond yet settling in place—but they rode the waves until there was no Bowen and no Kaia. Only them.

Together.

One last time before the final spin of the wheel.

Chapter 62

It's time.

—Dr. Atalina Kahananui to Bowen Knight

THE OPERATION WAS done.

Bowen's skull sealed back up.

Hours had passed without a response.

Bowen Adrian Knight existed in an unnatural sleep even his mate couldn't penetrate.

His chest rose and fell.

Pressing her fisted hand against her abdomen, Kaia blinked back the burn in her eyes, and she waited.

Chapter 63

I still have no trail. They're both off the grid and Heenali's now twelve hours past the date she told Domenica she'd return.

—Message from Lily Knight to Cassius Drake

IT WAS THE dull *thud, thud* of sound that first reached him, but it took Bowen almost a minute to realize what it was.

His heart.

Mechanical. Strong. Human.

Exhaling on that understanding, he opened his eyes . . . and looked into those of an inky black he'd never mistake for any other. "Hello, Siren." His voice was a rasp, but the words sounded as they should.

A brilliant smile, sunlight over a turbulent ocean. "Bo, it's done," she whispered. "You made it through."

Bo flexed his fingers and toes. "My brain feels . . . fuzzy."

"That'll pass." Dr. Kahananui's crisp voice. "You've been out for eighteen hours."

Bo wove his fingers through Kaia's, held on to this heart of his that lived outside his body. "Success?"

Dr. Kahananui looked up from the data panel. "You're rational and appear to have full control of your faculties, but we won't know if there's any neurological damage until after we run the full battery of tests."

Bo nodded, and in the long hours that passed, he cooperated with every test the doctor had for him—from completing childish jigsaw puzzles to solving high-level logic questions. When he did hit a glitch, it was on random questions to do with entertainment celebrities. "Not info I've ever had, Doc."

Dr. Kahananui, who was still *very* heavily pregnant, grinned. "Just checking if you're awake." She shifted in the comfortable chair Dex had brought in for her. "It's been a long day."

It grew longer yet.

Kaia was a constant presence through it all, both in his room and deep inside him in the way of mates. She disappeared only for short periods—and would always return with food or drinks. When the doctor told him to get some sleep and that they'd continue the next day, he and Kaia spent the night wrapped around each other.

They didn't speak of the inevitable tomorrow.

But tomorrow did come and with it, Dr. Kahananui's conclusion that the experiment had been an unqualified success. "I feel confident I can repeat the procedure on the others of your people who have the chip." A stroke of her belly. "After a slight delay."

It turned out she'd been having contractions all morning.

Dex almost lost his mind when she finally told him. The couple disappeared into the black with the healer only minutes later. Heart thundering and his head crystal clear in its precision, Bo stood at the seaward wall with Kaia. "Is it usually quick?"

"Sometimes, sometimes not." She leaned her body into his. "The next submersible arrives in three hours."

Bowen's blood froze. "Not yet." A harsh repudiation.

"I heard you talking to Lily—and I've seen the reports in the media. The Alliance is beginning to fragment at the edges." Her face lifting up to his, her fingers petting his hair. "They need you."

"You need me, too," he said bluntly. "As badly as I need you." Leaving her would shatter him.

"If you stay here," Kaia murmured with a chiding shake of her head, "you'll slowly begin to despise yourself."

That, too, was true. Bo had made promises, given his word that he'd lead his people from the darkness. He wouldn't be able to live with himself if he betrayed that trust by walking away. "I don't know how to be without you." He'd been self-sufficient for so long, but now he had a need for her that nothing else would ever quench.

"I shouldn't have mated us." Human eyes meeting his, her other self sliding away in a shame he felt as starkly as if it were his own. "You would be free without the bond."

"Siren, I haven't been free since the day I first opened my eyes and saw you." He kissed her, right there in the heart of the atrium, with the sea a silken darkness beyond and her clanmates watching.

He kissed his mate who knew him to the core and whose love was a fierce force of nature. "I will *never* regret our bond."

"Visit when you can," she said against his lips, the desperation of her need as potent as his. "I'll watch for you."

He crushed her to him—and over her head, he saw Alden's red face. But the other man didn't approach, didn't try to intrude, didn't bring up Hugo's name. He just stood there with angry eyes as Bowen held the woman who was his forever.

KAIA swam up alongside the submersible in her human form, her gills keeping her alive. It was somehow fitting that he'd press his hand to the window when the light from the surface began to spear through the water, and she'd press back before fading away into the deep, like the creature of the black that she was.

He walked silently from the submersible to the jet-chopper BlackSea had arranged to take him to the island runway, the sea too turbulent today for small craft. As it lifted off, he watched the water for her even though he knew she'd stayed in the deep. Kaia had her hand around his heart, and the higher he flew, the tighter she gripped. But the jet-chopper kept lifting and lifting until he could see the city from above. But Bo wasn't interested in the startling view of waves crashing up against a glittering and green oceanic city that was a marvel of engineering.

He was interested only in the siren who rose up out of the ocean below the jet-chopper, her face lifted toward him. Bowen pressed his hand to the window. She was his and he was leaving her behind because he'd made promises he had to keep . . . promises she wanted and needed him to keep. His mate understood that if he didn't, it would be a toxic poison inside him.

But keeping those promises meant leaving Kaia and that was unacceptable. So he'd figure out a way to change things. Bowen wasn't about to lose his mate at the first fucking hurdle. "I'll come for you," he promised, his jaw set. "You're mine, Kaia, and I'm not about to let you go."

Chapter 64

This is weird. I'm getting pings again. If he keeps to his current route, Trey is heading back into Italy.

—Lily Knight to Bowen Knight and Cassius Drake

BO'S SISTER RAN into his arms the instant he got off a jet-chopper that had landed on top of a Venetian building. The Alliance craft had been waiting for him when he disembarked the plane. Heart wrenching at seeing Lily alive and well after the horror of their last moments together—though she was far too thin—he lifted her up and spun her around. "Looks like you missed me," he said, putting her down on her feet.

"Maybe a little." She hooked her arm through his, her smile huge, and led him away from the chopper.

Turning, Bo sent the pilot a thank-you salute. The other man returned the gesture before taking off to make the journey back to his base at the airport.

Bo almost flagged him back down. He'd left part of himself in the deep, and how the fuck was he supposed to function without his heart?

His lungs tight, he drew Lily to the edge of the roof so he could look out over a Venice gilded by the gold of the setting sun. The glorious hues of the buildings dusted with snow, the winding canals, the gondolas, the buskers, it was all so familiar and it had always before soothed his soul. Today, however, he strained to glimpse the ocean that was Kaia's home.

"Do you think it'd be difficult to shift Alliance HQ?"

His sister threw him a startled look. "Well . . . we've been here a long time. The land the HQ stands on belongs to the Alliance and because we've been here so long, we have intricate security measures in place that it would take years to re-create in another location."

He could feel her examining his face with those big gray eyes that had been so bleak and stunned when his parents first brought her home. "Is it Kaia?" A gentle question. "You always smile when you talk about her."

"Yes." Bo blew out a breath. "She's my mate, Lily. And she's a world away."

"You could run a lot of things remotely. Our comm center is strong, and—"

"And our people need to see me here, in the thick of things." He shook his head at her, this sister of his who'd back him in any decision. "We're still so fragile." Like the finely blown glass out of Murano; a single crack could destroy everything. "Heenali?"

"Still nothing." Shadows drifted across Lily's face, the gold of the sunset eclipsed by an inner darkness. "It's not looking good for her, is it?"

"No." Bo turned his gaze back to his city. "Cassius is on her ex's trail?"

"Yes. He checked in a couple of hours ago, is following the new financial trace I picked up." She slipped her hands into the pockets of her coat, her breath frosting the air. "We're fracturing, Bo. It's good you came back now. Any longer . . ."

"The first thing I'm going to do is set up a stronger line of succession."

"It won't work." Lily's eyes appeared like Malachai's pale gold in this light. "We're too young in our current incarnation. Someone has to be the anchor for every new creation—and you're ours." Her sleek black hair was gilt under the sunlight. "But that doesn't mean you aren't allowed to have love. We'll figure this out. Venice is the least landlocked city in the world. Kaia could swim out to the ocean anytime she wanted. Lots of water changelings call it home."

Bo thought of his siren with her need for the safety of the black around Ryūjin, of her heart so tied to the blue, and shook his head. "She's a creature of the deep, Lily. It would be like trying to cage a butterfly."

KAIA didn't cry. She lavished her love on her newborn clanmate. She made treats for the entire station. She swam until her breath was lost and her heart thundered. And she spent every night dreaming of a human tied to her by a bond that would never break but that was stretched painfully thin across the vast distance that separated them.

The creature inside her swam in agitated circles, unable to think.

Nothing was right. Nothing was as it should be.

Bebe took one look at her four days after Bowen's departure and said, "Well? I told you your time would come. Make your choice, girl." Harsh words, but her hand was gentle where it patted the back of Kaia's. "You either fight or you curl up and die. Only two choices."

TEN days after his return and Bowen was still missing two of his senior people. Heenali remained off the grid while Cassius continued to track her surprisingly slippery ex. Added to that, the slew of recent media stories about the Alliance crumbling from within meant Bo had to show his face at certain events when he'd far rather be alone.

He was also going out of his mind missing his mate, though he could feel her inside him in a way he couldn't explain. He just knew that Kaia lived and that he'd realize at once if anything happened to her. But he couldn't reach out and touch her, couldn't kiss her, couldn't dance with her on the streets of his beloved *Venezia* while a busker played a love song.

Releasing a rough exhale, he glanced at the comm. He called her every morning and every night, and she sent him little messages throughout the day, but today, the comm was silent. She hadn't been on the station when he called—probably out for a swim in the black—and he hadn't yet received any messages.

"Bo?" One of his knights appeared in the doorway to his office. "We still on for the meeting?"

Bo forced himself to look away from the comm. "Yes." And he got to work—the stronger he could make the Alliance, the more time he could spend away from the HQ without devastating consequences for the organization he'd spilled his lifeblood to grow and keep strong.

It was around two o'clock that he decided to comm Ryūjin again, but he got an alert on his phone before he could get to the comm. A jet-chopper was about to land on the roof: *ID pings as BlackSea.*

Bo left his office at a run, taking the stairs three at a time. It was unlikely to be Kaia, but he swore he could feel her closer than usual. Then he was at the door to the roof and pushing it open against the wind of the chopper's landing. One look at the machine's sleek profile, along with the wave sigil on the door, and he confirmed it was a BlackSea craft. He couldn't identify the pilot from here, but he felt his siren.

Waiting only until the jet-chopper was safely parked, though its blades continued to spin, he ran toward it. The door opened before he reached it, Kaia jumping out into his arms. He crushed her to him, his entire body a buzz of delight. Above them, the chopper's blades began to slow before coming to a standstill.

"I missed you." Kaia's lips on his, her hands on his face, her scent swirling around them. "God, I missed you so much."

Having identified the pilot by now, Bo fell into the kiss like a starving man, the need in him an endless ocean. *"Kaia."* Another kiss, another wave of piercing rightness. "What are you doing here?" He grabbed her shoulders. "You took the fucking meds." The healer had told him exactly how bad those meds were for her system long-term.

"Stop scowling." She poked a finger into his chest. "I've been working with the healers and the counselors and Ivy Jane Zen. I hitched a ride with Mal for a short test, to see if anything's working." A deep breath, another. "I *am* on the meds, but it's a lighter dose. I have you deep inside me now and it's changed the balance."

"How?" he asked roughly.

"I can lean on you." Simple, powerful words. "You might get a backwash of my fear."

"Throw it all on me if you can." He'd shoulder every ounce of her pain if she'd let him.

"It doesn't work that way, but"—a determined smile full of affection—"let's see how I go."

"I still want to shake you." Bo gripped her by the upper arms. "You're in pain."

"No pain, no gain." Then she leaned in and nipped playfully at his lower lip.

Unable to hold on to his protective anger in the face of her innate mischief and his joy in seeing her, Bowen led her out from the shadow of the jet-chopper and toward Malachai, who'd gone to stand on the edge of the building.

"Mal." He shook hands with the BlackSea security chief. "How long can you stay?" How long could Bo keep his mate close?

"Only a couple of hours." Malachai's eyes were human today, but his presence remained that of a serious power. "I figured we might as well hold our meet in person."

That meeting was so Bo could update Malachai on what was going on with the hunt for the traitor in Alliance ranks. Bo continued to refuse to give Mal a name, but he'd shared all other data—trust took two, and Mal had already done his part. "I'm not going to argue."

Lifting his and Kaia's clasped hands, he pressed a kiss to her knuckles right as his phone buzzed. He took it out of his pocket to glance at the screen. "It's Lily."

He answered the call audio-only, while Kaia walked over to the edge of the building to look at the view. Their hands entwined, Bo moved with her. "Lil, if it's not urgent—"

"Trey Gunther's been spotted in Venice. Sending through the image—Cassius took it half a minute ago."

Kaia turned to smile at him just as he lowered his phone to look at the surveillance shot. Her smile faded. "Bo, let me see that." She tugged down his hand to get a better view of the screen.

Alerted by her response, Malachai moved so he, too, could view the image. Bo saw no reason to hide it—Heenali wasn't in the shot, though she had to be close; she was as well trained a hunter as Cassius and while she wasn't using Alliance tech resources, she knew Trey Gunther better than all of them.

"Bo"—Kaia's voice shook—"why do you have a picture of Hugo on your phone?"

Chapter 65

I fucked up, baby. I really fucked up.

—Message from Trey Gunther to Heenali Roy

KAIA'S BRAIN STUTTERED as it tried to absorb the unexpected new input. "When was this taken?" she asked before Bowen could answer.

"Less than a minute ago," he said grimly, then returned to his call for a short moment. "Lil, send me the location."

Malachai stirred as Bowen hung up. "I think you'd better explain."

"We know this man as Trey Gunther." Bowen's words made no sense. "He was deeply involved with one of my lieutenants for months." Her mate's hand tightened around hers. "She's the one we suspect of directing Fleet ships your way—and she's currently AWOL, searching for Trey." His voice had turned ice-cold during the briefing, the glance he shared with Malachai filled with something Kaia didn't want to see.

"No," she said. *"No."* There was no way Hugo would've sold them all a lie.

Bowen caught her gaze. "I don't know what's going on, Siren, and I'm not going to judge your friend before I meet him—but we find out the truth today." His phone pinged.

One glance and he was moving, tugging her along with him while

Malachai prowled at their backs. "His hotel is within walking distance." Shoving through the door, he began to head down the stairs. "He had to know we'd spot him once he entered Venice. It's almost as if he came here on purpose."

Kaia, her heart pounding a staccato beat, could only think of one thing. "Hugo's alive." Her other half dived in a dance of joy. *"He's alive."*

Bowen led her out a door and onto the snowy cobblestones of Venice. She'd never before visited this city full of water that many of her clanmates loved, and for a moment on the roof, she'd wondered . . . but now, she barely glimpsed anything of what they passed, the sun glittering off the snow to shatter brightness against her irises.

Hugo was *alive.*

But there was a dark thread in the joy that she couldn't ignore. If Hugo had escaped his captors, why hadn't he let anyone know? And why did Bowen say his name was Trey? Surely that had to be a mistake.

Her breath coming in rough pants, she barely managed to keep up with her mate as he took them through the streets and alleys of Venice. Water and snow sparkled around her. She'd read that Venetian canals had been filthy once upon a time, but that had been more than a hundred years earlier. The residents of the city had funded a massive system that meant you could swim in it without coming to harm.

And why was she thinking about that when *Hugo was alive*!

Bowen came to a sudden stop, his hand locked with hers. His breath puffed the air, but he wasn't out of breath any more than Malachai. As for Kaia, she wasn't afraid, her fear subsumed by the chaos that twisted black tendrils through her mind.

"My man is in that building." He pointed three buildings down on the right. "Trey—Hugo—is in the small hotel directly opposite."

"I want to see him," Kaia said. "Hugo never lies to me." Yet, if he'd been living a secret life as Trey, he'd told her many lies.

"You're both sure it's the same man?" Bowen asked.

Kaia nodded, while Malachai rumbled a flat "Yes."

"Did he disappear for days at a time from Ryūjin?"

"Yes, but that's just Hugo," Kaia pointed out. "He liked to swim to visit faraway clanmates. Then he'd work a chunk and disappear again." It was no more odd a pattern than any other for a water changeling.

"Trey told us he was a salesman." Bowen's eyes swept the alley. "It made sense he'd be in Venice for a few days, then on the road for a couple of weeks."

Her stomach twisted, her face hot. "I need to speak to him. I can't believe it otherwise."

"I know." Her mate brushed his hand over her hair. "You'd never betray a friend."

Swallowing hard because he knew her, understood her, she tried to break their handclasp—but Bowen wouldn't allow it.

"I want to speak to him alone."

"It's too late," Bowen murmured, his eyes on a petite dark-eyed and dark-haired woman who'd just run into the building. "Heenali's here. No time for stealth." He moved rapidly toward the door of the hotel, his phone to his ear. "Cassius, can you see through to the room?"

Whatever the answer was, Bowen slipped away the phone and they entered the hotel by the front door. The man on duty at the small desk looked at them with wide eyes. "Third floor," he whispered. "Room 308."

Realizing the hotelier must've been the original informant, Kaia followed Bowen up the stairs, Malachai at their backs. The door to room 308 was wide open . . . and Kaia heard the sound of a desperate "No!" echoing down the hallway before they reached it.

All three of them slammed into the room—and Kaia lost every whisper of breath in her body.

Hugo was lying on the crisply made bed as if he'd come into the room and decided to have a short rest. But his eyes were open and he was smiling up at the woman who held his head in her lap. Blood trickled from the corners of his eyes. ". . . fucked up." Husky words.

"Hugo." Kaia ran to the bed, and this time Bowen let her go.

The petite woman Bowen had called Heenali gave her a savage look before her attention flicked to the door and to the men who stood there. "Bo," she said, her voice as harsh, "we need medics."

"I've already sent the alert."

Hugo's reddened eyes turned to Kaia, the smile in them brilliant. "Kaia." He gripped at her hand. "I'm sorry."

"No, you don't get to be sorry." Kaia held on tight. "You stay alive and then we'll figure it out." She could smell a chemical trace around him. "What did you take?"

He coughed and blood flecked the air. "Didn't. Was given." He touched a small prick on the side of his neck. "Didn't even notice. Don't know when."

Heenali brushed his hair back from his face. "Just breathe," she ordered. "You breathe, Trey."

"Hugo." He looked up into the other woman's eyes, a plea in his. "Don't hate me. I love you. Came back for you."

"Hugo." No hesitation, no anger. "I could *never* hate you. I love you, you idiot."

Hugo's lips trembled. "Was so stupid, lover. Poker debts. Bad. Said they'd forgive if I—" His body racked by a worse spate of coughing. "If I convinced you to move a few ships off-route, made that dossier, spread rumors about Bowen Knight."

Even as Kaia struggled to accept what Hugo had done, she was listening desperately for the paramedics. When Bowen came to place a hand on her shoulder, she looked up at him. "Where are they?"

"Close," he said, a darkness in his gaze that told her he didn't think it would matter.

But Kaia couldn't believe that, couldn't imagine her best friend gone from this world. He was foolish and feckless and careless, but he laughed with all his heart and he was meant to be the crazy friend who'd spoil her children and teach them mad pranks.

"I thought you were smuggling," Heenali said as Malachai came to stand in Hugo's line of sight. "I didn't care about a little smuggling if it made you happy."

Hugo's eyes were losing focus, but he found Malachai. "I didn't know," he said desperately. "Until they sent me that picture of two of our own the night before I left, along with the reports of the ship movements and how they linked up to our vanished, I didn't know they were the ones taking our people. Didn't know what was true in the dossier and what wasn't."

Kaia's heart grew cold; his words were so close to what George had said. How many of her clanmates had been taken in, made to play a small role in a much larger and deadlier game?

But Hugo wasn't done. "Knew you'd figure it out once Kaia gave it to you."

"You shouldn't talk so much," she said. "Save your strength."

Heenali nodded. "Yes, be quiet."

But Hugo's eyes were fixated on Malachai. "Tell Miane I didn't know." Tears in his voice. "Please, Mal."

Malachai shifted to touch his hand to Hugo's brow, giving the other man the comfort of clan. "I will. I give you my word."

An exhale before Hugo said, "I tried to fix it. I tried to fix my mistake."

"What did you do?" Malachai's deep voice.

"Hacked everything." His eyelids fluttered. "Ran and hacked. Inserted Trojans earlier. Hated being blackmailed. Hacked them. They found me, but I found him fir—" His words trailed off into nothing.

"HUGO!" The cry came from Kaia and Heenali at the same time, two women who loved this man in different ways. Bowen had been ready to dislike the changeling male for the rumors he'd spread about Bo and for having a place in Kaia's heart, but all he felt at that moment was pity and sorrow. Hugo could've been a younger brother who'd lost his way, he was so oddly innocent in his stark acceptance of his mistake.

Sirens sounded close by, but nothing could save Hugo. Whatever poison had been shot into him, it was lethal—and it had been done stealthily enough that Cassius hadn't noticed—*or* it was slow-acting and Hugo had carried it with him into Venice.

Hugo struggled up into consciousness again, his unfocused gaze somehow locking with Heenali's. "I found him. Tell Miane I found him."

"Who?" Malachai demanded. "Who did you find?"

"Sold out our people." Slurred words. "My friend. Your friend." This time, the coughing was so violent it shook his entire body.

"*Who*, Hugo?" Malachai demanded.

"Stop it!" Pulling out a weapon, Heenali pointed it at the BlackSea security chief. "Let him rest!"

Bo put his hand on Heenali's wrist, gently pushed down the weapon. "He needs to do this," he told his knight. "He needs to go out knowing he put things right."

A tear rolled out from Hugo's left eye. "Love you, Heena."

"Love you more, Hugo." Dropping the weapon, she crawled to lie in the curve of his arm, her own arm over his waist.

Somehow managing to wrap both arms around her, Hugo said, "KJ," on a rattling exhale that could have only one end. "Found KJ."

Chapter 66

Heena, my love, my sweet, deadly rose. (Too goofy? I can't help myself around you. I open my mouth and goofy comes out.)

—Note attached to roses sent by Trey Gunther to Heenali Roy

"GO," HEENALI SAID as Hugo's dying words echoed in the room. "Please go."

In front of Bo, a trembling Kaia pressed a kiss to Hugo's cheek, her friend's eyes already closed, then let Bo lead her out of the room.

He was conscious of Mal staying long enough to say, "You did good, Hugo. You fixed it."

Kaia didn't cry, just stood frozen in Bowen's embrace in the corridor outside. When Malachai came out, his face was so grim it appeared chipped out of stone. As Bo watched, hearing nothing but silence from inside the room, the other man made a call. "Find KJ," he told someone. "Hold him."

As shell-shocked as Kaia, Bo rocked her in his arms. "How could it be him?" His brain had defaulted to cool logic and strategy in the face of the agony swamping him—Kaia's agony, Kaia's terrible sorrow.

Bo embraced it, embraced her.

"This traitor was pinpointing people in distant regions, and KJ is based on Ryūjin."

"There's a medical database," Malachai said tonelessly. "Our people are encouraged to check in at least once a year so we know who hasn't seen a healer for far too long, and arrangements can be made to get someone to their geographic location." His body was rigid, his eyes flat. "But we won't know for certain until I've run a full investigation."

As Bo had done with Heenali. Except—"Hugo spent his last breaths sharing that name." Kaia's best friend must've been brutally certain.

Kaia, still mute, stared at the paramedics who ran up the steps. Bo indicated the open door and they entered . . . only to return mere seconds later, their faces telling the story long before one of them said, "He's gone."

Stiff as a rock, Kaia closed her eyes and he could almost hear her silent scream. Bowen squeezed her tight, but felt her begin to slip away from him regardless. When she shuddered, he scooped her up in his arms and made his way down the stairs as fast as possible. This old building had no elevator and the journey took far too long.

The cold, fresh air had Kaia gulping desperate breaths when he set her down on her feet, but her respiration was far too shallow, her eyes dilated. "Focus on me, Siren. Lean on the bond." Cupping her face, he held her gaze with his; everything else could wait. Only Kaia mattered.

"Bo." A wheezed-out whisper of sound. "Can't breathe."

"Where's your medication?"

She began to reach into her pocket, but he was already there. Grabbing the preloaded injector, he said, "Can you take more? Is it safe?"

A jagged nod, Kaia extending her arm.

Shoving up her sleeve, he jolted her system with the medication. She sucked in more air, and deep inside him, he felt her presence become closer, impossibly more intense. *Leaning on him.* It took ten long minutes for her to stop trembling and for her dilated pupils to shrink back to normal size.

Cassius had called in an Alliance squad by then, his job to secure the scene while Malachai organized a BlackSea retrieval team. Enforcement might have something to say on that point, but they could argue with BlackSea about jurisdiction—and Bo knew exactly who'd win. But Kaia, she still hadn't cried.

Walking her away from the scene, he took her into the dark shadows between two buildings and enclosed her once more in his arms. “Cry, baby,” he begged. “Don’t hold it inside like you did as a child. *Please.*” Whatever progress she’d made in conquering her fear of land, it had splintered into razor-sharp slivers in that room filled with a dying man’s last words, but Bowen couldn’t bear to let her return to the black while she was in such horrific pain.

Who would hold his Kaia in the deep? Who would rock her as she cried for the loss of one of her closest friends? It didn’t matter what Hugo had done or the crimes he’d committed. Not now. Not to Kaia’s heart.

“I can’t.” The words were distant . . . and he realized she was under the full impact of the anti-anxiety medication. “I don’t feel anything.”

Malachai appeared on the edge of the shadows. “The retrieval team will be here in an hour. I’ll be leaving then.” His gaze went to Kaia, the question unasked.

“We’ll be coming with you.” Bowen had given his adult life to the Alliance, but today, he was being asked to choose between his mate and the Alliance and it wasn’t a choice at all.

“No.” Kaia pushed away from him. “Heenali, she needs you. She needs her alpha.”

“Cassius and Lily are with her.” He’d seen his sister run into the hotel not long after he and Kaia exited. “I’m coming with you.”

Kaia stared at him, the flatness of her expression belied by her next words. “I’m sorry,” she whispered, emotion creeping in on the edges of the medicated calm. “I see land when I look at you. I see death and pain and loss.”

Bowen staggered inside at the blow, at the chilling realization that he was the embodiment of her greatest fear. *“Kaia.”*

Shaking her head, she kept her distance. “There’s so much panic inside me, Bo. The medication’s the only thing keeping it back. I’m scared I’m going to start screaming if I don’t dive far, far into the black.”

Far from him, from her mate who was so totally a creature of land that he’d forever remind her of it. Every breath felt like a knife blade.

Shifting his gaze to Malachai's pale gold eyes, he said, "Take care of her. Don't leave her alone."

The other man gave a hard nod, his expression holding an unexpected sympathy.

AN hour later, Bo watched the jet-chopper lift off. Kaia pressed her hand against the window, looking at him until she was too far up and he could no longer see her. Still he watched, until the jet-chopper disappeared from sight far on the horizon.

And though his heart felt broken into a million tiny pieces, he clung to the feeling of her inside him. She was traumatized, in shock, heavily medicated. He'd wait, give her a few days, then go to her. As long as he could feel her in his heart, it would be all right. She was his mate, and mates were forever.

His siren had told him so herself.

He just had to be patient—even if it felt like he was bleeding inside with every second that passed.

Forcing his mind to go quiet, his control ruthless because that was the only way he could deal with this, he went to Heenali. She'd refused to leave Hugo's body, and it was Bo who'd had to wrench her away—he'd left her in Cassius and Lily's care while he said good-bye to his heart.

She came at him like a Fury when he walked into the bedroom in a nearby apartment building owned by the Alliance. "I hate you!"

Catching her in his arms and very aware of her deadly skills, Bowen used his own to immobilize her against the wall without causing harm. "I know," he said. "But he had to go home, to the blue."

She twisted in his hold until she had no breath left in her. "I won't get to say good-bye." So much pain. So much anger.

"I asked for you. They'll tell us the funeral date—as the woman he loved, you're welcome to join all rites and to sit with him the night before."

Stark brown eyes looking into his. A second later, his tough knight crumpled into his arms. He held her as she cried out her heartbreaking loss and he thought of a woman who hadn't cried at all.

His own heart hurt so badly that he didn't think it was mechanical any longer.

"I thought he was making a little money on the side smuggling things into BlackSea territory that he was able to offload from the ships by using his other form."

"You knew he was a changeling?" That explained so much of her fascination with the water changelings.

"Trey . . . Hugo told me. He didn't always lie." She lay against him, her cheek on his chest. "I'd already figured it out by then—it's hard not to when you're so close to someone."

Bo thought of how Kaia moved, how her eyes changed color from human to her other self, how there was an intrinsic, beautiful wildness to her. The only reason he'd picked up none of that in the man he'd known as Trey was that he'd spent very little time with him. "Why did he let us think he was human?"

"He told me he was in trouble with the clan and he'd rather just play human until he'd sorted it out, especially since we were building a relationship with them. He didn't want his track record to interfere." Grief thickened her voice; underlying it was love, raw and lost. "I didn't think it'd do any harm to indulge him with the ship movements, with what I believed was penny-ante smuggling. We've all crossed a few lines—it made him more real that he was just as imperfect as me."

How could Bo chastise her when he'd been willing to leave the entire Alliance to flounder so long as Kaia needed him? He couldn't. "There was a photo of two badly beaten changelings on one of our ships," he said, because they both fell back on work when things hurt.

"Which ship?"

"The *Quiet Wind*."

"Small crew—ten people, five on, five off. Easy enough to put to sleep if you know exactly where they'll be." She released a trembling breath. "I let him see the security charts, Bo. He was so interested in my work and . . . I loved him. I was foolish and gullible and I loved him and I still do."

"I'm glad you loved him." Bo knew the wounds on Heenali's soul; that she'd been able to love at all, it was a gift. What the damage would be after this, he couldn't predict. "Incapacitate the crew on duty without them being aware of it," he murmured. "Stage the photo, leave." If the intruders were silent enough, the sleeping half of the crew would never wake.

"No one would speak up," Heenali added. "Each would think they'd fallen asleep at their post. Classic case of covering their asses." She sounded like the old Heenali, crisp and no-nonsense . . . and she was nothing like the old Heenali. "Who was she? Did he love her?"

He heard her pain, did what he could to assuage it. "She's my mate. They were childhood friends who grew into adult friends, but they were never lovers and didn't want to be."

Bowen thought of how the dying man had looked at both Kaia and Heenali and knew that some part of Hugo *had* wanted more from Kaia—but life hadn't worked out that way, and in the end, he'd made his choice. "You were the one he loved as a man loves a woman."

"He conned me."

"Yes. But when it counted, he came back." Bo considered what he knew about Hugo. "He was a comms expert—and smart enough to hack into systems no one else could, but he let Lily see him, track him. He was running and trying to find information to fix his mistake, but he wasn't hiding from you. He just moved too fast for you to catch up."

"Do you really believe that?" Such haunting hope in her words.

"You can read Lily's reports yourself." Bo stared at the wall over the top of Heenali's head. "He was imperfect and flawed and he made the wrong choices, but he loved you."

In his arms, his tough, hard knight began to cry again.

Bowen just held her; they'd talk about trust and where to go from here later. Right now, Heenali needed a friend more than she needed the security chief of the Alliance. He gave her everything he could, and when he was finally alone, he messaged Malachai, aware the other man and Kaia would still be in the air: *Has she cried?*

No. She's barely spoken.

Bowen set his jaw; if she wouldn't allow him to hold her, he'd care for her another way. But before he could say anything, Malachai sent another message: *She doesn't know what she's saying right now, Bo. This is how she was after her parents died. She shut down. She wouldn't talk to anyone for weeks.*

Staring out at the night that cloaked Venice, Bo thought of that angry little girl and he thought of all the things Kaia had told him the nights they'd spent together on Ryūjin. All the stories she'd shared about that heartbroken girl's journey back to the world.

And his tactically minded brain saw a way to reach his mate through her grief.

Chapter 67

Chess is a game of patience and strategy.

—Jerard Knight to Bowen Knight (8)

KAIA STEPPED ONTO the deck of Lantia with a sick feeling in the pit of her stomach. It was the worst anxiety she'd ever felt, a nauseating, twisting sensation that she'd made the most horrific mistake of her life. But the realization hit up hard against a wall of cold that separated her from the world. She saw it, knew it existed, but nothing could reach her.

"Bebe?" she said, spotting her beloved many-times-great-grandmother not far from where Malachai had docked the boat they'd taken from the island. "What are you doing here?" Bebe rarely visited the city, preferring to spend time on Ryūjin, or on her island.

"I've come to take you to my island," Bebe said, as if that was perfectly self-explanatory.

And it was.

Not waiting, Kaia stripped off her clothes right there on the deck and dived in, shifting form as she hit the water. It took Bebe longer, but Kaia swam near Lantia until Bebe slipped in quietly beside her. Her island wasn't so far—close enough for even an elderly changeling to make it without undue stress.

Once they reached it, Kaia shifted, found the blanket she'd stashed under some rocks, wrapped it around herself, and tucked her body against Bebe's shell. She didn't know how long she slept, but she had terrible shivers at some point as the medication wore off. Still, they passed, and when she next opened her eyes, the sun was rising on the ocean.

They went swimming again and her other self fed because Bebe made it clear she was to feed. It didn't taste like anything. Back on the island in their human forms, the sun's rays warm on their skin, Kaia clasped her arms around her knees and thought she should cry, but the tears wouldn't come, her eyes as gritty as the sand on which she sat.

She clung to the bond inside her, afraid she'd float away without it. "Why did I leave him?" It seemed a madness now, when she needed him so desperately.

"Because you carry your fear like a third soul." Bebe's tone wasn't harsh, just pragmatic. "Now it's stolen your mate from you."

Kaia snapped her head toward her grandmother who was so old she was an ancestor. "He's still here." She slapped her palm over her heart. "He's still *mine*."

Shrugging, Bebe said, "Who's holding him while he hurts? Not you."

Kaia thought of how strong Bowen was, how much weight he carried on his shoulders—and how she'd silently vowed to show him joy, to be the person with whom he could be young and carefree and playful. "I told him I saw land in him." Horrified, she dug her fingers into the sand. "I didn't mean that! It wasn't me saying that!"

"No." Bebe bit into a hard fruit that grew on a tree on her island.

"Hugo died, Bebe." She couldn't deal with the rest of it, could only handle one pain at a time. "Hugo *died*."

"I know, child." A wrinkled arm around her shoulders. "And you'd already been so brave while your mate underwent Atalina's experiment. You walked with him even knowing he might not make it through, only to be reminded that he could die at any instant. Just like Hugo."

Agitation inside her skin, fear stealing her breath. "It took all my courage to be with Bowen while he was undergoing the experiment. I haven't got anything left."

"Will you give him up, then? Repudiate your mate?"

Jerking away to end up on her knees, Kaia stared at her grandmother. "He's *mine*." It came out furious, cracks shattering the cold that isolated her from the world. "He's mine!"

Bebe bit into the fruit again, as if she hadn't brought up a subject anathema to Kaia. Chewing with relish, she swallowed before saying, "Why isn't he here with you, then? A true mate would be here with you."

"I told him not to come!" Kaia was outraged Bebe would blame Bowen for this. "It was my choice."

"What kind of man accepts that?" Another bite. "Probably because he's human. Repudiate him," she said, like that was a thing that happened every day instead of being so rare it was more fable than reality. "Find a new mate."

"NO!" Kaia had never yelled at her grandmother in that tone of voice. "I will not!" Deep inside her, the mating bond warped, then settled again. What was that? Was it Bowen's pain? Was her mate hurting because she'd abandoned him? "Don't you dare blame him for my choices!"

"I'll do what I please." Bebe finished off the fruit and threw the core into the small bushes on the shoreline. "Anyway, the security chief of the humans isn't a good match for you. All these people out to kill him."

Kaia's breaths hurt, her abdomen rigid. "He's strong and he's smart. He's not easy prey."

"Are you sure?"

"Of course I'm sure! He survived a gunshot that destroyed his heart, came back from the dead, and had three injections in his brain using an experimental compound! Bowen is *tough*." And as she spoke the words, the scared child inside her realized their truth.

Bowen wasn't Hugo, a gambler and a charmer who'd fallen prey to professional predators.

Bowen wasn't her mother, a physician who never had a care for herself.

Bowen wasn't her father, an artist who saw beauty in the world but ignored the darkness.

Bowen saw the dark, Bowen saw the evil, and Bowen was a predator, too. One who chose to walk on the side of good, but who'd strike out against the dark if threatened. Bowen would fight like a berserker to his dying breath.

"I still think you should repudiate him." Bebe's expression was intransigent. "Let him find a nice biddable human woman. Then you can stay in the blue and he can stay on land."

So enraged she could barely think, Kaia splashed past the foam-white breakers hitting the sand. "No, no, no! He's mine!" And she was going to make sure he knew it.

She dived into the water.

SIGHING, Bebe creaked up to her feet. Maybe she should let the healer do the knee surgery he kept going on about. Impudent young man that he was, he'd told her he'd have her dancing in no time.

"Hmph." Finding the rock she wanted, she sat down on the sand again and pushed at the rock until she revealed the thick metal container hidden beneath.

It was Edison who'd given the container to her.

She kept snacks in there for when she didn't feel like swimming or doing anything. She was old and she'd outlived too many of her descendants. She hadn't planned to outlive her mate, too, but two days after his death, a heartbroken little girl had curled up next to her shell and then how could Bebe give in to her own terrible heartbreak?

She was allowed to be lazy and to eat chocolate bars five days in a row if she wanted.

Digging through the chocolate bars that the special container kept hard even when it was hot—she didn't know how and she didn't care, just that it worked—she closed her hand around a sleek black device.

The phone was cutting-edge, given to her by another one of her grandchildren. There were too many greats to fuss about at this point. It wasn't like she wanted to be reminded that she was positively ancient. Armand kept worrying she'd hurt herself on the island and no one would know. What worrywarts her descendants were!

Inputting the call code by memory because her brain worked just fine, thank you very much, she wasn't surprised when the call was picked up on the first ring. "Young man, do you play chess?"

Bowen Knight's voice had a crack in it when it came on the line. "It's been a year or two since I last had time for a match."

"I'll set up a game on my end and you do it on yours." Kaia's human had a strategic brain that intrigued her. "Did you let her go because she asked, or because you think three steps ahead?"

"I wasn't thinking much . . . for the first few minutes." His voice was no longer uneven. "Then I remembered that Kaia is possessive of her people and that she'll talk to you even when she shuts down with everyone else. She told me about your island and how she used to sleep curled up next to your shell."

Bebe chuckled. "It will be a good game, I think." She went to hang up, because men as beautifully devious as Bowen Knight shouldn't always be rewarded for their stratagems, but then she remembered her own beautifully devious mate and how soft his heart had been when it came to her. "It worked as you said it would."

Then she hung up.

A man should wait a little for his woman. Even if he had reached out across oceans to claim her.

Bebe smiled. "I like you, Bowen Knight." He saw her Kaia in a way others never had, not even her cousins who'd become brothers and a big sister; he saw her fears and he saw her flaws—but most of all, he saw her incredible heart.

Kaia Luna never let go of those who were her own.

Bebe included.

"I'm going to smack that boy's fin in a minute," Bebe muttered bad-temperedly when she spied a familiar form in the water. "Now not only do I have to deal with worrywart grandchildren, I have to stay alive long enough to win a chess match against Bowen Knight." And to make sure

Kaia had another pair of arms she trusted to hold her when her world fractured.

Because sooner or later, death came for them all. If you were lucky, as Bebe had been lucky, it was after decades and decades and decades of love and joy and children and grandchildren and even worrywart who-knew-how-many-greats grandchildren. Her mate had seen Kaia born, had held her in his wrinkled hands and kissed her on her plump little cheeks.

Such a life she wished for Kaia and for Bowen Knight, a human who loved Bebe's girl enough to fight for her through fair means or foul.

Chapter 68

KJ is gone. We found his wife hysterical near her yacht. They took it out half a day before I gave the order to find him, and at some point, KJ dived in to check something underneath the yacht and never came back up. She almost drowned diving to look for him—Miane had to haul her out because she wouldn't stop looking.

—Malachai Rhys in a call to Bowen Knight

BO LISTENED TO Mal while standing barefoot under a glittering night sky on an isolated stretch of Italian coastline. KJ wasn't dead, that much was apparent to both of them. Someone had obviously noticed Hugo's hacking and warned KJ to get the hell out. Whether or not KJ would *stay* alive was another question.

"Any indications why KJ turned against the clan?" he asked, his eyes on the horizon and his feet digging into the sand.

"Nothing so far, but we're still excavating his life. Regardless—the fact he married a woman only to abandon her to save his own skin tells me he's not who we all thought he was."

Bo had been racking his brain for signs of evil in KJ, but all he could remember was the other man's good nature. The *only* indication of anything "off" was that night after the second injection when he'd stirred awake because someone was in his room. He'd assumed it to be George, but there'd been a scent he hadn't been able to put his finger on at the time.

Peppermint.

Like the gum KJ was always chewing.

On the other hand, with all the layers of corruption and deception they'd uncovered, Bo wasn't taking anything at face value. "Doesn't make sense that he didn't take the opportunity to do me harm."

"It does if KJ was meant to be a long-term mole," Malachai pointed out. "Any action against you would've put the entire station under a spotlight. His bosses must've weighed it up, decided it wasn't worth losing KJ."

Bo had no counterargument to that, but his doubts continued to hover. "Mal, is there any chance he could've been set up?" What better way to hide a traitor than to have that traitor be found out? "Hugo could've truly believed he'd unearthed the name of the betrayer, but was being used the entire time."

"We're looking at that." Malachai's tone was as cold as the ocean; his anger hadn't abated any during the search for the truth. "If Hugo's intel is right, though, then these Consortium assholes have been smarter than we thought. Having all these people doing small things for them, no one knowing about the others, while distracting us with the big hits."

"Yes." While Malachai tried to ensure BlackSea was now free of moles, Bowen had Lily and Cassius digging for any other indications of trouble within the Alliance, however slight the problem might be—like BlackSea, they had to eliminate any tiny holes the Consortium had put in their wall of security and loyalty. "I don't want it to be KJ."

"None of us want it to be KJ. Especially after Hugo." Flat words. "I should have funeral details in the next forty-eight hours. The pathologist is still running tests on the poison."

Bo continued to watch the water. "Heenali will come, no matter when the funeral. But she needs time to say good-bye."

"I'll make sure she has it. His parents have already agreed to her nightwatch—they're glad their son had a chance to fall in love before he was murdered."

All these broken lives, Bowen thought, all this pain, just because the members of the Consortium had an endless lust for power. They couldn't bear to see a world at peace, made more profit when Psy, changeling, and humans stayed in their separate corners and suspicion hung in the air.

"If it wasn't KJ, he's dead," Malachai said into the quiet that had fallen between them.

"Yes." He'd have been the sacrificial lamb to lend credence to Hugo's discovery. "But hard as it is for me to accept, it also makes sense that it was him."

"A man no one would suspect."

"Exactly." A friendly, easygoing surfer type who was training in a profession that was all about care. "Any assistance I or the Alliance can offer, just ask and it's yours."

His eye caught on a break in the wave in the far distance. "I have to go."

"Is she there?"

"Yes." Bowen couldn't see her; she was too far out, but he *knew*. The same way he'd known which beach to come to tonight—the tug of the mating bond had become stronger and stronger the closer Kaia came, until she became the signal and Bowen's heart the antenna.

Though the sea was night dark and turbulent, he stripped off his clothing and waded in to the waist. The cold water lapped against him as he searched for her. He still couldn't see her, but he could feel the wildness of her deep in—

Something bumped his leg.

He looked down, gleaned nothing through the water.

Another bump, this one on his hip.

Lips wanting to curve, he began to "listen" to the sea, and the next time there was a shift that couldn't be explained by the waves, he reached out . . . but she was too fast, his playful mate whose other form was designed for the ocean. Whooping like a madman, his blood too hot to fear the icy chill, he dived into the water. She surfaced with him this time, and she wasn't in her human form.

Her eyes were vibrant and intelligent—and mischievous. "I knew you were a dolphin." Even before the mating bond and the knowledge it had thrust into his soul. "All that playfulness, such a tight-knit pod of family, these beautiful eyes."

Another nudge, this one at his chest before she dived under, and when she next surfaced, she was far enough out that she could dive up out of the water then back in. Showing off for him before swimming back in and sliding up against him. He ran his hand gently over her delicate skin, astonished and delighted and so fucking happy it hurt.

When he petted her dorsal fin, he noticed the small notch near the top. Curious, he bent to examine it, wondering if it was the result of an accident at some point in her life or if it was the counterpart to her "diva nail."

She nudged at him impatiently.

Laughing, he got the hint and began to stroke her again.

Light sparkled . . . and then there was a brown-eyed siren under his hands.

She wrapped her legs around his waist, her arms around his neck, and kissed him wild and wet and with keening need. He could do nothing but kiss her in return, drinking her in like she was water and he was parched. "You came back." The words were torn out of him.

He'd played every card he held, but in the end it had been her choice and all Bowen could do was wait.

"Because you're mine." Implacable words. "I was half-mad when I said what I did. I don't see land when I see you, Bo. I see my heart and it terrifies me."

"Me, too," he said huskily. "You swim in the ocean and it's full of dangers even without those who're hunting BlackSea. I had to force myself to breathe when I learned you were out there on your own." He'd never expected her to take off from Bebe's island and head straight for him. "God, baby, you came such a long way all alone."

Pride in the smile she gave him. "I had to come claim my mate."

"You own me, Siren. You always will."

"Forgive me, then?" A nuzzle of her nose against his. "I hurt you."

"Ah, Kaia, I'd forgive you the world."

This kiss was gentler, slower, tenderness in every fragment of a moment as they soothed hurts in each other. He knew she remained badly wounded, the losses piling up on her soft heart. And she knew he was bruised from her rejection. It hadn't been real, he understood that, but it had hurt all the same.

So he let her heal him and he tried to heal her, and when their bodies joined, it was with a devotion that lit up both their souls. Afterward, as he carried her to the sand he'd cleared of snow to lay down a thick rug and create a warm bed of blankets, Kaia said, "I miss Hugo," and her voice, it broke.

In the hour that followed, Kaia finally cried for her friend who'd lost his way, the sobs rocking her whole body as she lay curled up in Bowen's arms.

KAIA had never cried as she cried that night, held safe against her mate's strong, warm body under a thick blanket he'd chosen because it'd be soft on her skin. She cried for her parents, taken so young, and for Hugo, who'd made such foolish mistakes—and she cried for herself, for the wounds that scarred her. She cried until her tears ran dry and then she cried until her throat was raw.

Through it all, one thing remained a constant: Bowen.

Her love. Her anchor. Her mate.

She lifted swollen eyelids.

The world was silent around them but for the soft, soothing sound of the waves. Above, the night sky glittered like a thousand tiny lights had been turned on just for them. And though the temperature bit with winter's sharp teeth, she was lazily warm. The blanket was comfortingly heavy and her mate had set up self-contained heaters around their bed on the sand.

He was wonderful. And he was hers. "The sand's probably already in places I don't want anything," she said in a vain effort to banish the echoes of sorrow.

"I'll help you wash," he replied in the same playful tone, though his voice held a roughness that told her he'd cried with her.

"How is Heenali?"

"Broken." Bowen pressed his lips to her drying hair. "All we can do is give her time."

Kaia hurt for the other woman and for Hugo, who'd won a woman of substance and courage but who would never know what they could be together. "I'm going to make friends with her," she vowed. "She can talk to me about Hugo. No one in the Alliance knows him like Heenali and I do."

"Heenali can be a tough nut to crack."

"I'm stubborn." Kaia would watch over the soldier her friend had loved, a gift to his memory. "I wish you could've known him, Bo. I think you'd have liked him."

"Tell me about him."

So she did, and at times they laughed at the memories and at times she cried again. But she shared her friend with Bowen, and in doing so, she kept him alive a little longer. "I'm so happy to be here with you," she whispered. "I feel myself again." No frantic agitation, no sense of claustrophobic imprisonment inside her own skin.

"It took you a long time to swim here." Grim words, his embrace tighter. "I've been waiting for days—I'm fucking proud of you, but I'm not sure my heart can take it."

"I'm built for the water and for swimming long distances." Kaia rose up on her elbow to look down into his face, the hard lines and angles of it so precious to her now. "I know it might be dangerous, but I'm so tired of being afraid."

"What do you need me to do?" Unwavering devotion.

Kaia fell in love with him all over again. "Give me time enough to find my wings again."

"Not even a question, *tesoro mio*."

She felt like his treasure, adored and cherished. "I was driven by raw emotion this time." Sighing as he played with her hair, she petted his bare chest. "My return trip will be a conscious choice." It wouldn't be easy and she'd have to break her journey into many segments in order to beat the fear, but this time around, she was playing for keeps. "I'm going to start with the blue and work up to land."

Bowen reached to cup the side of her face with one big hand. "Are you hurting now?"

Kaia wanted to lie, wanted to tell him she'd conquered her demons, but he was her mate and he deserved nothing but the truth. "It's starting to build." The ugly churning, the flashes of cold and heat, the erratic heartbeat.

Running one hand down her back, Bowen cradled her close. "Go," he whispered roughly. "I'll see you soon."

For Hugo's funeral.

Her scarred heart stretched despite the pain. Because this man, he'd never surrender, not even to her fear. "I'll swim for a day, then catch a high-speed jet from one of our cities." Both so she could be there when her friend was laid to rest and so she could see her mate again.

"Call me as soon as you hit a BlackSea city." A hard kiss. "I'd microchip you if I could."

Kaia laughed but she held him, too, as afraid for the dangers he faced daily as he was for her swimming alone in the blue. "I'm going to buy you a bulletproof coat."

KAIA dived high out of the water for Bowen as she swam out. She saw him raise his hand, and part of her wanted to swim right back to him. But she was determined that the next time she came to him, she'd do so with enough strength to last the night, then to last the day.

She'd speak to the healers and to Bebe and she'd contact Ivy Jane Zen again.

Most of all, she'd lean on the mating bond. Her mate wouldn't mind.

Hope and determination a winged being in her heart, she made her first waypoint several hours later and shifted to call Bo. Her friends on the small floating town waved her off thirty minutes later. Two more waypoints. Two more calls. Two more kisses blown across an ocean to her mate.

She was halfway through the longest stretch between towns, her next stop where she planned to catch a jet, when something shimmered in her vision.

Fear, visceral and cold, tore a scream from both parts of her nature.

Then the net was closing around her and cutting into her skin and she fell into a nightmare.

Chapter 69

How many of our vanished are dead, Mal? How many of my people will I never be able to bring home?

—Miane Levèque to Malachai Rhys, one dark rainswept night

KAIA HAD LEFT in the middle of the night, a strong, beautiful woman who'd waded out into the water without fear. Standing submerged up to her hips, she'd turned and whistled at Bo in a complicated pattern. He'd done the same in return and she'd grinned with utter delight . . . then dived. Only to reappear far in the distance, her dolphin form arcing over the water to splash back in.

Bo had watched until there was no hope of seeing her again. Going back to Venice afterward, he'd waited for her to call in from the waypoints she intended to pass. His siren was a wild creature, but she understood his worry, had laid out her entire path back home so he could track her on the massive map of the world's oceans that he'd put up on his office wall.

The first call had eased the fist clutching his heart, Kaia had sounded so joyously delighted in herself for making the trip alone. The second and third calls left him smiling. He waited for the fourth one, when she'd haul herself out of the ocean and get on a jet.

It never came.

Lungs in a vise, he called Malachai. "Kaia should have reached Miraza by now." He'd marked the floating city on his map. "She hasn't called in. She's only half an hour overdue, but I have a bad feeling about this."

"Fuck." Malachai hung up on that single harsh word.

He called back minutes later to confirm that Kaia hadn't made it to Miraza—nor had she been spotted by the city's long-range scouts.

BlackSea was initiating a search.

Bo thought desperately about what he could do. BlackSea was better equipped to search the deepest parts of the ocean. So he'd search the areas closer to land. Commandeering a small boat, he began to crisscross the water starting from the beach and heading along the route she'd told him she was taking.

Yes, she'd made three waypoints before disappearing, but perhaps by following her trail he'd find a clue to what had happened. Maybe he'd run across a yacht or ship that had seen another vessel on her tail.

Kaia might've surfed the bow wave of a ship, could've been caught on camera.

"It might have nothing to do with the Consortium," he told himself. "KJ is gone." But the security chief part of his brain asked, if KJ *was* the dangerous central mole, what had he left in BlackSea's computer and comm systems? Back doors where others could listen in or download data? Kaia would've tagged her family from the waypoints, too, likely given them her intended route. What if the enemy had a way to monitor comms? Or could be they had spotters near the cities and they'd figured out Kaia's likely path.

When a dorsal fin appeared in the distance, he felt his heart skip a beat, but it proved to be a shark. That shark turned out to be huge and it swam alongside him for long enough that he realized it was changeling—and it was searching to his right. So he went left. And when other creatures of the sea appeared out of nowhere, he was very careful with where he piloted his craft.

Together, they all searched, Bowen's heart leading him deeper and deeper into the blue. The mating bond told him Kaia was alive, and that was all that kept him sane.

Malachai called back four hours later, his hair damp and his upper body clad in a black T-shirt that had patches of wet on it. "No sign of her and we've got hundreds of people in the water looking. You?"

"Nothing." Not even a hint of a familiar playful dolphin. "Is it possible she took a detour?"

"With the vanishings, we've got strict rules in place for all our people. She was mad when she left Bebe's island, but when she ran across Armand just off the island, she told him exactly where she was going. And she filed her return path at the first settlement she hit after leaving Italy." Malachai shoved a hand through his hair. "She knows exactly how terrified we'd all be if she went off-route."

Bowen's mind chilled to Arctic coldness. He couldn't afford to feel fear right now. "Are those filed routes on a networked system?"

"No." Malachai folded his arms. "I isolated that data to a local unit at each city or town; those units are accessible only by me, Miane, and the commanders of the cities. Griffin's at Miraza—he's as loyal to BlackSea as I am, and he considers Kaia a close friend."

Bo took Mal at his word; the other man knew his people. But . . . "No one new in Griffin's life?" Bo would've never thought Heenali would do what she'd done.

Mal's face tightened. "No. Trust me, Bo. None of the commanders along Kaia's route could be turned—we've lost too many people to be anything but fucking suspicious."

Bo shifted tack. "Humans have pleasure and race boats all over the place," he said. "They know not to go into BlackSea territory"—a command he'd reiterated after his return, with any accidental incursions to be immediately reported to him—"but Kaia's route home would've taken her through areas where humans might've spotted her in the distance."

"Sea is a vast place, Bo," Malachai said bluntly. "It's ours, but I'm not arrogant enough to turn down assistance. Canvass your people."

That was when Bo asked a question he didn't want to ask. "Mal, what does it mean if a mating bond is patching in and out like a bad signal? Still there but strong one second, flat the next."

"I'm not mated but I know who to ask." Returning a minute later, he said, “She’s either unconscious or drugged is the best guess.” Ruthless lines on his face. “Can you get to her?”

“I can feel the general direction.” Like a homing beacon in his chest. “But it’s *far*, and the signal keeps switching off.” The first time it had happened, he’d almost thrown up, but a moment of panicked concentration and he’d realized she was still inside him but “quieter.” “I’m going to get in a plane, try to trace it.”

“The call of the mating bond isn’t always that specific,” Malachai warned. “But if you can narrow it down to a general wide area, we can at least focus the search.”

“Have you asked Vasic?” Some teleporters could lock onto faces as well as physical locations.

“Yes. He’s being blocked the same way he was with the other vanished. They were deliberately scarred so their faces no longer matched available images.” A vein pulsed in his temple. “The survivors we’ve recovered say the bastards moved quickly to cut and brand them. Within minutes.”

Bowen realized at that moment that he was capable of cold-blooded and violent vengeance. “Go. Keep looking.” Ending the conversation on that order, he activated the same network he’d used when they’d been hunting George. But this time, he limited it to those who’d checked in as being on the water. That done, he went to power his way to land and to a plane . . . when he realized he had one other option.

It might not work, but it was worth a shot. If he used it, however, he could put the Alliance in debt to a man who’d use that advantage without compunction. So he’d have to think, be smart in what he gave up.

Picking up his phone, he input a code not many people had. “Krychek,” he said when the cardinal telekinetic answered. “I need a favor. Can you ’port to me? I’m not in my office.”

“I’m on my way.”

Kaleb Krychek appeared in front of Bo almost before he’d hung up the call. As always, the cardinal teleporter was wearing a black suit. But there was no tie today, his white shirt open at the collar. And his hair wasn’t as perfectly in place, the black strands tumbled.

"An unusual location." Krychek looked out at the water lapping against the small but fast vessel, his balance so perfect you'd think he'd grown up on boats. That was the thing with teleporters—they had a preternatural physical grace.

"I'll give you a human mind for the PsyNet," Bowen said, his hands clenching on the control panel that was currently humming in wait for his next order; he'd stopped the boat in anticipation of the conversation with Krychek. "Mine."

"It's not that easy," Krychek answered, the eerie white stars on black that was a cardinal's gaze impossible to read. "The connection must be a true emotional bond to be of benefit to the PsyNet. Or the unscrupulous would've already forced humans into the network."

"You have empaths." He might not trust powerful Psy, but Bo wasn't a monster; he worried about the millions of Psy who *weren't* powerful and who'd die horrific deaths should the PsyNet fail. As a result, he'd been thinking about the implications of Krychek's request since the day the other man made it—and today, driven by desperation, he'd seen something the Psy seemed to have missed. "I like empaths. Friendship with one won't be difficult."

"Friendship." Kaleb's midnight voice was musing. "Love works to create the right type of psychic bond, but friendship? No one has considered it."

"Probably because Psy-human friendships are all but extinct."

"Possible. It's also possible I'll be the loser in this bargain."

Bowen held the other man's inscrutable gaze. "I won't sell out the Alliance." If Kaia discovered he'd bargained humanity into bondage for her freedom, it'd destroy her. "But my mind is my own and I'm handing it to you. Any experiment you want to run, I won't fight it."

Krychek raised an eyebrow. "You have a shield."

Bo had never thought he'd want to rip out the shield inside his head. "Break it," he said flatly. "I know Psy can smash changeling shields with massive use of telepathic force." It usually led to death or to severe brain injuries, but Krychek was clever enough to recover enough of Bowen's mind to make it worth his while.

Kaia would hate him for the choice, but Bo wasn't about to leave his mate in enemy hands. "And if none of that works, then I'll owe you as many favors as you want. *Me*, not the Alliance, but I'll owe them for a lifetime." It'd be a millstone around his neck because he had no illusions about Krychek's ruthless nature, but the price was one Bowen was more than willing to pay.

"A fair deal," Krychek accepted. "As for the attempt at joining the PsyNet via a friendship bond, why would you agree to an action you find abhorrent? You've made it clear you don't trust Psy to respect the sanctity of the human mind—should friendship be enough to form a bond, you'd be surrounded by millions of telepaths on the PsyNet."

Bowen kept his roiling gut under vicious control. "You can teleport using a face as a lock, correct?"

"Yes."

"I need you to find my mate." Krychek was undoubtedly *the* most powerful teleport-capable telekinetic in the world; Bowen had to try this, had to know if Krychek could pick up "signals" that were invisible to Vasic.

"I need a clear image of your mate's face."

Taking out his phone, Bo showed Kaleb the picture of Kaia he'd snapped in the kitchen one day while she'd been laughing. "I have more." He swiped through.

"No lock," Krychek said almost at once. "You're sure she's alive?"

"Yes." Bo thumped a fist against his heart. "She's right here."

Krychek might be a pitiless bastard, but he was also mated to another Psy. That was how every changeling Bowen knew described the cardinal's relationship with Sahara Kyriakus. It felt like a mating bond to those who'd been close enough to the couple to get a sense of their emotional connection. So it didn't surprise Bo when Krychek just nodded. "Is she wearing anything distinctive?"

"No." Kaia had gone into the water naked, would've shifted out of it naked. "What else can you use?"

"Something that can lead *only* to her—or to a strictly limited number of people. Eye color won't work. Neither will hair color or even a tattoo unless that tattoo is unique. Most scars won't work unless it's a collection. There can be no blurred ID lines for a lock."

Krychek rode the rocking of a wave with ease. "When I try to find her this way," he said, "I'm effectively treating her as a place—and to find a place, I need a detailed image of the location. The smaller the 'location,' the more specific the image has to be because there's nothing around it to give it context or to differentiate it from another similar location."

Kaia had no tattoos or other distinctive markings on her body, except—"What about a small toe that's twisted inward and slightly overlaps the fourth toe?"

"Too general. Too many likely hits."

"The toe also has a scar and is missing the nail. Kaia had small multicolored dots tattooed on it with ink that lasts through a shift and back." Such a small thing that her abductors might've missed it; the colors on her "diva nail" blended in with the polish she liked to wear on her other nails.

"Yes," Krychek said. "That's probably unique enough, but I need an image."

Bo went frantically through his photos. So many of her laughing face, her body in motion, none of her feet. Fuck, fuck, fuck!

Chapter 70

Say "I'm going to bake my favorite man a blackberry pie."

—Bowen Knight taking a photograph of a laughing Kaia Luna

BO WENT THROUGH the photos again—and halted on a video of Kaia he'd taken one morning while lying in bed. She was sitting up making faces at the camera and had suddenly pounced on him.

He'd dropped the phone . . . and *there.*

Freezing the image, he turned it to Krychek. "Is this clear enough?"

The cardinal took almost a minute to examine it, zooming in and out. "I have a lock," he said without warning. "Faint but usable."

"Do it." Bowen put his hand on Kaleb's shoulder. He had a feeling the telekinetic was too powerful to need the contact, but he had no intention of being left behind.

A shift in time and space, and then he was standing on a floor that rocked under him. *A boat.* Even as the thought passed through his head, he saw Kaia sitting on a bunk inside the small room. Head hanging low, she was shivering, wrapped only in a thin blanket. She also had a massive bruise down one side of her face as well as thin cuts that crisscrossed her face on both sides.

Dropping to his knees in front of her, he gently stroked back her hair as she stared at him as if he was a ghost. "What did the bastards do to you?"

"Bo! You're real!" She hugged him tight, the blanket still gripped in her hands. When she drew back, she tried to smile. "Ouch." Wincing while he fought his rage, she said, "Punched me when I bit one of them." She sounded very satisfied by that, but her voice came out slurred, something inside her face broken or badly bruised.

"They cut you."

"No, it's from the net. My dolphin skin marks easily." A glint in her eyes. "I bit the asshole so badly he dropped his knife into the ocean. Others said the bruise plus the marks from the net would hide me until they got his hand bandaged up. He must be the designated cutter." Her voice slurred even further, her eyelids flickering. "Shit, I—"

Scooping her unconscious form into his arms before she could slump forward, Bowen looked at Krychek. "Can you get back here?"

The cardinal nodded. "I have enough specific location markers." A glance at Kaia. "Where?"

Bo's instinct was to take her to an Alliance hospital facility, but he wouldn't hurt Kaia by bringing her to land. Neither would he betray BlackSea by taking her—and thus Krychek—to Ryūjin. "Do you know Malachai Rhys's face?" The other man should be on Lantia coordinating the search.

"Yes. I leave the water changelings alone but I know who they are."

The answer put Bowen's final concerns at ease; if Krychek knew Mal's face, he could've teleported to Mal at any time. Bo wouldn't be breaching BlackSea's wall of security by showing the other man a photograph. "Go."

Wind and saltwater spray hit his face a heartbeat later. In front of him, Malachai's muscles bunched before he focused on what Bowen carried. "With me!"

Bo was conscious of Krychek staying in position on the edge of the deck while he pounded inside the city with Kaia. Healers swarmed over her the instant he put her on a bed in what appeared to be a large infirmary. A wet Miane Levèque appeared seconds later dressed only in a large black T-shirt that hung off one bare shoulder; she put her hand straight on Kaia's skin.

Unable to break his own skin-to-skin contact with his mate, Bowen looked at BlackSea's First. "Will she be all right?" It was impossible to ignore the brutality of the blow to her face; the bright light in the infirmary highlighted every break in the skin, every inch of black bruising. How had she even spoken to him? Her cheekbone looked to be shattered and one eye socket was dangerously sunken in.

Miane snapped her head toward him, her eyes nothing human . . . nothing animal, either. Not as Bo understood it. She was a wholly alien creature at that instant, with thought processes he couldn't predict. "Does Krychek have location markers?"

Bo nodded.

"Go." The order was directed at both him and Malachai. "Find the bastards—keep at least one alive for questioning." A sudden, unexpected touch of her fingers to his shoulder, the punch of alpha power behind it a thing that rippled along the mating bond. "I have her."

Conscious they could lose the cowards who'd taken Kaia unless they acted at once, Bowen forced himself to break contact with her and headed out with Malachai. They arrived on Lantia's eastern deck to find ten cold-eyed BlackSea men and women pointing guns at Krychek. The cardinal had an amused smile on his face. As well he might—he was so fucking powerful he could probably telekinetically push all ten to the far corners of the city before they ever pulled the trigger.

"Stand down," Malachai ordered before taking guns off two of his men. "We may be bringing in unfriendlies. Re-arm and stay alert."

Nodding, the two men raced off.

"Krychek," Bowen said at the same instant. "We're ready."

They were inside the room where Kaia had been held less than a heartbeat later. Krychek broke the lock using a small pulse of telekinetic power. Taking the gun Malachai held out, Bo went and opened the door with care. A glance outside showed a narrow and dark wood-paneled hallway that led to a flight of steps. Whatever this boat was, it was small. Which meant it probably didn't have much of a crew.

But Kaia had said "others" so there had to be at least three.

Going quietly up the steps, conscious of Malachai and Krychek behind him, he took extreme care emerging into the light. No bullet whizzed past his head. No shout went up. He looked around, realized they were on a small fishing boat. A net lay crumpled against the hull to his left alongside other tools of the trade. He could see the silhouette of one man at the helm out front, complete with a captain's hat.

Another man stood at the opposite end of the ship—behind Bo—and seemed to be scanning the retreating horizon with binoculars. Bo could just barely glimpse a third man along the right side of the boat, closer to the captain than the one with binoculars. He, too, had his attention outward.

It was the male with the binoculars whose hand was bandaged. *Fucker.*

Moving his own hand back behind him, he counted off the number of sailors for Malachai and Krychek's benefit. A touch on his wrist told him the message had been received. He changed the hand motions to point in the three directions where the men were located. Then, once that message was understood, he pointed to the stern, telling the others which target he was taking.

After that, there was nothing but speed.

Bo erupted out of the belly of the ship, heading straight for the man with the binoculars. Shouts went up as he was spotted, but it was far too late. He took down the man who'd brutalized Kaia before the bastard could do anything but drop his binoculars to the deck. And yeah, Bo took great pleasure in smashing the butt of his gun into the fucker's face, crushing his cheekbone and smashing his eye socket. "That's for Kaia."

He was ready to murder this asshole and dump him in the ocean, his rage a cold wave, but his mind flashed to Kaia's sadness as she spoke of BlackSea's vanished, Miane's words about bringing in at least one live abductor ringing in his head. "You're alive only on sufferance," he said as the man coughed and tried to rise from where he'd fallen to the deck. "Stay the fuck down or I'll blow off your pathetic head."

Sadly the asshole wasn't stupid enough to disobey.

Gun on him nonetheless, Bowen looked over to see both the captain and other crewman similarly captured.

Krychek's capture was floating five feet in the air, helplessly flailing his arms and legs. The whites of his eyes showed bright against the deep tan of a man often out on the water.

Krychek slipped his hands into the pockets of his pants. "Would you like to return to the city?"

A single hard nod from Bo and the entire boat appeared next to Lantia. Meanwhile, Krychek looked like he was out for an evening stroll, not as if he'd just transferred a large vessel and multiple people across half an ocean.

Bowen looked to the other man. "These three Psy?" He'd felt no psychic strikes against his mind, but that could simply be because the three were disoriented and terrified.

"No, human."

"We'll take it from here," Malachai said to Krychek. "BlackSea owes you."

"No. The payment's been made."

Malachai's eyes connected with Bowen's after Krychek teleported out, a silent question in them. Bo just shook his head. Now wasn't the time to speak of his devil's bargain. A bargain he'd make again and again to bring Kaia out of danger. "Later."

Nodding, Malachai threw a rope over the side and the boat was soon secured against Lantia.

Their three captives quivered as they were made to disembark, then get down on their knees on the exposed deck of the city. Miane appeared seconds later, still dressed in nothing but that large black T-shirt that hit the tops of her thighs and fell off one shoulder. Bo suddenly realized it was the same one Malachai had been wearing during their call. It should've made her look like a teenage girl playing dress-up with her boyfriend's clothes.

But Miane Levèque was no girl, the power that burned in her a chilling cold.

Her inhuman gaze found his for a split second. She nodded.

Kaia was safe.

His heart slamming, Bo kept his gun trained on the captives—and forced himself not to pull the trigger on the one with the bandaged hand and the broken face. He'd made the call not to kill on the boat and now he was on Miane's city; this was her show to run.

"You took one of mine," Miane said silkily to the three. "Talk."

The captain began to babble. "We rescued her. She was flounderi—" His words ended in a fleshy thump of sound as Miane backhanded him so hard that he hit the deck with violent force; he spit out a bloody tooth when he struggled back up onto his knees.

"Lie to me again and you go into the ocean." Miane didn't raise her voice, the menace of her all the more deadly for being so contained. "Now, I'm going to ask again. Why did you take one of mine?"

Chapter 71

Miane Levèque is beautiful the same way a shark is beautiful. Sharp, clean lines and lethal strength—but with a vicious bite. Do not underestimate her.

—Consortium briefing on the major changeling alphas

"I JUST GOT paid!" It was the crewman with the smashed face, his words thick but understandable. "Easy money, he said!" Indicating the captain. "Just had to help him snatch a dolphin for a black market collector. I didn't know she was a person until she shifted in the net!"

"Then why did you have a knife to cut her face?" Bowen's finger began to press down on the trigger.

"Bo." Miane's voice, a soft reminder of what was at stake, not an order. Alpha to alpha.

Grinding his teeth, he nodded to tell her he was back in control.

Miane said, "Throw him in the blue."

Screaming, the male tried to fight but it was no use. Malachai and Bo threw the fucker overboard and Bo kept him in the icy water at the point of his gun.

"And you?" Miane gave the other crewman the full impact of eyes gone eerily *other*. "Would you like to lie to me, too?"

A sudden wetness in his pants, the acrid scent of ammonia rising into the air.

"Seawater," Malachai said shortly and was soon passed a dripping metal bucket.

The BlackSea security chief doused the crewman.

Whimpering, the crewman hugged his arms around himself. "He's my uncle." A glance at the captain. "Said he had a big contract, needed crew."

"You knew you were taking a changeling."

The captain's nephew threw up at Miane's quiet words. Malachai washed that off, too, but it was obvious the spineless male who'd been willing to stand by while another man brutalized an unarmed woman was too fucking terrified to speak now that he was faced by predators with far sharper teeth. Miane turned her attention back to the captain with the bloody cut lip and missing tooth. She smiled at him and it was a smile that was of the black, of sinuous, cold-blooded things.

"Fuck it," the captain said, a tremor in his voice. "I wasn't paid enough for this." He began to tell them everything he knew, while the crewman in the water started to turn blue.

In short, the captain admitted he was known for being open to gray-market or black-market jobs. He'd carried illegal drugs, smuggled exotic animals, indulged in other criminal behavior. When he was suddenly offered a significant five-figure sum for work that didn't even take him out of his preset path to another job, he'd jumped at the chance.

"I was already in the area—I got sent a general location and told specifics about exactly which dolphin I needed to snatch," he continued. "Larger than an ordinary wild dolphin, tiny notch in the top part of her fin, swimming without a pod in a specific direction. Man I spoke to said they'd spotted her heading my way."

The captain used the back of his arm to wipe the sea spray off his face, smearing blood from his lip across his cheek. "If we got her, we got the whole payment. If we didn't, we still got ten grand. Not a bad deal."

"Did they tell you to cut her face?"

Blood draining to leave his skin the color of old parchment, the captain nodded. "I decided it was fucked up enough with the bruise and the marks from the net." His eyes jittered to the man in the water. "I use him as crew but he's a twisted fuck. Volunteered to cut when I hesitated over that part of the deal."

So much for honor between thieves.

Smile cold, Bowen shot into the water, causing the "twisted" fucker to scramble back, farther into the unforgiving blue.

"Who was your contact?" Miane asked the cringing captain.

"His name's Gianco. Guy's the go-between for a ton of stuff at the docks." He was happy to provide them with Gianco's contact details, as well as more information on how to track the man down. "He's gotten me good lines on work before so I knew the deal was legit."

Bo shifted to press his gun to the back of the captain's head, while Malachai kept an eye on the crewman in the saltwater that had to be hell on his bashed-in face. "You've done this before," Bo said. "You've taken others."

The man froze.

Miane smiled. "He's not going to blow out your brains," she said gently. "You took his mate. He wants to torture you by flaying off your skin inch by square inch until you beg for death. Make it easier on yourself and tell us everything."

"Just one other time." The captain swallowed convulsively. "Gianco supplied the crew that time and those guys were vicious—they cut up the changeling's face with razors like they were carving meat." Sweat broke out along his forehead. "I dropped them off with Gianco and I don't know what happened after that."

"What did the changeling look like straight out of the water?"

When the captain described the male, every member of BlackSea on deck went motionless. They'd recognized a clanmate—and each and every one wanted to do the same kind of violence as Bowen.

Miane's face was expressionless when she said, "Describe the crew Gianco provided."

Giving her a sickly smile, the man said, "I always get a photograph using my hidden camera. Just in case anyone tries to stiff me." He reached very slowly into his pocket to draw out a small phone. "It's on here."

"This bastard's gonna drown," Malachai drawled. "Bo?"

Turning to see the crewman in the water struggling to keep his head afloat, Bo took his time making the call. "Bring him in. I'm not done with him."

Mal nodded at one of his people to throw out a net. They used it to haul the blue-lipped and nearly unconscious male to the deck, where he was left inside the net to shudder in front of his fellow assholes.

"Was that previous crew human, too?"

The captain jerked his gaze from the crewman back to Miane. "No, Psy."

"And Gianco?"

"Changeling. A fish, like you all."

Miane examined the captain's sweating face. "How do you know?"

"I followed him once, the first time he came to me with a job. Smuggling that time. Saw him dive into the ocean, then saw a big-ass fish swim out. Never saw Gianco come back up." He swallowed again. "And his eyes . . . they did that black thing a couple of times when he was pissed."

Miane's obsidian eyes stayed unblinking on the captain's face. "Do you have a photo of Gianco on this phone?"

"No, he never got on my boat. Couldn't use my secret camera—but I can describe him."

A painful wave of shock and betrayal rippled through the deck when that description matched KJ to a fine point. Right down to his gritty voice and habit of chewing peppermint gum. "At what time did Gianco contact you for this job?"

"Only about two hours before we took her onboard. Like I said, we just lucked out by being nearby. Our other job was legit so I filed a route with the authorities and all."

That answered the question of whether KJ had survived his dive into the ocean.

"What else do you know?" Miane asked with no indication of the rage that had to be coursing through her blood.

It turned out to not be much, though the captain did tell them the specific "docks" at which he usually dealt with Gianco—a predictably slippery character who went missing for long periods of time. No doubt it'd line up with KJ's work schedule.

"Lock all three up," Miane said flatly.

Only after Kaia's captors had been dragged away with zero care for their injuries did Bo speak again. "KJ."

"He's mine." Miane's voice was like stone. "No one else is to approach."

As Heenali was Bo's to handle. "If you want me to blast his face across the human network, say the word."

Miane didn't answer with either a yes or a no and he didn't assume that was an answer in itself. It paid to assume nothing with the First of BlackSea.

Malachai's eyes went to the boat bobbing beside the city. "I'll go through the vessel, see if we can find anything useful."

Logic wove a cold line through Bowen's fury. "You should unhook it from the city."

When both Miane and Malachai looked at him, he said, "This deal might've been made while the vessel was already at sea, but the captain worked previously for KJ. If I were KJ, I'd have put a tracker on it somewhere, along with an explosive that could be detonated remotely. As soon as KJ checks the tracker, he'll realize the boat is nowhere near its intended location."

"Fuck, he's right." Malachai was already running to undo the rope.

He and a number of other BlackSea changelings jumped into the water and literally pushed the boat out to a safe distance before anchoring it again. Waiting only until he could see that the city was no longer in danger, Bo gave in to the driving need inside him. "Is Kaia still in the infirmary?"

Miane didn't immediately give him an answer. "How did you get Krychek's cooperation?"

"That's between me and him." He held her gaze, alpha to alpha. "All you need to know is that BlackSea owes him nothing."

Miane inclined her head a fraction. "Kaia is with the healers—and irately demanding to come to you."

A massive boom split the horizon, the sky colored yellow and orange and red and the sea reflecting the same. Flaming debris rained down from above, but all the changelings in the water had dived at the instant of the explosion, and reappeared well beyond the danger. The boat was gone, with it any physical evidence.

"We have a starting place to track KJ," Miane murmured. "We also have the photos on the captain's phone. It is enough to begin a hunt."

That hunt would end in blood.

Good.

Chapter 72

Changeling healers share multiple gifts with M-Psy and yet this convergence has never been studied in scientific literature.

—Draft paper by Dr. Natia Kahananui

KAIA SAT SILENTLY under the healer's touch as the older woman worked on her face, but her insides were a chaos of emotion. The only reason she hadn't run out to Bowen the instant she heard the boom of the explosion was that she could feel him safe and strong inside her—and because of how he'd looked when he'd seen what had been done to her face. If a little patience would soften the evidence of the blows she'd taken, then she'd find that patience.

Warmth emanated from the healer's fingers, the energy of the clan flowing from her hands. It had been extraordinarily more potent while Miane was in the room, the rage of her power a black wave that protected rather than drowned.

"I've managed to heal the fractures," the healer murmured, a frown of concentration between her brows. "The swelling isn't looking too bad, but the bruising's going to linger a few days."

"*Mahalo*, Rani." Kaia was reaching up to pat at the bruised side of her face when her mate walked into the room. "Bo!" Jumping off the infirmary bed, she ran into his arms.

They locked around her, warm steel and protective heat. Kaia was only vaguely aware of Rani slipping away and shutting the door behind herself, her focus on her mate—who was shaking in reaction.

"I *fought* them," she said, pressing kisses along his jaw. "I was only afraid for a few seconds right at the start—and then I got mad." More kisses, his scent in her lungs. "I bit him so hard he bled. Even after he punched me, I wasn't afraid. I was just angry I was too woozy to knee him in the groin."

Bowen pressed his forehead to hers, his expression hard with pride. "You're not a scared little girl anymore."

"No," she whispered with a smile that cracked open the scars, allowing in healing light. "No matter what happens, I will *never* again be unable to help the people I love." She'd been naked on the deck of that boat after shifting into human form to better fight, and she'd *still* managed to inflict enough damage that three grown men bigger than her had thrown her in that small room and locked the door. "I was plotting how to take apart the bunk and bash them over the head with one of the ends when they came in again."

Bowen laughed, the strain finally fading from his features. Rough-tipped fingers featherlight over her bruises as he took stock of the damage. "That makes this a badge of pride." He pressed a soft kiss to the bruise.

Eyelids closing, her eyes hot but her smile wide, Kaia said, "I knew you'd come. I just had to keep myself alive long enough and you'd come." It had been an absolute truth inside her, a driving flame.

"I will *always* come for you." A harsh voice, more tender kisses. "You're a little disappointed I came so quickly, aren't you?"

She found herself giggling. "I did really want to do some head-bashing-in."

Their eyes locked and laughter filled the air.

When he picked her up in his arms and swung her around, she didn't even care that she was in a stupid hospital gown that flapped with the rush of air. She felt like a warrior princess with her prince, a woman with bruises earned in fighting for herself—and to return to her mate.

She was strong. She wasn't afraid.

"I'm going to come to land with you," she vowed to him when he finally stopped spinning her around and pressed her up against the wall.

Smile erased, her stubborn mate shook his head. "No."

But Kaia had spent the time in the infirmary well. She cupped his face. *"Listen."* Scowling at him when he glared instead, she said, "The root of my fear has always been this terror of losing the people I love on land."

Arms braced on either side of her, he continued to glare at her. "A trauma that deep doesn't just disappear, Kaia."

"I asked the healer. She said it happens rarely, but shock can work both ways." Pressing her hand over his mouth, she said, "Don't you see, Bo? I was so afraid of losing you on land, but *I was taken in the blue.*"

Her words hung in the air, a potent ripple.

"I was taken in the blue," she repeated. "Far, *far* from land. If the kidnappers had killed me, you would've lost me in the blue. Nowhere near land." That truth had struck her deep in the heart while she sat in a locked room trying to regain her bearings so she could take apart the frame of a bunk. "I lost my parents on land, but land didn't kill them. A disease and a bunch of selfish people did. Those exist everywhere."

Kissing her palm, he tugged away her hand. "It's easy to be logical, baby, but God, it fucking tears you up to be on land." His voice turned to crushed stone. "I can't bear to see you in pain."

"Bo." She kissed him, sweet and deep and with all of her. "Let me try. If it doesn't work, if it hurts, I'll be honest about it with you and we'll do this the slow way." It *was* possible she was simply euphoric in the aftermath of holding her own against armed aggressors who wanted to harm her . . . but Kaia didn't think so.

She felt different inside in a fundamental way.

"Venice is surrounded by water." She ran her fingers through his hair. "The Adriatic isn't far for my other form." She could swim powerfully as a human, too, but her dolphin form was a sleek knife in the ocean. "Let me try."

"No, it causes you too much pain." Intractable resistance. "We'll find another way."

But Kaia held his heart in her hands and she was determined.

Which was how, two weeks later, Bo found himself moving into a home big enough for two—and that had a kitchen that passed Kaia's stringent standards. The one thing on which he hadn't budged was that the home have as many water views as possible. The Venetian lagoon lay on their doorstep, while the Adriatic was close enough that—from the top of the house—they could see the masts of large yachts heading out of Venice and toward the sea.

The house was also connected to a biosphere below the surface, an entire lower floor surrounded by transparent walls that reminded Kaia of Ryūjin. That was to be their lounge, a welcoming space for both humans and water changelings.

Her aunts, uncles, friends, cousins—Malachai included—*and* Miane turned up to move them in. Miane's elderly grandmother, an unexpectedly sweet and gentle woman who obviously adored her dangerous granddaughter and who made her home in Venice, sat in an armchair and supervised.

Dr. Kahananui and Dex had been disappointed to miss out on the impromptu gathering but had eagerly accepted an invitation to visit once the baby was a little older. Lily and Lily's doctor beau were also in the thick of things, along with Cassius and the other knights.

Bowen's best friend wasn't too good around strangers, but it was clear he liked grumpy Taji. Together, the two of them muttered about how baseball was going to shit these days and how they couldn't stand morning people. Teizo and Tevesi quipped about calling him Tassius now that he was an honorary triplet.

The most surprising person on the team was Heenali. She'd turned up silent and grief-stricken, and hadn't left Kaia's side for more than a few minutes all day. It had been that way since BlackSea consigned Hugo to the sea in a haunting song-filled ceremony that said nothing about his crimes against BlackSea.

Miane had made that call.

"Whatever his mistakes," she'd told Bo as they stood on the windswept deck of Lantia, "he gave up his life for the clan. We will honor that."

As a result, Hugo's family had been able to mourn him as a hero.

As for Kaia, under her own grief, she was pure light. No hint of the phobic pain that had followed her through time. The same couldn't be said of her family and alpha. Not a single member of BlackSea looked anything but grim—until they realized this home was partially submerged, the first two floors below what was a permanent floodline.

Kaia loved the presence of water so close. Especially when, on the day they took possession of the keys, he told her of his overhaul of the original front door; it was sandwiched in between the dry top part of the house and the biosphere-shielded bottom floor. Except for one protected passage to allow them to reach the first floor, the second floor was reinforced and permanently flooded—something to do with how the biospheres and houses were kept stable. A delicate but steady balance. "I had engineers go down, fix the door, and create an airlock so you can swim in and out safely."

All but jumping up and down, she'd made him put on a wetsuit and breathing gear so they could go explore their home and the surrounding waterways. Bo was a basic scuba diver at best, but he'd signed up for extensive lessons. If his mate was going to be swimming out into the blue and into the deep, he'd be coming with her until the fear clawing at his heart let go.

She saw that fear, kissed him deep in the night with her palm over his heart, and didn't try to stop him from coming along on her swims—even though he was slow and clumsy at his current level of skill. Kaia understood such fear intimately, though she no longer seemed to feel any terror of land.

Bo wanted to believe the change was real, but he'd witnessed the horrific depth of her pain, couldn't bring himself to accept that an act of violence had brought her happiness instead of agony. The only thing that would fix that was time—which they had now, thanks to Dr. Kahananui's experimental treatment.

Cassius, implanted second, would begin his own treatments in a week.

"Do you know you two are linked on the psychic plane?" Kaia said to him one night in bed after meeting his best friend—and charming him as much as anyone could charm Cassius. That she'd brought along his favorite pecan pie hadn't hurt.

"Doesn't surprise me." Curious, Bo asked her how she knew.

It turned out that as a changeling telepath, her brain didn't work the same as Psy brains apparently did; she couldn't see the network to which she was connected, but she could feel it.

The mating bond had pulled her out of the network she'd been blooded into as a child when her clan realized she was a telepath and needed that psychic network to survive. "Good thing Bebe's so old," Kaia whispered. "She knew exactly what was wrong when I got sickly as an infant."

Eyes glowing with light, she sat up to look down at him, a siren with hair that cascaded over his chest and perfumed the air with hints of coconut and tiare flowers. "Want to know how many humans are connected to you?" Her fingers weaving in the air, as if she could sense hundreds . . . thousands of threads. "So fragile, so fine, not like changeling bonds, but there are so *many* of them that they've become unbreakable."

Bo had spent much of his life hating telepaths, but all he felt at that moment was wonder. "How is that possible? Cassius and the knights I can understand. We've been through hell together. But so many others?"

"They acknowledge you as alpha." A soft murmur, her face kissed by the moonlight pouring through the window of their new home. "Even if they argue with you, they see you as their leader."

Despite the switch in networks, Bo had no fears about her psychic health; he could feel her bright with life inside him. Yesterday, she'd met a Psy child in the street and the little girl had taught her a telepathic game. "Pippi couldn't believe I was a grown-up and didn't know." Throwing back her head, she'd laughed. "Also, apparently my telepathy 'smells' different. Wild."

As wild as her.

As for Bowen's parents, they were ecstatic at both the result of the experiment and that Bowen had fallen in love. Having stayed with Bo and Kaia for the past couple of days, they'd quickly come to adore Kaia.

Life was more beautiful than Bo could've ever imagined . . . but for one dark cloud.

"Bo," Kaia had asked in the aftermath of their reunion in Lantia's infirmary, "what did you barter to get Krychek's help?"

She still hadn't forgiven him for what he'd done, especially since Krychek hadn't called in his psychic marker. It was a sword that could fall at any moment.

Epilogue

†あ8zǯ9i

—Entry tagged: Malachai Rhys (image attached)

KAIA SAT IN the gondola as Venice, a stately lady dressed up for the night, glittered past on either side of the canal. Music whispered over from some of the restaurants, conversation and laughter from others. She'd thought about opening a restaurant here, because of course the idea of simply sitting on her hands was ludicrous.

And cooking was a love for her, a delight.

Then Bowen had turned up with a petition signed by all of his knights demanding he offer her a position as the official Alliance HQ chef. She'd had them all to dinner by then, and it delighted her that they'd loved her cooking so much—they certainly needed to be well fed; it was obvious none of them ate particularly well.

She'd glared at them and told them as much. In return, they'd decided to claim her. For Kaia, to be in the thick of this human *ohana* that now held the same place in her heart as BlackSea, it suited her changeling nature right down to the ground.

She missed everyone on Ryūjin, but she'd spent too long hiding. It was her time to spread her wings and live a life with her mate. Tansy and Sera were already planning a long visit and others would come, too, nosy and affectionate and welcome, and she'd cook for them as she had on Ryūjin.

Bebe was too old to travel so far, and for her, Kaia would return as often as Bebe wanted to see her. In between, she'd chat with her grandmother while Bowen and Bebe mused over chess moves and argued the merits of a sneak attack versus a full frontal assault.

Her new human family was building her a kitchen deep inside the HQ, in the underwater biosphere section that looked out at Venice's sparkling water.

"You're making us a family."

"What?" She turned her eyes toward her gorgeous, obstinate mate who had bartered his psychic freedom for her. Even if Kaleb Krychek decided not to exercise that option, Bowen had bargained away a *lifetime* of favors to one of the most ruthless men on the planet.

Gods, she loved him. And gods, she wanted to push him into the water and yell at him for giving up so much of himself. He'd put himself in chains for her. He'd also put himself in a position where he might have to walk away from the Alliance if Krychek attempted to manipulate the organization through him.

"I'd do it again in a heartbeat."

That was what he'd said to her when she'd pounded her fists on his chest in anger.

How could she do anything but adore the man? Even if she was so very angry with him.

"Us, everyone at HQ," he said, his voice gruff with emotion. "We were close before, but there was something missing. The heart." He poled them past a trattoria festooned with fairy lights where a woman in a velvet dress was playing an upbeat tune on the fiddle. "It's there now, in the kitchen we're building and how everyone's always dropping by even though you currently only have a single working stove. The HQ isn't just about work now, it's about *ohana*."

The cool night wind kissed her cheeks. "It feels like that, too," she said with a smile that hurt with all that she felt for him. "A new family that's becoming entwined with my old family."

"You're happy" had been Miane's determination when she dropped by two days earlier. "Good. If you ever need anything, you remain one of mine."

That wasn't quite true. Kaia's first loyalty was to Bowen. But she knew her First's meaning, understood the love that drove it. Miane appeared hard to the outside world, but to her own people, she was a fierce force of love—and of vengeance. KJ had disappeared into the blue, but Miane wasn't about to allow him to hide. She would find him and she would make him pay for his heinous crimes.

The one good thing to come out of this was the idea of every member of BlackSea getting a unique miniature tattoo in a hard-to-find location. On the inside shell of the ear, in the bottom crease of a toe, under the heaviness of curls, hidden along the hairline, or in the complexity of an already existing tattoo. A nonsense collection of characters from the world's different alphabets, mixed with numbers. Random strings of short code that were each unique enough for a teleport lock.

Vasic Zen had tested the idea after speaking to Kaleb Krychek about how he'd found Kaia, and it worked. It apparently required a slightly different kind of telekinetic focus, but the Arrows were willing to learn that focus in the name of Trinity.

It'd take time to roll out the tattoos across Kaia's vast clan, but Armand was in charge and he could be meticulously organized when he wanted to be; he'd already split the entire globe into tiny grids and assigned people to find their most far-flung and vulnerable members first. Whether to get inked was a choice, of course, but so far, everyone had agreed to the practically invisible marking that would allow a teleporter trusted by the clan to find them if they were taken.

The information about which string belonged to which clanmate—and the images of those tattoos—was kept in a database unconnected to anything and accessible *only* by Miane and Malachai, with an intentionally anonymous third person holding the access codes as a failsafe. The Consortium would not be getting their hands on the database and using their own teleporters to snatch BlackSea's people.

"Adrian Kenner said humans are the bridge," Bowen murmured after long moments in the silken dark. "But this time, it's you."

Kaia tilted her head slightly to the side. "No, it's us." Despite all the efforts of those who'd destroy their friendship, the Alliance and BlackSea were now linked together for all time. Mating was forever. "Do you like children?" It was a question he'd asked her, but she'd never had the chance to ask him. "You'd make a wonderful father." Protective, honorable, loving.

He sucked in a breath. "Yes," he said roughly. "But Kaia—"

"I know." So long as Bowen was beholden to Kaleb Krychek, they couldn't bring a child into their world, not when they had no idea what the cardinal would demand from Bo—whether that meant smashing open his mind or forcing him to effectively work for Krychek. "I just thought you should know that."

Face setting in pitiless lines, he said, "I'll never regret my choice."

Kaia wanted to throw something at his head. "You're impossible." But he was hers.

"We're home." Poling the borrowed gondola to a stop exactly where the gondolier had requested, he hopped out, then helped her out.

They were walking down the cobblestoned lane toward their home when Kaia's gaze caught on a couple who stood looking out at the water. The woman wore a white beret and a matching ankle-length coat with bright red boots. The profile of the man's face, it was oddly familiar. He turned at that instant and in the white stars of his eyes glittered the reflection of the colored lights of a nearby tavern.

"Krychek." Bowen's voice, nothing in it of harshness or anger; he'd made his bargain and he'd honor it. "Are you calling in your marker?"

As Kaia fought the urge to scream, one of the deadliest men in the world glanced down at the woman with eyes of midnight blue who stood next to him. "Sahara has made it clear to me that our bargain cannot stand."

"It was made in good faith." Bowen set his jaw. "You don't have to worry I'll back away from it. You held up your end. I'll hold up mine."

"I'm afraid I'm the one backing away from it." The cardinal raised an eyebrow, his face so handsome it was intimidating. Kaia shifted an inch closer to Bowen's warm humanity.

"We'll make a new bargain," Krychek was saying. "You owe me nothing but a single personal favor. Not political. A thing between two men, as was my favor for you."

"Kaleb." Kaleb Krychek's mate scowled up at him, as if he weren't lethal and merciless and a shark in a well-cut suit.

He didn't smile but there was an unexpected softness to him when he said, "Knight won't accept a favor for nothing."

"I pay my debts." Bowen's body was rigid. "We hold to the original bargain."

Rolling her eyes, the woman named Sahara spoke to Kaia. "Make him understand."

Kaia squeezed Bowen's bicep with the hand she'd curled around it. "It's a gesture of good faith." Not friendship, that didn't exist yet, but a step in the right direction. "Kaleb won't take advantage of your need to push you into a corner."

"Actually," Kaleb said in a voice that reminded her of the darkest hour of night, "*I* would. But Sahara prefers I act as if I have a conscience." He held Bowen's gaze. "We must both answer to our mates." The faintest hint of a smile. "You are a braver man than I if you attempt to take them both on."

Kaia's eyes widened; what would Malachai say if she told him she was ninety percent certain that Kaleb Krychek, deadly cardinal and all-around dangerous predator, had a sense of humor? That particular fascination, however, could wait.

Tugging Bowen out of earshot of the other couple, she said, "Bridges are built over thin air. Someone must lay the first plank, the first brick, take the risk."

A grimace. "Friendship with Kaleb Krychek?" He sounded like she was asking him to swallow knives.

"You don't have to go quite that far yet," she reassured him with her hands on his chest, his heartbeat so strong and sure under her palms. "I don't think he's good at friendship, either." A man like Kaleb Krychek probably only trusted a rare few—exactly like her own mate. "A personal favor for a personal favor. It's fair and exactly the bargain you'd make with Malachai in the same situation."

Bowen's jaw worked. "My ego is dented," he muttered.

"He came to you because his mate made him." Kaia poked him in the chest. "You can have matching dented egos."

Narrowed eyes from Bowen, but when she drew him back to the others, he said, "You're certain about this?" to Krychek.

The cardinal nodded once.

"Then I accept." Bowen held out a hand.

Krychek slid his own out of his pocket to shake it . . . and the psychic ripple of that act was an invisible quake that jolted the air.

Across from her, Sahara's face glowed with an open and intense pride. All of it directed at the lethal telekinetic who engendered fear in the vast majority of the world.

"Come up for coffee," Kaia said impulsively, suddenly certain she would like this woman who loved as openly as Kaia. "I made a batch of tea cakes this afternoon and there are plenty left."

"I love cake."

Kaia stepped forward, Sahara joined her, and the two of them began to walk side by side shadowed by two dangerous, beautiful men. When she snuck a glance back at them, she saw they continued to walk a foot apart, as silent as the women were not.

Bridges took time to build.

But on this night, Bowen Adrian Knight and Kaleb Krychek had, together, laid the first brick.

ABOUT GOLLANCZ

Gollancz is the oldest SF publishing imprint in the world. Since being founded in 1927 Gollancz has continued to publish a focused selection of bestselling and award-winning authors. The front-list includes **Ben Aaronovitch**, **Joe Abercrombie**, **Charlaine Harris**, **Joanne Harris**, **Joe Hill**, **Alastair Reynolds**, **Patrick Rothfuss**, **Nalini Singh** and **Brandon Sanderson**.

As one of the largest Science Fiction and Fantasy imprints in the UK it is no surprise we have one of the most extensive backlists in the world. Find high-quality SF on Gateway written by such authors as **Philip K. Dick**, **Ursula Le Guin**, **Connie Willis**, **Sir Arthur C. Clarke**, **Pat Cadigan**, **Michael Moorcock** and **George R.R. Martin**.

We also have a strand of publishing in translation, which includes French, Polish and Russian authors. Gollancz is home to more award-winning authors than any other imprint, with names including **Aliette de Bodard**, **M. John Harrison**, **Paul McAuley**, **Sarah Pinborough**, **Pierre Pevel**, **Justina Robson** and many more.

The SF Gateway

More than 3,000 classic, rare and previously out-of-print SF novels at your fingertips.

www.sfgateway.com

The Gollancz Blog

Bringing you news from our worlds to yours. Stories, interviews, articles and exclusive extracts just for you!

www.gollancz.co.uk

GOLLANCZ
LONDON